I0739497

The KEEPER'S VOW

GUARDIANS TRILOGY
BOOK ONE

FRANCINA SIMONE

CHUNKYCATBOOKS
IDAHO

THE KEEPER'S VOW

GUARDIAN'S: BOOK ONE

ChunkyCATBooks

This is a work of fiction. Names, characters, businesses, places, events and incidents are either the products of the author's imagination or used in a fictitious manner. Any resemblance to actual persons, living or dead, or actual events is purely coincidental.

Copyright © 2014 by Francina Simone

All rights reserved. No part of this book may be reproduced in any form by any electronic or mechanical means including photocopying, recording, or information storage and retrieval without permission in writing from the author.

ISBN-13: 978-0-9977103-0-4

Cover art by Kimberly from KimG-Design
Interior design by Francina Simone

www.Francinasimone.com

For more information regarding this book visit:
thefrancinasimone@gmail.com

Twitter: @francinasimone

First Edition

Printed in the U.S.A

Alan Heathcock once told me never to apologize for myself.

And so,

to Juan—who has never asked me to.

There are vows you break.

And vows that break you.

1

Tristan

KATIE SHOULD HAVE known this morning that it would be a bad day. The smell of edible breakfast should have tipped her off.

If anything, she should have known when Mr. Rhineheart didn't care that she'd asked to go to the bathroom five minutes after class started—she should have known that very moment, when he said, "Don't forget the hall pass."

Not now, with this strange boy staring and talking to her like she was mentally ill.

"Look," he said, "I need you to come with me." He had "attitude" written all over his long face. One of those kids who thought they were above everything.

"And I need to pee." She walked past him toward the bathroom. To be honest, she really wanted to run to the library and hide there until the end of class. They'd just started Shakespeare, and it was better to fall asleep in the library than in front of Mr. Rhineheart.

"Katalina," the strange boy said with way too much authority. No one called her that. Why was he still following her? *Who* did he think he was?

"Do I know you?"

"I already told you. I need to talk to you."

And? she thought. His shirt was a little wrinkled—like he didn't care—his black pants fit not too big or small, and he wore ankle-high boots. He wasn't in full dress code. Either he was one of those kids who thought he was above the rules or the kind of kid who just liked to test the teachers. He could have been cute if he combed his hair—and didn't come off like a giant douche-bag.

He narrowed his blue eyes and she changed her mind. He couldn't have been cute if he tried. Not with eyes that probed and prodded like that. "Too bad," she said, pushing the bathroom door open and leaving him behind.

She stood in front of the mirror, scrolling through her phone. Only two minutes passed and she was already going crazy. There was no one to text. The only person she could talk to was Allison, but Allison would only lecture her for skipping class again. The same Allison who'd, just last week, said, *"Ew, skipping is like wearing a knitted hat in the summer. It's embarrassing when you're caught and there is no benefit."*

"I happen to like wearing knitted hats in the summer," Katie had said, knowing Allison was referring to Katie's favorite orange and white, hand-knitted hat with the lopsided puffball. It was the first and last thing she ever knitted; no matter how much it resembled a traffic cone, she was proud of it.

"Which is why you see nothing wrong with truancy."

But Allison was wrong. Katie did see the problem. The problem was her, standing in a bathroom staring at wads of toilet paper and tampon wrappers.

.ஒஉ ஐஎ.

"Just go to class. Study once in a while. It's not that hard," Allison said, stuffing her math book in her locker. Math was the only thing Katie was better at than Allison. Watching Allison slam the book all the way to the back of the locker gave Katie a little satisfaction. Maybe she sucked at making fashion statements in her school uniform or *always* being right, but Katie had a C plus in math and Allison only had a C minus—it was a start.

"It *is* hard. Brian understands. *He's* my best friend," Katie said.

Allison eyed Katie as she closed her locker, her red, silky hair swinging back and forth in a high ponytail.

"I'm kidding—second best-friend. Lighten up a little. I have next year to worry about grades and college. No one ever counts your junior year."

"Are you serious? You're going to end up at some no-name community college *if* you even make it out of high school. You'll end up like Olive Branch Knowles—aspiring to be a protest leader of free love. Teachers blame MTV, I blame her hippie parents."

"Be quiet, she's right there," Katie said as Olive marched down the hall in her knee-length, Hamilton High School navy-blue skirt, smiling and shaking hands with anyone who either didn't see her coming or was too dumb to avoid eye contact. For a week last year, Katie obsessed over farm animal rights and boycotted all dairy products until she realized she was boycotting her favorite and most important food group. Even though she went back to slurping milkshakes, chomping cheese-sticks, and downing gallons of ice cream, Olive *still* considered it a perfect conversation starter.

Katie grabbed Allison and headed toward the science hall. "Alright, alright I won't skip anymore," Katie said. "At least not this week," she added, catching a glimpse of Brian in the classroom just across from hers. He was sitting on top of his desk talking to someone she couldn't see. Even though his back was turned to her, she knew by the way he slouched that he was smiling—those eyes probably squinty and leprechaun-green. She could walk over to him now, and they could hate school together—but he'd probably ignore her for his "more popular" friends.

"Katalina," a voice, too familiar, said. It was the same boy from this morning. He frowned, shoving through bodies as if his destination were more important than anyone else's.

"Who's that?" Allison said just as put-off at hearing Katie's full name.

"I don't know. He was harassing me this morning after I left class."

"Not another hall monitor reject?"

"Those kids have no lives." Katie agreed. Last year, Principal Boyle got the brilliant idea to have hall monitors in a high school. An incident involving pepper spray and handcuffs shut down the program. However, some super do-gooders still lingered—probably in some underground club scheming to keep the halls free of Taco Tuesday wrappers.

"I need to talk to you," he said when he reached her. If he had said please or hadn't been looking at her like she spit in his cereal, she might have stood there and listened. One thing was for sure, he acted like a bully—and just like he missed the memo about her name, he missed the one about her being a bad target.

"We need to talk in private," he said, raising his eyebrows and placing a stiff finger on his left temple. All of his long fingers were calloused.

He suddenly stuffed them in his pockets.

"About what? I don't know you. We don't have anything private to talk about." The more she stood there, the uneasier she felt. Hamilton High wasn't a big school. It was private. Everyone knew everyone, and yet she had never seen him before.

"My name is Tristan. Now you know me."

"Unless you can think of a reason for me to go running off into some dark corner with you, don't count on it."

"Smooth, Kay," Allison said.

Katie blushed. "I didn't mean it like that." She hit Allison with her chemistry notebook as the bell rang. She opened her classroom door and shrugged, uncaring, at Tristan. Whatever he wanted would have to wait.

⁎⁎⁎

After school, Katie saw Brian standing near her locker, surrounded by a crowd of girls complaining about weekend homework. His short brown hair looked a little too dry and his lips a little too cracked. She wanted to douse him in moisturizer. It was a mystery how he stayed popular with those dry lips. If anyone knew the real him, the Brian whose room smelled like moldy Doritos and cheese—the kind of cheese she wouldn't touch even if it were deep fried and dripping marinara—he'd probably die of shame and she'd be his only friend.

They locked eyes for a moment before he turned his attention back to his fan club. The girls giggled and Katie continued to her locker.

"Hey Katie," Brian said, pulling on the back of her bookbag.

"The Brian fan club is getting bigger," Katie laughed, "And so is your head—stop flipping your hair like that. It makes you look like such a poser."

"It's not posing if you're the real deal."

Katie rolled her eyes and gagged as she opened her locker and shoved her books inside. She wasn't going to go anywhere near that ego.

"I'm so glad it's Friday. Let's go to the movies," Brian said.

"Aren't you grounded? Lucy specifically said, 'If you can't keep your room clean you can't have a life,' to which you said—"

"I'll just tell her I'm studying at your house. She's been way uptight lately. God, she's annoying."

He wasn't being fair. He was never fair about Lucinda and that bothered Katie. Lucinda was the perfect mother. He was lucky and he took it for granted.

Allison appeared from around the corner and Katie felt the tension as soon as Allison's eyes glanced over Brian. "You guys done now? We're supposed to be at your house in twenty minutes," Allison said, ignoring Brian.

"There goes the movie," Brian complained.

"Oh happy-happy, joy-joy," Katie grumbled as she adjusted her bookbag and followed Allison out of the school.

She had completely forgotten today was the day they were going to help her with the yard work. Ever since her dad found out she'd turned her room into a hamster-breeding laboratory he gave her yard duty as a learning exercise: *how to be responsible and tell your parent you're breeding rodents in the house.* He'd only found out because she accidentally bought a gerbil with a nub for a tail and introduced it to its not-so-friendly mating partner. She had no idea, when she put the poor dead gerbil in the plastic lunch bag, that it would fall out of the trash can and onto their driveway for her dad to find.

But, she did know the "learning exercise" was just an excuse to pawn off yard duty. Their yard was no paradise. Weeds didn't just grow there, they had originated there. And worse, the grass was on some type of steroids and grew ten times faster than everyone else's. It was already catching the neighbors' attention, but their stuck-up neighbors could afford gardeners. They had to be the only house in the neighborhood that didn't have landscapers.

Her dad had banished her to Hell.

"I'm not picking weeds. I'm saying that now," Brian said as they neared her house.

"I don't care what you do, I'm just glad you guys are going to help," Katie said, dragging her feet.

It was extra hot today. No breeze. No clouds. She was minutes away from backbreaking pain and itchy skin. It didn't help that every house she passed was fit for one of those *Home and Garden* magazines.

"We should split the yard into three parts, we'll get it done faster that way"—Allison eyed Brian—"and no one will get stuck pulling all the weeds."

"Good to see you're using those tremendous math skills you've got," Brian said.

"Well Brian, I'm so busy succeeding in *all* my other classes, math gets pushed to the back burner. But I would consider *one* 'C' acceptable, wouldn't you?"

Brian frowned and stared at the sidewalk. "Don't be annoying, Allison."

"You started it," she snapped back.

Katie sighed. They hadn't always been like this. Only for the last two years. One summer everything was great, but within the first year of high school, they couldn't stand to be near each other. It took a lot of begging to get them *both* to agree to help her. This would be the first group activity they did since sophomore year when they all got detention for starting a food fight with Christi Taylor.

"Hey," Allison said. "Isn't that the kid from earlier?" As they moved closer to Katie's house, she saw *him* standing on her porch, with his wrinkled shirt, fitted pants, and that same pissy look.

"Who's that?" Brian asked.

Katie squinted. "I don't know."

Allison slowed her steps and furrowed her brows. "How does he know where you live?"

Katie played back every conversation she had with him. He had come from nowhere. She tried remembering his name but could only come up with the names of people she already knew—people she had known for years. People who didn't know where she lived.

He stood there, watching, as she walked up her driveway.

"What are you doing here?" she said, glad Allison and Brian were standing next to her.

He frowned. "What do you think?"

"I think you can leave." She was creeped out by the way he stood staring at her. His hair was too black, his eyes too blue, and his skin too smooth. Even in his stillness he was too alive. She felt something deep in the back of her mind; stirring, inside a rattling cage.

Tristan.

He said his name was Tristan.

Tristan sighed. "I'm only going to tell you this one more time. In fact, I'll make it easy for you. Let's go inside and talk."

Allison and Brian stared at him. Surely they could see it too. He was off—on some brand of crazy.

"Get off my property. I don't know you, and we have nothing to talk about." She said it and meant it, but she was curious about what he wanted. After all, he had tried to talk to her twice that day; however, he was at her *house*. This was creepy. She didn't want him thinking he could stalk her.

She walked past him and to her door—to show him he didn't faze her.

He grabbed her arm. "This isn't a game. We need to talk now."

"Get off me!" she yelled.

Brian pushed his way in between them. Tristan grabbed Brian and threw him so hard against the wood railing, it creaked.

Katie pulled her arm, but it was useless. Panic seized the back of her neck. He dragged her down the stairs towards the driveway. Toward a car parked on the curb. Katie screamed for him to let go. Allison ran past her and stopped midway between them and the car.

She held up her hands. "Look, if all you want is to talk, we can calm down, sit on the porch, and you can talk to Katie."

Tristan stopped.

"Let go of me," Katie said, yanking her arm back, but it was like pulling at a pipe stuck in a cement wall.

"Kay, he only wants to—BRIAN STOP!"

Katie turned to see Brian lunging at them with a knife in his hand. Tristan shoved her onto the grass, and she rolled. She tried to stand; when she looked up, she sank back down. The knife stuck out of Tristan's chest. A knife.

"Oh my god. Oh my god." Katie couldn't breathe. She couldn't move. She could only watch as the blood stain grew, bigger and wider, on his shirt.

Allison cursed. She ran over to Tristan, but he pushed her away and pulled out the knife.

Katie swallowed down vomit as blood gushed out.

"Fucking great," Tristan stumbled onto the grass next to Katie. "Who the hell carries around an iron pocket-knife?"

Brian stuttered. "How…how'd you know? You couldn't know unless you're a—"

"Shut up," Allison snapped. "Brian, you have no idea how lucky you are."

"What are you talking about?" Katie screamed, eyes still on the growing puddle. Blood poured out of the rip in his shirt. "Oh my god. Brian, what did you do? Oh my god."

Tristan's face started to pale and his breath grew short and hollow.

"I…he's not like us. He can't be," Brian said, standing in the middle of her yard, just as pale as Tristan.

"Kay, can you do me a favor?" Allison said, her eyes darting up and down the street. "Put your hands on his chest and press down hard. Okay?" Allison knelt down and rummaged through her bookbag like a madwoman.

"What?" Katie swallowed down more vomit and started to cry. How had this happened? Why had this happened? Tristan tried to sit up but fell back down.

Tristan grimanced. "This is all your fault."

"Kay, do what I told you. Now." Allison pulled out her phone.

Katie reached out trembling hands over his chest and pressed down lightly. The warm blood welled between her fingers. *Harder*, she thought, but she couldn't stop shaking.

Tristan screamed. "You're making this hurt so much more than it should."

"Sorry," she cried, shaking even more.

"Lucy?" Allison said into her phone, "Brian just—can you come to Katie's house immediately? There's been an accident—no, Brian's fine. He stabbed someone—no, not like that—Katie is here too. Okay, hurry."

Katie looked at Allison. "We're supposed to call the police, right? We—we should call the police. Why would you call Brian's mom?"

Allison knelt down next to Katie. "You're doing really good, Kay. We are going to press down a little harder. Okay?" Allison placed her hands firmly on top of Katie's.

Why the hell hasn't she called the police? Katie pressed down harder. There was so much blood. Too much blood. What could Brian's parents do? This boy might be dead by the time they get here. He was going to die. Here. On her lawn—all because she didn't give him five minutes of her time. She cried harder, gasping, as her tears mixed with his blood. They were all going to go to jail. Her life was over. They had killed a boy.

"Kay, I need you to calm down. Okay? Lucy is going to be here any minute and everything will be fine."

"He needs blood, he's losing so much," Katie said. "Why haven't you called the police? We could explain we thought he was kidnapping me. It was an accident. It was an accident, right?" Katie looked at Brian; he offered no answer. He turned around and vomited on her dad's rosebush.

"Kay, we aren't calling the police. This is a special situation."

"What? Allison, he's going to die!"

"Shut up, Katalina," Tristan said between breaths. She stared into his eyes. They were calm, and if anything, aggravated.

"Why? Why aren't you guys freaking out? Why did you say Brian was lucky? Am I the only one seeing all of this blood? He needs a hospital!" Katie cried.

Before she got any answers, an SUV screeched into her driveway, and Brian's parents, Will and Lucinda, got out.

"Tristan? I told you NOT to leave the house," Lucinda said, kneeling next to him. Everyone stared at Lucinda, even Brian, who was still bent over the roses.

"Lucy, how do you know—" Allison started.

"He's my nephew," Lucinda said.

Brian gasped. "But he's a—"

"Shut up, Brian," Will said, moving to the other side of Tristan. "Help me get him in the car. Katie, keep your hands on that. Got it?"

Katie did as she was told and they all moved him into the back of the Andersons' SUV.

"I'll clean up here and take his car back," Lucinda said, pulling a set of car keys out of Tristan's pocket. "You're going to have to *earn* these back, Buddy."

Katie watched as Tristan's face turned from pale white to a morbid gray.

"Get home as soon as you can, Lucy. He's lost a lot of blood. I'm gonna need help," Will said.

"Aren't we going to the hospital?" Katie shouted. She trusted Brian's parents—she had spent more of her childhood with them than her own dad—but *this* was wrong. She began to shake violently and her bloody hands slipped over his wound. He screamed.

"Katie, just sit tight. Everything's going to be fine," Will said, pulling out of the driveway. She looked out the window to see Lucinda spraying off the puddle of blood Tristan left in the grass…covering up a soon to be murder scene.

Katie had just taken part in a murder cover-up.

"I'm not dead." Tristan grimaced. "And I'm not going to die. Takes more than that to kill a vampire."

2

The Board

IN THE REAR-VIEW mirror, Katie caught Will's eyes. "That's enough, Tristan," he said as they took the left turn into Brian's neighborhood.

Allison cursed under her breath.

Katie waited for him to pass out, for his head to go limp and fall to the side. That was what happened when people were badly injured. They became delusional and passed out—but he continued to stare at her with blue, probing eyes.

"I can't believe you don't know anything," Tristan said between breaths.

"Quiet," Will snapped.

Tristan coughed up blood. "I just want to know, who the hell carries a *hunting knife* to school? Isn't that against the law, no matter what kind of school you go to?"

"I—I didn't mean to—" Brian mumbled next to Katie.

"*Shut up,* Brian!" Will yelled. His voice boomed throughout the car as he pulled into the driveway of his house.

"Will," Katie said anxiously. She couldn't take anymore. They needed to go to the hospital. Not their house. What could Will and Lucinda do? They weren't doctors. She choked back fresh tears. The blood kept pouring out between her fingers.

"Katie, I know you are confused, but we need to get him inside. We don't have much time." The car jerked to a stop. Will got out and flew to the back door. He pulled Tristan out fast and gently. "Brian, get the door. Allison, I need you to get everything I tell you. Fast."

Tristan put all his weight on Will as Will helped him to the door. They moved into the house and Will took Tristan into one of the back rooms.

Katie stood in the doorway. She couldn't stop shaking. She shivered as air hit her blood-soaked shirt. There was blood everywhere. The smell of it burned into her nostrils; the smell even stained the back of her tongue.

She moved to the living room and sat down. She had lost her mind somewhere in between Brian stabbing Tristan and Will telling her they weren't going to the hospital. Tristan had said he was a "*vampire*"—that's what she heard while she was losing it—or maybe *he* was losing *his* mind while spiraling into death's arms.

"Bring me water… I need that rubbing alcohol in here," Will shouted from the back room. Allison ran from the hallway to the kitchen, and Brian dazed, moved out of her way. "I need more blood. Where's the blood?" Will shouted every time Allison stopped to rummage in the kitchen drawers.

"*Do* something, Brian. We need your help," Allison said. Gauze stuck out from under her arms and packs of blood balanced atop a basin of water that sloshed onto the carpet as she rushed back down the hall.

Katie looked at Brian standing in the middle of the kitchen. Doing nothing. She wanted to do something. She *should* do something. But she was like Brian—frozen. Of all things, why did he have to *stab* Tristan? She didn't know whether to be grateful or scared. She couldn't take her eyes off him—his soft, round face and puffy green eyes. She had to keep watching him. If she didn't, he would cease to be Brian; his round face would turn sharp and his eyes would become hard and dead. If she looked away—even to blink—he'd turn into someone who could stab another person.

"Katie!" Lucinda shrieked as she came into the house. "Brian, go get her one of your shirts and a pair of pants. She's covered in blood. On—the ivory Valdi. Katie?" Katie watched Brian disappear up the stairs. "Can you hear me, Sweetie?"

She looked down at herself. The baby blue tank-top she wore under her white blouse was now purple. The blood stuck to her stomach. Her navy skirt was darkly stained.

She flinched when Lucinda pushed hair out of her face. "He needs a hospital," Katie said.

Lucinda waved a finger in front of Katie's face. "Follow my finger." She checked Katie's pulse. Why her pulse? She wasn't the one bleeding out. "You're just a little shook up."

"He lost too much blood," Katie said.

"Let's get you off this very expensive couch and cleaned up. Of all places to sit, you know how expensive that Valdi is." Lucinda gently helped her up and led her to the bathroom. This house was foreign. This couldn't be where she had all of her birthday parties until she was too old for backyard parties. This couldn't be the place where she learned how to do cartwheels and climb trees. This was not the bathroom door Brian had tied a string to, to help her get rid of her loose front tooth when they were ten.

"Lucy, w—what's going on?"

"Remember when you were six, I used to run your bath water every night? You were so particular about using the jasmine bubble bath. You were addicted to it. I think I've got some jasmine body wash under the sink."

"Lucy. Brian—" She couldn't say it. Not out loud.

"You loved it when your dad worked nights. You'd come over carrying your overnight bag and spent hours in the bath—"

"Lucy!"

"Tristan is going to be fine."

A scream filled the house. It rumbled through the walls. Lucinda's eyes were wide and worried. He wasn't going to be fine. It was written all over her face.

"Oh my god," Katie cried. She tried to wipe her face but stopped as she felt the blood coat her cheeks. She turned and saw herself in the mirror. It couldn't have been her. She looked down at her hands. They were someone else's. Not hers—hers could never be that red. She rubbed them on her wet skirt.

"Listen to me, Katie." Lucinda gripped her shoulders tight. "I need you to keep it together for just a little bit longer."

"I can't," Katie said, trying to rub the blood off her arms. It smeared like lotion.

"Katie, remember when Brian fell out of that old tree-house and his bone stuck straight out of his leg? You were the bravest ten-year-old I'd ever seen."

"He wasn't going to die!" Katie's heart pounded. "I wasn't covering up a murder." She shook harder.

"Tristan isn't going to die." Lucinda turned on the shower and checked the water. "I promise, things will be fine. You just need to get out of those clothes and cleaned up."

Lucinda left the bathroom and it took every ounce of self-control not to scream as Katie peeled off the bloody clothes. She stood under the shower head and watched the tinted pink water swirl down into the drain. No matter how many times she scrubbed, she couldn't get the red stain from underneath her nails or the smell out of her nose.

Ten minutes passed, or maybe twenty. She couldn't move. Didn't want to. She turned off the water. Only the sound of water being sucked down the drain echoed in the bathroom— the house was silent. She hesitated before she pulled back the shower curtain. What would she do with her clothes? Burn them? It was evidence of whatever they had just done.

She squeezed the curtain in her hands and moved it. It came more as a relief than a surprise that her clothes were gone and replaced by Brian's old shirt and basketball shorts.

Lucinda. She was like that. Thorough.

Katie dried her hair and her body, expecting to see blood every time she pulled the towel away. She had to stop looking in the mirror because every patch of pink blotchy skin looked like a permanent stain, and she'd rub on them until they burned.

She got dressed and opened the bathroom door. Silence. Tiptoeing down the stairs, she checked the living room. What if they'd left her in the house? What was she supposed to do?

She jumped when she walked by the dining room and saw everyone sitting at the table. Everyone except Tristan. Her heart pounded and her stomach lurched. She swallowed back vomit and breathed deep, using the door frame for support. Lucinda said Tristan was her nephew, but Katie had never heard of him before. From the look on Brian's face, neither had he. Why would she not take her own nephew to the hospital? What— who—

"Katie?" Lucinda got up from the table and hugged her. "He's going to be just fine. Don't look like that, Sweetie. He's okay. He just needs a few days to get back on his feet."

"A few days?" Had Lucinda not seen the way blood spilled from his body like a knocked-over carton of milk?

"Katie, sit down," Will said. He sat at the far end of the table.

He had changed his shirt, not a drop of blood to be found. His hands were spotless.

"Will—"

"Lucy, we don't have time. They're coming. The longer we wait, the more we put her at risk." Will's eyes were soft and green. The same soft eyes she had seen nearly her entire life— eyes that were—that *seemed*—honest. She looked away. Why did everything about him, and the way Lucinda held her close, make her want to run for her life? She pulled away from Lucinda and opened her mouth to scream all of the questions that had been building ever since she saw Tristan standing on her front porch.

She sat down in the chair farthest from them all.

Will sighed. "Katie, there are people coming here. They are going to give you two options. We can't make the decision for you. All we can do is tell you that no matter what, we will always be here for you," he said.

"What decision? Who's coming?" Katie could feel her muscles tensing, telling her to get up and run.

Lucinda sat in the chair next to her. "Katie, Tristan is a vampire. We couldn't take him to the hospital because the people there, who *could* help him, can't know that. In fact, no one can know that especially the people coming." Lucinda reached for her hand.

Katie pulled away and looked around the table. They were all watching her, waiting for some type of reaction. "What's *really* going on?" she said.

The doorbell rang, echoing throughout the house. Katie looked at them and then the hallway.

"I'll stall them for as long as I can," Lucinda said, getting up from the table.

"I know we are asking you to believe something that seems crazy, but you have to listen to me," Will said. "There is a lot more to this world than you think, Katie. The people who are here are bringing someone who is going to erase your memory unless you choose to become one of us."

"Erase my memory?" Katie's insides squeezed. She could hear Lucinda open the door. Muttered voices filled the hall. "Will?"

"Trust me, Katie. Don't say a word unless I tell you to." He looked at Allison and Brian, "Repeat the story I told you. Don't so much as mutter Tristan's name."

"Got it," Allison said. Brian nodded, his face just as pale as before. His eyes never left the table.

Will got up and moved to Katie as the voices grew louder. "Trust me Katie. Everything I'm about to say about you is true. Everything. But once they tell you everything, it's your decision."

"Will—" Katie stuttered.

He put his hand on her shoulder and squeezed. Nothing about what he said was reassuring.

A big voice drifted in from the hall. "My wife and I are looking forward to another one of your dinners, Lucinda. Don't tell Mariam I told you this, but I dream about your steaks."

"Nonsense, Jim," Lucinda said, walking into the room. Her voice was light, but Katie knew by the way her eyes darted from Will onto her that she was on edge like the rest of them. A large man followed Lucinda in and laughed.

"Will, if Mariam was half as good at cooking as your wife, I'd have to have all my clothes custom-made!"

Katie took in Jim, the man that made the room smaller. He was as big as his voice, almost as tall as the door frame, and—staring at her.

"This is her?" A sharp voice said behind Jim. An old, thin woman fixed a pair of glasses on her face and peered at Katie. Not a hair strayed from her tight, white bun. She moved past Jim and closer to Katie.

Will squeezed Katie's shoulder one more time. "Yes, Katalina Watts," Will said. "Drew and Katalina's daughter."

"Oh, Katalina Rockwell? From New York?" Jim said, nodding. His voice booming as he looked back and forth between Will and Lucinda.

"That would be her," Will said.

"Well," the woman said, looking away from Katie and on to Brian and Allison. "What exactly happened?" Her eyes pierced them through her glasses.

Allison sat up straighter than a board and cleared her throat. "We were walking to get ice cream. We took a shortcut through the alley between Second and Third Street and a D-Range vampire attacked us. She was feeding off a homeless man and tried to attack Katie. But she ran off when she smelled the iron in Brian's knife. As soon as she hit the sun she crystallized."

"A D-range in the middle of the day?" The woman said with an arched brow.

"It wouldn't be the first time, Henrietta. Women are always getting turned and then thrown out. The north gate is right there next to that ice cream parlor."

Henrietta looked between them; she settled her gaze on Brian. "Where exactly, sir, did you get an iron knife, and why did you have it while walking home—*from school?*"

"I—I—"

"Speak up, boy." Jim cleared his throat. He too had hardened his gaze on Brian.

"I took it from my dad. I didn't mean to—I just wanted to—I don't know. I—"

"That's enough," Henrietta snapped. "You know the rules. We have them for a reason. If you can't follow them—I don't care *who* your father is—we will send you to an omitter."

Brian didn't move. If it weren't for the tiniest lift of his chest, he could have passed as dead. No one in the room moved. Katie had been wrong. It wasn't Jim who had made the room small— it was this woman, and she stood no taller than five feet.

"Glock," she said to the doorway. A tall thing walked into the room. It wasn't a man—it couldn't have been a man. It had no face—nothing Katie could see. Just a single black eye peering out from a head wrapped in gauze. It wore a suit, but she could tell the clothes were meant to hide something. Something hideous. Its hands were a color between gray and white, the veins clearly webbed and green.

"Don't worry. You won't remember a thing," Henrietta said.

It reached toward Katie and she jumped back in her chair.

"Wait." Will moved between Katie and the thing, Glock.

"Will, you know the rules," Jim said, seemingly bored and ready to move on to something new.

"She's a guardian."

"She isn't on the list," Henrietta said.

"She was born with the mark. Drew didn't register her. He didn't want her to know about us after they lost her mother." Will seemed unfazed by the thing standing only inches from him. A smell, like dying flesh or rotting fish, seeped from Glock. It was inhuman.

"I thought that was a little suspicious given the lineage," Jim said, eyeing Katie. "Why didn't you say anything three years ago? You know we're short on recruits. Especially ones with a solid bloodline like hers. If you knew, it was your responsibility to say something."

"It wasn't my place. Drew made his decision clear," Will said.

Jim scoffed. "It's *her* decision, not his. Really, Will. You let an old friendship cloud your judgment. I told you he was no good when he deserted"

"We can't change the past, Jim." Will turned around to face Katie. "But, it's her decision now."

As soon as Will moved, she was flooded with the putrid smell wafting from Glock. She tried to avert her eyes, but his single black eye was like a magnet forcing her to look.

She was mesmerized. It changed colors from black to green-gold. Like an animal in the night. "*I know you. I've tasted you before. I know what you are. I've consumed the horror that is your past.*"

"What?" Katie said. Her heart pounded in her chest and her skin itched with disgust.

"I said, it's your decision now." Will looked between her and Glock. "Glock, could you wait outside? We'll call you back in if we need you." Glock's orb returned to black and he left the room, leaving behind his smell. Had no one else heard him?

"I—I don't know," Katie said, looking between all the eyes staring at her.

"This isn't fair. Brian and I had three months to decide," Allison said. Katie wished she had sat next to Allison.

Henrietta shook her head. "Unfortunately, this isn't a normal situation, Miss Stonewall," she said. "You were under the protection of the school and you and your classmates were sectioned off from the rest of the world to learn about our world and make your decision. Miss Watts does not have that luxury given she wasn't properly registered. We have rules for a reason." She turned to Katie and took off her glasses.

It was the first time she looked kind. The wrinkles around her eyes lifted as she knelt next to Katie. "My number one priority in life is to protect as many people as I can. But, it's my personal agenda to make sure the children in this world have a fighting chance. I would be going against that if I let you walk out this door without deciding. When the evil in this world knows you can see it, it's only a matter of time before it seeks you out."

"How can I make a decision when I don't know anything about any of this?" Katie wanted to get up and fight her way out of the room, but there was no way she'd make it past Glock.

"We can make all of this go away. That's what Glock is here for. He is an omitter. He erases memories." Henrietta looked at Katie with clear blue eyes. "Or we can tell you what you need to know."

Katie thought about the blood that was smeared across her face and arms. How it coated her hands. She'd give anything to forget it. To forget the smell, that even now, lingered. "Will I just forget today?" Katie looked between Will and Lucinda.

Darkness passed between them. Lucinda frowned. "We don't know. Sometimes people only forget a few days, sometimes they forget months—or years."

"Years?" Katie couldn't believe that. How could they erase someone's memories if they didn't know how it worked? Henrietta had threatened to do it to Brian. Now Katie understood why he was still staring at the table—still stark white.

Jim leaned against a wall. "The omitters don't talk. When they take more than they are supposed to, we don't know if it's something they can control."

"They don't talk? At all?" Katie glanced at the dark hallway. Glock was still there, lurking. Listening.

"No one has ever chatted one up before. Not that I know of." Jim said.

I've tasted your memories…I've consumed the horror that is your past…

She started to say something but stopped. She didn't want anything more to do with Glock. She didn't want him touching her—there was something sick about him. But how could she agree to become a guardian? She didn't even know what that meant.

She looked at Allison. Allison had been so calm and collected when Katie panicked and cried over Tristan's bleeding body. Was that what being a guardian was like? Was that why Allison always walked with confidence? Could it be so bad if Allison and Brian, who she'd known her whole life, were a part of it?

Jim cleared his throat. "You could always choose to be one of us," Jim said as if he were talking about joining a team. "Ignorance is not always bliss, darling. Sometimes it can get you into odd situations, like the one you've found yourself in today. What you saw must have scared the daylights out of you. As guardians, we are secret keepers. We make sure that our human world stays ignorant of the demons that live below us and amongst us—don't look at me like that, Henrietta. Demon is a perfectly acceptable word these days.

"Anyway, if you become one of us, you'd be professionally trained to spot a demon—'other being'—and interact with them socially. We have many different departments in our line of work, but most people like to patrol known areas where—'other beings'—frequent to make sure they leave normal people alone. That D-Range you saw was a perfect example of someone not doing their job and some lawless demon thinking he can do whatever he wants. That woman's life was taken from her twice: once by the monster that changed her and again by the evil it turned her into. You can protect people from that." Jim smiled gallantly as if to emphasize the pride he felt for his work. "You can be a part of that, Katie."

Katie stared blankly.

"In so many words," Henrietta eyed Jim, "we also broaden relations amongst our different communities—"

"Dress it up how you will Henrietta, they're still demons," Jim laughed to himself.

"—And we strive to learn the laws of each community, as to keep peace between our world and theirs. Yes, we save people from becoming victims of heinous crimes, but that is only a small part of the bigger picture," Henrietta said as if Jim had never interrupted her.

Katie took in a breath. Her chair was uncomfortably warm against her legs.

"Do you understand the choice you have to make?" Henrietta raised her eyebrows.

Katie nodded, but did she really? Was it that simple? No—it couldn't have been, Tristan wasn't human. Nothing was simple about that. Nothing was simple about deciding her future today, at this very moment.

Katie looked to Allison—Allison, who always pushed her to take life more seriously. No amount of perfect attendance or completed homework could have prepared Katie for this moment.

Katie wished she knew what Allison was thinking.

Allison nodded and smiled at her.

"Miss Stonewall," Henrietta said in warning. Allison broke eye contact, but the smile was still there.

It was this or the monster. *This*, or possibly not remembering the last year of her life. "I'll do it," Katie said. "I'll be a guardian."

Henrietta nodded. "It's not an easy choice. You won't be a teenager anymore. You'll be expected to study hard. Failing in the classroom isn't an option—yes, we've seen your current transcripts—and you will be enrolled in a vigorous training program that will challenge you mentally and physically. Life as you know it will be over."

"If I get my memory erased, my life could be over anyway," Katie said. What would life be like if she woke up and didn't know who she was?

"Fair enough," Henrietta said, standing up. "You were born with a gift, and gifts should never go unused."

Katie shook her head without meaning to. She had no gifts. She could barely color in the lines.

"If Will is right, and you were born with a mark, you are untouchable like the rest of us. You possess a power that renders you untouchable to anyone who isn't human. But being *born* guardian isn't enough. It requires discipline and hard concentration." Henrietta paused. "She'll need a mentor to get her up to speed."

"I'll do it," Lucinda said. All the heads in the room turned—even Brian looked up from the table. "I'm ready to come back. She needs someone she can trust."

"Lucy," Will said.

"Will, I can do it. I'm okay now." Lucinda ran her hands across the table cloth.

"I'm glad to hear it," Henrietta said, putting her glasses back on. "Will, I'll do the paperwork for her transfer along with your nephew's. Tristan, was it?"

"It's so rare we get transfers. To think, all of this in one day, what are the odds?" Jim laughed. "Where did you say he was from?"

Lucinda smiled tightly, gesturing for them to follow her out of the room. "The—"

"Southern part of Texas," came a voice from the hall. Tristan walked into the room looking pale as ever, but a smile stretched across his face. Everyone except Henrietta and Jim froze. His hair was wild and his shirt was wrinkled and blood free. He strolled into the room as if he hadn't had a blade in his chest an hour ago. He sat down in the chair next to Katie.

"A bit pale for Texas, aren't you?" Jim reached out to shake Tristan's hand.

"Well I'm originally from the northeast." He flashed a set of white teeth at Henrietta.

"That's a lot of transferring for someone still in training," Jim said.

"Yeah, it is. I only left the northeast because our house burned down. My dad said it was time for a new start. I had to agree, I felt like I was living in a prison cell." Tristan laughed at himself.

"That's too bad," Henrietta said.

"Yes, absolutely terrible," Lucinda said, still gesturing for Jim and Henrietta to follow her out of the room.

"Not as bad as the tornado that hit our house in Texas," Tristan hung his head.

"String of bad luck you've got!" Jim said, sitting next to Tristan. Fury flickered in Lucinda's eyes.

"No, the bad luck hit when my mom found out my dad had an affair with the guy who burned down our first house. My poor mom. Broke her heart. Literally."

Henrietta blinked a few times and glanced between Will and Lucinda. "I—I'm so sorry to hear that."

"Dear, God. That's a—a tough situation," Jim said. He patted Tristan's shoulder with a heavy hand.

Tristan grabbed his chest and bent over. His face contorted with pain.

"Are you okay?" Henrietta said as both she and Jim moved in closer.

"It's just so hard," he said between his teeth.

Katie's mouth dropped. This kid was a class-act. A nut case. A whack job. Who told people that? Complete strangers no less. Was he even serious? Was this why Lucinda never mentioned him or his parents?

"Okay, well if that's all we have to discuss," Lucinda said, moving to the hallway. "I'd love to have you both for dinner, but it's been a long day, and I still have to get Tristan situated."

"Oh. Yes, of course." Henrietta looked relieved to leave. "Will, you've got a bit of paperwork piling on your desk."

"Gone for one day, and you can't get on without me." Will left the room with Henrietta, Lucinda, and Jim in tow. Their voices moved slowly down the hall.

"That was intense," Allison exhaled when their voices were indistinguishable.

Tristan sat up. "Of all the knives to use, you used an iron knife. My blood is on fire." He pulled his hand away from his chest; there was a small blood stain. He was sitting so close, Katie could see it rise and fall. Brian got up and left the room without uttering a single word. Tristan's eyes zoned in on Katie as if Brian hadn't moved at all.

"What do you want from me?" she said, watching him. He couldn't have been the same boy from before. A boy who dragged her with no effort across her lawn. A boy who threw her out of the way as Brian ran up to him with a knife. A boy who was more concerned with getting her out of the way than saving himself.

"*Now* you want to talk?" He tilted his head back and studied the ceiling.

3

DIRTY LITTLE SECRETS

LUCINDA STORMED INTO the dining room. "I swear to God, Tristan, if you do anything like that again, I will lock you in a basement until you're old enough to wear diapers again."

"Considering my current *lifestyle*, I'd say that might be a few hundred years," Tristan said, closing his eyes. He was the poster child of spoiled brats. Everything about him made Katie hate that she wanted to know more about where he came from and what he was and—what he wanted to tell her.

Will appeared from the hallway and leaned against the door frame. He closed his eyes and sighed. "Tristan, you're wearing out your welcome. Go back to your room before that wound opens up more."

"Do you know what you just put us through? And Katie through? Will had to lie for you. He put his job on the line," Lucinda said. Her arms twitched and Katie was sure Lucinda was going to smack him.

"*He* didn't ask me to lie, Lucy. Don't put that on him." Will stared at Lucinda. Silence passed between them.

Lucinda slunk into a chair. "Will, what else did you expect?"

"For once in your life you could have—"

"Not now, Will," Lucinda said between her teeth. "We have company."

"When don't we?" he said.

Katie blushed. She had never really seen them fight before. The look on Allison's face told her she hadn't either. Tristan's eyes were still closed as if he were asleep, unaware of everyone in the room. The slight smile creeping on his face said otherwise. This was all his fault. This entire day.

"You know, Lucy," Will exhaled. "The funny thing about damage control is you have to cause damage first."

"What are you suggesting?" Lucinda said under her breath.

Tristan opened his eyes and sat up. "Don't worry, Will. Every good guardian family has a dirty secret." He looked at Katie. "Like Katalina."

Though she could feel all the eyes in the room on her, the only ones that mattered were his. She couldn't decide whether he was being rude or willing her to understand something. A voice in the back of her mind rattled; a thought had appeared and vanished before it could be heard.

Will rubbed his temples. "Tristan, you haven't even been here one day. I'm regretting my decision."

"Okay. Okay. I'm going back." Tristan got up. He frowned at Katie as he pushed in his chair.

"Will—" Lucinda started.

"I'm getting tired, Lucy. *Really* tired," Will said, running his hand down his face. He left the room behind Tristan and with them Katie's courage to look Lucinda in the eyes. Though it was obvious, she didn't want Lucinda to know she had heard what he really meant.

Lucinda cradled her head in her hands. "Today is a fine day for a glass of wine. Don't you think girls?" She looked at Katie for a second and sighed. "I'm sorry, Katie. Today must feel like a nightmare for you. How about some ice cream and a movie? We can have our girls' night early this month."

The last thing Katie wanted was ice cream and a facial. How could Lucinda think *girls' night* was the solution to spending— what felt like—hours soaked in more blood than she had seen in her entire life, meeting a deranged lunatic of a boy, watching the worlds most perfect couple admit they aren't so perfect, and worst of all, agreeing to be something she didn't know a thing about. She looked at Allison for help—for some desperately needed sanity.

"Maybe we can take the ice cream to-go and call it a night," Allison said. Her eyes were wide, and in them, Katie could see a plan stewing. They needed to be alone. They had a lot to talk about.

"I don't want Katie alone tonight," Lucinda said, eyeing her. "Why don't you both just stay over? I'll get the guest room upstairs set up." Lucinda sighed deeply as she raised herself up and started pushing in all the chairs as if it were already decided.

"My dad—"

"Don't worry about him. We'll let him know you're staying over. Everything else can wait until the morning." Katie knew Lucinda wasn't going to call her dad. She'd get Will to do it, even if he was mad at her. Lucinda hadn't said a word to Katie's dad in three years—the year she was supposedly supposed to learn about all of this—and today wasn't going to be any different. "Help yourselves to anything in the kitchen. I don't think I'm up to cooking tonight," Lucinda said, leaving the dining room.

"Allison," Katie said as soon as Lucinda was out of earshot.

Allison put her finger to her lips to silence Katie and told her to follow her into the kitchen. Allison walked past the spotless island, past the other kitchen door and walk-in pantry, and all the way to the breakfast nook on the far side of the kitchen. It was a cozy spot under a darkening window. They could see someone coming from both doors if they needed to.

"This is so freaking exciting. You're one of us now. Ohmygod. I'm so mad this didn't happen before. *You* could have been my partner instead of Brian. If I had known—ohmygod. Kay, *this* is freaking awesome."

"I need you to take three steps back because your idea of awesome is grossly skewed." Katie leaned against the table and sighed. Already everything started to feel like a jacked-up dream.

It hadn't happened. There were no such things as vampires, or *whatever* Glock was. Nothing about Tristan screamed anything more than teen boy—except his death grip on her arm and him walking around hours after being stabbed.

"Once the shock wears off, you'll see what I mean. I finally get to tell you *everything*. Do you know how hard it was *not* calling you the first time I met a werewolf, or telling you how incredibly awesome it is to be the only level-3 in my class?" Allison rummaged through the cabinets and pulled out two bowls. Katie opened the freezer and shifted a bag of frozen broccoli to get to the rainbow sherbet ice cream she knew was in the back just for her. For a second she expected it to be gone. How could it be there—so normal—while Allison was spouting off things about creatures that only existed in fantasy?

She grabbed the sherbet and found the chocolate for Allison. "What exactly have I signed my life over to?" Katie wanted to sound sarcastic and calm, but her voice cracked.

"Don't be so dramatic, Kay. If anything you've just been offered a once-in-a-lifetime opportunity. You are a guardian now. Well, technically you've always been one, but now you get to *actually* be one."

Katie stared at her blankly as she sat the ice cream boxes on the table and slid into the booth. She scooped ice cream into her bowl, but not even the sherbet could ease the anxiety she felt in every inch of her body.

"It really isn't anything scary, just—cool."

"That is the vaguest thing you've ever said to me." The sweet flavors of her rainbow sherbet were gone, and she wasn't even two spoonfuls into the bowl. She let go of her spoon and moved the bowl away from her.

"Kay, I've been studying for two and a half years. All I've done, so far, is meet a bunch of normal-looking people and take tours around a city. It really isn't a big deal. We're just in on a secret that no one else is. That's the cool part. I mean, if you're hard core, when we graduate you could go into a department that does bounties."

"Bounties…like be a bounty hunter?" Katie's eyes widened. "A bounty hunter?"

"Normally that's a Level-0 job." Allison stopped mid-spoonful and put the spoon back in the bowl. "But it's really rare to get a job like that. You have to be, like, really good. That story I told Henrietta doesn't happen often. Most of a guardian's work is to keep people from going downside, and keeping an eye on our non-human friends, and in some cases integrating newly changed people into both societies. There's a department for that, but it's pretty lame. No action there—it's like, 'here is a blood bank where you can buy your ounces, and raw steaks are cheapest in these locations—blah blah—here's a pamphlet—blah blah—give us a call if you want to join the: Cry About Your Adjustment Problems group'." Allison looked up and shrugged at Katie's blinking eyes. "What? It was the worst field trip of my life."

Katie bit her bottom lip. How could she freak out when her best friend was sitting across from her eating chocolate ice cream and grinning?

Allison threw her head back, her red hair rocking back and forth in her ponytail. "You're gonna flip," she laughed. "I've got *the* biggest and juiciest gossip."

Katie grabbed her sherbet and mixed the liquid and solid swirls. "You could strip down and dance naked on the counter tops and it wouldn't phase me. I'm all out of shock for today."

Allison laughed harder. "Okay, then. Mr. Right, our math teacher. guardian. Mr. Rhineheart. guardian. Even Myrtle the office lady. All of them."

Katie was wrong. There was still a little shock left. "*Mr. Right?* He's so—*so boring.*" She imagined her dad freaking out after he found out the private school he'd been paying for was a hoax. Then again, he knew, didn't he?

"Yep. The teachers, the principal, the secretary, the nurse, I think even the janitors are all guardians. That accelerated program I'm in is a cover up. They're my training classes."

"Wait, why? At our school of all schools?"

"We live in a guardian community. Apparently, It used to be a school that only taught guardians, but then some starting marrying outside of the community and more kids weren't born guardian than were—so in order to keep the secret and not risk looking suspicious, we just blend in. We can weed out most of the normal kids from guardian families by pretending they don't meet 'Hamilton High standards,' but there aren't enough of us in training to make up a real school. And that's how you get an accelerated program." Allison shrugged.

"You mean to tell me Christi Taylor is a guardian?" Katie scowled, thinking about every time that girl said, 'Accelerated program,' as if she were a toe away from Harvard.

"I like how *that's* the first thing you think of," Allison said, scooping out more ice cream from the box.

"They really shouldn't call it that, it's misleading."

"I think that's the point, Kay. She really doesn't have anything to boast about, she's mediocre at best." Allison laughed and threw up her hands dramatically. "OMG. I can totally tell you what *really* happened to Crispy Christi now!"

Katie laughed too. "How could you keep a name like *Crispy Christi* from me?"

Allison stopped laughing long enough to say, "You remember when you found out she wore that wig?"

Katie's mouth dropped. Christi used to flip her hair in Katie's face and say, *"The other day my stylist said she'd die for hair like mine. She's in love with my volume."* That stupid girl hated the way Katie's hair was frizz-free with natural looping curls throughout. Time and time again she'd come to the school with some weird puffy copycat version until the year they started high school, when her hair miraculously transformed, bouncing with every step and shining with silky sheen. Even Katie was envious for a few months—until she found Christi in the bathroom shifting the "head of curls" on her head.

"She said she wore a wig because her 'stylist' gave her a bad hair cut," Katie said, reliving that glorious moment Christi spun around so fast her wig tilted.

Allison burst into a new set of giggles. "That summer before high school, remember we went off to that summer camp?"

Katie could never forget that summer. She wanted so bad to go to camp with Brian and Allison. She'd begged her dad week after week until he snapped. They couldn't afford it and he told her that she needed to grow up. It was the first and only time he'd ever yelled at her. She still wasn't completely over it. If she had known they had money problems she never would have brought it up. She never asked him for anything extra again. "I remember," Katie said, taking in a small mouthful of ice cream.

"That's where they told us about the guardians. Christi smuggled in *at least* twenty candles." Allison rolled her eyes. "She'd always light them around her head board and on her night stand. One night she laid down on her bed and the next thing I knew she was screaming bloody murder as her hair went up in flames." Allison laughed herself to tears. "I swear to God, you know how much hairspray she wears, I thought the whole camp was going to explode."

Katie laughed hard. It felt good to laugh.

"She pretty much had a buzz cut until camp was over. It was either that or leave early and forfeit her right to be a guardian."

"I'm surprised she didn't opt to have her memory erased," Katie laughed.

"Even Christi wouldn't risk that." Allison paused. "Remember Neil Tanner?"

"Scanner Tanner?" He was the only kid in their middle school with a photographic memory. It was starting to click for her. "Let me guess. He's not at some ivy-league private school in Washington?"

"Nope. He went to camp and had a breakdown. Said he wanted to go back to his normal life. They called an omitter and now he goes to a public school in Meridian."

Katie looked up. When everyone found out Neil wasn't at Hamilton High, rumor spread that he'd gotten a scholarship to a college prep school. A public school the next county over was far from that.

"Last I heard, he's still in the ninth-grade and can barely remember his own name." Allison looked down into her bowl of lumpy chocolate soup and shrugged. "I wouldn't have let them do that to you. I would have fought them off and taken you to the mountains or something."

Katie smiled and stared down at her own melting rainbow swirl. Her eyes burned. It didn't matter what else anyone told her about this world or any other. She'd be okay because she had Allison—even Brian was only trying to protect her in his own way. Her two best friends were on her side. She scooped up her soft ice cream, and it never tasted better.

"I'm glad that I have you guys," Katie said.

"Ha. You have me. Brian got you into this mess." Allison rolled her eyes. Katie thought for a moment and realized why her two best friends never told her why they started hating each other—why they stopped calling themselves "*the tripod.*"

"What happened after you guys found out you were guardians?"

Allison frowned. "At the end of summer camp, we had to pick partners. I picked Brian—obviously. By the end of freshman year—I don't know." The words began to rush from Allison's mouth. "At first, we were good. We learned things and we had a lot of fun. Then I picked things up faster than him—he resents me for being better."

Katie watched Allison grind her teeth. "Why didn't you just change partners?"

"We tried. You aren't allowed to change partners until you graduate. It's supposed to teach us how to work closely with someone and overcome problems. But that's pretty pointless when your partner is spiteful and lies to everyone and himself." Allison stood up and put her bowl in the sink. The spoon raked across the bowl.

Katie checked the kitchen doorways out of guilt. She expected him to walk in at any moment with a look of pure betrayal written on his face.

"He's lucky he didn't get expelled for having a bounty hunting knife, let alone bringing it to school." Allison slunk back into the breakfast nook.

"Where'd he even get it? I mean, Will? *Will?* A bounty hunter?"

No. She baked cookies with these people.

"Used to be. Now he's on the board. Lucinda used to be a level-0 bounty hunter too, but a long time ago she got hurt so bad she had to retire."

"What happened?" Katie asked, remembering the way Lucinda sometimes rubbed her hip.

"I don't know, they never talk about it." Suddenly, Allison slapped her hands down on the table making Katie jump. She looked at the doorway and lowered her voice. "There's only one reason why Lucy would come out of retirement." Allison's eyes were wide. "There are only two types of vampires that can walk around in the day, purebloods and halfbloods. I'm positive Tristan isn't a pureblood, there are only a handful of those left. Plus, Lucy got him into our school. No way he'd pass the hand test if he were a pureblood."

"What—"

"No wonder Will is pissed. *We* probably weren't supposed to know about any of this. That's why he made us lie about what happened."

Katie leaned in closer, waiting for Allison to continue.

"Halfbloods are taboo. At least, giving birth to one is. Lucinda's sister must have been a guardian."

"Allison, I'm not completely following." Allison had a way of forgetting that others couldn't read her mind.

"Guardian women aren't supposed to have relationships with vampires. It's taboo, especially if she gets pregnant. Something messed up happens to the baby after it's born and they die. But sometimes they live. The teachers try and tell us they don't, but *everyone knows* it's propaganda. When the baby lives it's half-guardian and half-vampire. They're called shades because they will never truly live in the light or the dark. They are cursed in the shadows. A bit pretentious to think us guardians are *'the light'*, but you know how that goes."

"No, I don't."

Allison shrugged as if Katie hadn't said anything. "I've never met one, and as far as the school is concerned they don't exist. I'll bet my new purse *and* pumps that Lucy came out of retirement to be his mentor. She wouldn't trust anyone else with that secret. That's a secret that can ruin a family's reputation."

Every guardian family has a dirty secret. Tristan said it earlier. He was talking about himself. "But Lucinda said she was going to be my mentor," Katie said, but she was sure what Allison was going to say. It didn't take a genius to put the two together.

Allison nodded. "It's one mentor per pair. You and Tristan are going to be partners."

❧ 4 ❧

A Mother's Gift

THE REST OF the evening, Katie and Allison exhausted every topic they could think of in relation to Tristan: where he came from, why he came to live with Lucinda and Will, if he was dangerous, what he ate, how long he would live—but their conversation kept coming back to what he wanted with Katie.

Had he found her name somewhere in this house? She always left things when she came over. Sometimes Lucinda labeled food she'd bought just for Katie. Katie checked the rainbow sherbet. The cherry Pop-Tart box. The bag of Pink Lady apples. Nothing. And anyway, that didn't answer how he knew her full name or what she looked like.

Long after Allison had gone to sleep, under the fluffy down blanket Lucinda put out on the queen-size bed in the guest room, Katie still couldn't think about anything else. He couldn't be dangerous or Lucinda wouldn't have let him stay there. Not in the same house Katie had considered a second home. The very same house Katie had pretty much grown up in. All those years her dad worked hundreds of odd jobs just to pay the mortgage and put her through private school. He worked days and nights it seemed—especially when she was younger—so it was *this* house that she called home.

She looked around the dark room. There was only a small amount of light coming in through the window, but she knew this room like she knew every room in this house. By heart. She could see the dresser right across the bed and how now, a TV sat mounted above it where an old ocean painting used to hang. She could see where the door to the little walk-in closet was even though it really melted into a shadow casted on the wall. She could feel the soft cream-colored rug without stepping on it. This room was just as much hers as her room back home. There was no way Will or Lucinda would bring someone into the house that was dangerous.

Katie rolled onto her side and adjusted her pillow. Her head was heavy. Though her eyes were just as heavy, vivid thoughts from the day flashed across her mind, and one in particular repeated over and over: Tristan's eyes. There was something in them she couldn't shake—a type of urgency behind them—a type of anger.

*

Sunlight woke Katie up. She had hoped, that maybe for a second, she would have forgotten yesterday. However, like a heap of dirty laundry, it was there waiting for her the moment she opened her eyes.

Allison was already gone, probably eating the pancakes Katie smelled. All she had yesterday was her dad's eggs—edible but gross—a peanut butter sandwich for lunch, and rainbow sherbet ice cream for dinner.

Her stomach led her to the kitchen.

It was nice to see Will reading the paper at the table and Brian pouring what looked like a second bowl of cereal. This was normal. Katie sat at the booth next to Allison, who was scarfing down pancakes with as little grace as ever. Katie smiled. Normal.

"How are you this morning?" Will said, looking over his paper. His hair was a mess, but that was standard for a Saturday morning.

"Fine. I guess," Katie said. On the table was an empty plate waiting for her to fill it with the loads of food: bacon, eggs, pancakes, a fruit mix, a box of cereal, milk, orange juice.

Everything was normal. Too normal. Or just the same.

Why did that put her on edge?

She looked at Lucinda, who was pouring a cup of coffee at the other end of the kitchen.

"Where—" She couldn't bring herself to ask. It was clear why she couldn't stop blinking blindly at Brian drinking milk from his spoon. They were acting normal. Like Tristan didn't exist. Or were they? What difference did it make that he was there? Why did she expect *them* to be different just because Tristan had walked into their lives?

"What was that?" Will said, looking up from his paper.

"Nothing." Katie forked a few pancakes onto her plate. She needed to be cooler about all of this. There was no point in making anything a big deal if they weren't.

"Looking for me?" said the reason she couldn't be cool about any of it. She didn't want to turn around and look at him. No, it wasn't that she didn't want to, she couldn't. But that was stupid. She had no reason to be bashful.

"No," she said, focusing on the bowl of eggs she picked up.

"A little self-absorbed, aren't you? I wasn't talking to you," Tristan said, sliding into the booth next to Brian. Katie blushed.

Brian shifted. Katie realized he'd been staring at his bowl of cereal like Kellogg's was going out of business. His "pity" face.

"Yes, Tristan," Lucinda said. "I need to know your pant size."

"What for?" he said, picking up one of the discarded news columns.

"You only have three pairs of pants, four shirts, and you need a uniform. Did you think clothes just popped out of thin air?" Lucinda said. She leaned against the kitchen counter and crossed her legs. "Morning, Sweetie," she said to Katie.

"I like to travel light," Tristan said behind the paper. Katie couldn't stop staring at where his face would be. She felt like she was starting to forget exactly what he looked like. It was an odd feeling to have, like a compulsion. She just wanted a peek.

He abruptly dropped the paper. Everyone briefly looked at him as if he'd had a spasm, but he smiled. Directly at her, as if he knew she'd been staring.

Katie looked away.

"I was under the impression you were done traveling. Why else—"

"Alright, I'll get more clothes," he said, cutting off Lucinda. "But I'll buy them myself."

"You'll also need some school supplies—"

"Got it," Tristan said a little louder. He hid behind the paper again.

Lucinda breathed hard and changed the subject. Katie sat and half-listened to the idle chatter between Will, Lucinda, and Allison. Mainly because she didn't understand what they were talking about and partly because she couldn't help but feel Tristan was staring at her from behind the paper.

She knew that sounded dumb, but he hadn't turned the page once. His messy black hair didn't move from one side to the other, and she could still feel those blue eyes probing her. He was a vampire after all. Maybe they could do that. *See* through things. It would explain the smile when he caught her staring the first time. Then again, intuition could explain that.

Will closed his paper. "I'm taking them to the Pony Express to meet Fenkly."

"You couldn't arrange a meeting anywhere else?" Lucinda said, putting her coffee mug in the sink.

"You know Fenkly. If he's going to put on a show, he's going to make it difficult. He doesn't sell to minors anymore so it's not a big deal, Lucy," Will said.

"What's the Pony Express?" Katie ate the last piece of bacon on her plate.

"A drunk's pub," Tristan said, looking at her. When had he put down his paper? Stealth wasn't even the word.

"We're going to meet a fate aren't we?" Allison smiled.

"A fate, indeed," Will said.

"Seriously?" Brian asked with a little bit of color in his face. Katie knew this face. It was the one he wore to remind his parents he was an innocent, good kid. It rarely worked.

Will frowned. "Remind me to search *you* at the door." He turned his attention to Allison. "You'll like this, Allison." He gestured for Tristan and Brian to move so he could slide out of the booth.

Allison nearly pushed Katie out of the way too. She followed Will out of the kitchen rattling off so many questions Katie couldn't keep up. Brian watched her with contempt. Katie studied him for a moment. Now that she'd thought about it, it wasn't the first time she'd caught him staring at Allison like that.

Whenever Will was around talking to Allison, his eyes would flicker.

Tristan chuckled to himself. Or maybe at her.

"Brian, you better go get ready. You're lucky he's taking you." Lucinda glared at him. She definitely was not over yesterday. It struck Katie as odd that Tristan didn't seem to care about yesterday. He sat next to Brian as if he'd been doing it his whole life…sitting *there* in *that* seat. Katie changed her mind. That wasn't it. Earlier, Tristan reached over him to grab the paper. Even now, as Brian left the room, it was like he didn't exist to Tristan. Tristan wasn't over it—he was ignoring him.

Petty. Warranted, but petty.

She was doing it again, staring at him, and he noticed. She focused on the lines in the table and finished her food.

"That will be us soon, Katie," Lucinda said, clearing the table. Katie helped. "Will is Brian and Allison's mentor. He's getting them familiar with Gray City and the type of people you find there."

"Gray City?" Katie said.

"You'll find out about it soon enough," Lucinda smiled.

They finished clearing the table and washing the dishes as Tristan pretended to read the paper. She knew this time he was pretending because he was turning the pages. Her reasoning was mental, but she just knew. She could feel his eyes on her, even when he wasn't looking. There was a crooked smile on his face every time she gave in and looked. It was a game. She was going to beat him by not playing.

She left the kitchen, and Will stopped her on her way upstairs to find Allison. "Katie, I'll stop by your house on the way back so we can let your dad know what's going on. I know it will be hard to explain by yourself."

She wanted to nod her head and say, "*Sure,*" but the back of her mind said, "*No.*" She didn't want her dad to find out from his ex-best-friend who he barely talked to except on forced occasions.

"No. I'll do it," she said. She knew her dad. He'd feel uncomfortable with Will in the house, might even refuse to talk to him, just to avoid the awkwardness.

"I don't know," Will said.

"I'll do it, Will." They looked at each other for a long moment before he nodded and headed to the front door. Katie exhaled. She felt like she'd dodged a bullet. A big bullet and she didn't know why. She just knew it wasn't right—not the way she wanted her dad to find out. *He* had been hiding this from her after all.

In the room, she found Allison putting on her shoes. "I have to run home to change and get ready. Are you headed home? Want to walk together?"

Katie shook her head. She didn't want to go home yet. Here everything was still hanging on by a string, but she didn't know what going outside would be like. She found her washed clothes from the previous day folded in the dresser. Not a bloodstain to be found.

Lucinda never missed anything.

It didn't take long after Will, Brian, and Allison left for Katie to get restless. As much as she dreaded it, she knew she *had* to go home. She needed to tell her dad what happened and find out why he kept everything from her. She let Lucinda know she was leaving and took her first step outside since yesterday.

She didn't even make it to the sidewalk.

She felt anxious. Sweat beaded on her forehead and the hair on the back of her neck rose. She couldn't go back inside, Lucinda would make a big fuss and tell everyone. Katie couldn't risk that embarrassment. She needed something to soothe the feeling of impending doom. Books.

She didn't care much for reading them; she just liked to collect old ones. She headed out of the neighborhoods with her bookbag slung across her shoulder, toward her favorite bookstore.

Barnaby Books was a sanctuary. A book buyer's dream. Katie wasn't always a book buyer, but looking for first-edition odd-end books was an emerging hobby. Something about collecting an original made her feel like a distinguished hoarder. The scholarly kind.

She made it out of the neighborhood, and into the belly of downtown. She waited for the crosswalk light to change. It wasn't so bad. Being out in the open. The way the lady from the board talked about "protection," Katie thought she'd be dodging paranormal activity left and right.

Nope.

It was just her and the normal downtown crowd. The regular homeless working the crowd coming out of the theatre. A few joggers. Someone with a dog so small, its little legs were on full throttle to keep up. Kids from the nearby public school. She could always tell they were from the public school because they all looked the same as if a fashion hurricane swept through it every three months. Skinny jeans in this month? Yup. How about shirts with the neon-colored writing? Check. Fringe bang? No, not this month. This month all the girls were rocking bobs.

Katie laughed. Impending doom? Good thing she didn't go back to Lucinda with that. She skipped the last few feet into Barnaby's and was welcomed by light jazz and the smell of coffee. Why the bookstore smelled like coffee she didn't know, because they didn't sell coffee, and she never saw anyone with coffee, staff or customers alike.

She made her way to the antiques section. Walking through Barnaby's was different than all the other local bookstore because it was a house. A house filled with books. The walls were floor-to-ceiling bookshelves, and everything in between was filled with books. Floor stacks. Tables full and oddly placed spinning racks. It was the mirror image of its owner, Barnaby— odd and disorganized.

Katie had met Barnaby a few times before she realized he was the owner. For a while she thought he was the homeless male-version of a crazy-wicked cat lady. He had hair longer than any man with a giant bald spot on the top of his head should, and huge eyes that drifted off to the side when she talked to him. It must have been a condition. He was there now by the classics. Just standing and staring at the books. He did that a lot. Katie used to think he was looking for a book, but now she knew better. He was really sleeping—with his eyes open.

The antique section was the smallest in the store, but also the hardest to get to. Katie had found it by accident once, when she mistook a stack of books for a wall, leaned against it, and fell right through. She'd found a first edition, *Peter Pan.* She never really liked the story, but the idea that the dusty tome in her hands had once been in England, was trippy. So she bought it.

She scanned through the books and didn't see anything new, besides a small copy of Othello—it looked nice, but she hated anything that reminded her of school—and a book on formaldehyde. She cringed at the memory of dissecting a pig fetus in biology. Her fingers had smelled for hours.

She wandered around the store for a few minutes, slowly making her way to the front. She heard the door open, as the bells tied to it jingled, and looked up.

It was him.

Tristan.

She ducked behind a pile of books and ran to the other side of the store. What was he doing here? Why was she asking herself that question? Of course he followed her. Everything about him screamed stalker the moment he showed up on her front porch. The real question was, why was she crouched down, sneaking around the bookstore?

She began to stand up but stopped and made a dash for the door instead. Who was she kidding? She was jumping over book-piles and running ninja-style through the bookstore because she didn't want to be alone with him. He was nuts. Not to mention a vampire—half or whatever.

She waited for him to disappear into a room, and made it out of the bookstore and back out onto the street unseen. Her heart pounded—absolutely jumping out of her chest. A part of her wanted to laugh and call Brian because she totally pulled off some high-level evasive moves, but she didn't. Tristan showing up at the bookstore made her nervous. She completely doubted it was coincidental. He didn't seem like the coincidental type.

She walked to Sunny Music, looking behind her every few seconds to make sure he hadn't seen her. But, the coast was clear. No Tristan.

Sunny Music was past her favorite ice cream shop: Kat's Ice Cream. She'd known the guy who owned it for forever. Larry. He always gave her discounted or free ice cream, ever since she told him she liked his new signpost of a fat cat licking ice cream. He was nice, but dumb. There was no profit in giving away free ice cream. Not when she went every Friday. She passed by it but made sure to wave at him as she went.

Sunny Music was anything but sunny: black walls…black floor…black lights. The only 'sunny' things were the little bit of light coming through the window by the door and Bob Marley's "*One Love*" playing in the background. Bob Marley was the only music ever played on the loudspeaker.

Katie tried to browse through some indie rock, but Tristan was all she could think about. Why was he following her now? Maybe she should have stayed and confronted him. That's what would have made sense. Why did she always think logically *after* the fact? She couldn't go back now, she'd just look stupid.

She shuffled through some alternative rock, not seeing a single title. She sighed and moved to leave when she saw him again. Just outside the window, pulling on the door. She ducked down as light spilled down the main aisle. He was *really* stalking her.

Again.

What kind of nutcase just follows people to random places?

She couldn't sneak out like she did in Barnaby's. He'd see her the minute she stood up. But, if she stood up now, he'd know she'd purposely ducked down.

She pretended to tie her shoe and took a deep breath before she stood up.

He wasn't looking at her. His back was turned to her as he shifted through a section, finally pulling up a CD. She made her way to the door and stopped at the sound of his voice.

"Hey?"

She turned around expecting to see him smiling at her with that stupid crooked smile, but his back was still to her as he walked up to the counter.

"Can you tell me if their new album came out yet?"

Was he serious? He hadn't seen her?

She grabbed the doorknob and ran out of the store before he did. She needed to get far. Somewhere different. Joe's Coffee Shop. She'd even take the long way two blocks over.

She looked over her back every five seconds, sure he'd be right behind her. There was no way he'd *coincidentally* end up at

Joe's Coffee Shop. There were at least two other coffee places between Sunny Music and Joe's. If he so happened to want coffee, he'd go to one of them. Not Joe's.

The long way took another five minutes, but so far, she was in the clear. She'd even worked up a thirst for an iced coffee with whipped cream and caramel syrup. When she walked into Joe's she stopped dead. He was there, at the counter ordering something. There was no way. No way…

He turned around and looked at her, his eyebrows raised in an accusatory manner.

"Don't look at *me* like that," she said. "You're stalking me."

"I was here first," Tristan said, paying for his order.

"What about Barnaby's and Sunny Music?" Katie crossed her hands over her chest.

"So you followed me there too?" he said, backing up like she'd jump on him at any second.

"That's *so* not cool. I'm not the crazy one. *You* showed up on *my* front porch."

"That's old news, Katalina."

There it was again. Her full name. "Seriously, what do you want?"

"Isn't it obvious?" Tristan said, looking around.

"Obviously not," Katie said.

"Tristan?" the barista called out. Tristan walked over and picked up his order. An iced coffee with whipped cream and caramel syrup.

"What the—"

"What?" Tristan said, walking back over to her.

Katie was stunned. There was no way. How could he—

"Like the same drink as you? A little self-absorbed don't you think, Katalina?"

Katie's eyes grew wide. Her thoughts. He finished her thought. All along—in the kitchen, he *was* talking to her. *Was* staring at her.

She backed up toward the door and into someone. She jumped as if a three-eyed dog had jumped out and bitten her.

"Oh sorry," she said breathlessly to a girl who looked thoroughly affronted.

Tristan rolled his eyes and walked past her and out the door.

"Wait," Katie said as the door closed. She needed to know. What just happened? She ran out of the coffee shop. Tristan had already crossed the street and was headed away from her. She called out to him, but he ignored her. Of course, now that he had gotten her attention he didn't care about her.

When she caught up to him he didn't look at her. He stared ahead, expressionless. She walked next to him, a thousand questions flying through her mind with no idea how to ask them. But then again, she probably didn't need to.

He walked fast; she could barely keep up, especially after running most of the way to Joe's. Her throat was dry, but she was determined to keep up with him.

He held out the iced coffee to her. At least twenty scenarios ran through her mind. What if he poisoned it? Or worse, *drank* from the straw.

He looked at her from the corner of his eye and held out the drink over a trash can as they passed it.

"No!" Katie made a grab for it and saved it before it fell into the trash. She sucked down a fourth of it before her throat eased up. "So— Um." She had no idea what to say. Or was she saying it all now? Could he really read her mind, or was it just a coincidence?

His eyes flashed in her direction.

Not a coincidence.

"Do Will and Lucy know you can read their minds?" she said as he slowed down enough for her to drink and walk at the same time.

"I can't read their minds," he said.

"But you can read mine?"

"Yeah," he said.

"Anyone else's?"

"Nope," he said.

"How is that possible? Why is that possible?" she said.

His face was still expressionless. "Gift from your mom." He stared straight ahead.

Katie knew that wasn't possible. Her mom died giving birth to her. Not exactly enough time to send gifts—let alone some jacked up ability to read her only daughter's mind.

"You still believe everything your dad told you? Nothing about yesterday made you question a few things?" he said, making an abrupt left turn.

"What's that supposed to mean? What do you know about

my mom?" It was strange saying that word. Mom. It was something she didn't have but had always wanted—like a cat, E-Z Bake Oven, a sixty-piece oil pastel set. A mom. Something she'd grown out of and would never have. A mom.

Tristan held her gaze for a few steps, then stared ahead for a whole block before making another left turn. He didn't say anything else.

Next a right...straight...a left. He was walking her home. No matter how many questions she thought in her mind, he didn't say a word. The only hint that he was truly listening was the way he looked at her when she wondered if he could turn into a bat and fly. It was a stupid thought, maybe, but plausible given the circumstances.

He stopped at her street corner. She didn't know why she expected him to continue all the way to her house, or why she'd even want him to. It crossed her mind that maybe he didn't want to return to the place he was stabbed.

"You've been avoiding going home since you left Lucinda's, right?" he said, looking at the house down the street. She had, hadn't she? Even now she could feel the anxiety she felt earlier creeping up again. Going home meant confronting her dad. It occurred to her, the anxiety attack, the reason she didn't want Will to stop by...it was all to avoid telling her dad. "Then," Tristan said, turning around, "I don't think it's a good idea for me to be seen by your house. Drew might recognize me."

Tristan stuffed his hands in his pockets and looked at her.

"How do you know my dad?"

Nothing.

"The same way you know my mom, I'm guessing?" she said.

Nothing.

"Fine," Katie sighed. It was strange. Yesterday, when he was on her porch, he scared her. Now, he was kind of annoying.

"See you Monday, Katalina," he said, walking away from her. She forgot he could hear that—she didn't like that he could hear that or anything she thought.

"Wait!" She had so many other questions that the pile was starting to topple.

He continued down the street.

⁘

As soon as she walked into her house, she could hear her dad in the kitchen. Not her dad exactly, but the radio. He always listened to it when he tried to cook.

Katie took a deep breath. "I'm home," she said. The radio quieted.

"Katie Bug? I'm in the kitchen. You gotta try this spaghetti sauce."

Katie walked into the kitchen. He was listening to country music and dancing in his sweats and slippers. She stood in the doorway watching his fuzzy brown-gray hair sway back and forth.

"Katie Bug?" he yelled as he turned around. "Oh, I didn't know you were right there." He was all smiles—his eyes and his toothy grin.

"Hey, Dad."

"Who peed in your cereal? Everything go okay over there?"

"Yeah," Katie said, sitting in one of the two kitchen chairs.

"You're not uh—the mother nature stuff?"

"Dad."

"Just asking," he said, turning back to the stove. "Would you stop looking like someone shot Santa Claus if I told you I'm not mad about the yard?"

Oh right. She had forgotten yard duty. Mrs. Field, the all-in-one neighborhood watch probably came over bright and early to remind him. She didn't care. "Sorry."

"No worries. Will called," he said.

Katie watched him stir the sauce, still swaying his hips to the music. "What he say?" Katie held her breath.

"That you were staying over. Something about issues and needing Lucinda for some lady-talk. I get it, Katie Bug."

Katie sighed. But froze again when her dad looked at her.

"You'd tell me if something were wrong, right?" he said, frowning. She could see him swallow hard. It was his way of beating around the bush with uncomfortable conversations.

"Like what?" she croaked.

"You know—stuff." He stared into the sauce pot.

"I—I don't know what you mean." Katie held her breath as her stomach leaped.

"You're not thinking of—you know. I'm sure sex seems like what all the cool kids are doing but it's not," he said in one breath, stirring the sauce faster.

Katie exhaled. "What? Jesus, Dad. No."

He smiled again and let out a long breath. "Good—good. These days there's all sorts of diseases going around and girls are giving their stuff away like candy."

"Dad, please. You're killing me. Let's not have this talk," She said, relieved.

"I'm just checking. You know, if you were you could talk to me, right? I wouldn't judge you—too much," he said, flashing her another toothy grin before picking up a pot. "Help me over here?" He nodded at the strainer and she went over and put it in the sink.

She leaned against the sink as he drained the noodles. "I'm sure whatever parenting book you got that line out of says *not* to judge your daughter."

"Tell you what. Don't have sex till I'm good and dead and we won't have to worry about any of that." He kissed the top of her head and laughed.

"I might as well become a nun."

"That works." He ran water over the noodles. "You going to taste that sauce or what?"

Katie looked at it simmering in the pot. If it was anything like his lasagna, she'd pass.

"It's not going to kill you."

"The eggs you made yesterday almost did," Katie said.

"I put in too much onion. I was trying to make an omelet. You have to give me some credit on presentation."

"Sprinkling green things on top didn't make it taste any better." Katie couldn't help but grin. It was her first time all day.

She helped him set the table and they sat down for dinner. The spaghetti was better than she thought it would be. *Too* good, in fact. After going back for seconds, she teased him until he admitted the sauce was from a jar.

"I commend you on your jar selection, sir," she laughed. They cleaned up like they did almost every night—he washed, she dried and put away. They watched a little TV until he fell asleep. She'd laugh at the way his head dropped back, jolting him awake until he threatened to make her watch Matlock and Jag reruns.

On the way to her room, she stopped in the hallway at the picture of her mom. If she told her dad now, what would he say? Would he tell her why he kept the truth from her in the first place? Would he tell her a different story about her mom?

She had passed that picture a thousand times; never once had she stopped and wondered anything more than what her dad told her. She could turn around and tell him about yesterday. All she had to do was open her mouth and say it. But she couldn't. She couldn't be sure her dad would tell her the truth anyway.

5

GREAT EXPECTATIONS

KATIE WOKE UP early to get started on the yard. Anything to avoid a conversation with her dad. She was knee-deep in weeds when he came out to help. Every time they were within twenty feet of each other, she'd find something somewhere else to work on. The entire morning passed with only a few grunts here or there between them: "What do you want for dinner?" he'd ask. "Eh, whatever," she'd reply. "What do you wanna watch?" he'd mumble. "Eh, I don't care," she'd yawn. It wasn't that hard or unusual for them to murmur that way. That's how they usually talked unless there was something specific to talk about. The only unusual behavior that day was the way Katie froze anytime he'd grumble out a question. When he said "Hmph, it's hot," she froze as if his words had slapped her. Or when he said "Hmph, water?" she felt her own words drowning in her throat.

He never noticed, or if he did he made sure to pretend like he didn't. They were both masters at avoiding anything close to an awkward situation. It was good he didn't feel chatty or ask too many questions. All she thought about for two days straight was Tristan. Him *reading her mind*. How did it work? How far did he have to be before he couldn't hear her thoughts? How *long* had he been hearing them? That last question she'd spent hours on, wondering if he'd heard her most private thoughts. It was a complete invasion.

How the hell had this happened to *her*?

It was Monday.

Katie was out of bed, dressed and eating her cereal an hour before it was time to go. It was Monday. This never happened on any day of the week, let alone a Monday. It was still dark when she got out of the shower. The fact that she had time to take a shower *and* dry her hair was a phenomenon.

She couldn't stop wondering what would happen at 7:25 when it was time to leave. Would they all walk to school together?

Would *he* be there?

What would school be like?

She swirled the cereal around in her bowl. Who else was in the program? How many already knew what she'd just found out? Her school. *Her* school was more than a bunch of teachers hustling to get her to do homework. And *homework*. Did this mean no more papers on irrelevant dead people?

Katie considered herself terrible at school. She worked just hard enough to stay in the middle of the pack, and that in itself took a lot of strategic planning: which assignments to do, which ones to do to the minimal degree. If only her math teacher knew how often she *did* use math, he wouldn't shake his head every time she entered the room. But her heart sank a little as she thought about Brian and Allison. They were always busy. They stayed at school longer than Katie on most days, and they were always studying. Katie had always thought they were just more serious about school. It had never occurred to her they were keeping a secret.

Her cereal sat soggy in the in the bowl, and she poured it into the sink as the clock slowly ticked closer to 7:25.

It was time to go.

Just as she grabbed her bookbag she heard her dad opening the bathroom door. There was a pause.

"Katie? Are you up yet? Katie, you're going to be late!"

"I'm downstairs," she yelled back, looking for her keys.

"Really?"

She opened up all the pockets in her bag fingering for her keys. When she found them, she yanked them out and yelled, "Bye, Dad!" before rushing out the door.

She hurried to the edge of her neighborhood. She ran away from her dad and into a strange new chapter in her life. As she neared the usual meeting spot, sweat beaded on her forehead and her chest tightened.

This was it.

She was being pulled to a new world completely. Everything was going to change. She turned the corner out onto the main road and stopped.

No one was there.

She looked at her watch. It was exactly 7:25. They always met at this spot at 7:25. Why, of all days, did they choose today to be late? Or worse, not show up at all. Had they gone straight to the school and no one bothered to call her? She pulled her bag around to grab her cell phone but sighed when she remembered it was still at school. She'd discovered that she'd left her cell phone Saturday night when she wanted to call Allison.

Katie hated not having a phone.

She waited.

Nothing.

Thirty more seconds.

Nothing.

Her hands were clammy and she scratched her arm more times than necessary. Panic settled in. She didn't know why. It wasn't like she didn't know how to get to school on her own. It wasn't like she'd never walked to school by herself before. But today—today was different. Today was like going to a new school. She didn't know what to expect. Maybe there was a secret entrance she was supposed to go in through. Why hadn't anyone prepared her for today? Why hadn't anyone prepared her for any of this?

She tapped her foot as she stood on the corner trying to decide whether to wait or leave.

Katie scanned the street.

Finally, she spotted Allison walking toward her—five minutes late.

"You're late," Katie said, trying to pull it together. She felt like an idiot.

"Actually, *I'm* two minutes early. You're always seven minutes late," Allison said. Her expression told Katie the next question was going to be, *"Are you okay?"* but instead she said, "I called you last night, but your phone kept going straight to voicemail— are you okay? You're totally spazzing out."

"I'm not spazzing out." Katie adjusted her bookbag.

They started off down the street. Katie was irritated. All weekend no one bothered to contact her. Maybe they did call her cellphone, but there was email too. It wasn't that she really needed someone to call just to find out how she was, but why hadn't they tried harder? Stopped by her house, or sent a telegram. What if she had spent the rest of the weekend having panic attacks? Didn't anyone care that her life had just been turned upside down?

"Kay?" Allison said, breaking their long silence. She put her hand on Katie's shoulder.

Katie felt a wave of guilt and shame. Why was she mad? Where was it all coming from? Her stomach twisted with each step as she thought of a response. "Mmhmm?" was all she could muster. Tears threatened to blur her vision. Why was she about to cry? She felt so stupid.

It's just school. I'm just going to school. She'd spent yesterday trying to convince herself that it was just school. But no matter how many times she told herself that, she knew it wasn't true; every time panic crept in and she'd remember Glock's horrid, beady black eye drawing her in and the smell of death rolling off him.

That was what waited for her if she changed her mind.

Allison stopped her. "Kay? What's—did you tell your dad? Did he say something?"

The dam was overflowing. Katie hated how caring Allison could be. She was almost as bad as Lucinda, and it always made her close to flooding the gates.

Katie stood in the middle of the sidewalk trying not to cry like an idiot. After Allison pulled out a handful of tissues from her bookbag and Katie blew her nose a few times, they continued walking to school. Katie told Allison that she hadn't told her dad, or slept well the last two nights. She told her about her recurring nightmares of Glock.

"I don't blame you," Allison said as they walked up the steps to the school. "Everything about him is nightmare-inducing."

Katie started to agree when she heard someone call her name. She turned around to see Lucinda waving as she climbed up the school steps towards them.

"Lucy, what are you—" Katie started, but instantly knew the answer to her question. He was staring at her with his funky blue eyes behind Lucinda.

"Katie, I've been trying to call you since Saturday. Did you get my messages?" Lucinda said, turning back to make sure Tristan was following her.

Katie felt another wave of guilt. "I left my phone in my locker. Why doesn't anyone email me?"

"I was under the impression you wanted to be left alone."

There was a hint of sadness in her voice. Katie sighed. Lucinda had been expecting her to call. Why didn't she use her dad's cell to call anyone? Katie kicked herself for it. She'd thought about it, but pride had stopped her multiple times.

Lucinda checked for Tristan one more time even though he was standing next to her in the school uniform, looking as normal as ever. Not a hint of vampire on him. "Well," Lucinda said, looking back at Katie, "I'm glad Tristan spotted you. We have to go to the front office to get your new schedule. Unless, of course, your father came to do that with you today. How did that go anyway?"

Katie could hear the strain in Lucinda's voice. They avoided talking about her dad just for this reason. It had been three years since the day Katie had heard Lucinda scream that he could never come back to her house ever again. She was in the backyard with Brian, and they hadn't heard anything until that. Katie was sure the whole neighborhood had heard Lucinda. Still no one would speak of that day or what made Lucinda snap like that.

"It went fine," Katie said, eager to change the subject. "I have a new schedule? What? Werewolf 101?"

Lucinda and Allison stared at her. Tristan stared off as if he weren't interested in the school and even less interested in the conversation.

"Katie. It's important you don't say anything like that unless you're in one of your—accelerated—classes. You saw the trouble it caused when you found out. Imagine if it were someone whose only option was an omitter."

Katie felt the blood rush to her cheeks. "I didn't—mean to—"

"It's alright. Let's get to the front office before classes start. Can't be late on your first day, right?" Lucinda said, doing her routine check on Tristan. He raised his eyebrows at her and shoved his hands in his pockets.

Katie couldn't help notice that some of his facial expression sparked an instant spike of dislike…paranoia…shock.

He scowled at her, which meant one thing. He was reading her mind again.

⚬⚬⚬

Katie hated going to the front office. Myrtle, the front desk lady, gave her the creeps. She was kind of spacey.

They walked to the front desk with Lucinda. Myrtle waved, wearing a bright blue frilly shirt, her frizzy straw-yellow hair in its usual beehive location, and her usual strange smile.

Lucinda and Myrtle talked for what was achingly too long while Katie and Allison sat in waiting chairs. Myrtle took Tristan's picture for his new school ID card and waved Katie over. Her eyes sparkled when she asked to take Katie's picture for a school ID card.

"It's me, Katie. Katie Watts. I already go here."

"Sure. Of course you do." Myrtle said, still smiling. "I've been waiting for you. I have your new schedule. You weren't on the active list since birth, so you'll have to take an evaluation with Mr. Carver before winter break. If you pass, you'll be a permanent member of the program." She handed Katie a piece of paper: a new schedule.

Her schedule wasn't as new as she'd thought it would be. The first half of the day she had regular classes: English, Math, Chemistry—except she'd been moved into Brian's chemistry class—and Study Hall (normally that was her seventh period class where she napped). The second half the day was what she didn't recognize: Natural History, Field Study, and Practical Application. Last on the list made her cringe, but she knew it was coming: After School Activities. For three years, Katie had counted herself lucky that she got to go home to her comfy bed after seventh period, while Brian and Allison went to their after school activities four days out of the week.

She already worked hard at being average. How was she going to get the little bit of homework she *did* do done? She suddenly realized Myrtle was still talking. Something about an extra midterm test.

"What if I fail?" Katie asked.

"What?" Myrtle smiled.

"The test. What if I fail the test."

"Well, sweetheart, we'll cross that bridge if we get there, won't we?" she said, her eyes sparkling and glazed. "Oh! I almost forgot!" She fumbled through some papers on her desk. "Ms. Tisdall will be your study hall tutor. Oh, here it is." Myrtle handed Katie a stack of papers. "This is the material you'll need to go over by winter break—oh, no need to look through it now, Ms. Tisdall will go over that—oh you dropped a paper right there. Should I staple those for you?"

Katie shook her head as dread filled her soul. This was a mistake. If they had told her she'd have this much more homework to do, she would have jumped into Glock's arms.

Tristan had only one sheet of paper in his hand, and, without a single word, he put it on top of her stack. It was an exact replica of her new schedule. *Why doesn't he have a stack of homework papers?* Annoyed, she looked from Tristan to Lucinda and to Myrtle's smile.

The bell rang.

"You kids better be off to class then," Lucinda sang. She moved to straighten Tristan's shirt, like Katie had seen her do a dozen times to Brian but stopped. He turned as if he didn't notice.

They said their goodbyes to Lucinda and left her to talk with Myrtle.

Katie handed Tristan back his schedule as she left the office dragging Allison with her.

"Aren't you going to show me around, Katalina?" he called from behind her. She turned around to his easy smile and tripped over her own feet. Why did seeing that smile creep her out?

"Don't call me that here."

"But that's your name."

"People call me Katie."

"Katalina sounds better."

Allison snorted and stopped at her locker.

"Tristan," Katie said.

"Katalina?"

She sighed and turned away from his mocking smile. How could she ever think he was menacing? The only thing he was capable of being was irritating…annoying…pesky…*and there was probably a hint of self-centered there somewhere.*

"You want to let up on the compliments?" Even though she wanted to slam his face into a locker, she couldn't help but stare in awe. She let out a short laugh. This was *absurd.* Pure insanity.

⚬৪৫ ৯৯⚬

A new type of doom and gloom hung over Katie as she realized she hadn't done her English homework. She needed to do a short journal entry on the first act of Othello. That would have given her enough points to skip out on the paper. Out of the corner of her eye, she could see Tristan shake his head.

Mr. Rhineheart introduced himself to Tristan and told him to take a seat wherever he'd like. Tristan picked the seat on the other side of Katie. Brian's seat. It didn't escape Katie that he wasn't there.

She found herself staring at her teacher as she pulled out her copy of *Othello,* from her bookbag. It was impossible to think of Mr. Rhineheart as a guardian. He was just a high school English teacher. Even stranger was knowing some of the kids in her class were guardians, just sprinkled in with normal kids. Had she really spent the last two years of high school with kids who believed in monsters?

"Katie? Katie—come in, Ms. Watts. Over," Mr Rhineheart said, doing his walkie-talkie impression. "Do you mind sharing with Tristan?" he asked. "We're out of Othellos."

"Sure," she said, realizing she had been staring at him the whole time. He looked at her a little longer than usual, no doubt contemplating if he should move her to the slower-paced class.

"I'm pretty sure I know this play by heart," Tristan said, once Mr. Rhineheart moved on.

"Did you read it a lot at other schools?"

"No. I had to recite it once. How many times do you think I've been in the eleventh grade?"

She stared at him.

"When I was a kid—*how old do you think I am?*"

Katie looked away. She couldn't help it if she thought he was a kid in the 1800's. He *said* he was a vampire.

Tristan opened his mouth but changed his mind.

Mr. Rhineheart put on a theatrical reading like he did every class, and Katie relaxed. She expected everything to be different, but English was still Mr. Rhineheart's chance at being a Shakespearean actor.

She paid attention more than usual as Tristan pointed out his favorite parts. He marveled at the way Iago manipulated Othello. "Genius," he said. "Genius."

The next two periods (math and chemistry) passed the same way: Tristan sat next to Katie and made her look incredibly stupid. He was good at everything. It was disgusting. He sat in class, took notes, answered questions…what was he doing? Wasn't this a hoax? Why was he trying so hard?

Katie almost died when her math teacher, Mr. Right, walked over to their desk and told them to exchange numbers. "If Tristan has questions about the school, he can ask you, and if you have questions about math, you can ask him."

"I see. My only talent lies in knowing where the classrooms are?" Katie said, eyeing Mr. Right.

"Katie, your talents go farther than spacial recognition. I've seen you in the lunchroom haggling with the lunch ladies. Maybe you can get him a cheap lunch."

Katie smacked her head against the desk as the class laughed. "Aren't teachers supposed to *encourage* students and *build* their self-esteem?"

"Aren't students supposed to have a *hunger* for knowledge and a *thirst* for learning? By the look on your face I think you know what I'm getting at. Exchange numbers." When Mr. Right left Tristan was still laughing.

"It wasn't *that* funny," Katie said.

"No, I'm laughing because he's under the impression that I'd ever give you my number." Tristan laughed harder while jotting down more problems.

When the bell rang, Katie was glad to go to study hall. She left the class so fast she forgot to wait for Allison to pack up her things. They always walked from math together. In fact, they usually sat next to each other in math, but Allison had forsaken her to Tristan to sit next to her newest crush. Typical.

Katie slowed her pace to the library. She was supposed to be meeting her new tutor. A tutor. It wasn't that she cared how it looked. She worked hard at not caring what other people thought of her. But she couldn't help hating the idea. It didn't matter that the subject was paranormal. A tutor was a tutor. She'd be subjected to a speech about trying harder and living up to her full potential.

Katie let out a long breath. Today was proving more normal than she thought. Troublesome, but normal.

As soon as she walked into the library, she spotted her. Her new tutor. It was obvious. The lady was the dorkiest looking thing in the library, and waving like she was manic. Katie took a deep breath and inched her way over, periodically looking over her shoulder to make sure the lady wasn't waving at someone else.

"Hi, Ms. Tis—"

"No, Call me Traci!" Traci said, blinking behind the biggest bifocals Katie had ever seen. They made her eyes look bigger and rounder than they should have been. Beside her face, her thick, bushy black curls made her look no older than Katie

"Hi, Traci. I'm Katie." They shook hands. Traci's hands were so small Katie felt like she could break them if she squeezed. Traci couldn't have been that much older than her. Yet, everything about her pea-green sweater and binoculars for glasses made her look like she belonged in a nursing home.

Katie looked away, trying not to stare or judge. It would be just her luck that Traci could read minds too. Her eyes drifted to the door as Tristan, Allison and a few other students piled into the library. Allison called to Tristan, inviting him over to a table, but whether he heard her or not, Katie couldn't tell. He sat in the far side of the library with his back to her.

"I'm very excited. You're my first student—but that doesn't mean I don't know what I'm doing or anything. It's just, this is the first time they've let me do anything, really. They think because I'm not good at hunting things or giving life advice that I'm not much use for anything, but of course, that's not all people are good for, right? Oh—sorry. I didn't mean to go on like that—you're new right? This is your first day? That's different."

Katie blinked. Was that a question or statement? The way Traci stared from behind her large frames indicated that she was looking for an answer. "Yeah, I guess I'm new," Katie said, averting her eyes. Traci smiled anyway and pointed to the stack of papers Katie still had in her hand.

"Is that a study plan?"

Katie handed her the papers with a shrug. Study plan? Fuel for fire? It was all the same to her.

"Oh yes. Indeed. *Oh, look.* We even get to cover the Lycan Empire! That's my favorite really. Lycans really don't get the respect they deserve amongst the lore. It's not like they *choose* to be big and hairy. You know, there's something about having a tail that really makes them fascinating." Traci shifted through the papers, smiling to herself as her finger found more topics she liked. Katie tried to look interested, and for the first minute or two she even felt sincere, but the more Traci talked, the more Katie felt the weight of her new life. She tried to swallow down the anxiety that had been building all day, but it just rose higher and higher.

Just when her hands began to shake, Traci stopped talking and turned to her. Not a single blemish on her toffee colored skin.

"You know, I know it looks like a lot of work, but I've got an idea..." Traci bent over in her chair and rummaged through a large flower-print bag Katie hadn't noticed before. Traci surfaced again with a brown leather notebook. There was a pink flower in the center. It was hideous. "I hope you don't mind, I bought you this as a sort of good luck token."

"I—Thank you," Katie said as Traci handed it to her. Katie blushed as guilt welled in her. She was never good at getting gifts. She didn't know what to say. What was the proper protocol? Squeal and say something nice about it? Instead, she drew her hands across the cover. It was soft. She tried to think nice things about it as she forced a smile. She felt like an ass.

"Oh no, you don't have to thank me. I just want to help you as much as possible. I know what it's like to be behind. And, well I just want it to be kind of a reminder that, if you use this, you won't be for long. Also it's a planner, so it'll help organize your time." Traci smiled big, obviously proud of herself. Katie felt even worse.

Katie reached into her bookbag and pulled out a pen. She opened up the planner—cringing a little at the flower print paper—and asked, "So how do I use this thing?"

Traci laughed. It was the cutest thing Katie had ever heard until Traci snorted.

❧ ❧

It was the longest fifty minutes of Katie's life. Traci planned out nearly every hour of Katie's day, even her new "sleep time," for the next ten months. Guilt or not, she was going to take that little book of hell and stuff it into the darkest depths of her locker. Just before the bell rang, she caught a glimpse of Tristan hovering over a book. His back was still, and he was the only one wearing the jacket to the school uniform. It made Katie angry that even then he looked more in his element than Katie felt listening to Traci mumble on about "The Vampire Dynasty." This was her school, not his. Her life.

Her life.

The bell rang and Katie thanked Traci for the notebook again before leaving. It was a relief to be out of the library, but not for long.

"Why, exactly, do you strive to be mediocre?"

What bothered her most wasn't what he said, but how he walked next to her. Like he was pretending *not* to walk next to her.

"Why are you here?" She checked her syllabus. She was headed to a new class with a teacher she'd never had before, but history, whether it was "Natural" or American, was still bound to be boring.

"Because we have the same class," Tristan said.

"No, why are you *here*. Bothering me, at my school, why do you exist? What is the point of you?"

He was silent, and Katie found that more aggravating than his banter.

They walked together, and yet apart, to the classroom. She scanned the room, curious to see who was in it. She didn't expect a greeting of gaping mouths. *New students must be a rarity.* She knew a lot of people in her grade, and apparently most of them were normal because she only recognized two people. Christi Taylor and Ethan Brown.

She cursed. She hated Christi and she only knew Ethan because he stalked Allison all last year. The only other person she knew was Tristan—*and he's annoying like Christi and just as much of a stalker as Ethan. Great.* She frowned, looking at his face and wondered if he heard what she had thought. If he had, he didn't show it.

"Hello, Katalina? Tristan?" Mrs. Barnes said. Katie only knew of Mrs. Barnes because Brian would point her out and complain about her hard-to-pass test last year.

"Katie," she responded. Mrs. Barnes nodded, smiling behind a wall of make-up. Mrs. Barnes' face reminded Katie of her clay pots: blotches of bright paint here and there with no sign of artistry. She wore her hair in a fluffy bun on the top of her round head.

"I'll remember that, Katie," she winked. "You will take the desk there—in the back next to…Christi—Christi, raise your hand—okay, and Tristan you can take the next one over. I'll go get your books before class starts." She gestured for them to take a seat and went into a tiny office.

Katie laughed at her luck. Of course Mrs. Barnes would make her sit next to Christi. She moved to the seat next to Christi and contemplated smiling at her. An offering of a silent truce. The last thing she needed, in her increasingly complicated life, was another problem with Christi.

Time to be the bigger person. When Katie turned to face Christi, she was staring at Tristan.

"Hi, I'm Christi. And you're Tristan?"

Tristan turned slightly in his chair and looked at her.

"I've never seen you before, are you new?"

"That's generally what it's called," he said, shifting back to his original posture.

"Well, I'm the president of the Junior Guardian Honors Society. We only let a select few people in. That is," she paused and glanced at Katie, "We don't allow just *anything* in. You should come to one of our meetings."

Katie cursed herself for ever thinking she'd smile at that snot-nosed pig. She wanted to punch her in the face and break her pig nose, but Mrs. Barnes walked in and handed Katie and Tristan their new books. *Why do I let her get to me?*

"Christi, can you show them the two chapters we've already gone over in class? Thank you." Mrs. Barnes didn't wait for a reply.

Katie glanced over her book. It looked like a regular textbook—heavy with glossy, boring pages.

"Don't worry, Katie. There are plenty of pictures in it. You'll be able to understand at least a few things," Christi said loud enough for the back of the class to hear.

Katie snatched up her book, ready to swing. She didn't care that she'd get kicked out of class and probably suspended for a week. She got a thrill out of seeing Christi flinch—but she stopped. A hand grasped her wrist. It was firm, like it could break her bone with a little-added pressure. A chill went down her body because she knew the hand belonged to Tristan.

"You've got to work on that temper," he said, letting go as soon as she put the book down. Katie choked on a response.

"She's obviously unstable," Christi said.

"You have a death wish?" Katie spat back.

"How about both of you shut up?" Tristan said, back in his lax position.

Katie spent the next twenty minutes on the same page in her book, not hearing a word of what Mrs. Barnes said about Louis the Great, a guardian who stopped a war between vampires and werewolves in the fifteen hundreds. She tried to shut out the chill that ran down her spine when Tristan touched her. It was an electric pulse she'd felt in her bones.

"And this leads us to the rise of the Fates," Mrs. Barnes said, walking towards Katie. "Page eighty-nine, dear. Who can tell me where they came from?" A boy three seats in front of Katie raised his hand. "Yes, Michael."

"No one knows. Most people think they came from the fae, but that's not a fact." *Could it be?* Michael Heckler sitting three seats in front of her. *And knowing it all, what a surprise....* She hadn't seen him when she walked in.

"Very good, Michael. Someone read ahead," Mrs. Barnes smiled. "The fates showed up in Europe and Asia around the same time and helped kill many high-profile people. They were used as trackers. Anyone know how?"

This time, it was a girl in the first row who raised her hand. "All they need is to see the person they're tracking once. It doesn't matter where in the world the person goes, they can find them again."

"Correct, Jennifer. That's exactly how they got their name. There is a translated quote from Louis the Great saying, *'Once he have seen thy face, thy thread of life has been cut.'* He was referring to the Greek Fates of course, but as time went on they became the embodiment of the word."

"Is it true they have fangs with venom?"

"Yes, Michael. Depending on how much is taken into the body, it can cause permanent paralysis."

"Are fates involved with the recent sightings of D-Ranges?" Michael said.

"We are not discussing current events or crack-pot theories."

"But my dad said an increase in the D-Range population only means one thing. A pureblood is building an army to overtake another coven, and they always use fates to take out major players. My dad says purebloods are the only ones with enough money to pay for their service."

"Enough, Michael." Mrs. Barnes rolled her eyes.

"He said even the vampires and werewolves are scared of them."

"Michael!"

"I heard the omitters are fates," a boy sitting next to Michael said. Like a pot of boiling water, the classroom erupted into chaos.

"There's evidence fates have been stalking the streets in Gray City!"

"I heard they sent a message to headquarters demanding guardian allegiance!"

"I heard they're getting inside help, which is why no one is reporting the increase in D-Range population!"

"Quiet!" Mrs. Barnes shouted, red in the face. "Enough. All of these rumors are ridiculous. Turn to page one-hundred."

After forcing everyone to read silently, Mrs. Barnes ended class with a three-page paper on fate behavior and their impact on the Holy Roman Empire.

Katie sighed, stuffing her textbook in her bookbag. *This is more work than regular history,* she thought. Happy to escape Mrs. Barnes' squinty eyes, Katie went to the cafeteria in search of food and Allison.

Tristan didn't follow her. She refused to acknowledge that it both did and didn't bother her. As she waited in line for her food, she wondered what Brian was doing. She missed him in English and in the hall between classes. They always joked around like they were the only people in the world that could laugh. Swapping lunch with Brian and eating off of each other's lunch tray was the best part of her day. *How could Brian miss Taco Salad Day?*

"Looks like it's lunch with me and the track team," Allison's voice said behind Katie.

Katie paid for her tray of taco salad. "You make it sound like a punishment," Katie said, feeling like it was. Katie loved Allison, but all she did during lunch was study.

Allison looked around the cafeteria, and Katie knew the question before Allison could form it.

"I don't know where he is, and I don't care," Katie said, not sure if the last part was true. Her eyes darted to the door every few seconds since she'd arrived.

"Kay, he's new. He needs friends. Everyone needs friends," Allison said, looking between the crowds of bodies.

"He looked real friendly in the library when you asked him to sit with you."

"So he's a little aloof. He's new. All new kids act weird at first." Allison swung her lunch box back and forth as she crossed her hands.

After lunch, Katie walked with Allison to her new Field Study class. On the way, Allison explained that it was an internship class. They took field trips and had job training. When Katie walked in, Tristan was already there, pretending he hadn't seen her walk through the door.

"Come on in, everyone. Come on in." A man wearing brown plaid dress pants and a yellow polo shirt walked up to Katie. Mr. Carver. Everyone knew who he was. Checkerboard Carver. "Katalina? Oh," he said after she corrected him. "Katie then? I'll try to remember that. So your partner is Tristan, am I right?

That's what the paper says. Because you two are a little behind on the partner thing, I'm going to send you home with some projects that Lucinda will have to sign off on. But I see Tristan is a transfer student, so you've got an experienced partner if you have questions. Great relationship-building opportunity—Michael! How many times do I have to tell you not to touch those? Good grief, kid—Anyway, Katalina—no Katie, see, I caught myself. Why don't you go on over there with Tristan? I've made you two a worksheet. We're reviewing some material today, so you're not missing out on much." Mr Carver handed Katie a small packet of papers and pointed to a door at the back of the room. "You and Tristan can use that training room. Just don't touch any of the buttons or you'll end up somewhere completely different—MICHAEL, STOP TOUCHING THAT!"

Mr. Carver walked off to continue yelling at Michael. Katie had heard about half of what he said and, yet again, was left with a packet of papers. Were these papers supposed to prepare her for fates and lycans and vampires and who knew what else? Allison grabbed the papers from Katie and looked them over.

"Oh," she said with a hint of caution. "It's a team-building worksheet." Allison handed it back.

"What?" Katie looked through the worksheet. It was a questionnaire with questions like: *What is your partner's favorite food? What is your partner's favorite weapon type? What challenge do you set for your partner?*

The final bell rang. Katie looked around for Tristan and saw the door Mr. Carver pointed at, cracked open.

"Hello, partner," she said, walking into the room and closing the door behind her. The room was smaller than she expected and empty. Nothing but white walls and floor. And quiet except for a slight hum from the florescent light. Tristan sat on the floor with his legs crossed, flipping through the worksheet. He looked like a boy. A regular boy.

He looked at her.

"Stop doing that," she said, blushing.

"Doing what?" He went back to the worksheet.

"Are you ever going to tell me why you can read my mind?"

Tristan sighed and stared at the worksheet. "What's your favorite color?"

"You're just going to ignore my question?"

"How about saddest memory?"

"Why are you like this?"

"My favorite color is yellow. No, maybe red. Write down both."

Katie stared at him.

"Are you going to write that down?" he said.

Katie sat down and pulled a pen out of her bookbag. "If I write it down will you answer my questions?"

"Sure. As long as they're on that worksheet." His glint in his eyes mocked her. And a smile crept across his face when she thought how nice they were—or could have been if he wasn't annoying.

They spent the rest of class filling out the worksheet. Tristan gave Katie a challenge of studying harder, and she wrote that he should be honest and straight forward, especially since his saddest memory was when he found out *Titanic* was one of the top-grossing movies ever.

Katie lay on the floor and stared at the ceiling. She had two more periods to go, and she was already exhausted.

"It's because you don't fuel your body correctly." Tristan stood up.

"Blah, blah, I know, *'food pyramid, protein, exercise,'* and all that crap they feed you in elementary school about health." She yawned and stretched.

Tristan stood over her and cast a slight shadow over her face. His gaze made her aware of how much she didn't know about him. "Are you really half-vampire?"

"Yes." He grimaced.

An honest answer. "Your parents?"

"Murdered."

Any other questions she had stopped in her throat. "S-Sorry."

He offered her a hand, and she hesitated before she took it. He pulled her up with ease, and she almost lost her balance. His grip steadied her. It was firm, yet violently electric. Her body was betraying her, urging her to know something and he knew it. She could see it in his eyes—they too were urging her to know something. It wasn't anger she'd seen in his eyes, it was a kind of desperation.

She pulled her hand away and cleared her throat. There was a split second where she wondered if she imagined it all—the way he looked into her—but his stiffness told the truth.

Who are you?

He left her in the room with no inclination of whether he heard her or not and ignored her for the rest of the day—which must have been an art he perfected given they were default partners for everything they did in the Practical Application class (which turned out to be gym on steroids). Their teacher, or *"Sensei Steve"* as he called himself, didn't care that she hadn't had a Karate class for at least four years. He judged her like she was training for the Olympics. When she fell while stretching, he told her he hoped she'd be better in judo tomorrow. She'd never even seen judo.

Not surprising Tristan knew what he was doing. Everything he did was effortless, including ignoring her. This time, it bothered her. The way he looked at her earlier was tattooed in the back of her head. It was almost helpless.

Hopeless.

The more she thought about it, the more vacant he became. Which didn't help when they broke off into pairs to work on the same kick they'd done all class—his almost mechanical in accuracy.

By the time the bell rang Katie was tired of Robo-Tristan and ready to change back into her clothes and go home.

Tristan shook his head and spoke for the first time in over an hour. "We have activities every day except Friday. It's Monday." He pointed at a schedule on the gym wall. "Just pick one. I don't care what it is."

"You want me to pick yours too?" Katie said. Even though he'd ignored her, he still wanted to be tied to her hip?

He gave her a long side glance and then looked back at the top of the poster:

Activities Must Be Done With Partners!

"Oh," Katie said, feeling stupid. "Okay, swimming then," she said.

"No."

"But you said—"

"And now I'm saying pick something else." Tristan looked at the list. "Track. You need to run more."

Katie cursed. "I'm not running."

"It's either running or *"Sensei Steve."* He's teaching everything else. I'm sure he'd love another hour with his favorite student."

"*I picked* swimming."

"And I unpicked it. Besides, I have nothing to swim in." He picked up his bag.

Katie leaned against the wall and closed her eyes. She hated running. Running was the fastest way to set fire to her lungs. She sucked in a deep breath. "Fine." She exhaled. At least he wasn't ignoring her now, and she'd be running *with* someone. She grabbed her bag and almost lost her balance when she saw his face. It was there again until he blinked it away. Why was he looking at her like that? Like she'd burned down his house and made him watch?

"I know you can hear me—but I didn't—"

"I'll teach you how to breathe," Tristan said, slinging his bag onto his shoulder.

"Wh—What?"

"It helps when you run, so your lungs don't burn."

"Oh, okay—are we just going to ignore the awkwardness?" Katie said, following Tristan out of the gym.

He looked at her thoughtfully. "I am."

6

It's Complicated

THEY RAN FOR fifty minutes straight. Or rather, Tristan jogged next to Katie as she limped and wheezed for thirty minutes. She bent over in the most severe pain of her life. Tristan's breathing exercise didn't help. Not in the least.

"Well," Tristan said, looking under-worked, "You don't have to like it, but you do have to get in shape. Maybe you should cut the snacks and drink more water."

"Wow. You must be a popular with the ladies."

"I'm just telling you the truth," he said. They walked back towards the gym to change. Tristan matched his pace with her slow one.

"Now you're Mr. Honest?" Katie laughed. "Just when I'm about to go home. It's a shame really."

"What do you mean home? We still have to train with Lucinda. Katalina, do you *read* anything? You should have gotten a schedule in that stack of papers they gave you."

There it was again, her full name. "What do you mean train? What did I just do?" She didn't have an ounce of energy left to "train."

"You just did 'school'. Now you do work."

What did training entail? She wasn't prepared for this. All she did today was stack up homework and run her body into the ground. Now she was expected to *train?*

"I don't know," Katie said. Again, her life was moving faster than she could hold on. Training meant it was real, all of it. After seeing Tristan stabbed, she never wanted to see anything like that again. That was what she was training for, wasn't it? To intentionally hurt someone. Or worse, to be stabbed by someone and live through the pain…or die.

"It's not hard when it's for someone you care about." Tristan followed her eyes to his chest.

Her insides froze.

"That's why most people fight. To protect the people they care about."

Katie cringed. What did *she* think he meant? Did he know? Awkward…

"I'll tell Lucinda you'll start after-school training tomorrow," Tristan said, turning his back on her.

"Oh, yeah. Thanks."

Tristan started to walk away, and Katie felt abandoned. She

was exhausted, mentally and physically, and alone. The anxiety clawed its way up again, faster now that she had no way to fight against it. What was she supposed to do? Go home? Tell her dad? Pretend this wasn't her life?

Her breathing quickened, and she tried to blink back tears. This was it. Her life was over, and she was all of a sudden expected to know all these new things. She was alone. Alone and confused and—she was spinning, spinning, spinning…

"One, two, deep. One, two, deep. Like we practiced earlier. Come on, Katalina. It's not that bad. One, two, deep."

One, two, deep. One, two, deep. She repeated it over and over, or at least she thought she did. She heard it like a mantra. There was a tight feeling across her chest to the rhythm of her breathing and the constriction seized her. She didn't want to open her eyes because she knew he was holding her. If she opened her eyes she'd cry harder—if she opened her eyes, he'd see the dark parts of her soul that even she didn't want to see.

"You're having a panic attack. Just breathe and it'll pass," Tristan said as he moved her into the shade. She was mortified, and so she cried harder. It was finally coming out. All the shattered pieces of her life. All day she'd tried to hold them together, but they'd slip out of her hands and spill. She'd pick them up, and it'd be okay, but now—she was too tired.

What the hell was happening to her? She couldn't explain any of it: Glock, the guardians, the mother she never had, Tristan *hearing* her thoughts. Nothing made sense anymore.

It was a while before she stopped crying. Every time she was close to stopping, she'd remember Tristan was there holding her, and the embarrassment would send her body racking. She buried her face into his chest because she hated crying in front of people and it was the only way to keep him from seeing her face. Worse, his shirt was wet with her tears, and probably her snot, and she needed to blow her nose badly.

He moved his arm around, unzipping the bag that was on his shoulder. The bag dropped to the floor. "Here," he said quietly.

Without looking, she moved her hand out slowly, and he put what felt like a towel in it. A part of her didn't want to move from his chest. Being that close to someone, no matter how mortifying it was, comforted her. Nevertheless, she cursed her thoughts and transferred her wrecked face from his chest to the towel.

She expected him to move away. Or drop his hand from her back, but it stayed. "You can blow your nose in that if you want," he said.

She tried to blow quietly at first but realized how stupid that was.

"Sorry," she said between breaths.

"We're partners," he said. "If you can't lean on me then who can you lean on?"

Katie wanted badly to see if there was a mocking smile on his face or not. The thought of him making fun of her brought on more tears.

"Katalina, really I'm not. I was—I was being serious. Christ, you think I'm a monster."

She laughed in between a sob because she did. She'd been painting him all day as her personal terrorist. How could she not? He just showed up on her front porch. Bled out on her lawn. Shattered everything that was normal in her life. And worst, invaded her mind.

He stiffened. She felt him add space between them and realized quickly that though he had come into her life like a tornado, at this very moment he was the only thing holding her together. She didn't dare ask him to move closer. She tried not to think it.

He didn't.

She needed to say something, apologize for what she'd thought, but she couldn't bring herself to open her mouth. She was a coward.

"I'll walk you home," Tristan said after a few moments. His voice was tight. Katie had managed to make an already humiliating situation worse.

She nodded and wiped her face. She handed him the soiled towel without looking at him.

"Maybe you can keep it," he said, pretending to be busy looking through his bag.

"Sorry," was all Katie could muster.

He didn't reply.

They walked to her neighborhood in silence, and like last time he stopped on her street corner. They barely waved before parting. Katie felt like she should have said something— thanked him or apologized. But she couldn't. She let him walk away without uttering a single word. It didn't count if he could hear it in her mind.

⁖⁖⁖

Her dad wasn't home yet, to her relief. She took a shower and lay on her bed with the intention of taking a quick nap before dinner, but didn't wake up until ten minutes before she was supposed to leave for school the next morning. She half-walked, half-jogged, to the front of her neighborhood. Allison was already there, staring at her phone.

As Katie walked toward her, the only thought on her mind was if Tristan would walk to school with them. It wasn't something she expected, but she couldn't lie to herself.

"Hey, Kay," Allison mumbled without looking up from her phone. "Are you kidding me?"

Katie waited for the news.

"He's not coming to preliminaries? God, what a dick." Allison squeezed her phone in her hand, her knuckles turning white.

"What?"

"My dad, he's not coming to preliminaries. All parents go to the preliminaries, how embarrassing."

"Allison, I have no idea what you're talking about."

Allison shot her a look so violent it made Katie rock back. Allison paced back and forth. "If Brian doesn't hurry up, we're leaving without him. I do not have the patience for his crap today."

Katie didn't respond. This wasn't new to her. Sometimes Allison got into moods where saying anything was the wrong thing. Allison buzzed around like an aggravated wasp. Every second that ticked by only made her more aggravated.

Finally, Brian appeared around the corner, but looking just as grim as she felt. When he saw Katie's expression, his eyebrows rose as his eyes flickered in the direction of Allison. Katie shrugged and tried to ignore her disappointment when it looked like Tristan wouldn't be there after all.

"So how was your first day?" Brian said, unbuttoning his shirt, showing his undershirt. Allison marched off in the direction of school, leaving them to follow.

"It was." All she could think about was her panic attack and how warm Tristan had been. "Interesting."

Brian smiled, obviously unaware of her thoughts. "So, what crawled up her ass?"

It didn't matter that Brian had outwardly said things like that about Allison for years, it always bothered Katie. *"Nothing,"* Katie said disapprovingly.

Brian rolled his eyes. "Okay, okay. What's wrong with her?"

"Her dad isn't going to preliminaries? What is that?" Katie said.

"Seriously? It's really not *that* big of a deal. Preliminaries is like our Sports Day. We compete for our places in the finals at the end of the year. It's not really that serious. But go figure, Allison is pretty uptight about most things."

"Are you doing it?" Katie asked. She caught herself looking over her shoulder. She still expected *him* to be there following them.

"We all have to. It's not really voluntary."

"What? When is it?" Her heart skipped a few beats. She'd have to compete. *Compete.*

"This Saturday. There are posters in the Field Study room." Brian patted her on the back and assured her it wasn't anything serious. That didn't help. *He* didn't take *anything* seriously.

"Easy for you to say. You've been doing this for as long as everyone else. You're good at it, I can barely run for five minutes."

Brian laughed, but it was forced.

When they finally made it to school, Katie hardly recognized it. Before, it was a place she knew the ins and outs of. She had a napping spot in the library, she had a lunch table and people she knew. She had a life here. Now it was a foreign place out to kill her with homework and exercise. They all expected her to just know things. It was a fluke she'd found out she'd be competing at the end of the week. And competing how?

She felt alone. Even her friends weren't much help. These things were normal to them. They didn't get it. She still hadn't spoken more than three words to her dad in the last two days. How was she going to tell him, or even bring it up? Where would she start?

As they walked to their English classroom, she realized Brian was talking to her. "My mom still won't let up. She follows me around the house like I'm a criminal. I'm going to have to sneak out if I want to go out tonight."

"Out?"

"—A movie."

It was a lie. Why did Brian always think he could lie to her? "Movie? What movie?" Katie asked, maneuvering through a sea of white and navy-blue. Why was it so crowded today?

Brian looked guilty. "Nothing good. Just going to go see something with a few friends."

Ouch. I guess I'm not invited. "Cool."

"Are you in a hurry or something? You're literally almost out of breath."

Katie stopped in the middle of the hall. He was right. She could hardly breathe and her calves were burning. Her purpose had been to go straight to the classroom, not their usual hangout spot by the staircase. She wanted to see if *he* was there. She didn't dare think his name incase he was in a dark corner somewhere listening.

"I think I'm still a little freaked out from yesterday," she blurted. She needed to tell someone about what happened. But she couldn't, could she? It would sound stupid.

"You'll get used to things." Brian looked around the hall, bored. "You mind if we go over there?" Brian was pointing to a group of people by the science hallway, next to the trophy display. Right under the biggest trophy stood the biggest headache. Christi Taylor.

Brian didn't wait for her to answer. Katie hesitated. Even if Tristan was in class, what would she say to him if she went there now?

Katie followed Brian over to the group. They opened up their circular form enough for Brian. Katie had to squeeze next to him. She felt so out of place, but Brian put his arm around her shoulder. She didn't know whether she liked it. A few guys slapped hands with Brian. He laughed and made a few jokes about passing teachers and a few socially awkward kids.

Everyone slurped up his jokes like dogs dying of thirst. *As popular as ever.* It bothered Katie that he was popular. At first, she thought it was because it made her feel jealous, and then petty, but more and more she realized it was because Brian always changed when he was the center of attention. He always became invincible.

"Hey, you're new, right?" a guy said to Katie. If she could remember correctly, his name started with an "*A.*"

"No. Are you?" she said, ruder than she'd meant.

"I meant to the program." The guy looked around the group to confirm that he had said it right the first time. Eyes stared back at her full of confusion. Silence never felt so awkward.

Katie felt stupid. "Yeah," she said, nodding her head. No one asked her any more questions.

The bell rang, and they dispersed to their classrooms.

Finally, she made it to their English class with Brian walking lazily behind her. She walked in and there he was. There he was and here she was thinking about how he was right there.

He looked at her—confused.

She turned around and walked back out, brushing past Brian. What was wrong with her?

"Uh, did you forget something?" Brian said, standing awkwardly in the doorway.

"It's Tristan, he—makes things incredibly awkward," she said.

"I know." Brian's face fell. "He lives in my house." Brian stepped into class and Katie took a deep breath.

⁘

School passed the same way it had the day before, with just as many awkward moments. The only difference was in Field Study, when Mr. Carver brought out an array of weapons from different time periods, reaching to modern day. There were guns, clubs, swords, and knives that Katie didn't catch the name of, and Mr. Carver carefully lectured on the uses of each. When they were free to walk around and look at them, Tristan explained, in detail, the more modern-looking ones. It was creepy how much he knew about weapons. And killing. Weighing heavy was the of invasion of these weapons in her classroom. Everything in her told her they weren't supposed to be here. They were dangerous. No one seemed to care, though.

"Oh, this one is nice, it's very light."

"I like that this one is so heavy. I always forget I'm holding the dinky ones."

"Last year's model was better, I think."

"Oh, I should write down this model. I'll ask my mentor about it."

She was the only one not talking about them like new chemistry supplies.

⁘

After another grueling run after school, she'd nearly forgotten that it wasn't over. She'd gotten out of her mentor-sponsored training yesterday, but there was no avoiding it today.

"We're supposed to meet Lucinda at her house," Tristan said to Katie as she gulped down as much water possible. She noticed he said *her* house even though he lived there too.

"What if I die between now and then?" Katie said, lying down on the concrete. It wouldn't be so bad to close her eyes and sleep there for a while.

"Then I guess we'd both be screwed." Tristan wiped the sweat off his brow. He hadn't run with her today. He ran at his own pace, which was too fast for far too long. Every time he lapped her he'd shout, *"Breathe."*

"Yeah, you'd need a new partner," she said, signaling for him to block the sun out of her eyes.

He didn't move. "Something like that."

⋅ༀ⋅

Katie didn't bother changing. She figured whatever lay in store at Lucinda's house would probably require more sweat. They walked to Lucinda's house in silence. Was it going to be like this everyday? The two of them doing *everything* together?

Her thoughts shifted away from whether Tristan wondered that too when she saw Lucinda in the front yard, waving at them enthusiastically. "Who's ready to go shooting?" she called.

Katie didn't respond. How was she supposed to respond to that?

"Hey!" Katie turned around and saw Allison running toward them. She was plastered in sweat and looking determined. "Am I—late? Wanted to run—so I took the long way here. Will didn't leave—without me—did he?" Allison put her hands on her hips.

"You ran here?" Katie said.

"Preliminaries—are this—Saturday. I can't—slack off," Allison panted.

Lucinda waved Allison inside to get water. "Will has an emergency at the office. So I'm going to take you and Brian out today. Where is Brian?"

"Really? Are you serious? You're going to train us?" Allison gasped. "OMGOMGOMG youhavetoteachmehowto—"

Katie couldn't make out the rest.

They waited almost an hour before Brian got home. That hour buried the little confidence she tried to muster. She tried waiting in the house, but the talk of guns and knives made her nervous. She tried outside, but the lingering summer sun burned her skin. There wasn't a cloud in the sky. Just the sun. Like an eye…watching her, a reminder that there was nowhere to run. This was it. This or being hauled off in the back of a van with Glock, screaming bloody murder.

"Ready?"

Katie jumped as Lucinda came out of the house with two pop cans. Allison, Brian, and Tristan followed, piling into the SUV.

"All or nothing, right?" Katie said. Lucinda handed her a can and opened her own. The cold sugar and caffeine cooled and calmed her.

"Did you know I grew up on a farm?"

Katie shook her head.

"Yup. It was where my dad taught me how to shoot. I was about your age and a laughing stock because everyone else learned when they were ten. But my dad, he just told me when I was ready I'd learn. It was a *real* hot day—everyone was at our neighbor's pool, and I stayed behind to help my dad clean out the barn. We shared a whole six-pack of Coke." Lucinda laughed and held up her can. "This was way back when pop came in glass bottles." She took a long swig before she continued. "When we were done, he grabbed his small twenty-two pistol, the bottles, and told me to follow him. We went to our fence in the back of our property and lined up each bottle. I didn't miss one. Still haven't," she winked. "Guardians aren't made, Katie. They're born." Lucinda laughed.

Katie stared out the window not entirely soothed. Katie didn't even know how to hold a gun. She'd likely shoot her own face off.

⁕

She thought they were going to a building with booths, earmuffs, and personal shooting targets. She was wrong. Lucinda drove them out of the city and deep into the foothills, far away from hiking trails and roads.

It was dry and windy where they stopped. Patches of green hovered near trees, but mostly rock and brush surrounded them for miles. Lucinda warned them to watch out for rattlesnakes.

Brian and Tristan unloaded the truck while Lucinda and Allison set up a table with guns of different sizes, bullets clinking and rolling as they fell out of packages.

Katie watched, useless and in the way.

"Check the actions for me, Allison," Lucinda said.

Allison cocked each gun. The constant sound of metallic springs recoiling and snapping put Katie on edge.

"Can you smell the sage?" Lucinda said.

A gust of wind picked up and slid down the hills. Smells of sage and dust whirled around Katie. She choked on it.

Lucinda walked over with a pistol in hand. Katie recoiled as Lucinda presented it to her. Lucinda covered gun safety, and Katie found it hard to focus. How could she remember every step? Every detail? *If it's such a killing machine, why should I be allowed to use it much less touch it?*

"If you forget everything I said, just remember one thing," Lucinda said, putting a single bullet in a small pistol. "Muzzle control. Always know where you point your gun. Also, never point it at someone unless you intend to kill." She showed Katie how to cock and hold it. "Just stand there and get used to the grip. I'll be right back." Lucinda disappeared into the truck and came back seconds later holding Katie's pop can. She put it on a stump about twenty feet away.

"Okay," Lucinda said. "Hold it steady, aim, and shoot."

Katie waited until Lucinda was far behind her before she held up the gun. Her hands shook so badly she thought she was going to drop it, killing everyone. She heard footsteps behind her.

"Knowing how to use a gun won't make you a killer. You're going to need to defend yourself," Tristan said, just loud enough for her to hear. She was still afraid. Afraid of how it might change her life. There was no going back after this.

"Stop thinking there's something to go back to. Life moves forward, Katalina. Never backwards. Either move or get left behind," he said. He was standing so close that even if she wanted to turn around and bolt, he would be there blocking her way.

Are you always this pushy?

He was right, though, what did she have to go back to? Her life was changing whether she wanted it to or not.

She didn't need to turn around to know Tristan had moved from behind her. She was alone. It was her decision.

She pulled the trigger.

The report was loud and she completely missed the can. She didn't care. The exhilaration of being in control of something so powerful made her brave. *What was I even afraid of?* She turned around and everyone ducked before she realized she was pointing the pistol at them.

⋅⊙⋅

Katie tried an array of pistols of all different sizes and calibers. When she put a small, heavy revolver down on the table, Lucinda told her that Tristan was going to be more of an assistant coach than an actual partner in her physical training.

"What? He's my partner! Isn't *he* supposed to *have* the same training as me? That's so wrong, Lucy. The school would never agree to that." Katie eyed Tristan as he sharpened a set of knives in a bit of shade under a tree.

"Due to the time constraints, we need to accelerate your training. I've decided, Katie. Tristan's agreed, and he has a lot to offer."

Katie shook her head. "Lucy, you can't just hand over my training to a kid I barely just met."

"If you don't trust him, At least trust me. It's very complicated, but I trust Tristan. He *wants* to train you. He's more capable than me," Lucinda rubbed her hip the way she always did out of habit. Katie never knew what happened to her. "Don't tell him I said that. Besides, I'm going to be right here watching." Lucinda gave her a slight push in Tristan's direction. "Tristan's already knows what to cover today—go on. Go learn something, Sweetie."

It's complicated. She was sick of that being an excuse. *Just trust me…it's complicated….* She watched Lucinda pick up three knives and stick a target thirty-five yards away. Arguing wasn't getting her anywhere. Instead, she walked over to her new make-shift teacher.

Without a word, Tristan stood up. "You should take that off," he said, pointing at the necklace Brian had given her for Christmas. It was a little jade-green turtle. She looked over at Brian, throwing knives at a flimsy tree, each knife bouncing off into the surrounding bushes. When he gave her the necklace, she promised she'd never take it off. She wasn't going to break that promise now, or ever.

Tristan studied her hard. "You know, the harder you hold onto things, the more likely they are to break?"

She scoffed and put the turtle under her shirt.

He explained how to hold a knife and use it. At first, she refused to touch it, but he showed her it was fake. "Never stab, not unless you're going for the kill and your opponent is unable to stop you."

She nodded, though thinking about killing someone, even if they were technically *not* human, didn't sit right with her.

"You still need to know this," Tristan said, openly probing her.

"How am I supposed to do anything if vampires can read my mind?" she mumbled.

"Vampires can't read your mind. They aren't psychic. I can understand you because you let me. I can feel you because you're careless with your feelings. That's it." His eyes were stern, and he nodded for her to get into the defensive stance he'd shown her.

"You realize that is essentially the definition of psychic?"

"Just stab at me."

"You just told me not to."

"Just do it," he said. She hesitated, then half-heartedly jabbed in his direction. He knocked her hand out of the way roughly. "Be serious."

She lunged at him. He grabbed her arm and smacked at the bottom of her elbow. Pain seared up her arm and pulsed as she dropped the knife.

"That's why you don't stab. Now slash."

"What was the point of that?" she said, rubbing her elbow. A dull throbbing pain settled into the bone.

"So you'll remember not to stab. Slash," he said.

Katie glanced at Lucinda expecting her to step in and scold Tristan.

Lucinda waved for them to continue.

"Are you serious?" Katie breathed. No one acknowledged her, so she sighed and moved back into position.

She slashed at him and expected him to grab her again. Instead, he backed up each time. "See the difference?"

Tristan went on, showing her different ways to block, all of which she found relatively easy. After twenty minutes of repeated drills, he showed her some offensive moves that she had never seen before, but once she got the footwork and understood the motion, they were just as easy.

Never once did he compliment her. He wouldn't say *one* nice thing. And her kicks were pretty awesome. How was he supposed to be a teacher if he couldn't give positive reinforcement? Lucinda had dumped her off with another "*Sensei Steve.*"

In one move, Tristan kicked Katie's legs out from under her and she hit the ground.

"*Shut up* already. Be more focused on what *you're* doing, not me. Do you think the werewolf trying to kill you will compliment you on how you stabbed him in an artery? Do you think the vampire trying to rip your head off will say you have a nice kick? Get over yourself. I'm sick of listening to your crap. You *never* shut up."

"Tristan," Lucinda scolded.

Covered in dust and dirt, she yelled, "Then get out of my head!" How dare he complain about invading *her* privacy?

"You think I enjoy this? Do you realize I spend my entire day trying to shut you out!" Tristan yelled back. Lucinda, Allison, and Brian were staring at them, but Katie didn't care if all of

Boise was staring at them. She was tired of him. Tired of not knowing whether to hate him or not.

"I can't stand you," Katie said.

"Funny, I didn't hear you saying that yesterday."

"I never asked you to do anything. I didn't show up at *your* school. I didn't mess up your life!" she screamed. Maybe it wasn't fair that she was taking out *all* of her anger on him, but he asked for it.

"Katie," Lucinda warned.

"I didn't ask for *you*. I didn't ask for *this*. I didn't have a choice." Tristan glared, balled up his fists, and walked off.

The look in his eyes before he walked away was the same look he had yesterday. The one where it seemed like *she* was the one who'd torn apart his world. It was worse than a punch in the gut.

For an instant, like a distant murmur, she could feel him in her mind.

He was screaming.

❧ 7 ☙

FINDLEY PARK

THE RIDE INTO town was awkward. Katie didn't dare look at Tristan. *I heard him…or you…I actually heard you….*

Her mind—it was full of him. It was only for a small second, but it was real. He was angry, sad, and he was hurt. *How is this possible? Tristan—capable of feeling? What am I saying? I'm sitting next to a vampire. I wouldn't be surprised if I could sprout wings and fart pixie dust.* She wondered if he heard her just now…

She inched her eyes to the far side of her head. He was staring dead at her. His brow furrowed and his stiff black sweaty hair stabbing into his face said, *"unamused."*

That death stare isn't attractive.

He turned away.

She hated that he knew everything she was thinking, but now she knew it worked both ways. *Why can't I hear your thoughts all the time? Because you're shutting me out?* She didn't need a response to know it was true. She *wished* she could shut him out.

She imagined building a wall between them, none of her thoughts getting past it. Picking up each of her thoughts, one by one, putting them in a jar and closing the lid. Him looking at the jar, pressing his nosey ear to it in vain. The wall building higher and higher until he couldn't even *see* her jar.

Tristan snapped his head in her direction, confused.

Me: one. You: none.

⁓⁓⁓

Katie, relieved to be out of the truck, was sure everyone felt the same way—everyone except Lucinda.

"Let's celebrate," she said, unlocking the front door. "Katie's first training was a success—" she paused at their blank, wide-eyed stares "—At least most of it, anyway."

As soon as the door was open, Tristan went directly to his room.

"I have plans," Brian mumbled, following Tristan's lead.

"Plans for what?" Lucinda said sharply.

"I wanted to study at Michael's house. He's going to help me with the history exam we have," Brian said defensively.

Katie seethed. It was a flat-out lie. A lie she wasn't even invited to.

"Fine. You need the help." Lucinda's eyes bore into Brian as he climbed the stairs to his room.

"Okay then. Just the three of us girls. We can have a ladies' night instead," Lucinda said, leading them to the kitchen. "I know, we can have a sleepover like we used to. I can give you girls facials, and you can get me caught up on everything. Go home, pack a bag, and make sure it's okay with your parents. Today's been exciting enough without a call from—when *do* you plan on telling your dad?" she asked Katie.

"I—" Katie started. How did she know?

Eyebrows arched, Lucinda nodded and said, "Preferably sooner than never, Katie."

⁓⁕⁓

Katie decided to *tell* her dad she was staying at the Anderson's, rather than ask. He started his usual flow of subtle objections. but stopped when she added that it was a girls' night with Lucinda and Allison.

"Oh. Have fun then," he said, sitting on the couch. He looked tired and lonely. Between his work schedule and her deliberately not waiting up and watching TV with him, he really didn't have anyone else to spend time with. "I know you think of Lucy like a mom, but try not to forget about Dear Old Dad. I haven't seen you much."

"Sure, would you like pink polish or red? I personally think a black would go nice with your attitude," she said. He was predictable.

"Lucy can't recite *Star Wars* episodes four through six with you like I can. That's a hard act to follow." he grinned.

"Maybe, but Lucy's the only mom I've got."

"That's not true."

"It is." Especially since he'd neglected to tell her anything about her real mother, besides the fact that she liked gardening and arts and crafts.

"How about Saturday we go to the zoo or something."

"I've been to the zoo a thousand times, and the sloth bear is still as boring as ever." She stopped when she saw his face. "But I do want to see the lions again."

"Me too," he said, smiling. His eyes were soft, but they panicked a little—as if they wished they could reach her, but with each try, the distance became farther and farther. "I'm not sure you should stay at Lucinda's on a school night."

"See you later, Dad," she said, ignoring him.

"Yeah, yeah. One of these days I'm going to expect you to do what I say. Be careful, Katie Bug."

The click of closing the front door startled her. The sound echoed throughout her mind. That smile—the soft, lonely eyes. For a split second, she wanted to go back in and sit with him like she used to. But she had already closed the door. There was no point in going back now.

⁂

She returned to Lucinda's house, pulled in by the smell of steak, fresh steamed vegetables, and potatoes. Her mouth watered. She hadn't realized how tired and hungry she really was until Lucinda put the food on the table.

"So what happened out there with you and Tristan?" Allison

said, stuffing her mouth with broccoli. It was a marvel how she could fit so many pieces in, all at the same time.

"Um. Nothing."

"Kay, don't be dumb."

"Allison," Lucinda said.

"I'm just saying. There is *a lot* going on with them. You two act so weird when you're in the same room." Allison's eyes lingered on Katie as a large cut of potato disappeared into her mouth. Katie's face burned under her gaze. She wanted to say, *Really, Allison? You pick now of all times to bring this up?* But instead, she settled with, "Can you eat your food like a normal person?"

"He just came from nowhere," Allison said, ignoring her.

"Everyone comes from somewhere, Allison," Lucinda said.

"I'm serious, Lucy. He shows up on your doorstep. Stalks Katie, and then says he didn't *"choose"* her. That he spends all day trying to get her out of his head. It's a little mental."

"It's complicated," Lucinda said, centering the vase of orchids in the middle of the table. She moved it an inch to the left, half an inch to the right…

"Fine, Lucy. Forget the crazy story. He's half-vampire isn't he? You know what will happen if the Board finds out."

"Allison! I'm not an idiot." Lucinda's brushed her hands together as if the vase had stained them.

Katie exhaled, feeling like her head was going to explode. Why was it no one wanted to be honest? Then again, she just left her dad in the dark about recent events. Katie was no better. A secret keeper like the rest of them.

Lucinda smoothed out the table, which was strange considering it was wood—*what is there to straighten?* She shouldn't have been surprised, though. It was Lucinda's way of letting out anxiety. The same way she'd go over a recipe ten times before she collected the ingredients, or wipe the counters until her hands were raw and red.

After dinner, they watched a one-hundred percent predictable comedy romance—cliché montage and all—movie. Katie loved laughing at every second of it up until everything went black and her face slammed into the popcorn bowl.

"And you call me a pig," Allison laughed.

"Ha ha," she yawned, picking kernels out of her hair. She fell asleep before the girl realized she was a completely selfish person and chased after the man of her dreams. Actually, she'd fallen asleep before they broke up.

Katie's eyes started to close again. Her arms and legs weighed a ton and a half. Her eyelids longed to fall to the floor, dragging her into a deep, dark abyss.

"Go to bed, Katie. You've had a long day," Lucinda said.

Katie grumbled and left.

As soon as she dragged along to the guest bedroom, she collapsed onto the soft, cool sheets.

She saw herself taking down bricks from a wall, and waving at Tristan on the other side. He walked over to her with his arms spread out, ready for her to fall into them. The smell of him made her smile. His long fingers and broad shoulders. He kissed her forehead. It felt like home. His lips moved down. His tongue slipped into her mouth. She didn't want to let him go, but a blackness was coming, the world began to shake, and he was disappearing. She rocked back and forth until the blackness took her whole.

She opened her eyes and she was back in the room—still rocking. When her eyes adjusted to the light, Tristan was staring down at her.

"Quit being a pervert," he said. His words smashed into her like a car into a brick wall.

She pinched herself. This was another dream. Another horrible unwanted dream. "Oh. My. God."

"Yeah, and I was there with you for every second of it. Pervert."

She threw her pillow at him. She wanted to curl into herself and implode. "It was a dream. Argh—why didn't you just pretend you didn't see it? What's wrong with you?"

Tristan smiled before he left the room. "What would be the fun in that?"

I don't like you, she screamed loud in her mind. *Omg, I do not like you. I don't even like your hair. Or your creepy, beady blue eyes. Omg, I do not like you.*

"Pervert," she heard back. She wasn't sure if it was her brain echoing him, or his thoughts. *Of all people, why him?* It was obvious. He was someone new in her life and for the last five days he'd been invading her space and thoughts. It was only natural that you dream about someone you've been around constantly.

She thought of her thoughts in a jar, but this time with a jar made of soundproof glass, and a wall that reached to the stars. Not too long after she considered a sonarproof wall, Allison walked into the room, yawning.

"You're still up?" Allison asked.

"I had a nightmare," she said, frowning at the wall.

Allison cocked her head to the side and offered a sympathetic smile. "Still feeling overwhelmed?"

"No. But thanks for reminding me. I made out with Tristan."

"You what? When? Just now?"

"Dear God, no. In my nightmare. It was terrible."

"Seriously? That's what you call a nightmare?"

"You weren't there. It was horrible. He called me a pervert."

"What, did you try and cop a feel? Unrequited love can be devastating."

"No, he ninja-stalked my nightmare, woke me up, and then called me a pervert."

"*Ninja-stalked* your nightmare?" Allison arched an eyebrow.

It was time to tell Allison the truth about the fight Tristan and Katie had earlier—what he really meant about getting her out of his head.

Allison listened intently. "You're trying to tell me he can *hear* your thoughts?"

Katie nodded.

"Wait—so I'm clear—not only can he read your thoughts, but he also saw a dream you just had where you made out with him."

"Correction: nightmare. And yes," Katie said, feeling a whole new sense of violation blanket her.

"And then he came up here, woke you up, and called you a pervert?" Allison nearly murdered herself in a fit of laughter.

"You're supposed to be my friend," Katie said.

"I can't b-believe he called you a pervert. How embarrassing."

"My mind gets hijacked on a daily basis, and you laugh." Katie threw the covers over her face and ignored Allison's jeers.

Allison pulled the covers off Katie with a new look on her face. "Seriously though," she started, "That's creepy. Does Lucy know?"

"I don't know. If she did, what good would that do?"

"Well for one—well—well, I guess it doesn't change anything." Allison pulled at a few strands of hair. "It explains a lot."

Katie waited.

"He always looks like he has a headache—I don't mean like that, but seriously. He looks at you a lot, randomly. I noticed when we were in the library today, he'd shoot glances at you every few minutes, and sometimes he rubs his temples and he'll have this look on his face like—well, it kind of makes sense."

"That I'm a headache?" Katie said, trying desperately hard to ignore her body's response to learning that he *looks* at her.

"Imagine if you heard my thoughts all the time. All of them, *all the time*. The sheer amount would give anyone a headache."

"Poor Tristan He has to listen to my private thoughts all the time. The things I *don't* want him to hear. The things I don't want anyone to hear."

Allison frowned. "Why? Why can he?"

Kate and Allison spent an hour talking about it. Where exactly Tristan came from. What he knew about her mother. Why he wouldn't tell her the truth. What Lucinda knew. Whether or not he was listening to them at that exact moment… Always they came to a dead end. Back to square one.

⋰⊱⊰⋱

In the midst of Allison's rhythmic nasal honks, Katie heard a car door slam and went to the window in time to see Brian waving as a car pulled out of the driveway. It was after midnight.

She paced the room trying to figure out what she should say to him. *"Couldn't help but see you waving at your friends. Tell me who they are and maybe I could wave next time too."* No, that sounded too desperate. *"Those your new friends? Names and numbers please."* No, too stalker-ish. *"You don't have to hide your new friends, Brian. I only want to know why all of a sudden I'm not invited to sneak-out (insert smile)."* If only that one hadn't made her feel like an ax-murderer.

She held her breath as heavy, dragged footsteps climbed up the stairs. She opened the door just as he reached the landing.

"You were out late," she said, trying to hide the bits of hysteria she felt. She knew she probably looked manic with her hair falling all over the place. Stupid. Why didn't she check her hair?

"Mom already yelled at me for not calling. I don't need it from you," he said.

"Why would I yell at you?"

He laughed. "I was just kidding." He hesitated before opening his room door.

Katie caught a whiff of something. Maybe alcohol? "Oh, well how was the movie?"

Guilt spread across his face like butter on toast. "Uh, it was a piece of shit."

"I bet." Why was she getting so angry?

He paused, and she stared at his familiar half-smile, trying to make sense of the tightening in her stomach. "Err, night," he said, closing his bedroom door.

⁂

The tightening in her stomach was just the beginning. It was like she couldn't stand to be around Brian. The next day, after study hall, he saw Katie with Traci and started laughing with his *"movie" friends*. "Look, it's Train-wreck Traci! I heard she's not even allowed to go within a five-mile radius of a gun."

Maybe Katie would have laughed too, or asked the follow-up question, *"Why?"* if it hadn't pissed her off. Traci was standing right there in the hall when he'd said it. She had heard him. Katie knew it. It was in the way Traci adjusted her rucksack and scratched her nose.

It was this *Invincible Brian* that Katie never liked. She had tolerated it because he was hardly like that, maybe an hour out of the day or when he was around the wrong people. But as the week progressed, *that* Brian showed his face more often than not.

On Thursday, Allison got a certificate for being the only level-3, which was pretty big (according to Mr. Carver, who looked like a proud father). Katie clapped and congratulated Allison, even though the only thing she knew about a level-3 was that it was higher than her level-6. Actually, everyone was higher than her level-6. Even Tristan's fake records put him at level-4.

Everyone stopped clapping when a bubble of laughs erupted from the other side of the classroom. It was Brian cracking a joke about Allison having "*level-3 man hands.*" Allison's hands were a little bigger than the average girl, but they were *not* man hands.

Allison pretended not to hear it—she was always too dignified to react to stupid jokes—but Katie saw the way she gripped the certificate.

Brian was a giant jerk, and Katie made it a point to give him the cold shoulder for acting like a douche-bag, but it wasn't just him that had her aggravated and on edge. This one week was more torture than Katie had endured since she joined the swimming team two years ago. There was a reason she'd quit this year. She wanted a relaxing junior year, and now it was like she couldn't escape stress.

Homework piled up, and between classes and training, she was tired even when she was sleeping. Ever since their first training session, Tristan didn't say much more than what was necessary. He only beat the crap out of her during their training sessions and grunted when she didn't turn in assignments.

All the while, Sports Day loomed over her like a stalker in a dark alley. She'd already conceded that she'd come in last, she just didn't want to do it in front of everyone and their parents.

She sat down on the school steps and watched cars pull up and drive off. She could always invite her dad and tell him that way. She laughed at herself. The thought was stupid. Her dad would know right away that something was up. Katie spending a Saturday at school?

She froze. They were supposed to go to the zoo tomorrow. She smacked her forehead.

Tristan cursed under his breath behind her.

"I know," she said, hanging her head between her legs. What a headache.

"No. I'm talking about that."

Katie lifted her head and followed his gaze out onto the street. Her heart constricted in her chest. Her dad sat in his truck staring at her. Her and Tristan.

He knew.

Everything about the disgusted look on his face said he knew. His eyes bore into her.

Katie sat on the steps unsure of what to do. Her dad's face didn't say he wanted to talk. It was the look of a man completely betrayed. But why did she feel like she'd stabbed *him* in the back? Why was her heart in her throat? He was the one who'd lied to her.

She stood up and prepared herself to walk over.

Tristan grabbed her arm. "You don't have to go over there."

Katie's hands shook. It didn't matter whether she did or not. Her father started up the truck and left.

Time froze, her body still and encased in panic. Why was this happening now? How did he know?

She took off running. Something told her if she didn't show up at home ASAP, things were going to be worse.

She made it a quarter of the way before she started coughing.

"Katalina—" Tristan was right behind her.

"Shit. Shit. I'm in so much trouble. He's going to kill me. How did he find out?"

"Katalina, you haven't done anything wrong." Tristan shook her. "Look at me—you haven't done anything wrong."

"I can't deal with this. I can't. I don't know what to do. He's so pissed."

Tristan gripped her shoulders so hard it hurt. "If he threatens to do anything, run."

Katie shook her head. "What? He wouldn't hit me. No. Christ, no. He's not crazy." Tristan's eyes pierced straight into her mind.

"There are worse things." He let her go. She was completely thrown off. Why were there always worse things?

When she made it to her house, the truck was in the driveway. Katie took a few deep breaths and walked to her porch.

"You've done nothing wrong, Katalina." Even though Tristan said it over and over again, she felt like she'd been caught half-naked with a boy.

She left Tristan and went inside. It was silent except for the sound of the TV. He was in the living room, in his usual spot on the couch. She stood in the doorway waiting for him to notice her.

He didn't move a muscle. The long wait made her feet ache. He wasn't going to say anything? He always said something. Her heart pinched and pounded. She turned to leave when he spoke.

"Who's that boy?"

She didn't say anything. That wasn't what she expected. "Just Tristan—he goes to my school."

Silence.

Her feet throbbed from running and anticipation. Was that what he was angry about? Did he know Tristan or did he just dislike the fact that she was with a boy?

"Do you realize what you've done? Do you know what I've gone through—*sacrificed*—to make sure you were safe?"

"I haven't done anything wrong," Katie said in a small voice.

He looked at her through the slits of his eyes. "If you ever talk to, look at, or speak about that family or that boy, I swear to God, Katie."

What was he saying? "Dad—"

"I had to hear it from *him*. Of all people. You're a liar and a coward. Look at me when I talk to you. Never again are you allowed to go near those people."

"You can't—you can't say that. They're family."

"*Stupid* girl. I'm your family. They'll get you killed!"

Katie shook to the bone. It was true she was scared—she was a coward, and a liar—but she wasn't stupid. She hadn't had a choice. Not a real one. She had made the right decision. "No," she said, barely audible.

"What?"

"I'm not stupid." Tears started to fall. Her throat burned with all the anger and fear she'd been keeping inside. It was his fault she was in this situation.

"Well, you're not smart."

"How the *hell* is this my fault?" she screamed. It came out like fire.

"Listen to me. And Goddammit you better hear me. You're done. This little game you think you've been playing is over. Never go to that house again."

"You can't stop me. They're my family. *They* took care of me when you wouldn't." Katie never thought she'd throw that in his face. Her childhood wasn't all roses and rainbows. Her and her dad had a tough time when she was young, sometimes she had to stay with the Anderson's for months because he worked at odd times of the day—and sometimes drank too much. It wasn't like that now, they were fine now. At least, that was the silent agreement they'd come to.

"I can make you forget your *family*," he spat.

In his eyes, she saw a monster who'd take her memories away—in his eyes she saw Glock.

She turned and ran.

⁘

Katie smacked into Tristan as she flew out of the house. She didn't stop to assess the damage. She couldn't stop. She had to keep running, her bookbag slapping against her back. It was amazing how much farther she could run when it wasn't around a track and when her legs pumped with rage. Rage she didn't know she still had about things that didn't matter anymore.

When she finally stopped, Tristan wasn't far behind her. What was she going to do? She had just officially run away from home. She laughed, trying to release whatever was making her shake, but stopped when it almost turned into a sob.

She sat down on a bus bench. She was still clenching her bookbag. "I take it you know what happened?" she said. There was a girl with blue hair walking down the street. There were a lot of cars out. Rush hour maybe. She looked for other things to focus on.

"Don't have to read your mind to know how that went." Tristan stood next to her.

She fidgeted on the bench. There was so much anger swirling in her body she thought she was going to explode. She gripped the wood, making her hand gritty and dirty.

"Come on," Tristan said. He grabbed her bookbag and started to jog. She followed.

Her legs pounded on the concrete. Her feet hurt, but the pain was better than the one unpacking all of her childhood memories. Calling Lucinda once in the middle of the night because her dad never came home. Who did that to a ten-year-old?

Tristan jogged into Findley Park and set her bag down. "Come at me, like I showed you yesterday," he said, unbuttoning his shirt. He threw it on the tall grass and untucked his undershirt.

"I'm not in the mood to practice," she said. Her dad had never even apologized. All the years she'd spent growing up with the Andersons. One day, he picked her up and acted like *she* hadn't been there for an entire month. He never mentioned where he'd gone, no one had bothered to tell her, and her father was probably on a bender. She had to figure that one out on her own.

Tristan kicked her leg and pushed her off balance. She caught herself before she hit the ground.

"Don't," she yelled. "I'm so not in the mood." Katie ground her teeth and dug her fingernails into the palms of her hands.

He did it again. She swung to slap him and he pushed her arm away. She tried to shove him, and he slapped her arms aside. She could feel her throat burning again. She swung at him again and finally landed a punch on his arm.

He laughed.

"Asshole," she yelled, and swung again, and again and again. Each time, he blocked and tried to push her off balance.

Without, thinking she faked a punch and went for an uppercut. It landed on his chin.

Tristan cursed and rubbed his chin. "I didn't teach you that one," he said, smiling. "Try it again."

Tears fell from her eyes, but she didn't care if he saw them. Not while she was punching.

They fought in the park until they couldn't see each other. Sweaty and tired, she lay out on the grass and stared at the stars between the trees. A weight was lifted, and she could breathe. It didn't matter that she was lying in the middle of a park, homeless.

Tristan sat down next to her.

"You stayed at my house that entire time?" she said.

Silence.

"You're such a creeper," Katie laughed.

"If I hadn't been there, where would you be now?"

She couldn't tell if that question was directed at her or himself.

"Where did you come from?" Katie said it before she thought it. She couldn't imagine what his life was like, or who he was.

"I left Idaho after my parents died. Since then I lived in New York."

"With other family members?" Lucinda did have a big family.

"No."

She couldn't see his face, but she imagined that blank mask he wore. "When did they—how old were you?"

"Seven."

Katie felt a deep unease slowly slide into her. "Sorry," she whispered. She wanted to know more, but she couldn't say it. Not out loud.

They listened to crickets and black leaves rustling in the wind.

"Do you hear all of my thoughts?"

"I try not to."

"When did you start hearing them?"

He was quiet for a long time. She figured he didn't want to talk about it.

"I had just turned seven—when it happened."

Katie's eyes widened. A thousand questions flew through her mind. How? Why? Did it have something to do with his parents' death? Could he hear her this whole time? All these years?

His breath quickened. "It depends on how close you are," he said, answering only one of them.

"What?"

"I hear your thoughts better when we are closer. The farther you are, the less I hear. But the last week has been like listening to talk radio nonstop."

Katie thought about what Allison said, that night after her first training session. He probably didn't get a kick out of it like she'd thought.

Tristan laughed, "You can be really annoying."

Katie grunted.

He laughed harder when she hit him. It struck her that she'd never heard him laugh like that before. It was light and unguarded.

He stopped.

Silence passed between them. Katie smiled. She couldn't help it. "You're so awkward. Oh my god. You really are. You make everything so much weirder than it has to be."

"Maybe if you didn't scrutinize everything I did," Tristan said defensively.

"That's what people do. That's how you—I don't know— learn about a person."

"You're *learning* me?"

She could hear him smile. "See, you just made the most natural thing sound weird."

She lay there and he sat there for hours. Like two homeless vagabonds. They spent most of the time arguing about movies, songs, and video games. Everything with him was an argument. She liked cowboy space operas and he thought they came from a special place in hell. She liked art, he thought it was a waste of time and energy. She thought it was perfectly normal to want to smack politeness into him and he thought she was a lunatic for trying. Nonetheless, he talked more in those hours than he had since she met him.

They were quiet for a while before she said aloud what she was thinking. "I heard you, the other day. In my mind."

"I know."

"So it works both ways?"

"Yeah," he breathed.

"Then why can't I hear you now?"

"I don't know. Maybe you forgot how—" He clipped the last word.

More questions rushed to her mind.

"Katalina," he begged.

Katie could make out his silhouette. He held his head in his hands. "Sorry," she said, trying to still her mind. It was the hardest thing—trying to not think.

"You can think. It's just I can't focus on what you're saying without hearing your thoughts too. Then, throw in your acute ability to think fifteen things at once…"

Katie sat up. "Maybe that's it."

"No," Tristan said at the same time.

"Why not? I only want to try." She stared at him. If she thought about hearing him, maybe she would.

"What if I don't want you in my head?"

She didn't have to voice how much of a double standard that was. She ignored his protest and stared at him. His dark eyes glinted in the moonlight.

"You call me creepy? You should see your face right now." He turned away.

Katie scowled. "I'm concentrating."

Tristan blurted out a laugh. "Don't ever do it again."

Katie pushed him, but he didn't budge. "Is that a vampire thing?" She had noticed how solid he was. He was like a wall most of the time. She watched the way he made an effort to relax his body.

"Sort of. Stop watching me." He turned away from her and played with the grass between his fingers.

"You know, you were right," Katie said. "In the grand scheme of things, Sports Day really doesn't matter." Katie reached for her bag and pulled out her cellphone. It was past four in the morning. She had no missed calls or messages. "So much for being concerned about my safety. He didn't even call." The way her dad said he'd make her forget set her on fire again.

"He knows you'd go to Lucinda's."

"How do you know that?"

"Wouldn't you?" Tristan turned to face her.

"Am I there now?" Katie said, realizing she could in fact be dead in a park, and her dad would never know.

"Touché."

She lay back on the grass and stared at the deep-blue patches of sky and stars—until she was waking up. The sky was morning-blue and hazy. She sat up, and Tristan's button-down shirt fell off her. He was sitting in the same spot. She checked her phone. It was half-past six.

"Thanks," she said, stretching. She handed his shirt to him.

"Actually, you just took it," he said, brushing loose dirt and grass off it. "What time does your dad go to work?" he asked, pointing at a bit of grass stuck to her face.

Katie wiped off the grass and drool. Under normal circumstances, she would have been mortified, but she had just spent the night in a park after running away from home. She was over having shame.

Tristan laughed under his breath.

"He has an early morning shift on Saturdays. He's already gone." Katie wondered if he had been looking forward to going to the zoo with her after work. *I think it's fair to say that's no longer on the agenda.* She stood up and grabbed her bag.

"I'm going to go home and grab some stuff—wanna come?" Katie half-expected him to pass.

He shrugged. "Sure."

8

PRELIMINARIES

KATIE SLIPPED INTO her house to pack a bag. Tristan followed her up to her room and analyzed it like an art gallery.

"I wouldn't exactly describe it as an *art gallery*," he said, touching the robot stickers on her dresser. He touched her giant green bean bag and stared at her purple-fur rug. "Nothing matches. It's like a whole bunch of crap thrown together. It suits you," he said, giving the room another survey. He stopped at the orange cat-shaped lamp.

"I'll take that as a compliment," Katie said, trying to figure out what else to take. What did people take when they ran away? How long was she supposed to run away? Almost none of her clothes were clean, as she'd neglected laundry all week. She grabbed the only clean tank top left and went to the bathroom.

She took a quick shower and washed her hair. She hated dressing in a steamy bathroom, but she had no choice. When she went back into her room, she caught him looking through her book collection.

"Is this what you buy at that weird bookstore?"

She nodded, looking for a pair of socks. For some reason she always forgot socks. It was a little nerve-racking having him in her room. She tried to pretend like it was fine, but it was odd how he studied her stuff.

"I'm '*learning*' you," he said. Even though she knew he was mocking her, she blushed. She turned from him to hide her face, knowing that it was pointless.

Katie rummaged through her dresser drawers for her old middle school gym clothes. She was going to do laundry last night—

"We could always skip the preliminaries," she said, finding the old shirt. She pulled it over her head. It was a little tight, but she *was* wearing the tank top too.

Tristan was staring at her. His eyes unblinking. "Something tells me it would be tight even if you took off the other shirt."

"What is *that* supposed to mean?"

He blinked.

"Stop calling me fat! I'm not fat."

"I never said fat." He shook his head as if to get rid of a buzzing fly. "That shirt looks like it belongs to a six-year-old."

Katie looked at herself in the mirror. Her old shirt was faded and clinging to her. To be fair, she was the size of a blade of grass in middle school. It wasn't until the last two years that she actually grew anything…

Tristan's eyes grew wide.

"EW!" Katie yelled. Had she been thinking about what she looked like naked? Had she thought about it clearly enough for him to see? Thinking about what she could have been thinking made images flash in her mind. She was just in the shower. He probably heard her in there washing herself… She smacked her head. "Get out! Get out!"

"It doesn't work that way."

"GET OUT OF *MY ROOM!*"

⚜

It was thirty minutes before she opened her room door and peeked down the hall. He was gone. Completely. She sat down on her bed next to her packed duffel bag. It overflowed with clothes, a tube of Play-Doh, her first edition *Peter Pan*, and her "Hang In There" kitty poster. She was kidding herself. How long could this last? She wasn't adult enough to run away. Adults packed essential things. Adults *had* essential things. Where was she running away to? Lucinda's? Sure, they'd take her, but it wasn't her home anymore. They didn't watch *Star Wars* from start to finish on random weekends. Lucinda would never try eating Flaming Cheetos and sardines for dinner. She couldn't sit around all weekend in pajamas collecting cereal bowls in front of the TV.

Katie breathed back the tears that were welling up inside of her. He still hadn't even called. He wasn't supposed to actually let her run away. He was supposed to be here when she got back. Angry, but glad she was okay. For the second time in her life, she hated him.

She hugged her pillow and lay back against her headboard. She needed to be angry again. Angry was always better than crying like an idiot.

Her phone rang. She jumped up and searched her room. It was under her duffel bag. Her heart sank when she saw Lucinda's name.

"Hello?"

"Katie. Hi, sweetheart. I hope you're excited for the preliminaries this morning."

"Well—"

"I don't mean to cut you off, sweetie, but I need to know if you've seen Tristan?" There was a light strain in her voice. Katie left her room and looked through the house for Tristan. Her heart sank. Lucinda was obviously worried about the self, sufficient totally independent nephew who didn't show up last night. Her dad didn't even send a text message. *Father of the year goes to—*

"Uh," Katie looked in the living room. She didn't know what to say. The whole truth? A half-truth? A lie?

"Katie, have you seen him? What's going on?"

"Well, I did see him—" She opened the front door. To do what? Look up and down the street? Why couldn't she just tell the truth?

"Katie? Katie, do you know something? Katie, talk to me."

She didn't have to say anything. He was sitting there on her porch. Katie handed him the phone.

She could still hear Lucinda on the other end. "*Katie?*"

"She's not here at the moment, but I can give her the phone back," Tristan said, sounding unenthused. "No, I stayed out late—I don't have a cell phone—Katalina has a weird thing about people using her phone—I'm not at her house, she just so happened to find me. We're at a bar—I'm kidding. I'm kidding—It's funnier than you're giving credit." He held the phone away from his ear and rolled his eyes. "I'm not a kid—fine, whatever—I'm not going to the preliminaries—well, I don't have a change of clothes—are you serious? I can wash my own clothes—I—Okay—OKAY." Tristan handed the phone to Katie.

"—This is completely unacceptable. It may come as a surprise to you, but people *worry* about you. Do you understand me?" Lucinda's voice was high-pitched and thin.

Katie tried to hand the phone back to Tristan. He ignored her.

"Hello? Tristan? Tristan?"

"Hi," Katie said in a small voice. "He—"

"I'll see you *both* at the school nine o'clock sharp." Lucinda hung up.

The only thing that pissed Lucinda off that much was politics. Now, Katie was incriminated in the disappearance of Tristan. "Please, try not to make her fly off the handle. At the moment, I'm very homeless and in need of a place to stay."

"Are you kidding me? That woman smothers. We're better off sleeping in parks."

⋅⊛⊛⋅

The streets were busy as they walked to the school. Katie felt like everyone knew she was running away. Her bookbag was full to the brim with toiletries and knick-knacks, and her duffel bag full of resentment, guilt, and Play-Doh. By the time they arrived at school, her shoulder hurt, and she felt a little annoyed that Tristan hadn't offered to help her as she fumbled around with both bags.

"Pack lighter next time," he said, walking up the steps. The school was busy. People chatting in groups, mainly adults.

"I don't plan on making this a regular thing."

He grabbed the duffel bag from her, and she almost fell over.

"Easy!" she said, nearly bumping into a lady laughing like a horse.

"Do you want it back?"

Why was he like that? As soon as he seemed tolerable, maybe even pleasant to be around, he'd turn back into a giant turd.

"Tristan! Katie!" Lucinda called from somewhere. It was amazing how easy it was to recognize someone's voice when the very sound of it put you on edge. She was still pissed, and it was written all over her face when Katie saw her marching up from the crowd. She was carrying two tote bags. "Here," she said to Tristan, handing him the smaller of two bags. "I brought you both a lunch, *since you were probably too busy to remember to make one*. Go get ready, the games are about to start. We won't be able to watch until the third event, but make sure to eat during the lunch break. Katie, what are you wearing—I don't even want to know." She handed Katie the second bag and stalked off. Katie watched her walk to Will.

She spoke to Will, and he looked up at Tristan, then Katie. He raised his eyebrows at her, then the duffel bag in Tristan's hand. His shoulders sank. Did he know? Katie turned around just as he started to make his way to her.

He was the one who called her dad. He said he'd let her tell him, yet he called. He knew how her dad was. He betrayed her. If he had let her do it on her own time, she wouldn't be wearing this dumb shirt or carrying around the stupid duffel bag at stupid sports day.

⚬⚬⚬

When Katie walked into the gymnasium, she was the only student not wearing this year's gym shirt. It wouldn't have been so bad if she wasn't the only bright blue in a sea of deep green. Not only was she going to lose every event, but she was also wearing her own loser flag.

Brian laughed at her while standing with his new posse.

What a friend.

Katie was relieved when she saw Allison, but quickly dodged behind a few parents when she saw the look of demonic rage on her face. She must have still been mad about her dad not showing up. At first, Katie thought it a stupid thing to be angry about. They weren't in elementary school anymore—but the more she looked around the gymnasium, the more she realized there were just as many adults as students. Maybe everyone's parents *did* show up. Everyone's except hers, Allison's, and Tristan's.

"Excuse me!" said a voice on the loudspeaker. The principal, Mr. Boyle, was on stage, looking as dumpy and confused as ever. It was the way his eyes were shaped. They always made him look surprised. "Okay, thank you, settle down—okay, can I have the students all come to the front, parents to the back—just like that, oh not you—you there in the blue. Oh you *are* a student? My mistake—"

Katie tried her hardest to hide that her face was starting to resemble a shiny tomato.

"You look more like someone's kid sister. Do you realize your shirt says Hamilton Middle School?" Tristan said behind her.

"It was the only clean shirt I had!" Katie spun around as the principal droned on about the annual sporting events and the rules.

Katie eyed Tristan's green shirt. It fit. Too well. Most of the boys' shirts were loose, waiting to be grown into. His fit.

"*—Please, last year we had an issue with marbles on the track field. I deeply encourage you not to cheat—*"

"Stop staring at me," Tristan said, furrowing his brow.

"I'm *not* staring at you." Katie turned her back on him. "Your shirt is just way too tight for a boy."

"*—Parents, remember your place is on the sidelines, not the wrestling mat. We do not want to repeat the episode with the broken nose—*"

She couldn't get the image of his shoulders in the shirt out of her mind. What the hell? She focused on the butt of the boy a few people in front of her. It was plump and cute. She squinted, focusing on it. It wasn't *that* cute. Actually, it was a little flat.

"Christ, Katalina."

"Then stop listening."

"I'm trying!"

"*Shhhh—*" she heard behind them.

"—And so, I wish everyone good luck! Remember, if it hurts, you're doing it right, if it bleeds, you're doing it wrong and should get assistance right away. You know who you are." Mr. Boyle looked at the crowd. "Let's get started! 1st years, stay here and help pull out the mats, 2nd years please go to the pools, 3rd years if you will follow Mr. Carver to the tracks. And 4th Years to the Field Study classroom."

The gymnasium erupted into noise and movement. For a second, Katie wondered if she could be considered a 1st year. She'd have a fighting chance with the 9th graders, but Traci had already told her it didn't work that way during one of their long tutoring sessions.

The first person Katie looked for was Tristan. She needed to stop doing that. She looked for Allison instead. Allison wasn't hard to find—she was the redhead charging through the crowd to get to the back doors.

On the way to the track, Katie felt heavy. She hadn't eaten since yesterday's lunch. When she saw the obstacle course, she wondered if she could feign dizziness and sit this one out. She lost her nerve as Mr. Carver split them into five groups and lined them up based on rank. Where did he find a green-and-white checkered tracksuit?

Katie and Tristan were in the first group and in the last lanes. He explained the obstacle course, but most students ignored him, placing bets on their times. They might have done it before, but Katie had to pay attention to the order. Was she supposed to climb the wall first, or after crawling under the rope…or after swinging over the pit of mud? If she got this wrong—if she failed today—she'd be the butt of every joke. Did it matter? Maybe it did, maybe it didn't. But as Mr. Carver waved them to the starting line she knew one thing: she didn't want to be a loser.

Three.

She wasn't ready for this.

Two.

She should have taken it more serious.

One.

She didn't want to be the loser. God, she didn't want to lose the whole thing.

Go.

She never made it over the wall.

She could take the fact that everyone had scaled the wall before she even reached it. She could take the fact that she was never going to get over it. What she couldn't take was the way everyone's parents cheered their kid on as Mr. Carver shouted encouraging words for her not to give up. "—Come on, Katie.

I know you have it in you—you're a fighter!—Oh don't let that stop you, beat that wall! Beat it to a pulp—oh *that* was a nasty fall. Are you okay?"

She gave up. Mr Carver wrote on his little wooden clipboard. She sat on the track trying not to feel like an epic loser as Tristan flew through the obstacles. He was leagues in front of everyone, and it was so effortless. He looked...bored. He trotted across the finish line and walked towards Katie. He looked at the wall and frowned.

Allison was second. And looked desperately pissed when she saw Tristan. Everyone else made their way across the finish line. Katie tried to muster a smile as Brian made his way over. He was third to last and though he saw her, he didn't return the smile.

Michael Heckler walked up to Brian, gulping down a bottle of water. "Don't try so hard, man."

Brian laughed, "If I did you'd get tired of me winning. I like to leave that to Allison."

Michael laughed as they gave each other high fives. Sometimes Brian was the biggest ass Katie knew.

⁕

After everyone finished the course, they rotated to the Field Study classroom. Katie had no idea how everyone was supposed to fit into the classroom or what they were expected to do in there.

"Five at a time please," she heard a man say. It sounded like Mr. Rhineheart. And there he was, looking as dramatic as ever, waving people into the small room Katie and Tristan had worked in on Monday. When it was their turn, Mr. Rhineheart smiled at her. "Katie, nice to see you participating in the sporting events. Doing well, I hope."

"Ha, something like that," she said, walking into the room. Allison and a few parents walked in behind her.

"Allison, hit the button for me?" Mr. Rhineheart said as he closed the door.

Allison tapped a yellow button by the door, and the room began to move.

"Woah," Katie said, reaching to grab onto something.

"It's an elevator, Kay," Allison said.

"Oh." It was strange. That was the first thing they had said to each other all morning. So much had happened yesterday. Normally Katie would have picked up the phone and called Allison at the slightest bit of news—like when she decided she wanted to dye her hair blue (luckily, Allison talked her out of that). Now, she felt like there was nothing to tell her. Maybe *too* much had happened.

"Who knew Tristan was that wicked fast? I could break his face." Allison crossed her arms.

"Wha—what?"

"The race, he beat me by twenty seconds. He totally shouldn't be allowed to compete."

"Why?" Katie said. She felt like she didn't know what to say to Allison. Like she was walking in a glass room with giant mallets for arms. Why was she being so weird? It was just Allison.

Allison stared at her, then raised her eyebrows.

"Oh!" Katie nodded. Of course. He's a vampire who acts like he's lived a life full of back alley deals. —And where did he get money from? The school uniforms were expensive. Katie heard Lucinda offer to pay more than twice. Then again, maybe he had a job. She would have asked if he wasn't so shady when it came to talking about himself.

"I swear, if he beats me in targets, I'm going to scratch out his eyes," Allison said, stretching her arms. One of the parents moved away from her when she cracked her neck.

Katie smiled. "You're kind of scaring me, and everyone else right now."

"Can't win if you're not in the zone," Allison said as the door opened again.

Katie gaped as she walked out into a room the size of the track field. It was set up like a maze. Maybe an obstacle course? Though, the course itself was less impressive than the entire room she never knew was there.

"We're underground?" Katie said, following everyone like a lost kid in a crowd.

"Yeah, it's the weapons room. We don't really use it until next year. Except today, of course. Come pick out your gun."

Katie stopped dead in her tracks. Gun? The hell? Did they expect her to shoot targets? They had kids shooting guns? *Her* shooting guns? Didn't they know she was liable to kill someone?

"—I think I want pink—Kay?" Allison laughed at her. "Kay? You look totally freaked out right now. It's a paintball gun. You have to pick your color."

Katie breathed. She was relieved, but that didn't stop her dread of losing yet another event. She wasn't that good at shooting either. She picked the color yellow at random. Funny enough, Tristan's favorite color. *Or no, yellow was just one of them.*

When everyone made it down to the room, Mr Rhineheart split the students into five groups. Katie was in the last group. She was glad this time, as she would have a chance to watch everyone else go first. She could study what they did and maybe use it to her advantage.

Brian was in the first group, and he missed all but two targets. He laughed about it during and after. Katie wondered if he would still have taken it so lightly if Will and Lucinda were there. All the other parents seemed to root their kids on seriously, and the other kids took it just as serious.

Allison and Tristan were in the second group. They both shot every target, beating last year's record. Allison lost to Tristan by three seconds. Allison taunted him as they put their guns away.

"You know, I don't count your wins because it's *cheating*," Allison said, contorting her face. She looked a little deranged.

"You don't count my wins because you're a sore loser. Besides, I really don't care."

"Then why don't you just lose!" Allison poked him in the chest, and Katie's stomach twinged.

"Would that make you feel better? Or would you feel better knowing your real competition is with someone like me?"

Allison opened her mouth to say something, but stopped short. "You know what, Tristan? I'll take that as a compliment."

"Take it however you want. I really don't care." Tristan moved toward Katie, but didn't say anything when he stood next to her. Allison looked pleased enough, but whenever she looked at the parents standing on the side, shouting at their kids, that dangerous look would cut across her face again.

It was Katie's turn. She put on her goggles, and she felt like everyone was watching her, mainly because she'd tripped over her feet when she stood at the starting line. She concentrated. At the start, she was supposed to shoot the first target, but then duck the oncoming blue paint that had pelted Brian across the face. The second target she should miss because it was an old lady. Then she'd hurry to the third one that she was supposed to shoot, then the fourth—

Mr. Rhineheart blew the whistle.

Katie shot at the first one but missed it. She ran to the second one and forgot about the blue paint. It stung as it hit her face. She ran through the third one and tripped over a cable. A cable? Who leaves those lying around?

"Move!" A girl spat at her. Katie got up and kept going. She missed all the targets and accidentally shot a girl on the side of her head. Yellow paint splattered across her black hair.

"Bitch," The girl screamed, but she kept running through the course.

When it was over, Katie wanted to die, and the girl she shot probably wanted to be the one to kill her.

"That was horrific," she heard a lady say to another mom.

She wanted to "accidentally" let off a few rounds of yellow on her stupid, pretty green blouse.

Tristan grabbed the gun from her. "Don't listen to her. You might have missed all the targets, but you did manage to shoot a moving one."

Was that supposed to make her feel better?

.ෙ ෙ.

Mr. Rhineheart gave them a break for lunch. Katie, Tristan, and Allison went to her locker to grab the lunch bag Lucinda had given her. It was unsaid, but they were officially team Screw Preliminaries. None of them had to say it out loud. It was in the way Allison stared at everyone with their parents in contempt, the way Tristan looked bored to death, and in Katie's score card.

They sat in silence until Allison said, "You know what. Screw this. I don't care if my dad is a douchebag who won't watch his daughter cream everyone except for this cheating asshole—no offense. I'm going to break every record. When his daughter is on the way to winning gold medals in the Olympics, I'll tell everyone it started on this day, when my father abandoned me." Allison laughed a little manically. It was contagious.

Katie caught up in her own giggles took a breath. "And when I get into the Guinness world book for most epic fails in a competition, I'll tell them it all started when I shot a girl in the head with yellow paint."

"Not morbid enough. We'll work on it," Allison said, pulling out three peanut butter and jelly sandwiches, an apple, and two bottles of water.

"You're going to eat all of that?" Tristan said.

"Got a problem?" Allison was obviously still *very* confrontational.

Katie opened the bag Lucinda packed and pulled out four sandwiches, two bananas, two waters, and two fruit cups. Katie gave half to Tristan, but he pushed it aside.

"Aren't you going to eat anything?" she said, feeling like she was missing something obvious.

He stared at her. He smiled just enough to show her his teeth. His tongue ran across his canines. They weren't fangs exactly, no sharper than her canines, but still, the way his tongue dragged across it—it was animalistic.

Katie realized his weird vampireness had become normal.

Tristan scoffed. "You're making too much of it," he said under his breath.

"Woah." Allison said, looking between them. "You just did *it*, didn't you?" She lowered her voice, "You read her mind. That's *so* freaky, and *cool*."

Katie focused on her sandwich. It was turkey and swiss. Lucinda always made good sandwiches, but she could never remember that Katie hated tomatoes.

⚬⚬

Being in the gym made Katie want to puke up her lunch. Some students were already putting on padding. It meant that they were going to fight. What else did they need mats, pads, and helmets for? And of course, Steve Sensei was the one making sure students were wearing their chest pads correctly.

"This is probably the only event you might be able to score in," Tristan said as they sat found seats in the bleachers. Allison was already changing into gear. Katie looked at the piece of paper one of the parents and given her as she entered the gym. It was a bracket. She had to fight at the third mat in fifteen minutes. She was fighting a boy named Adam. "You only have to get three hits. Your worst quality is you're slow, but you can land hits if you try hard enough. These people aren't that good."

Katie gaped as she watched a boy do a Karate kick in the air. It was like a movie. She laughed out loud. "I'm not just going to lose. I'm going to get the bejeezus beat out of me. Wonderful!"

Tristan patted her on the back. She tried not to freeze up. It always caught her off guard when he touched her.

"Come on." He led her to the third mat. She started putting on the gear while two girls fought. They screamed a lot, and Katie hoped she didn't have to make the same weird sounds. "You're doing it wrong," Tristan said, pulling off one of her arm pads. "You have to be able to move. Unless you *want* to lose." She stood still as he re-strapped the pads. Next were her legs. He watched her do it, only offering directions such as lower or higher. Last was her chest padding, and she managed to get her arms through, but felt like a small child when Tristan moved behind her and tied them.

Some people watched him tie her up, and she felt embarrassed and proud. She didn't know why and tried to bury it. Maybe because everyone else had parents helping and they just had each other. She flushed and could feel heat fill her at the thought. He made no sound or movement to show he was listening.

She wanted to focus on the fight, but she couldn't.

"Just remember not to cross your legs. You do that a lot—Stay loose. You move better when you're loose. Or angry."

How did he know that? They'd only been practicing for four days if she counted the unsupervised session at the park yesterday. For four days, all he did was show her a move and beat her up. She chuckled at the thought. She'd just spent four days straight getting beat up by the guy who was checking her pads.

He jerked a little, and she could tell he was trying to pretend he hadn't heard that.

"You talk too much," he said. She pretended to punch him, but he brushed her hand away. "Don't waste your energy."

"How do you do that?" He was too good.

"Are you ready, Katie-san?" Steve Sensei asked abruptly. It took a second for Katie to realize he was talking to her. "On the mat then."

As Katie took a deep breath, she heard Lucinda and Will cheering Allison on in her match.

"Stay loose," Tristan said.

Katie looked back at him. Easier said than done.

Adam. It was the guy who'd asked her if she was a new student. He was the guy she had been a complete turd to. He gave her a small smile. Maybe he had forgotten. Maybe he was nice—to bad he was wearing a helmet and sizing her up. They shook hands and it started.

He got the first hit immediately, but she moved fast enough for him to miss the second.

"Come on Katalina, quicker than that," she heard Tristan say. She flexed her hands. If she could hit Tristan, she could hit this guy.

Adam moved in for the second hit and Katie tried to sidestep. She crossed over one of her legs, and Adam hit her with a kick. She fell to the mat.

"Katalina, if you want to lose, have the decency not to do it on your back," Tristan said.

Katie got up. Was Tristan trying to motivate her or kill her self-esteem?

"Move faster or lose faster. Stop wasting time."

"Come on man, she's new," Adam said, looking at Tristan. Katie took Adam's momentary distraction as an opening and punched him on his left arm.

"Sorry," she mumbled.

Adam's dad yelled for him to hurry up and finish her. *What a gentleman.* Katie readied herself for another move, but Adam was already moving. Before she could switch to a defensive stance, he landed a kick on her right leg. She at least caught herself before she fell.

Steve Sensei called the match. Adam won. Tristan smiled. It was a real smile. She smiled too. She hit him. She got one hit. Granted, it was a cheap shot while he wasn't looking, but still she hit him.

"Doesn't matter. A hit is a hit. Never take your eyes off your opponent unless they're dead."

Katie shifted her eyes. Tristan had a way with words.

Katie didn't have another match for forty five minutes. She watched Tristan fight four times. The matches never lasted more than a minute, and each time he'd push the other person to the side and hit them. His fourth fight was with Brian. Katie found a seat next to Will and Lucinda. She wasn't the only one who didn't want to watch it.

Tristan changed. His eyes burned, and for the first time that day Brian didn't open his mouth to laugh. Brian circled the mat, hesitant to approach Tristan. Tristan waited patiently, watching Brian. When Brian made his first move, Tristan blocked his hit and punched him in the chest so hard his feet left the ground.

"Come on Brian," Will said.

"Stop it, Will." Lucinda reprimanded. "You know—"

"Lucy, they have to fight it out sooner or later. Might as well be now."

Brian got up and moved in quick. Tristan dropped down and kicked Brian's legs from out under him. Brian landed flat on his back with an audible thud.

Almost everyone was watching this match by now. The gym was quiet except for a few yells and the sound of feet hitting mats. Hate flickered and burned in her like fire. It fed on her soul. She wanted to break Brian—

Katie choked on her own breath. Tristan. His violence was overwhelming her. This was what vengeful anger felt like. She should say something. Stop the match. Brian was no equal to that. What if Tristan wanted to *really* hurt him?

It was too late. As Brian stood up for the final time, Tristan moved in, spun Brian around and smacked his back. Brian hit the ground and it echoed.

"Tristan!" Lucinda shouted, but Will held her back.

"You go over there and Brian will never get up."

"Foul!" Steve Sensei said. "One point to Brian-san."

Katie held her breath. She had hoped it was over. She felt sick satisfaction from watching him stand up. It made her heart quicken a little— No, not hers, *Tristan's*, but she couldn't tell the difference. It was hard to separate her emotions from his. Was this how it felt for him? Like an alien invasion.

Brian stood up, but Katie silently begged him to stay down. She knew what was coming. Brian screamed and charged Tristan. What was he hoping to do? Tristan wasn't even trying. Katie watched Tristan elbowed him in the ribs, smacked his head with the same arm, and kicked him flat in the chest in three quick movements.

Brian flew off the mat with the wind knocked out of him. Everyone felt it.

As Will grabbed Lucinda's arm, Katie tried to push Tristan out of her mind. His hate thrashed around inside of her.

Steve Sensei helped Brian to the bleachers.

"You wanted to see your son beaten like that?" Lucinda spat.

"Better it be Tristan, in a room full of guardians, than a werewolf, or a vampire who won't show him mercy," Will spat back. They stared at each other. Lucinda yanked her arm away and went to Brian.

Katie looked between Brian, slouched on the bleachers, and Tristan. She wasn't the only one. Even Allison, standing on the other side, looked sorry for Brian. That wasn't a match, it was a slaughter. Had it been revenge for stabbing Tristan? Tristan was looking at her from the mat. She couldn't read his face or thoughts.

⁕

Katie had one last match. If she could beat the girl named Jenn Black, then she would qualify for another. As soon as Katie saw who Jenn Black was, she knew she'd lost, and she wasn't wrong. It was the girl who she shot in the head. She still had streaks of yellow paint in her hair. Jenn made sure Katie knew what it felt like to be shot in the head.

It was over before it even started. Jenn hit her on the same spot three times.

In thirty seconds.

"I think she actually *tried* to hit me here," Katie said, rubbing her head.

"No, she *succeeded*," Tristan said, helping Katie off the mat.

The last match before the final rotation was between the two undefeated fighters: Allison and Tristan. Katie could hear everyone murmuring. *Would he do to her what he did to Brian? Does this kid have a point to prove? Where did he come from?*

Katie knew different. Tristan looked as bored as ever, even though Allison was flexing and throwing quick practice shots. If anything, she was worried that Allison might go berserk when she lost.

It wasn't a quick match. When Tristan blocked, Allison would block his counter. It wasn't until she got one hit in that Tristan started to look alive. The one hit was all Allison did manage, but it was more than anyone during all of his matches.

They finally moved on to the last event. Katie felt a glimmer of hope. Swimming—it was the one thing she could do well. They had three chances to dive and collect as many weights as possible. They went in five different groups. Again Katie was in the last group, but it didn't bother her. Being last gave her the advantage of knowing how much weight to collect to score high. As soon as it was Tristan's turn, he forfeited. Gasps and shocked expressions drifted from around the pool.

"You do realize," Mr. Right said, "That you're giving up the top spot."

"Yup." Tristan sat on the benches before Mr. Right could say anything else.

As all the groups went, Katie realized something. The only thing that mattered was if she could use her legs fast enough. Most people lost weights before they could surface because they couldn't swim to the top fast enough. It was deep. Twenty feet, so the push off the ground would only help about halfway. The boy she fought, Adam, brought up the most weight. Forty-five pounds total. Katie only needed one more pound to place first. She was going to go for it.

She stood on the edge of the pool and curled her toes over the edge. This was it.

She dived.

Getting to the bottom wasn't hard. She had strong legs, and she was fast. She grabbed seventeen pounds on the first dive. One ten-pound bag, one five-pound, and one two-pound. It was hard, but she knew she had to do the hardest tow on the first dive when she had the most energy. As she thought, the push off the pool floor only propelled her a little over halfway. Holding the bags meant she had to kick harder and faster before she lost momentum. She broke the surface just as she ran out of breath.

She flipped onto her back to preserve energy as she swam back to the edge.

She dived again. Fifteen pounds.

Before the last dive, Mr. Right announced the amount of weight each student had. Katie, thirty-two. A girl next to her had just twenty pounds. The next student thirty pounds. She had a good lead. She even beat out a most of the students. But she wanted to win. Badly. Just this one event. She was good at swimming. Her arms felt heavy and sore. Her legs burned.

She hopped onto the edge and prepared for her last dive. She bent her knees and leapt. Before she entered the water, she knew it wasn't strong enough to send her to the bottom. She had to kick more than half the way. Big mistake.

She grabbed a ten-pound bag and a five-pound bag. Her air was running out and she was twenty feet underwater. She propelled off the ground as hard as she could.

Ten feet. She was nearly out of breath. Her legs were on fire. She couldn't get them to swing right.

Five feet. She couldn't hold her breath anymore. She had to make a choice—let go of a bag and use her arms, or nearly drown. She tried to stroke with the bags in her hand. They were pulling her down.

Push. You can do it. Katalina, push!

She snapped her legs back and forth as hard as she could. Just as she took in a mouth full of water, she surfaced. She held the bags to her chest. She couldn't let go of them now.

"COME ON KATALINA!"

"KAY, YOU GOT IT!"

"KATIE! KATIE!"

She flipped onto her back, still choking on water. Her legs barely worked, but she kicked to the edge. As soon as her bags touched the edge of the pool, people were pulling her out of the water. She was coughing up water, still clutching the bags.

"Did—I—get—the—most?" she coughed.

Mr. Right took the two bags. "That makes forty-seven-pounds! That is the most collected all day. Just shy of the record, forty-nine. Well done."

There was clapping, but Katie didn't hear it. Not as loud as she heard Tristan. In her mind. Words. He spoke to her in her mind. Katie was laughing, but not for the reasons everyone else thought. Only Tristan, the boy who was smiling at her, knew why.

9

THE SIGN

WHEN THE SCORES were announced, Katie finished thirty-seven out of fifty. It was nice, considering she'd planned on finishing last. Brian finished thirty, Tristan third, and Allison first. Allison said she was happy, though every time someone would congratulate her on her huge trophy, they'd ask where her dad was, and she'd smile the way Katie knew she smiled when she was being overly polite.

Katie wandered outside and sat on the steps. There were too many people in there talking about too many things. She wanted to think quietly.

"You surprised me at the end there," Tristan said, appearing from nowhere. He did that too well.

"It's nice to know your faith in me goes so deep." Katie couldn't help but think, "*You surprised me too.*" There might have been a slight smile on his face. If there was, it was gone now. "We could totally cheat on tests this way."

"You are the saddest person I've ever met."

"Really? I've been told I have a cheerful look about me." Katie smiled as if to make her point.

"That smile right there, it's a smile that would scare even the bravest of men."

Katie felt a pang of disappointment. She'd meant to be silly, but to say her smile was something so hideous that it scared people went a bit far.

"I never said it was ugly."

"I know what you meant." She scowled.

"I meant what I said."

"Just when I thought we were getting along, you start with the riddles and '*ohhh I'm shady Tristan, look at me I'm all mysterious and cool because I never make sense and I always leave people wondering what the hell I'm talking about.*'"

"I don't sound like that."

"*I don't sound like that,*" Katie said.

"You're so annoying."

"*You're so annoying.*"

"Are you done?

Katie stood up. She didn't have to sit there and listen to his crap. Tristan grabbed her hand to pull her back down. As soon as their hands touched, he snapped his hand back as if he'd never meant to do it. She stood there, not sure what to do. His face made it harder to decide. He looked like he'd just been caught.

She sat back down. "If you want to be friends, you can't be such a dick."

He didn't say anything, but she knew he got the message. They sat in silence. Or in thought, or whatever, because technically it's never silent between them. Not for him, anyway.

"Katie? Tristan? Oh there you are. Katie, Will says you had a duffel bag this morning? What was that about?" It was Lucinda, walking down the school steps toward them. Will wasn't with her. Maybe with Brian? She hadn't seen Brian after the swim.

"Everyone has a duffel bag, Lucy," Katie said, avoiding eye contact.

"Not filled to the brim. And don't think I forgot about this morning. What is going on?"

"I—I sort of left home."

Lucinda didn't look surprised. Of course Will told her he'd spilled the beans to her dad. She must have been expecting a dramatic outcome. "When?" This time she looked between her and Tristan. The cat was out of the bag. The cat was screaming and scratching up the bag because it was violent and glad to be out of it.

Tristan looked at her, but offered no words.

"Technically?"

"Katie Watts."

"Yesterday."

Lucinda's eyes bulged. "*Where did you sleep yesterday?*"

"Al—"

"Think about that lie before you tell it." Lucinda rubbed her right temple.

"A park. But I technically didn't sleep there. Maybe for an hour or two I—"

"YOU SLEPT IN A PARK?" Lucinda pointed at the school doors. "Get your bags right now. We're going home. As soon as we get there, you're grounded. *BOTH* of you are grounded."

"You're *grounding* me?" Tristan said the word like a foreign concept.

"YES I'M GROUNDING YOU. NOT ONLY DID YOU SLEEP IN A PARK BUT YOU ALSO BEAT UP MY SON IN A ROOM FULL OF PEOPLE! SO MUCH FOR BLENDING IN!" Lucinda was red in the face. People were staring, "Don't you have teenage children? What are you looking at?" she snapped.

Katie and Tristan took her momentary distraction to slip away into the school.

"She can't ground me," he said, looking over his shoulder. "She can't even ground you. You're homeless."

Katie laughed despite herself. They grabbed Katie's duffel bag and bookbag. She congratulated Allison again and said her goodbyes. When Allison's eyes drifted to the bulging duffel bag, Katie realized it would be hard to tell her best friend that she ran away, slept in a park, and spent the entire day not telling her anything at all. One more problem to add to the growing pile.

When they went back outside, Lucinda and Will were waiting in the truck. Brian was nowhere to be found. No one mentioned his absence, so she didn't bring it up.

"Katie," Will said, talking to her directly for the first time today. "I called your dad on Friday to make sure he was handling everything okay. I didn't know you hadn't told him."

Since when do you call my dad to see how he's handling things?

"How about we ride over there and try and smooth things out?" Will said, looking at her in the rear view mirror.

How could she tell them that her dad blames them for everything and doesn't want her to see them ever again?

"I don't think that's a good idea, Will," Tristan said as if he was above the conversation. "He'll just cart her off to an omitter and move away."

"Tristan, how do you know that? Katie, did your dad say something to you? Exactly what happened?"

Katie cleared her throat and looked out the window. "He doesn't want me around you guys. He said he could make me forget you."

The only sound in the car was the engine.

"It doesn't hurt to try," Will said, turning into her neighborhood. It was a few minutes past four. Her dad was definitely home, and he wouldn't react well to everyone showing up on his doorstep like they were hosting an intervention.

Katie hesitated before getting out of the car.

"Well," Tristain said. "Worst thing that happens? He threatens to take you to an omitter or gets angry and throws you out." He shrugged. "It looks like that's already essentially happened."

"Thanks," Katie said sarcastically. She closed the car door, but Lucinda opened it again.

"You're coming too," Lucinda said, waving Tristan out.

"I think I'll sit this one out."

Lucinda's head snapped around. If they could, her eyes would have glowed red. "Get—out—now."

Katie felt like that was a bad idea, but she wasn't going to tell Lucinda that. Not with her eyes shooting out lasers and burning holes through concrete.

Will had already rung the doorbell when she stepped onto the porch.

Her dad answered the door and looked at all of them. "How dare you come here after what you've done?" Katie thought he meant her, but he was looking at Will.

"Drew, look. What's done is done. Can we stop playing the blame game and talk about your daughter?" Will said.

"The one you've stolen from me?"

"They didn't steal me," Katie said.

"Oh, no. They've been plotting this for some years now. Lucy's always been good at revenge."

Lucinda laughed violently. "You think I would use a child to get back at you? You've got to be kidding me. Only one of us is that cold-hearted."

Katie's dad looked at them all. One against four. It wasn't fair. "It's not anyone's fault. It just happened," Katie said, trying to defuse the tension.

"And they just *happened* to bring him here? Nothing *just happens* in life. I thought I raised you smarter than that."

Katie looked between her dad and Tristan. Tristan's eyes were dead cold. She tried to connect the pieces, but nothing fit.

Will cleared his throat. "Are we gonna sort this out or not?"

Katie thought her dad was going to slam the door in their faces. Instead he left it open as he walked inside. He leaned on the wall that led to the living room. "You know you can't take her to an omitter, Drew. It's against the law. It's her choice now. She's over the age." Will never had a quiet voice, but in their small hallway it boomed.

"Don't talk to me like I don't know *your* laws."

"Our laws," Will said. "You are still one of us, whether you act like it or not."

Lucinda stood in the middle of the hallway, not touching anything. Tristan was just as rigid. Katie wanted to suggest that they all sit down, but she felt so small.

"Drew–" Will started.

"No, Will. I get it. The boy shows up, and she"—he pointed at Lucinda—"starts feeling a bit vengeful, and somehow my daughter ends up in the middle of it. I can see through you like glass, Lucy. And Will, you've never had the balls to tell her when she's bat-shit crazy."

"I'm crazy? How dare you? HOW DARE YOU?! After what you did—"

"I did it to protect my daughter." Katie's dad went red in the face. "You've just exposed her. It's only a matter of time before—I can't believe you! After all I've done to *protect* her!"

Lucinda was shaking. "What about my sister? What about her family? You just didn't care, did you? How can you stand here and think what you did was right? For years, you lied to my face. *How* can you look at *his* face and think what you did was right?"

Her dad didn't budge. "Your sister? My *wife* was there too. I made my decision. Katie, make yours. I'm not going to bury my daughter. If *you* remember correctly"—her dad looked at Tristan with disgust in his eyes—"I didn't even get to bury my wife."

"You didn't bury her?" Katie's voice was so small the only person who showed signs of hearing her was Tristan.

"Decide now, Katie. I can make everything go back to normal, and we can get on with our lives." Her dad fidgeted.

"You know it's not that simple," Will said.

Katie started, "I can't—" she looked at Tristan and the pieces clicked together. What had happened ten years ago. Why she couldn't remember anything about her mother. "You took me to an omitter before, didn't you?" she said. She couldn't look her father in the face. She knew the answer was written all over it.

"And you've had a good life because of it. This world—"

"What about Allison and Brian and everyone else? Their parents aren't trying to erase their memories. I'm—"

"You're different, Katie. You can't be a part of this."

"Why do you think I'm so *stupid*? If they can do it, so can I. I *am* going to do it." She was starting to feel brave. She was starting to feel like she had a voice. "Whether you like it or not."

"*Whether I like it or not?* Okay." Her dad's face contorted with rage. She had pushed the last button. "Get your shit and leave." He turned around and walked into the living room. The conversation was over.

.ಂಲ ಲಿ.

Katie packed another bag full of clothes. When she packed the first one she didn't think she was *actually* running away. This time she'd been kicked out. This time Tristan wasn't there to look through her things. It was just her, packing as fast as she could, trying not to cry like a baby. She wasn't even sad. She was angry. What had just happened? Everyone knew something she didn't. It was no wonder she never remembered kindergarten or first grade. She'd always chalked it up to being too young or too unmemorable. But there weren't many baby pictures either, were there? No, there was one. She was sitting with her dad, maybe she was two. Who'd taken it? The mother who had died during childbirth? What happened to the rest of the pictures? Who was Tristan, and why did her dad talk to him like he was at fault for whatever happened? He would have only been seven…around the same time his parents were murdered. What happened?

Her mind spun faster than ever before. It worked hard trying to uncover clues. Every time it went as far as it could, she'd start to feel dizzy. She almost tripped going down the stairs, but she swore, for a moment, she saw a little boy with blue eyes and black hair.

No one said anything on the drive to Lucinda's and Will's house. Her new home until her dad came back to his senses— just like old times. It hurt that he kicked her out, but most of it was him being petty. She knew he'd get over it sooner or later. But did she want to go back home to a house of lies? Before she left, she wanted to smash every picture of her mother. What if the woman on the wall wasn't even her, but some fake picture that came with the frame? That's the life her dad wanted for her. Fake people to fill picture frames.

Lucinda didn't have to tell Katie which bedroom to set up in. It was the same bedroom she spent most of her childhood living in. She had more memories here than she did at her own house. Katie passed through the front door and stopped. When did those memories start? She ran to her old bedroom and searched the door frame. She found it in seconds. Several notches and their correlating years where Lucinda kept record of her height. Her stomach dropped. It started at seven years. She ran to Brian's door and looked. His started when he was one. As far as Katie knew, as far as anyone told her, she'd been coming to this house since she was born. She'd asked her dad once about that picture of them both, when she was two. Her hair had been in an elaborate up-do. She'd asked who did it and he'd told her Lucinda.

It was a lie. Another lie. She could feel it in her bones. The memory was fuzzy, but it hit her, the first day she'd met Will and Lucinda. Lucinda was making applesauce, and let Katie help. Katie had asked if Lucinda was her mother. No, maybe that was a dream. Maybe she was making it up.

Katie unpacked one of her bags and hung up her kitty poster. It was all she could do before she left the room to find Will.

He was in the basement watching pictures move by on the TV.

"How's unpacking?" His gaze didn't waver.

Katie walked over to the empty armchair. She leaned on it, rubbing her fingers over the fabric. "Okay, I guess."

She looked at the TV, pretending to watch it. They were both pretending, and she felt stupid. "Will—my mom didn't die in childbirth, right?"

"No, Katie. She didn't."

"When did she die?"

"About ten years ago. You and Drew moved up here right after."

What could have happened to make her father erase the memory of a six year-old? "—How?"

"I wasn't there." This time he looked at her. "Some things are best left alone. But I'm not going to tell you what you should and shouldn't go looking for."

She stared at the TV, waiting.

"You've had a long day. Maybe you should go get some food and hit the sack?"

He was telling her to leave.

On her way up the stairs, she saw Brian walk through the front door.

"What are you doing here?" he said. Katie thought there was a hint of annoyance in his voice, but she ignored it. She was on edge, and probably thinking too much of it.

"I got thrown out."

"By your dad?" Brian looked thoroughly surprised. "What the hell did you do?"

It struck her that he had no idea what was going on in her life. How much was because he didn't care to ask? At that moment, she felt a twinge of satisfaction that Tristan had embarrassed him in front of everyone. Someone had shown him he wasn't that invincible.

"I told him I was going to quit school and be a prostitute," Katie spat.

"What?" Brian shook his head, "Whatever, I'm not in the mood for your drama."

"Asshole." She could finally yell at someone and be heard.

"Go tell someone who cares," he said, going up the stairs. Katie wanted to run up the stairs and punch him in the back of the head. She wanted to take it all out on him. Why did everyone think she wasn't someone to take seriously? She went to her new room. How long was it going to be like this? She slammed her face into her pillow and went to sleep.

⁂

The ever-growing fall chill settled in Katie's bones as she woke up for yet another morning training. It had been two months since she left home.

It was torture.

Lucinda scheduled trainings twice a day, no matter if the mornings, like this morning, were freezing, or if the evenings were dark and dusty. Tristan didn't care, not that she cared if he cared. They'd gone back to being two awkward people who spent nearly every waking moment together—which was a type of sick hell. Worst was Brian actively ignoring her when they lived in the same house, but then again, he didn't seem to be on good terms with anyone in the house.

She dragged herself out of bed, wrapped up like a silkworm cocoon in her blanket, and shuffled to the bathroom, wearing nearly every shirt in her closet. From there, Katie went straight to the backyard, where Tristan waited to beat her up. The cold wasn't the only reason she wore extra shirts. She could use the padding. Her bruises from yesterday morning were turning a deep gray-blue. Her hip ached from landing on a tree root two days ago, her elbows still burned from being dragged across the ground yesterday, and her left leg twitched a little when she stood on it too long.

"No pain no gain," Tristan said as he set down a pair of knives.

"Out of my head." She was too tired for this.

"Then wake up. You're going to learn how to really use a knife today."

She couldn't help but smile. "Really?" She had been waiting for this ever since she saw Allison practicing. The way her body extended to the tip of any knife she held was unreal. The fluid stabs and quick recoils, the impossible accuracy of each throw. If Katie could perfect that, she could stunt double for action movies.

Tristan scrunched up his eyebrows. "No. I lied. But, now that I have your attention, stretch your legs out. You're going to do a lot of running this morning."

She could have pretended to be affronted, but a part of her had expected him to be lying. "Water break," she sighed, opening the back door.

"Oh, come on. You just got here," Tristan laughed evilly behind her. "Seriously, hurry up."

She was surprised to hear Lucinda pacing the kitchen floors. Normally she sat at the window in the living room, watching them practice, screaming orders and corrections.

In the silence, Katie heard her, "She's getting good. Really good," she said. She must have been on the phone, because no one else was in the house. Brian and Will had left earlier that morning.

Katie stopped in the hall when Lucinda smacked her hand against the kitchen counter.

"No!" Lucinda's voice turned to acid. "That's not the same. Drew kept Celia's death *and* Tristan from me. Letting a little boy be taken by some stranger is as bad as throwing a baby out in the woods—he claims that's why he left the system, but he's no better than any of us."

Katie stiffened, her pulse beating in her throat. She pressed her body against the wall as Lucinda's footsteps grew closer.

"No, William. He should have known I would have forgiven him. I knew what she was in the beginning. He's a liar and a murderer."

What Lucinda said pushed the breath from Katie and beat her down worse than all the weeks training with Tristan. A murderer? Her dad wouldn't *kill* anyone. Had he *killed* Tristan's parents?

Lucinda said her goodbyes to Will, and Katie hurried back outside. Being in the house made her feel like she couldn't breathe, but it was worse the moment she looked at Tristan. She felt a wave of his anger, frustration, and pity.

"Practice over," he said, no doubt knowing how all-sorts-of confused she was.

"Why won't any of you tell me anything?" she screamed.

He turned his back on her like they all did. Her dad the liar, Lucinda who swept everything under the rug, and Will who made it very clear that if she wanted answers she wasn't getting them from him. This wasn't some national security secret. This was her life.

⚬⚬

She spent days not talking to any of them. She trained because it was necessary, but she ignored them all—for less than a week because, though Katie was most definitely not being unreasonable, she had to give up *Operation: Don't Talk To Me* when she realized she hadn't talked to her dad in two months, Will and Lucinda were too busy to notice, Tristan didn't care, and Brian was already doing his best to avoid her.

Her fourth favorite holiday, Halloween, came and went, and she didn't even notice until the day after. It didn't help that it fell on a school day—a school day that was jam-packed with three tests and Traci shoving flash cards down her throat. She was on the third stack when she heard Brian and his new friends say it again. *"Train-wreck Traci."*

Traci always tried to pretend like she couldn't hear them, and Katie did her best to pretend like she didn't hear them either. Katie was embarrassed for her and angry that Brian was worse than usual. Whenever Traci would start to look like she might cry under her bifocals, Katie would tell Traci about one of her new hobbies.

That day it was origami, but as the days moved forward again, the only hobby she actually had was training and homework. She couldn't skip training to do anything fun, and it turned out her teachers were way harder on her when she didn't turn in assignments or did poorly on her tests. Mrs. Barnes would hand back homework with a raised eyebrow and a note that read, *"See me after class,"* Mr. Carver offered extra lessons any time she got something less than an high B on a quiz or essay, and Mr. Rhineheart called on her more in class whenever he thought she was drifting off.

Schoolwork was hard, but it turned out training was kinda fun. Every day she could actually see improvements. When she learned something new, Tristan would pair it up with moves she'd learned earlier. He didn't take kindly to forgetfulness. The tender spot on her rib cage, just above her left elbow, was a reminder of that. Every time she missed a step, he'd tap her there, in the exact same spot, just hard enough to make her recoil.

It wasn't so bad all the time, though. Sometimes her body moved on its own, as if it had a mind of its own. *"Muscle memory,"* Tristan would say over and over when she'd spend two hours throwing single, identical punches, one after another. It was numbing and exhilarating at the same time. Most of the time it was boring, but all of it—the movements, Tristan's dry low voice, *"again…again…again,"* and the pain—felt right.

Watching Brian train, however, felt very wrong. Will, Brian, and Allison always used the backyard before Tristan and Katie. Katie made it a point not to be around when they did because Will always told Brian he wasn't doing something right or scolded him for not practicing hard enough. He even once told Brian that Katie was better than him and it made Katie want to melt into the wall.

One night, Will asked Tristan and Katie to switch practice times with them. She had no clue that Will was going to make Brian join theirs. He called it a *"mandatory warm-up."*

Watching Brian try to block a punch or carry out more than three offensive moves at once made her stomach hurt. She'd look away when it was his turn, pretended to tie her shoe, or shield the nonexistent sun from her eyes.

She couldn't take watching him fall and trip over his own feet. Not again. She ran inside for water and waited by the door until the distant thuds stopped.

"You get to use a knife today," Tristan said as she closed the back door and stepped onto the grass.

She stared at Tristan, making sure to squint her eyes.

"I'm serious. Sort of." He pulled a white plastic knife from his pocket.

"Liar, liar, pants on fire." She regretted it as soon as she said it.

"Wow. Lethal rhyming skills. But a knife is a knife, Katalina."

"Whatever, just show me how to use it."

"That's the spirit." He smiled that disgusting two-dollar smile. "I think you mean *million*-dollar smile," he said.

Been in the mirror lately? She arched an eyebrow, but quickly put it back down as Brian eyed them. She'd forgotten he didn't know anything about Tristan's mind voodoo. She honestly didn't want anyone to know.

"Stop calling it that," Tristan murmured.

"Can we train?" Brian said, pushing up his dusty sleeves. The dirt on his face made his jaw look sharper than usual.

Tristan showed Katie how to disarm a knife-wielding opponent. He made her repeat the move slowly, twenty times before they did it at normal speed. Her body pulled and snapped in a dance. Fast, but smooth. Each time she missed the disarm, he'd slap her ribcage, and pain would shoot up her arm. They kicked up dirt, and sweat burned her eyes, but each time she was more determined than the last.

Until finally, she got him to drop the knife.

It hit the ground, and in one quick movement she picked it up. Her chest bobbed up and down and her arms burned, but she couldn't help the smile that stretched across her face.

"That's called pride," Tristan said, looking at the small white piece of plastic. "Hand it over. It's Brian's turn."

She gave it to him, but not before running her finger over the shiny bit of white. She moved to the edge of the yard to give Tristan and Brian space. She tried to ignore the fact that she saw Will looking through the back window. It was where Lucinda sat and yelled things while she watched Tristan and Katie practice.

Katie watched as Tristan went through the same steps with Brian. The first two moves he got easily, and Katie's stomach jumped a loop of joy. It was nice to see him standing on his own two feet. At first, she used to feel a little triumph when he fell. Seeing him covered in dirt and sweat, scrunching up his face in anger, was like payback. Payback for pretending she didn't exist. Payback for acting as if this space between them, this thick silence, was normal. But then she'd see the desperation in his eyes when Tristan hit him hard for missing a step. When Tristan would say, *"I've killed you three times in the last ten minutes. That's pathetic."*

Brian only made it through half of the steps before he started to lose balance and misstep. Even though she couldn't read his mind, she could feel the desperation seeping out of him. It was as if her smile, the electric pulse, and the pride she had felt about herself had turned against her, becoming a mass of bile in her stomach. Despite the tension between them lately, he was still her friend.

He fell to the ground. Again. She watched him, and each time he'd leave an opening for Tristan to land a fatal move.

"If you—"

"I'll get it," Brian said, cutting off Tristan.

Katie watched him fail ten more times. Each time, the dirt kicked up violently as he hit it.

She moved over, toward them. Each footstep heavy and thought out.

"It's your footwork," she said, offering him a smile. "You just have a small misstep. Try it like this." She showed him the maneuver slowly.

He wasn't even looking in her direction.

"You see, if you put your left foot higher, the swing will come more naturally." Just standing next to him felt utterly wrong, like being on a frail bridge as all the ropes creak with tension. All she had to do was run to the other side before the bridge collapsed. "You just have to move your foot—"

"Shut up, Katie." Brian's voice was low.

"I'm trying to help."

"I'm not doing it wrong. I'm doing it the way my dad showed me. I think he knows more than you do."

Her cheeks were on fire. He looked at her with disgust. A look she didn't deserve. *Does your dad know how much of a failure you are?* She wanted to say it, but she couldn't. "What's wrong with you? What have *I* done to you?"

"You think you know everything. You've been a junior guardian for what? A few months? And now you're living in my house. Trying to throw crap in my face. Get over yourself."

She didn't think her mouth could drop any further. *What is he talking about?* She lived in his house because her father *abandoned* her. She didn't think she was any better than him. She didn't even know what she was doing half the time. She had more bruises than she could count. She earned every little victory she got. She worked harder than she'd worked for anything. Never once had she flaunted any of that in front of him. And whenever he made an idiot of himself, she usually made it a point to look away, to spare him any more embarrassment. *You want me to get over* myself? "You're right, what do I know? I'm not the one who spends most of practice on the ground," she spat.

His nostrils flared and he bit his lower lip. Neither of them moved, stuck in the eye of a hurricane, waiting for the storm to hit. The longer they stared, the more she saw the desperation in his eyes. He was looking through her, and that was worse than anything he could possibly say. She wanted—needed—him to say something. Yell, scream or call her names. The only sound was the last strand of their friendship finally snapping.

He turned and left her and Tristan standing in the backyard. Her eyes burned and her hands shook.

"Now that the dramatics are over, can we get back to work?" Tristan said.

Katie sat on the ground. She couldn't train after that. Her mind surged, replaying the last few moments over and over in her head.

Tristan sat next to her. "Let's work on your meditation then. You really suck at it, and there is a test next month."

"No."

"Okay. Let's talk. You two always been this weird?"

She got up, grabbed her bag, and went inside. *Of course we haven't always been like this. Everything started to crumble the day you showed up.*

At school was no different. Instead of politely ignoring her, Brian acknowledged her presence with contempt. In chemistry, she watched Brian chat with his new circle of friends. She didn't hate him having other friends or for even being *Brian the Invincible*. She just hated two things: he had stopped being her friend, and Christi was officially a part of that new group.

Christi wore her skirt hiked up higher than the dress code allowed, and her button-up shirts always hugged her breasts so tight, Katie counted the days before one of the buttons would pop off and blind someone. Her perfume reeked, and the nasally voice she used when answering questions was horrid. What did guys like about her? Christi wasn't *that* pretty. Katie wasn't exactly a heartbreaker, but she knew she was definitely prettier than that smelly thing. How could Brian even be friends with someone like that?

Katie clenched her teeth and sighed. When did she sink so low? There were plenty of things to hate Christi for—her looks weren't one of them. *Brian is bringing out the worst in me.*

Tristan nudged her. "Sure. *He* is. Stop obsessing over Brian. Let it go."

"Get out of my head."

"I'm not in your head. You're staring—in a psychotic way."

"It's obvious you've never had a best friend before. You just don't stop being best friends. That's not how it works."

He looked at her. "Maybe Brian's right. You're a little know-it-all."

"He didn't mean that."

"Just like you didn't mean to say you're better than him?"

"Shut up—"

"Miss Watt, can you finish balancing this chemical reaction?" Mr. Beaver said, looking over his shoulder, a green dry-erase marker in hand. He had a way of somehow getting the ink from the green marker on all his white shirts. Always the green.

"No, sorry I—"

"Then you'll kindly refrain from asking your teacher to '*shut up.*'" He went back to writing on the board as chuckles filled every corner of the class—especially Christi's nasally one. Katie opened her notebook and drew a stick figure.

This is you, she thought, eyeing Tristan. When he glanced over at it, she scribbled all over its body. She looked back at him, waiting to see the shock or disbelief in his eyes, but none of that was there. His face turned red, and then he laughed. His laughter shook her bones and jostled her heart. She frowned, but her heart pounded even more.

"You're like a five year-old," he said. Tears glossed his eyes as he tried to stifle the noise, but he just laughed harder.

"Shhh, you're going to get us in trouble," she whispered, feeling his laugh bubble up her throat. She smiled, and then it was over. They laughed so loud Mr. Beaver threatened to give them detention.

◦෨෨◦

After school, even though it was cold, Katie, Allison, and Tristan went to get ice cream. They went to her favorite shop, and Larry, the owner, looked pleased to see them. Tristan didn't actually order anything. He looked uncomfortable when Larry tried to strike up a friendly conversation. It embarrassed her when he blatantly ignored him and walked over to the window.

Katie ordered a triple scoop of rainbow sherbet, and Larry plopped on a fourth scoop free of charge.

"Always the best for my best customer," Larry said with a smile. He had an accent that Katie still couldn't place. He looked fairly young, maybe in his thirties, but she could tell he was older by his eyes. He had gray eyes, like hers. "Your friend seems charming," he said.

"As charming as they come," Katie said, exaggerating an eye roll.

"You should date better boys. He's a troublemaker." Larry smiled at her, but she got the feeling he was being serious.

"Totally not my boyfriend," Katie said, wondering why he'd even think that. He could have easily been Allison's boyfriend, or they could have just been three kids walking into a shop to get ice cream. Katie paid and sat down.

Tristan looked more annoyed than ever. Obviously eavesdropping on her conversation.

She devoured half her ice cream in one sweet minute. She'd forgotten how beautiful the flavors of rainbow sherbet were.

Tristan asked her if she'd ever seen any out-of-shape guardians.

"Since I only know the small population Boise has to offer, no."

"It's because they don't eat—" Tristan stopped and stared out the window. A man with burn marks on his face and a wretched limp passed by. Allison gasped.

"Allison," Katie said, astounded. "Don't be mean—"

"Quiet," Tristan hissed, glancing at Larry, who seemed none the wiser. He rushed them to finish their ice cream. He didn't talk again until they were out on the street.

"It was a fate, wasn't it?" Allison asked Tristan as they walked past Sunny Music.

"Yes. And it was tracking. The nasty ones shape-shift to look like that when they're close to what they want. They know people's natural reactions are to stare, giving them a good chance to scan every face." Tristan said.

"What if that was just a perfectly normal man with burn scars?" she asked, feeling like they were being a little dramatic.

"His eyes. They were blank. You would have known to look for that if you read a book once in a while," Tristan retorted.

It wasn't Katie's fault she never had time for all her homework. Traci often pretended to understand when Katie would show up with half her work done, but Katie was running out of excuses.

"If fates are Downtown, the rumors must be true. What if that fate *was* tracking a pureblood?" Allison said, looking like a conspirator. "I read that the last time a pureblood was assassinated, a war broke out. Like a power vacuum. Everyone scrambling to gain power. The violence spread into our world like wildfire. The real precursor to the first World War."

"Katalina. How comfortable are you with a gun?"

"You mean to carry around? That's illegal for anyone under twenty-one," she said, laughing.

"I didn't ask you about the law. I asked you how comfortable." Tristan's black hair looked wilder every step he took, each movement shifting it into a more madden state of being. He reminded her of the stray cat she used to feed. Before it disappeared, she would sneak up on it, and its hair would puff up like a spiky cotton ball. "Katalina," he snapped.

"I'm not." He knew that. The last gun she held shot out yellow paint.

"Knives?"

"Plastic ones—"

"Start carrying at least three—real ones." He pointed at her. "There, by your ankle and one in your pocket, and one there." His finger lingered on her thigh.

"How am I supposed to wear one on my thigh?" Katie nearly burst into laughter. She'd most likely gut herself after two steps. Did he forget he only trusted her with a plastic knife? Plus, Lucinda would never let that slide.

"Just put it under your skirt."

"Jesus, Tristan. Before I go around looking like Laura Tomb Raider. Why are you acting like a crazy person?"

Allison shook her head. She looked serious, like Tristan. It was clear, Katie wasn't getting something. She was the one left out of the loop again. Her stomach started to turn.

"You have to protect yourself. You have to be prepared for anything. What if I'm not around?"

"Prepared for what?"

"Anything!" he yelled at her. A feeling told her that the mental wall she suspected he held up between them was about to be flooded. His hair stood on ends. Fear and mania seeped out of him and into her mind. She couldn't shake the cold that creeped into her skin, making her jump as a car next to them backfired. She didn't understand the fear, but she felt it anyway.

He studied her face and the terror that, she knew, was plastered on it. His expression changed, and his emotions pulled away from her like a vacuum sucking away wisps of smoke. He took a deep breath and frowned. "Just do it. Just in case," he said calmly.

"What aren't you telling me," she said to him silently.

Katie looked at Allison, and Allison shared her look of confusion. "He just means it can be dangerous when wars break out between clans or covens. Sometimes they spill over up here and people get hurt. Vampires are notorious for causing commotions." Allison rummaged through her purse and pulled out a bottle of pepper spray. "Maybe you can hold on to this. I have a ton of this stuff. We can't have knives at school, but carrying around pepper spray when I don't have my pocket knife makes me feel safer. Plus, you know, normal people can be dangerous too."

Katie took the pepper spray. Allison shrugged as they looked at Tristan again. He was gone in his own mind. Somewhere too far for them to find.

Snow started to fall the week before Thanksgiving break. The snow was better than the rain that had murdered any hope of a practice without wet puddles. Every day she'd go to school looking like she'd been in a fight with a bucket of dirty water, and every night she went to bed feeling like she got beat up by a hurricane. But today was the first snowfall of the year. Aside from it being the worst hair day she'd had in weeks—dirt and snow from the previous night plus one squirt of shampoo did not mix well—she was excited for what today meant. Tons of holiday breaks. Any break from Mrs. Barnes' constant essays on werewolf involvement in industrial age London, or Traci hassling her about working on her core, was a blessing.

Her core didn't mean abs. It was something they worked on every Friday in Field Study with Mr. Carver. They had to meditate until they felt a kind of coating over their skin. It was what made them guardians. They were untouchable by the paranormal. If anyone had bothered to explain this in depth before, Katie wouldn't have spent nearly every day being paranoid about having to join the fold.

It wasn't an easy thing though. Katie still hadn't figured out what it was, and it wasn't exactly something someone could show her. Mr. Carver compared it to putting on a coat. No one in the class could do it except Allison and Adam, and even then it was only for a few seconds.

Katie could barely meditate, let alone focus.

School probably wouldn't have been as tiring as it had been lately if Tristan weren't pushing her even harder in practice. But nothing was going to get in the way of today. Dry bar-soap hair, stiff legs, dropping her deodorant on the bathroom floor and then using the broken pieces to prevent a long day of bad body odor? Nope, none of that was going to taint the day that marked the—summer aside—best part of the year.

To start it off, it was Friday! The best day of the week, because there were no after-school activities. To make it better, Lucinda cancelled their morning training—most definitely auspicious. Katie had a chill in her spine when she woke up and was thrilled to stay indoors, warm and inactive. She even snuck in a few cups of hot chocolate before Tristan walked into the kitchen, ready to leave.

She almost skipped to school. It felt like a good day.

"I'm running an errand today," he said.

Yet another glorious sign.

"A sign for what?"

"Nothing." She smiled. "Why are you leaving this time?" she asked, feigning only a slight interest. He cancelled their training sessions every so often to run secret errands, but only in the evenings. For all she knew, it could be another lie. He could be going on dates. Vampire girls with no morals or self-respect. Come to think of it, what *was* his type? He never told her anything about himself—his hobbies, his likes, dislikes—aside from chastising her, books, and being called girly.

Your fault for having hair blacker than a fresh dye job. No one's hair curls that perfectly around their face.

He cut her a look from the corner of his eye. "I'll be back before this evening. Make sure you warm up before practice."

Katie shrugged, pretending she didn't care, but once they got to the school, her stomach jolted. She hadn't expected him to leave just then.

He waved at her with his crooked smile as he turned and disappeared around the corner, leaving her in a sea of student bodies. She felt confused and misplaced. He was gone, and she was...alone. No one to hear her thoughts all day. No one to chastise her.

She was free!

⋅ⓔⓔ⋅

School dragged. By second period, she was vacant and despondent. *And it's only the second hour....*

She let her head fall to her desk as Mrs. Barnes called roll. She eyed Tristan's empty desk, startled to find herself wishing he was there. He would be making a sly comment about her having coffee withdrawal, or maybe poking fun at her makeshift ponytail of twisted curls and pencils. *Hell is selling frozen Popsicles. I think we've become...friends.*

Cue the manic laugh. He wasn't exactly friend material. He was a jerk, always on her about doing homework, and downright brutal during their training sessions. Every other day, he bruised her so bad she wouldn't heal for weeks. These stiff legs were *his* fault. Although, she didn't make it any easier for him to like her. She was unrelenting when letting him know what she *really* thought about him. But he deserved it.

Yet, there was his empty seat. She missed him, that was for sure, but it was only the antics she missed. Not him in her head. She was a diary with no lock, and he was a book with empty pages. It wasn't fair.

"I'm glad you've started stalking someone else for a change. The way you used to follow Brian around was kind of pathetic," a suicidal voice said next to her.

Does Christi want to die? Sure, Christi probably could have beat her up a few months ago, but training with Tristan had changed things.

"If you don't shut up, I'm going to pound your face into the desk," Katie said, not looking at Christi.

"Look, Katie. I'm not trying to start anything. I'm just saying—I'm glad you've found someone else."

Katie had to see if the sincerity in Christi's voice matched her face. Katie was shocked. The venomous snake was actually being honest. Rude, but honest.

"I haven't *found* someone else. And I didn't follow Brian around. We were best friends." She wished she hadn't said, *"were." Are. We are best-friends.*

"Okay, well I'm glad you found a new best friend. I'm trying to be nice. Just accept it." Christi sounded exasperated but genuine.

"Why?" Dread filled her. If Christi was extending an olive branch, the world must be coming to its end soon. The apocalypse was near, and she hadn't stocked up on a year supply of rainbow sherbet.

"Because...it's obvious we see a lot of each other. You're in the program, and—I'm just trying to call a truce. Are you always this difficult?" Christi said, looking a little jittery. She stuck out her hand for a handshake, but Katie ignored it. She opened her textbook and stared at a picture, of a man transforming into a wolf, trying to piece together Christi's god-awful change in behavior.

"It's not a good idea, Kay," Allison said in their math class.

"Allison, you should have seen her. She tried to shake my hand."

"Kay…"

"It's not like I'm going to beat her up. Just burn down her house or something. I feel like today is a good day for that. All the signs point to my success."

"What?" Allison looked tired.

"Brian would support me," Katie said, knowing the old Brian would have. *The new Brian wouldn't care if I fell off a cliff.*

"Brian is anything *but* supportive," Allison spat, breaking the lead in her mechanical pencil.

"Allison."

"Seriously, Kay. He's an asshole. Stop talking about him. He's been treating you like dirt. He's pretty much replaced you," Allison glanced at her. "I mean, he might as well have with the way he's ignoring you."

Katie knew that Allison was covering something up. That small darting of the eyes.

It was her tell. "What do you mean, *'replaced you?'*"

"I just said it figuratively."

"Who?"

"No one."

"Who?"

"I don't know."

"Allison."

"All of them!" she said too loud. Mr. Right looked up from his desk. They put their heads down and worked through a few math problems.

"Explain," Katie said after a moment.

"He's been hanging out with kids from the Junior Guardian Society. They're his new best friends. Christi is the president, so there's no way you're going to get chummy with them. It's been pretty obvious for a long time now. He's pretty much traded you in, so stop being nice to him. Stop caring. "

Katie stared at Allison.

"Kay, I didn't say anything for a long time, because I thought it was a phase. I thought he'd stop ignoring you. I thought they were only his friends because of Will and Lucy, you know? Having parents on the 'Elite Force' is like having celebrity parents. I thought they were using him and that he would realize it and go back to you. But…I guess I was wrong."

Katie wanted to explode. She didn't want to care, but she did. She cared so much. She and Brian always had a friendship where they walked on the edge. At times, she'd think she was his closet friend, but then he'd do something like hug her in front of everyone and throw all of his attention on her. It was always a fine line. Were they best friends or two people who grew up together?

"So you knew for sure and didn't tell me? You've let me look like an idiot kid sister tagging along."

"What did you want me to say? Brian's a douche? Brian's a jerk? I hate Brian? I already say that. You just never listen to me. In fact, all you ever do is complain to me about Brian. But I guess I can understand that because it's not like you want to tell me anything else."

Was Allison serious right now? She was obviously still angry about Katie not telling her that her dad threw her out until a week after the fact. That was months ago though. She needed to let it go.

"Whatever, Allison," Katie said. She didn't want to talk about it anymore. She didn't care that Allison looked hurt. Katie didn't even care that she was being unfair. She just wanted to stop feeling like the butt of a joke.

She finished her assignment for the duration of class. She didn't say another word to Allison for the rest of the day.

∽⧉10⧉∾

Drowning

&

Other Unpleasant things

KATIE SPENT THE rest of the day at her own pity party. Without Tristan there to distract her, she watched Brian laugh with his new group of friends in chemistry: Christi, who she hated; Michael, the most annoying kid in the world; and Ethan, who called her weird last year for no reason.

She had to fix it. There was an empty pit in her stomach. Brian *was* her best friend. They'd had a messed up few months, but there must have been something else going on. At home, he avoided his parents more than he avoided her. It was normal for him to barely talk to them, but it was different now.

Katie made up her mind. She was going to get him to hang out with her after school. She wouldn't take no for an answer.

The final bell rang for them to finally be done with Practical Applications and Steve Sensei. Though, to her delight, today was swimming. An excellent end to the school week. Katie climbed out of the pool and cornered Brian before he could get out of the pool.

"Come with me downtown?"

He ignored her, looking for another stepladder.

"Brian, come on." She bent down and grabbed his arm. His muscles were warm from the countless laps they had to do. He didn't pull it away. "Please. I just want us to go back to being friends. I don't know what happened."

His green eyes looked her over. She wanted to tap on his nose like she used to, but she held in the impulse. When did she start doing that? Stopping her impulses around him?

"Your new best friend isn't here today, so you need a fall back?" he said, gripping the ladder. Why was everyone doing that? Calling Tristan her *new best friend?* She just barely accepted them being friends today. *Good grief.*

'Brian, you can't be serious. He's my partner. Just like you have to spend a ton of time with Allison, I have to spend a ton of time with Tristan. Katie was glad Allison was already in the locker rooms and out of earshot. Besides, it's *you* who's been avoiding *me.*" Katie softened her tone. "I'm sorry. About before."

"Fine. I'll meet you on the steps in twenty minutes," he said finally.

Katie opened her mouth, ready to plead her case before she realized he'd actually agreed.

She went into the lockers and changed, reapplying her deodorant and putting her damp hair in a high ponytail. Her heart skipped a beat as she waited on the steps. What if he stood her up?

To her relief, he came down the stairs and stopped next to her. "Pizza?" he said.

She nodded.

On their walk, they talked about all the old things: the secrets of the TV show *Lost*, Gandalf's lack of power, the ridiculous essay she had to do on the mating habits of trolls, Mr. Rhineheart's new obsession with audiotapes in the classroom… but something was off. They were…off sync.

They walked over soggy leaves as they journeyed to their favorite pizza shop, The Pie Hole. As they ate, things felt a little better, but they both danced around the problem. Why they stopped being friends? Brian didn't bring it up, and Katie tried harder than ever to avoid it.

They left after sitting for a while and walked using the same route they had all last summer. Most of the stores were closing up, as it was late, but they were kind of having fun.

They stopped in front of a Dudley's Music Store, and she burst into a fit of giggles. The last time they were here, Brian was trying to learn the guitar. He was so bad, his lessons teacher asked him if he would be interested in the drums instead. Whenever he tried playing for her, she'd take it from him. *"If you care about humanity, you'll never pick it up again,"* she'd tell him.

"What?" Brian said, smiling. She stopped laughing as she looked into his eyes. It was gone. The little light that shined in them whenever he looked at her. The way his eyes formed little half-circles when he smiled. How he bit his bottom lip right before he completely showed his teeth. It was all gone. He was smiling at her like she was no one special. Just a girl. A stranger.

"We should head back," he said. A slight coolness nipped at her spine. The sun was falling down, turning the sky a dim blue."It's getting kind of cold."

Katie nodded. Nothing would ever be the same between them again. And she'd never know why. As they walked past all the closed signs, she knew she might as well be walking with a stranger. They took a shortcut through an alley as the sun sunk completely into the horizon, taking the last bit of warmth with it.

"How sweet," a silky voice said. They turned around. A tall, slender man stood maybe thirty feet away. He had blonde hair, milky-smooth skin, and wore a long black jacket that molded to his frame.

Brian cursed under his breath.

"Woah, no need to be nasty, kid."

"What do you want?" Brian said, his voice deeper than usual.

"I just want to talk to your friend. It's Katie, right?" Brian looked at her, and she shook her head. She didn't know him. Not at all—deja vu. The last time someone knew her name and just wanted to talk, Tristan got stabbed.

"Get lost," Brian said.

The man walked closer, ignoring Brian. The speed in which he glided toward her wasn't humanly possible. His graceful movements were just like Tristan's. She backed up after seeing his eyes. Right before he stepped from the shadows, they glinted silver. He was a vampire, and there was no mistaking it. There was something else about him...the way he *smelled?*

Brian pulled a knife out of his pocket.

"You're really nice on the eyes," he laughed. "Why don't you take a walk with me?"

"I'd rather not," Katie said, her chest constricted. She was a caged bird being watched. Except there were no bars.

"Of course you wouldn't," the vampire said, sighing. "No one ever does until someone gets hurt."

Before Katie could blink, he moved. Brian tried to get away, but the man flashed like a shadow. He punched Brian in the stomach, but Brian managed to cut his arm before dropping the knife and hitting the ground hard.

Brian coughed.

Katie moved for the knife. Her legs twitched with fear. What was she doing?

"Really? That wasn't enough to make you think twice?" The vampire shook his head and pulled out a gun.

Small, like one Lucinda taught her to shoot. There was a silencer on the end. She panicked. She couldn't just leave Brian on the ground, and even if she ran, he'd catch her. Or shoot her. She fought every urge to wet herself and beg for mercy.

"I don't know what you want." Maybe she should just agree to talk to him? No. Her insides screamed no.

He laughed and pulled the trigger. A shot fired to the right of her. She ducked, shaking so hard she thought she was going to vomit. He told her to get up. She jerked her body up, even though it screamed for her to stay down. She cried.

"That was a warning. Cut the crap. You come with me quietly, and I won't kill your friend."

"Please—" she stuttered, still gripping her knife.

"Don't fuck with me, girl. It's been a long day, and I'm losing patience. Come with me, or I'll kill your friend." He flicked his gun toward Brian's limp body.

"I'm coming," she heard in her head. Tristan?

She tried to stand up straight. Maybe she could talk to him long enough to distract him. What was she thinking? What could she possibly do? She could hardly keep herself from peeing.

"Do you want me to kill him?" He steadied the gun on Brian.

"I'LL COME," Katie shouted.

He lowered his gun and laughed. Laughed.

"You know, you're a pretty girl. I bet you have soft thighs."

She lost her nerve and turned to run. The gun went off, muffled by the silencer. The side of her ribcage split and burned as she smacked into the ground. Her breath was knocked out of her, and she tasted dirt and road. She closed her eyes.

"Quick little thing, aren't you?"

Katie heard his footsteps as he slowly walked toward her.

"It's no fun if you just lay—" He was cut off by his own scream.

Katie looked up, her side burning like fire, as a colossal dog tackled the vampire. He dropped his gun as the momentum of the dog threw them past her and down the alley. She grit her teeth and stood up, pain slicing at her side. She grabbed her side, staring as the dog tore at the vampire's flesh.

She needed to get to Brian. She wasn't sure when Brian had come to, but when she looked behind her, he was up and gripping the pistol in his hand. He aimed it at the vampire and dog tumbling in the alley.

The vampire ripped open the dog's shoulder and it fell back. A howl tore through the night, and she was thrown forward as another muffled gunshot sliced through her ears. This time she didn't feel it. She saw it. Bits of red burst out of her stomach. She fell to her knees as a frenzy of pain blossomed in her. She screamed out, and Tristan answered back.

"Katalina!" Tristan grabbed the knife from the ground. With speed she'd never seen him use before, he tackled the vampire off of the dog and they crashed into the ground. Tristan was on top of him, stabbing repeatedly. He stopped and the vampire laughed, gurgling up blood.

"Tristan. Let me go now, and maybe I'll forgive you for being a traitorous coward. Maybe I'll let you watch me play with her. I—" Tristan never let him finish.

Tristan cut at his neck. The body spasmed and went limp as Tristan hacked at it.

Katie chocked out a scream as her body fell to the ground. The massive dog limped over sniffing at her body. At least what she thought was a dog. It should have occurred to her earlier that it was a werewolf. It was grizzly, its eyes a hazel color. Human.

It sniffed her and let out a low grumble. "Thanks," Katie managed between spasms of pain. Blood flowed freely from her stomach and over her hands.

The wolf bounded off into the shadows. As Tristan's face appeared over her. Wind cut through and whipped his hair. It blew his fury and bloodlust in her face. His eyes glinted silver, and he began to blend in with the darkness. He was saying something but she couldn't focus.

She winced.

Tristan moved his hand over hers but stopped. "Was it Brian?"

She could feel the blood pulsing through her stomach but she didn't want to think about it. She didn't want him to know, not when he looked the way he did now. Not after he just cut a man's head off. Not while she could feel his thirst for blood.

Brian stood a few feet away, frozen and staring at her. Tristan snarled, and in a flash, he was gone and on Brian.

Tristan threw him against the alley wall with one hand. "You worthless piece of shit," he yelled. "How could you shoot her? You could have killed us."

Us?

"Tristan." She wanted to get up, but dizziness overcame her. She looked down at her hand. Her jacket covered most of it, but she could feel the blood pouring out. She was going numb. She moved her hand, and torn fabric stuck to it, revealing a hole that pumped blood.

Tristan still had the knife in his hand, and it glistened with blood as he raised it to Brian's neck. "Give me one reason," he said. Blood ran down Brian's face, and his body jerked. Tristan's arm was against his neck.

Katie blinked, surely losing consciousness as Tristan was beginning to fade into the shadows. She dropped her eyes, catching a glimpse of her hand, her body, everything fading into darkness.

"Please," Katie pleaded. She was being burned alive. "Please. Help me." Katie forced her eyes open once again.

Tristan dropped the knife and Brian, and ran to her. As he lifted her, pain seared through her as if her flesh had ripped farther.

Before Katie could tell him to wait, he was running down the street, in a darkness, so fast it made her vomit.

Katie tried to keep her eyes open but passed out.

⁘

"She needs to go to the hospital," Lucinda screamed.

"No," Tristan shouted. "They'll find out." Katie felt weak. She was still in Tristan's arms, but he was laying her on Lucinda's white couch and leaving. Katie tried to protest. Her words fell out like slugs.

She closed her eyes. She heard Will and Lucinda talking, but the sounds were thick and long.

Tristan was back. She didn't need to see him or feel him to know he was back. He grabbed her.

"STOP," Lucinda screamed. It was high-pitched and crazed, but Tristan was shaking and he wasn't listening. He continued to lift Katie's head.

Stop what?

The taste was violent. As soon as it touched her lips, she wanted to scratch her own eyes out. She gagged and spit it back up.

Blood.

"Drink it," Tristan said, forcing her mouth open with his shaking hands. She tried to push him away.

"Drink it. Katalina. Drink it or we'll die." His eyes were hysterical. Did he hear himself? Lucinda fought against Will, trying to get to Katie. Why was Will holding Lucinda back?

"GET AWAY FROM HER," Lucinda screamed over and over.

Katie cried as Tristan forced more down her throat. She was choking on it. He was drowning her in blood.

She blacked out.

⁓⁂⁓

"You left him in an alley, barely breathing." Lucinda's voice cut through Katie's mind.

She opened her eyes. They were heavy. She'd had a nightmare?

"That's a gross exaggeration. Besides, she would have died if I didn't," Tristan said, sitting with his shirt off and blood smeared on his face and chest. They were in his room. She could tell by the Japanese cherry blossom picture above his head. That was always in the downstairs room.

"I understand that, but you could have killed Brian," Lucinda said. "Go take a shower. You smell like vomit."

"He *shot* her. I gave him some bruises and a sore face. He shit his pants *before* I got there."

"He said you put a knife to his throat," Lucinda hissed.

"I don't care."

"I do! He's my son, Tristan. We're family. You don't do that to family."

"Now I'm family? *Your son* has problems. He's out of control."

"Enough."

Tristan scowled and looked at Katie. She wished he hadn't seen her. She didn't want to talk. Not yet. He turned away and she went back to a drowsy, ache-filled blackness.

11

ANNABEL

NIGHTMARES FLASHED ACROSS Katie's mind. So many people dying or being murdered. All night, she awoke in cold sweats.

I'm sorry, she'd hear over and over again. Maybe it was Tristan. Maybe it was a lingering thought from the nightmares.

It was dark when she woke up for the final time. Her body was sore, but she felt fine. She sat up and swallowed a scream when she saw Tristan sitting at the desk.

"Are you trying to kill me?" She was having a heart attack. Everything felt too fast. Too real. Even the fibers of sheets felt alive against her skin. She tried to slow her heart down.

She stopped breathing when she saw his eyes. They were red. She didn't know if he was crying or if they were just red. She looked away. There was no reason someone's eyes would *just* be red, but she didn't want to think that he'd cried. Her chest squeezed.

Katie focused on herself. What had happened? She was with Brian, eating pizza, then... Her stomach dropped as her fingers brushed across her abdomen.

It wasn't a nightmare. What happened was real, and she should have been in a lot of pain. A bullet flew through her stomach just yesterday. Or maybe it was still the same night? How many days had it been? She should be in a hospital, hooked up to IVs.

She lifted up her shirt just enough to peek. Maybe it *was* all a dream after all. There was an angry red line just above her belly button. It looked like an old cut. Not a fresh gunshot wound. A thin red line where tiny perfect stitches held her together. Katie had seen Lucinda stitch enough things to know what her patch jobs looked like. Katie was a patch job.

"What's going on?" She couldn't look at Tristan without remembering how he forced blood down her throat, how she drowned in it.

The door burst open and smacked against the wall, bouncing back into the grizzly man that was her father.

"Get out. You, get away from her." He hadn't shaved in weeks, maybe. His beard made him look like a mountain man. He grabbed Tristan by his shirt and slammed him against the wall. Tristan didn't do anything to fight back. "How could you? Why didn't you just stay away?" The last word came out as a whisper. Her dad crumpled over and let Tristan go. "Please, just leave."

"I'm not leaving her," Tristan said.

"Can't you see you've ruined her life? You've ruined it. All because of you. You've destroyed my family."

Katie's mouth opened, but the words stayed confused and swirling in the back of her throat.

Tristan met her eyes. *Do you want me gone? If you want me gone, I'll leave and never come back.*

What was he saying? And why did she hear it so clearly in her mind? Hysteria swirled around her. Her limbs ached. Why did Tristan look like that? So weak and defeated?

The memory attacked her like a violent nightmare. The little boy with black hair and blue eyes. Walking away from her. Leaving her as she reached out for him. Tristan looked at her now with the same broken eyes.

"Just leave," her dad screamed.

"No!" Katie found her voice. "No." She couldn't make sense of what was happening, but she knew if he left she'd feel empty again.

Her dad sobbed. She'd never heard him cry. It made her cry.

Her hugged her. "I'm sorry, Katie Bug. I messed up. I messed up."

He held her for a long time, and they cried. She didn't know why, but this pain was like going home. It was something they'd been sidestepping her whole life. All the nights he'd left her in this house for another family to raise. The times he was too drunk to remember she needed to eat more than chips and water. They never talked about it. She didn't want to. She hated thinking about her dad that way. He wasn't like that anymore.

Tristan moved, and she panicked. He glanced at her before he slid down the wall and sat on the floor in the corner. His head leaned against the wall, as he watched her. Listening to the past she never told anyone.

Her dad pulled away from her. "Do you see why I tried to protect you?"

"Why don't I have giant bullet holes in my stomach? Why am I—Okay?"

Her dad didn't say anything. Neither did Tristan. They weren't going to tell her. Her breath quickened. They couldn't go on treating her like this. They were going to tell her something or she was going to flip-the-fuck-out.

"You're like me," Tristan said.

Katie stared. She didn't want a clarification. She didn't need one. She knew what he meant. It was impossible.

Tristain continued. "That's why I made you drink. You would have died if I didn't. You would have—"

"Please. Stop," her dad said again. His voice was small. He was begging Tristan, not telling him.

"You don't remember me because he made you forget me. I can read your thoughts because your mother made me take the Keeper's Vow. You don't remember her because—"

"I didn't want it to haunt you for the rest of your life, Katie

Bug. I wanted you to grow up happy. I wanted you to have your own life. Your mother wanted you to have your own life."

Katie was calmer than she expected. Her mother was a vampire. That was kind of cool, maybe? Tristan broke their eye contact, and she knew she hadn't heard the worst of it. Allison had told her once that vampire women couldn't give birth. They were infertile. It was only guardian women who could bear half-vampire children.

"You're a vampire?" she asked her dad. It was impossible.

His face contorted. He ran a hand across his face. "There's something I have to tell you. But you know, I'll always be your dad."

"Dad, don't." She didn't want to hear it. He was her dad, no matter what. No matter what they'd been through, the tough times up until her last year in middle school, it didn't matter.

"I knew your mother for a long time, but there was a time I hadn't seen her for years. I—she came to me looking for help. She was—pregnant."

"Dad, please—I don't want to know."

"Your mother wanted a place to start over. Her family kicked her out. I always loved her. I fell in love with her all over again. And you. Katie, you were the most beautiful thing I'd ever seen. I've always loved you."

Was that why he'd leave her with Lucinda? For months?

"Who is my—who was she with?" She couldn't say father. She couldn't even think of the woman that was her mother. She'd spent so much of her life not caring about the one she saw in the picture frames. Now she felt betrayed.

"She didn't know."

Katie sniffed. Her mother was a tramp. Her next question was directed at Tristan. "What's the Keeper's Vow?"

He looked into her. Deep. "It allows us to hear each other's thoughts."

"Why?" It didn't make sense to her.

Tristan shrugged. He was lying to her again, but he didn't budge. Her dad looked at him and sighed.

"Tell me what happened." She didn't have to clarify that she meant the event that seemed to start it all. The event that made Lucinda start hating her dad three years ago, the one that made her dad erase everything about her life ten years ago.

Her dad stood up. "I've relived that night over and over for the last ten years. I don't want to hear it again."

Katie looked at her blanket as his heavy footsteps thumped on the floor—they paused before opening the door. "I can't stop you anymore. But I erased your memories for a reason. Katie Bug. We can still go back to the way things were."

Katie stared at the floor. She was tired of being kept in the dark. "Life only moves forward, Dad. Never backwards." Her eyes never left the floor, but she knew Tristan was watching her. It was what he had told her at their first training session. She finally understood what he meant. She couldn't run away forever.

The door opened and closed. She didn't have to look up to know her father was gone. The only sound left in the room was Tristan's light breaths. He was so quiet, but she could hear them anyway.

She opened her mouth.

"We lived in the mountains," he said, "because my mother was blacklisted. I was five at the time, but my parents only fed me blood, so I developed faster. I didn't know that until I met you.

"You were almost five. Your mother brought you over because she wanted you to grow up around someone *like* you. I didn't believe you were like me. You had never had blood. You were just like a normal girl, and as dumb as a rock as far as I was concerned."

His sudden silence made Katie look up. He was staring at her—in her. "So calling me names is a force of habit?" she said, uncomfortable under his gaze.

Tristan smiled, but his gaze never broke. He was looking at her like he was seeing her for the first time in a long time. "You can say that. I wasn't nice to you at first. I used to talk you into eating dirt and worms. You were the first kid I had ever met. You were the first and only friend I ever had. One day, I put a mouse on your head, and your mom said she wasn't going to bring you anymore. I think that was the first time I had ever cried.

"After that day, I treated you like a slow friend, instead of my unequal rival. I read to you, and cleaned up after you when you made stupid messes. Annabel The Dim-watted. You'd always talk to this ugly doll you carried around." Tristan snorted.

"Annabel?" Katie asked.

"That was your name. Annabel Watts."

It made her uneasy to look him in the eyes. All this time she'd wanted him to be honest and share his secrets. The more he talked, the more he relaxed. He was talking about *them*. A life they had together, and she didn't remember a second of it. Whenever his lips curled, she felt guilty. They'd had happy times, and he was the only one who remembered them. No one to relive them with.

"Your dad didn't like it much. He thought I was an abomination. He tried more than once to get your mom to move back here. On your sixth birthday, we were popping all the balloons when we heard them arguing. He regretted getting Lucinda involved in finding us—" Tristan paused. Thoughtful.

He laid his head on the wall and smiled. "You used to torment me. There wasn't a day you weren't trying to slip and kill yourself. I stopped you from falling out of trees and falling into the lake when neither of us knew how to swim. It was always a countdown before you did something stupid." He laughed again, but it wasn't light, like the night in the park.

Tristan lifted his shirt, and she saw a small, silver tattoo on his chest. It was a sun, and inside was a crescent moon. "My dad had this mark too. He never told me much about it." Tristan looked down at the mark before pulling his shirt back down. "It dated him. The only vampires known with it were born to royal houses.

"The royals were the only ones with gifts. Some used their gifts to kill their fathers and 'cleanse' their houses. Others wanted to reform the vampire rule. My father didn't care about any of that. He knew that his would only be used by others. He had the strength of a thousand men."

He looked at the ceiling, and his eyes were like ice, crystal clear and close to melting. "Your mother wanted me to take the Keeper's Vow with you—because I have my father's gift." Tristan stopped, and Katie was overwhelmed with his anger and guilt.

She looked at him, but he wouldn't so much as glance in her direction.

"My dad never asked if it was something I wanted to do, or if it was something I was capable of doing. I imagine when made me speak the words and drink your blood, he didn't know he'd be murdered less than a week later. In the end, it didn't matter how strong he was."

This was it. Katie knew it was coming. The event that had changed their lives forever. The one that sent Tristan away, turned her father into a drunk, and even now was still ripping their lives apart.

"We were playing in the upstairs bedroom. I heard them break in through the front door. I could smell the blood before I heard my mom scream."

"Why?" Katie said. *Why couldn't things be different? Why did any of this happen?*

"Because if you kill a royal pureblood and drink his blood, you gain his power. It's against the law, but some people don't care about that as long as you don't get caught." Tristan adjusted himself on the floor. "They were fast. The only option was to hide. You were too slow back then to run. I wasn't strong enough yet, not to carry us both and out run them. Your mother was the first to reach our room. I grabbed you before you ran out of the cabinet we were in. There was someone behind her. And then she was on the floor. I covered your eyes, but you knew. I thought you would scream and give us away. But you never did. You didn't say anything that night."

"He made me forget it all," she said, feeling overwhelmed.

"He did what he thought was best for you."

"How did we survive?" Her heart pounded in her chest.

"A friend of my father. But I don't know if it was luck or cowardice."

"It wasn't cowardly to hide. We were children."

He didn't seem to hear her.

"Why didn't you stay with Lucy?"

"She barely knew I existed. Besides, I didn't belong here—with guardians. If I had come to live here, people would have found out what we both are."

"So? Is it *that* bad?" She could have remembered her mother. Maybe then her dad wouldn't have turned to drinking, or if he did, at least she would have had a friend to talk to who understood—instead of being ashamed every time an afternoon play date turned into a two-week sleepover.

Tristan got up and sat next to her. He put his arm around her, and she let herself be held. "It is here. Here, we are less than human," he said. She had a healed bullet hole to prove she was different.

"Then where did you go? What did you do? You can't tell

me you were just left to fend for yourself." Like a closing door, his wall was rising and blocking her out. She knew what he was doing. "Tristan, tell me."

"I lived with someone who took me in. A nice big house, with no one in it. But I left a few years ago and—"

"And what?" she whispered.

He didn't say anything.

She held her stomach, feeling like she'd fall apart. She got a new life, a new name, and he got what, exactly?

When it was obvious he wasn't going to answer, she asked a different question. "How did you know my dad changed my name? Where to find us?"

"A month after everything happened, I ran away and wandered around for a few days, listening to your voice, until I found you at the elementary school up the street from here.

"You were on the playground. You didn't know me. I called your name and—your new name was Katalina. We even played for a while...but you had no idea about anything and from then on, I knew I would never see you again. Not the real you anyway. I was sent to live in New York after that."

"Why?" Katie said.

"Punishment? I was a bit violent after that."

"No," Katie said, imagining a little Tristan who'd lost everything he'd ever known in one night. "I mean why did this all happen? Why did it turn out this way? Why does life suck like this? Why did I get shot?"

She turned to Tristan as if he'd have all the answers. He

was so much braver than her, and he was barely a year older. She wondered why he seemed to enjoy going to school and studying, why even though Lucinda yelled at him to mind his curfew or nagged for him to join her for a movie, he'd listen and comply. It was because he hadn't had a real home life since he was seven.

"Life sucks sometimes."

"That doesn't explain why *I* got shot."

"I don't know what he wanted with you," Tristan said, shifting.

"He knew you. He called you a traitor." There was still something he wasn't telling her. A something that got her shot.

"I killed him. He won't come after you again."

"Tristan. I was nearly killed—"

"Because Brian shot you. I saved you. I won't let anything happen to you."

"What aren't you telling me?" If that vampire knew her, it was because he knew Tristan. It wasn't a random act of violence.

"Katalina, I'll protect you with my life."

She steadied her breathing. She was almost killed. Extinct. Erased from the earth. That wasn't enough.

"Nothing else will happen. He's dead. I killed him. He's gone, okay?"

She nodded. He did kill him. He was gone. But what if there were others?

"There won't be others. He was the only one," Tristan said, gripping the sheets on the bed.

"How can you expect me to believe that? Just take your

word for it?"

Tristan's eyes darted around the room.

"Tristan?"

"I used to be a Death Dealer. My dad left me money, but I went into training so I could have a place to live and a real job."

"I thought you had a place—"

"That *place* wasn't a home." The sheets tore under his grip. "Death Dealers are the underground police force. They were more like a family to me than the place I ran from."

A thousand thoughts flew across Katie's mind, but one flashed brighter than the others. *Death Dealer.* He killed people.

"I didn't kill *people*. D-Ranges mostly. Ones that went around *actually* killing people. The vampire that attacked you was one of my lead commanders. He's been trying to find me ever since I left. He does a lot of shady shit and doesn't like deserters who could potentially talk. "

"Anyone else pissed at you?" Katie didn't want to sound angry, but she was. *He* had gotten her shot. Something *he* was a part of.

"I should go." Tristan stood up, but she pulled him back down. It was instinct to hold on to him. The guy was dead. It didn't matter anymore.

That's what she told herself.

They sat in silence. How did someone move past something like this? He'd joined some weird gang, and now it was following him around spraying bullets at her.

He flinched.

What if it had been her with no friends, or parents—related or not—to look after her and care about her? "What'd you tell Will and Lucy?" she said.

"Not everything. I'll tell them the truth."

"No." Katie said. It was stupid, maybe. She'd been told her whole life always to tell adults when something bad happens. Tell the truth. Always come forward. What would they do? Kick him out? He'd be back to the life he was trying to leave.

It was Tristan who'd saved her life. He knew she needed blood. She shuddered at the way he'd forced it down her throat. It was the most vile thing she'd ever tasted. "Do you ever get used to it?"

"No," he said.

She remembered how she choked on it.

"I had to."

"I know." Even though she said it, it didn't make her feel any better. "If we tell Will and Lucinda, maybe they can use connections or something to make sure no one else is trying to revenge-kill you."

"It doesn't work that way. They can't tell anyone. What we are…we'd be outcasted and kicked out of school. It would ruin Will's career. He's an elite. And they'd both lose credibility as guardians."

"All of that because we are—" Was she really half-*vampire*? Was that something she could accept? No. She was still Katie. Katie Watts.

"They don't care who you are. Not as much as they'll hate

what you are. You can't tell anyone. Not Allison, not Brian. They know about me, fine. But no one can find out about you."

Katie thought that normally she would laugh or tell him he was being dramatic, but she didn't. There was no desire to challenge him or anything he'd told her. She was numb. "People are better than you give them credit for," she said.

"You give people too much credit."

"How do I know when I walk out this door no one will put a bullet through my head?"

"I'd kill them first. I killed him."

"Exactly. You have to stop doing that. You have to leave all that gang crap behind you or you'll get us all killed."

"It wasn't a gang. It was a police force."

"Funny, the police department here doesn't put out hits on retired cops."

Tristan didn't say anything.

"Your life is different now. No matter what happened before it's in the past. You have to change too. No more going on errands or anything like that. From now on, we're normal kids going to a normal-ish high school, living a normal life. Okay?"

"Katalina—"

"Promise me. You'll stay. You'll stop keeping secrets and going off to secret places. I have to know things are going to be okay. I don't want you to leave. I want us both to have a decent life. Together."

The last word. She meant it, but she didn't mean to say it

out loud.

Tristan nodded.

It was good enough. She pushed him off the bed and lay back down. She needed to sleep.

❧ 12 ❧

HONEY POT

KATIE MOVED BACK home with her dad over Thanksgiving break. It was awkward between them at first, but eventually he stopped tiptoeing around her. Brian was home from the hospital, but she hadn't gone to see him. She couldn't face him, not after he'd nearly killed her. It was a relief that he'd be out of school for the rest of the term. Lucinda didn't say whether it was because he needed time to recover or if it was because he refused to go.

Between being shot, opening the Pandora's box that was her past, and moving back home, Katie was not prepared to go back to school either. It didn't help that she felt oddly groggy and sluggish for a few weeks. It could have been because teachers were cramming in material, trying to get through their lesson plans. It was always like that though. Hamilton High *was* an academic school. The problem was the big evaluation she had to take before winter break.

Traci followed her everywhere around the school. She'd pretend that she 'just so happened' to be in the cafeteria too! And with a pile of textbooks, no less! *"Katie, I hope you're using that noggin of yours today, because we have to get through half of this chapter!"* Or, *"That tuna sandwich looks nice. By the way, I made you math flash cards, want to go through some?"*

It wasn't just Traci either. Tristan and Allison hounded her daily to meditate, find her core, and harness "the power." At least twenty times a day, Tristan told her to breathe.

"What do you think I do? *Not breathe?*" she said in the middle of Field Study. They were supposed to review independently for a test on vampire defense. There were two pages of weapons, and she had to know the effect each one had on a vampire. It took her two days, but she'd memorized one page already. She scanned the page again. To be honest, it gave her the creeps. "Who knew there were so many ways to skin a dog?"

"Cat," Tristan said, taking the paper from her.

"What?" Katie reached for it back, but he held on tight.

"The phrase is about skinning *cats* not dogs. Anyway, you should practice your meditation now. Forget this test, you're going to fail it anyway. You've been studying the wrong list."

Katie snatched the paper back and groaned. She'd been studying the one for werewolves—a test they took two weeks ago.

She couldn't do anything right. She'd been trying over the last few weeks, but it was too much. Too much information about the dramatic history between vampires and werewolves. The debate on whether ghouls existed, and if the fates really were faerie which meant the existence of faeries were then in question. Everyone knew those things. Everyone meditated perfectly and made *Sensei Steve* "bow"—which Katie was sure was more incorrect than Steve's Japanese. Everyone, except her, knew what they were looking for when they meditated. They all understood what the untouchable power was. "This is so unfair. How am I expected to do it when most of the people in this class, who know what they're doing, can't?"

Tristan shrugged.

It didn't make sense. She was being set up to fail. And what would happen when she failed? Myrtle made it clear they'd get rid of her, guardian style. She'd be enrolled at the public school down the street and would most likely spend her days drooling on her desk.

"No one is going to erase your memories. Just breathe," Tristan said.

"What do you *think* I'm doing?" A few heads turned in her direction. She scowled.

"You know what I mean. Take deep, slow breaths, concentrate, and harness the power."

Concentrate? On what? Her center? She had yet to *find* her center, and she didn't think she'd be able to harness anything but a headache. Katie closed her eyes and groaned. Concentrate on what? The only thing she could think about was Tristan's cologne. It didn't smell bad. It smelled like him. But because their chairs were so close together, it suffocated her. Actually, she was starting to feel suffocated by *him*. Sitting so close, even though they weren't touching, felt like they were confined in a tight space, where neither one could move without colliding with the other.

It was like that now, ever since that night. He never left. Anytime they weren't in their separate houses sleeping, they were together. On days practice ran late, she'd stay at Lucinda's house and they'd sit in the backyard until midnight, meditating. How was she supposed to concentrate when she couldn't find her own space? They were *always* in each other's space.

Now, the smell of him alone was permeating off her own skin. *What?*

She opened her eyes, finding it hard to breathe. The room looked strange, like she had moved a seat over—like she was sitting in Tristan's seat…

Katie turned her head to the right and nearly screamed when she saw herself, eyes closed and still. In a split second, she was back, falling out of her own chair.

"Are you okay, Katie?" Mr. Carver said, moving from his desk to help her up.

"I'm fine," she said, staring at Tristan from the floor. He looked as confused and as surprised as she felt.

Katie picked herself up and fixed her chair. There were some chuckles in the class, but Mr. Carver went on answering review questions and announcing the homework. "Remember class, talking blood type with vampires is like talking politics. You should always know what the most popular type is at the moment. B positive is on the rise—Michael, *B* positive. There is no D."

"Tristan," Katie whispered.

He ignored her, watching Mr. Carver as if his words would be on a test. She was in his body. She was *in* his body. How was that possible?

The bell rang.

"Tristan?"

"Katalina, leave me alone." He grabbed his books and strode out of the classroom.

"What just happened? I was—we were—why aren't you freaking out?"

"You used to do it when we were kids. You sort of put yourself in my mind. It's—annoying."

"So, I wasn't imagining that? I was actually *in* your head?" Katie said, pacing by the wall of lockers and students. They only had five minutes before their next class, Practical Application. Steve-Sensei planned for them to do floor exercises. No time for talking there. She needed answers now.

"Just stay out. I didn't like it when we were kids. I don't like it now."

"Are you serious? You do the same thing to me!"

"It's not the same. I've never gone into your head, I just hear and feel everything you bombard me with."

"So it's *my* fault you eavesdrop on *my* private thoughts?" She laughed at the idiocy.

"With the way you shout at me, I'd hardly call it eavesdropping. What you used to do, and what you just did, is an invasion of privacy," Tristan said.

Katie laughed at his terrorized expression. It was nice to know she had—even for a short time—unnerved him.

She owed it to him to invade his privacy. He kept a wall between them, hiding all of his thoughts behind it while rummaging through hers. She was afraid of any idle thought, wondering if he'd heard it or if he could hear her wondering *if* he was wondering. It was madness.

But this....

This was payback.

Over the next two days, she concentrated on him. She'd even move her chair closer to him, smelling him, memorizing his facial features—the way his top lip was a darker shade of pink than his lower. Every time, he'd shift in his chair, aware of what she was doing. Each time, she'd feel that closed-space feeling, he'd cringe, and she'd feel herself being shoved away.

Each attempt was in vain, but the way he'd reach over and pinch her arm in warning made it worth it. She was breaking through his wall and evening the playing field—not by much, but it was a start.

They sat on the floor for yet another class in Field Study. Today was a special day, though, it was Meditation Friday. Katie resumed Operation: Torture Tristan. She thought about the way his body moved naturally in and out of punches and blocks, the way his hair was never combed, and how his eyebrows always arched when he made funny faces. She felt how close she was to touching him, how they always sat that close together. How he always sat that close to her, no matter where they were....

She lost control of her breathing. It was faster than it should have been. She opened her eyes and saw herself sitting in her chair, looking still and calm.

Her eyes closed against her will. She was in his body, but she had no control. It was *his* lungs she felt taking in too many breaths, his heart beating too fast. She didn't like it. Where was hers? How was this working? What if she couldn't get back? What if her mind stayed hijacked by his body forever?

'*Calm down,*' Tristan said to her, '*I want to show you something.*'

She tried to clear her mind of the panicky chatter. Is this what Tristan heard from her all day? How did he keep his own thoughts straight when he could hear hers too? '*It's worse with you here,*' he said. She tried to silence herself and waited in the blackness of his mind.

As if she had teleported, she was surrounded by forest. A wet, sunny day after a short rain. She smelled a mixture of wet wood and sun. Aggravation filled her. Though the day was still early enough for his dad to teach him how to swim, he had to meet a girl named Annabel instead.

Annabel? The wet wood smell and forest were gone in a flash. She saw black again. '*Was that a memory? Your memory?*'

Just watch, Katalina. I can't concentrate when you think,' Tristan answered. A new memory surfaced. It was still wet, but the sun was setting. There was a little girl standing a few feet away, and a tall, slender woman standing by her side.

"This is Katalina and her daughter Annabel, Tristan. Go on, introduce yourself," a woman with a silky voice said, standing next to him. She had beautiful black hair and a smile that made him feel genuinely happy.

He walked over to the woman and said hello. She shook his hand, and he turned his attention to the girl. She was supposed to be like him.

She wasn't.

She had an ugly ragdoll in one hand and the other in her mother's. Her brown hair was pulled back into a ponytail, and she looked moderately slow. "I'm Tristan," he said, holding out his hand. Just as he thought, she wouldn't shake it. She wasn't like him at all.

The scene changed, and he was standing in front of Annabel. She was a little taller, and her brown locks were flying around her face in the wind. She had a long stick in her hand, and she held it like a sword.

"I told you, Annabel. You're the captive, and *I'm* saving you," Tristan said, irritated. She was ruining everything. *Again.*

"No. I'll save myself. I'm not playing with you anymore."

"Why?" he said, losing his patience.

"Because you're mean." She frowned. "I *know* you don't like me."

He stomped his foot. Of course he liked her, she was his friend. Why couldn't she be more like him? Why couldn't she see she was being stupid again? Her large gray eyes sat just underneath a furrowed brow. Why was his Annabel so sensitive?

Everything went black again, and Tristan was in a dark room lying on a bed. A loud voice filled his head, and he couldn't make it stop. He pleaded for Annabel to stop screaming in his mind, but she continued to cry and babble. She had heard her mother yelling at her father, and she wouldn't stop the crying. Tristan was filled with her terrible emotions, and they were ripping his mind apart. He screamed, thrashing around in his bed.

"I told you he was too young," his mother snapped at his father as they came into his room.

"Help me," Tristan begged, squeezing his head.

"He'll learn to block her out," his father said, pouring dark liquor into a glass.

"Ivan, you took away his life."

"If the tides were changed, Lawrence would have done the same for me. I'm done discussing it."

Tristan's head was going to crack open.

Katie couldn't take it anymore. The screaming and the crying was becoming too much. She felt a tug, and when she opened her eyes, she was back in her body, gasping and relieved the screaming was over.

"I'm sorry. I've forgotten how bad that one is," Tristan whispered, his eyes searching her for something.

"Was that right after you took the vow?" she whispered back.

"Yeah. You're not so bad anymore." He smiled.

She was still too shaken to return the smile. "Because you use a wall," she said.

"To keep *my* thoughts from *you*."

She still didn't like that he could hide things from her and yet know everything she wanted to hide. They were *her* thoughts, no matter how stupid or annoying. The mind was the only personal thing anyone had. But he knew that. It was why he used a wall.

"It's not," he said, looking up to make sure Mr. Carver was still at the front of the room, shuffling through papers. He opened his mouth to tell her something, but stopped. And there it was—a prime example of his wall being handy.

"It's hard to believe we were friends," she sighed, looking at his hair. It was too black, like he was too mean.

A wide, crooked smile spread across his face. "It's hard to believe you're still so sensitive." She had seen that smile a hundred times, but this time she felt it—a tug, catching her off balance.

The bell rang, and they left for Practical Application.

ঙ ৯

They spent the first half of every Field Study class sifting through Tristan's memories. They'd pretend to read their books while he showed her every memory he had of her and her mother. Her mother's sweet jasmine perfume, her sad smile— always sad—her loud and heavy laugh. Katie had a mother, and she was more than amazing. She was real. Sometimes, Katie would pass by a jasmine tree on the way to school, and she'd remember her, a small smile, a whisper of a laugh, or the barest touch. It was her. She was real. She was hers.

After school, they'd con Lucinda out of practice, using homework as an excuse, and lay in his room, on the floor, racing through his childhood memories. One memory would trigger a new one, and he'd stop to explain what had caused him to jump. She had never seen him smile so much or laugh so hard and long.

However, at least once a day, he would jump to something dark, and she would feel a deep depression. She'd named it The Black Void. He'd throw up his wall between them and turn on her as if she'd given him those memories, or been in his mind without his permission.

That, at least, was what happened yesterday after eating dinner at Lucinda's. It was late, and Lucinda made her stay the night. So, they spent most of the night sifting through memories until he kicked her out mentally and physically. He shoved her out, of the room before she even knew what was happening.

She woke up the next morning expecting to go home and spend the day watching Saturday morning cartoons in front of a bowl of sugar, cereal, and milk. She didn't expect him to be in her room after she got out of the shower.

"Sorry," he said, jumping at the sight of her. She gripped her towel and threw the closest thing she could grab—a handful of pens. He held up his hands to shield his face.

"How did you *not* know I was in the shower? I was thinking about hot water." She kicked him out and didn't let him back in until after she put on clothes and towel-dried her hair. She was still mad about his bipolar episode last night and she wanted to make it a point that she didn't work on his schedule.

"Do you want to see more or not?" he said, sitting on her bed—his butt placed directly on one of her pillows. "Sorry," he mumbled, moving it. He was wearing the yellow shirt with the blue lining that shaped his broad shoulders nicely. It brought out his eyes too, but nearly everything he wore did.

He turned away from her and stared at the wall. She blushed. Of course he heard that. Of course he thought she was checking him out. "It's just a nice shirt. Jesus. Can't I think it's a nice shirt? It's just a shirt. I say lots of people have nice shirts." *Shut up. Stupid. Shut up!*

She felt him smile. She'd never understand how she could feel that, but she did. "Just show me another memory," she sighed, sitting on the bed next to him.

"Unless you think my pants look nice too," he laughed, stretching out his legs to show off his jeans. She slapped him with her pillow until they were lying back, legs dangling over the bed, memory-surfing.

He idolized his father, and every memory he showed her today was about him. The way his dad's laugh shook the ground, the wrinkles in his face when he smiled. How he only saved laughs and smiles for special moments. All other moments he was quiet and constantly thinking. When she looked at Tristan now, she could see how similar they were—contemplative, reserved, and stoic. But when he laughed—as he was now, explaining to her why his mom falling out of the boat was so funny—he shook the earth too.

It didn't take long for him to slip into The Black Void. This time, it was as his father started to tell him about an underground city. His father faded out, and silence filled her mind. Him in an empty house walking through quiet rooms—waiting and waiting.

She braced herself for him to throw up his wall and move away from her, as if she had brought on the memory. This time she would refrain from saying anything, she would just sit there and feel helpless. Try not to think anything because that would set him off too.

She prepared herself for all of that.

None of it came.

Tristan grabbed her hand. He squeezed it, breathing like he was running from whatever lay just under the surface of his mind. She didn't know what to say or what to do. She imagined anyone else would have known how to make him feel like everything was all right. He squeezed her hand tighter, and she glanced over at him, his eyes wide open as tears collected at the edges. She turned away.

He could not be crying. Tristan could not be crying. She wasn't equipped to handle this. She squeezed his hand back because that was all she could do. Good friends wipe away tears. She could do that. She looked back at him, but they were gone, and his eyes stared up at the ceiling with less alarm.

They lay in the bed, silent and unmoving, aside from his chest slowing down until it was smooth and natural.

He relaxed, and his body sighed. The storm had passed. She felt proud. He let her in. Not really *in,* but he didn't run away from her, and she could still generally feel him. That counted for something.

Tristan's hand twitched a little, and she became aware of them holding hands.

She didn't dare look at him, or move an inch. They were, after all, holding hands while lying on a bed....

He shifted, and his thumb brushed against her hand.

They both froze.

Her palm itched. Of all times. It was sweating. He would think she always had sweaty palms—not that she cared. But still.

He stiffened again, and this time she thought he'd stopped breathing. Their legs were touching too. She hadn't noticed it before, but there was a slight pressure...or was she imagining that? The more she thought about it, the more it wasn't there. Not that she wanted it to be. They were just friends having good old-fashioned mind-reading fun. *Not that I think this is anything else. That's not what I'm saying. I'm not saying anything...*

Silence.

I mean I...I...I've got a lovely bunch of coconuts deedly-dee, there they are just standing in a row. Big ones, small ones, some the size of a bed.

"Katalina?"

"..." She cleared her throat.

"I think you mean, *some as big as your head.*"

"I don't have a big head."

"No, you have a—I'm talking about the lyrics."

"..."

"We should probably call it quits today."

"Probably."

He cleared his throat before pulling his hand away from her and standing up.

She tried hard not to think of the shocking cold his absence left—not just from his hand, but from his body so close to hers.

"We should train instead."

"Good idea," she said, going over moves in her head. *That new one with the kick at the end. That was the most awkward—move— I've ever done. So awkward…the kick, just tossed in there like that, with no warning.*

Tristan cleared his throat. "Okay, see you in ten minutes then." He had that funny twisted frown on his face. The one that made his eyebrows pop up to the top of his head. "Okay then." He crossed the room in three quick steps and tripped over her bookbag as he left.

⁂

That moment between them—whatever it was—was forgotten as soon at is ended. Not because she didn't secretly wonder about it every night for the next three days, but because Tristan acted as if it never happened. Like they were just good friends, and that day was one friend being a good friend to the other. And that *was* what it was.

What am I, twelve?

Katie fixed her pillow and snuggled up in her green blanket. Her room was dark and cluttered like usual. She stared at her orange cat lamp, glowing in the moonlight.

She was being immature about holding hands. No wonder he nearly ran out of the room. *But what if….*

No, she had way more important things to worry about, like the test she had to take tomorrow. She had no idea how she was going to pass it. Tristan hadn't been on her about meditation like he had been. In fact, he hadn't been on her as hard in training either—and here she was, thinking about Tristan again.

She rolled over in her bed. There wasn't anything wrong with thinking about him. They spent all their time together. Like earlier today, they laughed more than they worked. Everything was funny—when she accidentally slapped his forehead, or when he'd take on Russian personas and say, *'I'm going to kill you.'*

But there were awkward times too. The worst she played over and over in her mind, humiliated by what she'd done, but secretly glad she'd done it.

She'd pinned him on the leaf covered ground.

"This is a weak hold," he'd said.

"I'll drool on you then," she'd said, making him laugh. His laugh always made her laugh, it was contagious and spread like wildfire.

"You'll have to do better than that." He'd started to worm his way out of her hold. *"As soon as I'm out, I'm going to kill you."*

She felt herself losing her grip, and so—she bit him. On his stomach. And he laughed, frantically trying to get her off. Then she laughed, astonished that of all places to be ticklish—he was nearly in tears.

"*I got you,*" she'd said in a terrible Russian accent—and then it happened. That feeling of unease when an imaginary line is crossed. He threw her off with strength he had never allowed her to feel before.

"*That just got weird,*" he'd said. There were tears on his face, and his eyes gleamed. "*You sounded like a hooker, or a really bad honeypot.*" He laughed harder.

"*It's not my fault. It was the accent.*" Her face burned, but watching him fall back laughing made her grin.

"*Next time leave out the accent, honeypot.*" He smiled up at her before shaking her world with his laugh.

What if it wasn't her imagination? She hadn't imagined the way they brushed their arms against each other whenever she ate dinner at Lucinda's. He sat next to her there too, like during lunch at school, and every class they had. He'd pick food off her plate when Lucinda wasn't looking and scrunch up his nose. Sometimes she knew he liked it. She wondered if he'd ever stop drinking blood and just eat food like her. She could never drink blood.

She turned over in her bed again and closed her eyes. Pitch blackness, like his hair. She wondered what it would be like to touch his hair. She'd smelled it the other day as a joke—said she bet it smelled like girl shampoo, but it didn't. It smelled fresh. Like bar soap.

⊷❀❧

Katie and Tristan were on their way to school. Allison had stopped walking with them a few weeks ago, deciding to jog there instead. Katie could have used a jog that morning. It would have calmed her nerves. She couldn't stop hyperventilating.

"Sometimes I wonder about you," Tristan said, when she told him she was going to fail the evaluation. He laughed, and it only made her more frantic.

"We are at the bridge, Tristan! We are going to cross it and get our memories erased. Okay, maybe not you, but I'm going to have my memory fried. *Again*."

"Katalina, you're not going to have your memory erased. You've been ready for weeks now," he said with his crooked smile.

"Oh my god. You've lost your mind." She wanted to slap him. He needed to be serious.

"Please don't hit me," he said, eyeing her. "You've been transporting your consciousness into my body quicker and quicker all week. What did you think memory-surfing was? In order to find your center, you just have to concentrate on *yourself*, not me."

"Why did you wait till now to tell me that?" Katie said, still not knowing how she was going to completely do that. She felt a little cheated. She thought he *wanted* to show her those memories, not use it as an exercise. Besides, concentrating on Tristan was easy. Concentrating on herself was like those stupid "tell me about yourself" surveys teachers hand out at the beginning of the school year. *As if they really care what my favorite color is.*

"Obviously you didn't read chapter seven. It covered the basics on using meditation to find your core. No wonder you got a 'C' on that test."

Now was not the time to chastise her. "How did you know I got a 'C'? You went through my bookbag?"

"No, that would be a violation of your privacy. I got it from Mr. Carver's grade book."

She stared at him. *There are so many things wrong with what you just said.*

"You're concerned about all the wrong things. When it's time for your test, just relax and think about what makes you feel strong. Imagine a pit of energy in your stomach." She should have practiced before the test. What was wrong with her? Tristan put his arm around her shoulder and his laugh sang into her ears. "It's not that serious. You *are* a guardian, the power is there. You just need to concentrate long enough for them to see it."

She looked up at him. He only had seven inches on her, but she still had to look up, especially when they were this close. "Are you sure?"

"You should actually *read* the book. Not just look at the pictures."

She punched him, and he laughed pulling her closer. She told herself the reason her heart was pounding so hard was because of the test.

At school, she began to calm down. At least there were four periods and lunch before the evaluation. She could warm up and find some confidence. Maybe do breathing exercises three through five. Then she could do a full cycle in second period; but when she walked into her English class, all her plans died an agonizing death as Mr. Carver smiled at her.

"Tristan. Katie. Just the two people I was looking for. I asked Mr. Rhineheart to excuse you from class. Now is the only time I'll be able to give you your evaluations," he said, wearing a red tie and checkerboard chess suit that made him look like an *Alice in Wonderland* executioner.

It's all over. At least I won't have to remember all the horrible things. Being shot, the blood, a decapitation...

Tristan nudged her as Mr. Carver ushered them to his classroom. "Who'd like to go first?" Mr. Carver asked, opening his office door in the back of the room. Katie looked at Tristan and silently implored for him to let her go last.

"It won't make any difference," Tristan said, glancing in her direction. "I'll go first."

Katie exhaled. He was right, it wouldn't make any difference, but she wasn't ready to say goodbye to the world as she knew it. She waited ten too short, minutes before Tristan came out of the office. She had been too busy having a mental breakdown to notice him walking over.

"You'll be fine. Just remember to breathe."

She nodded, her hands sweating.

"Want me to wait?" he asked in a way that startled her. Why was he being so nice if this was a piece of cake? "It's not that." He offered a smile.

She shook her head as Mr. Carver called her in.

Katie walked into the office and was surprised by the presence of another man. He was tall, lean, and dressed in a jet-black suit. *A stylish executioner.*

"This is Mr. Reynolds. He's a—good friend of mine, and he's going to help us with your evaluation." Mr. Reynolds stuck out his hand for her to shake. When she saw the moon tattoo on the inside of his wrist, he winked.

"I'm a werewolf, but I promise I won't bite." She shook his hand, and he gave her a firm but soft jerk. "How do you do, Miss Watts?" He had an English accent and sounded much older than he looked. His hair was the color of ditch water, and his chin was covered in stubble.

"I'm fine, thank you," Katie said, clearing her throat. She sat down in the only chair in the tiny room. A tiny, frail-looking window behind Mr. Carver's desk let in a little sun—dusk particles floating in the rays. All of his office looked like that frail window—seconds from falling apart. The walls bulged a little; his desk was wood, but flimsy; and the books stacked up to the ceiling looked older than her.

"It's a bit warm in here. No—maybe it's just me," Mr. Carver laughed. "Let's get started then. Katie, we'll give you about five minutes to find your center, and then I want you to imagine power right there in your core. You'll know when you are ready, at that time just hold out your hand, palm down." There was an eerie silence sitting in the room with them. "Is everything clear, Katie?" he asked.

She nodded.

"Then begin."

She closed her eyes and followed the same breathing patterns she did when moving herself into Tristan's mind, but instead of thinking about Tristan, she imagined a small circle in her stomach. It glowed like an ember. First a dull green, a violent orange, a fiery blue, and finally a blazing silver. It had come too easy, like it was there all along, waiting for her to see it. It moved, a flickering flame in her mind, and then throughout her body.

She tingled with excitement because she had never felt anything as magnified as this. She felt suspended in the air. Was this what it felt like? She held out her hand, palm down. But soon, she started to feel overwhelmed. The fire was growing with nowhere to go, getting bigger and bigger, as if it would blow her body to bits.

There was pressure against the back of her hand, followed by a deep growl.

A gust of icy wind slapped her face as she jumped out of the chair. Her head was going to explode.

Slowly, the sensation subsided, and she was left breathing hard, backed up against one of the bulging walls. Mr. Reynolds held his hand to his chest, letting out a string of curses. Books had fallen from a stack, and pages floated to the ground. Confused and shaking, she looked at Mr. Carver. He was standing by the window, frozen. Wind filled the room with cold air.

"What happened?" Katie said, looking from Mr. Carver to

Mr. Reynolds.

"That's a good question" Mr. Carver said with his eyebrows raised. He still held onto the windowsill. He looked from the books on the floor to her, and to Mr. Reynolds.

"I'll tell you," Mr. Reynolds said with a laugh. "That girl nearly seared my bloody hand off. You have a nasty bite, Miss Watts. And that's coming from me."

"Here, John. Put some of this on it," Mr Carver said, handing him a tube of ointment from his desk drawer. "That was extraordinary, Katie. You did it in less than a minute. I thought Tristan was remarkable. I kind of expected it from him though, he's a transfer, but you…"

"What do you mean?" Katie couldn't take her eyes of Mr. Reynolds. He didn't look angry, but she felt terrible. "I'm sorry. I didn't mean to—do whatever I did." But she did, didn't she? Wasn't she supposed to do what she did, or else get her memory taken?

"Well, actually you did. This"—he held out his hand with an angry red scar—"Isn't exactly what I signed up for, but Carver here didn't tell me these were advanced evaluations. I thought these were baseline evaluations."

"They aren't. I mean, they *were supposed* to be base-line. I didn't expect Katie to be able to—I had no idea you'd be this focused. Considering—well, you're new and all." Mr. Carver laughed. "You really did a number on his hand."

She felt all the blood rush to her cheeks. Katie apologized over and over.

"Oh, are you proud now, Carver?" Mr. Reynolds said, approaching Katie. Hesitantly, he put his hand on her shoulder.

She was embarrassed for smiling a little, and even more so for being consoled by a stranger. He was making her cheeks burn worse.

"Don't worry. My hand doesn't hurt all that much," he said, patting her shoulder.

"I guess we're all done then. We've got a starting mark for you. You can go now." Mr. Carver said.

She nodded, stepping over some of the books. She must have knocked them over when she jumped out of the chair. She started to pick a few up, but Mr. Carver waved her out of the room.

"A *starting* mark?" Katie murmured. She'd been freaking out this whole time and the evaluation was just to see where her starting point was?

"Yes, what did you think—Katie, dear girl, you have to start *reading* the handouts I give you. This was just to check your breathing exercises and to see if you were giving off any fluctuating sparks. No wonder you were sweating bullets—oh don't go blushing on me—off you go, you know I hate it when you kids look like I've been lecturing you—Go on."

Katie left, closing the office door behind her. She couldn't hold back the smile. She had to tell Tristan. She did it. Something she didn't even know existed. She was finally better at something than everyone else. She ran out of the empty classroom and straight into Tristan. He was like a rock.

She rubbed her head. "I did it." She smiled.

"I told you." He smiled back.

They turned as they heard clacking heels down the hall. Tristan put his arm around her shoulder. "Let's go hide in the library."

"Tristan. Skipping class?" Katie feigned a gasped.

"There's this girl. She's a bad influence."

"A girl?" Katie laughed.

"Yeah, she's my best friend. Crazy though." Their legs were in sync with each other, and she wished she were like him. He was confident, strong, rational, did everything deliberately, and always knew exactly what he wanted to say. He didn't freak out about anything, really. She was the exact opposite.

"That's not true. You're confident in your own way, you're stronger than you give yourself credit for, and…well, you *are* erratic and irrational, but those can be redeeming qualities."

"Oh?"

"Yeah, ever seen *The Gremlins*?"

She laughed despite herself, "I hate you."

"No, you don't." He smiled. "You love me."

"Ha!" She rolled her eyes. She couldn't think of anything witty. She was stuck on the word *love*. "Race you the rest of the way," she said, sprinting towards the library. It was the only way to bury the sound of her fluttering heart.

⚬❦⚬

The next time she saw Mr. Carver was in Field Study, and this time she was happy to see him. He announced they'd be going on a field trip. To Gray City. Katie was excited and freaking out at the same time. What would it be like? If it was a field trip, it couldn't be too dangerous, then again, they weren't in this program to live a safe life…

The field trip was tomorrow, Friday, and apparently everyone already knew that except her.

"The flier has been on the board for weeks, Kay," Allison said as they left class.

"She doesn't read the board," Tristan answered. She could hear him mocking her. "Katalina, it's not mockery if it's true. You don't read anything. It's like you're allergic to words."

"I just might be!" Katie shouted. Traci wanted her to read this and that and more of those. It was a miracle she still had working eyes.

The next day, Katie didn't *read* anything. It frustrated Traci, who gave her a lecture on self-betterment, but Katie couldn't help it. She was going to Gray City after lunch. *The* Gray City. How could she concentrate on anything else? A place where mystical creatures really existed.

She was the only one who seemed to care. Everyone else just chalked it off as a free half day. They were told to bring a pair of jeans to school—clean, no rips or tears, and preferably dark so they could match, because they were still Hamilton High students.

After lunch, Mr. Carver handed out black t-shirts with big letters in yellow print:

JG

Junior Guardians

They were walking billboards, but Katie didn't care as long as she wasn't the only one wearing it. They all changed. Except Tristan, who walked out still in his uniform. He said something to Mr. Carver and winked at her before he left. He was up to something, and as they loaded the yellow bus, she realized he wasn't going.

The giant pang gripping her chest was disappointment. When had she started getting these feelings? When did thinking about the way he smiled start making her giggle like an idiot? Allison gave her a confused look as the bus drove off.

The bus drove past Kat's Ice Cream shop, took a left at the one store that sold maps, and Katie realized they were moving into the heart of downtown. The bus stopped at a small restaurant, and no one seemed alarmed. Was it a pit stop? Was Gray City a small bistro called *Viva*?

"Okay everyone, please move in your pairs—Katie, Allison? Why don't you two pair up since both your partners are out sick."

Sick? Tristan sick? Katie rolled her eyes and smiled. She wondered what he was doing now…

"Admit it already," Allison said, opening the door of the bistro. Olive oil and balsamic vinegar filled Katie's nose. Her mouth watered.

"Admit what?" Katie said, hoping she hadn't spent the last minute ignoring everything Allison said. Mr. Carver was leading them all into a private room.

"That you're crushing. Hard."

Katie blushed. Was it that obvious? What if Tristan knew? How could he not? He was in her head all the time. But she was careful around him. And who said she was even crushing?

Mr. Carver cleared his throat. "Okay, four at a time. Wait at the bottom." He opened a door, and Katie and Allison were the first to go in, followed by Michael and Ethan. They were in an elevator, but the number panel was different. It was a keypad. Mr. Carver punched in a series of numbers while everyone pretended not to look. It must have been a secret. Katie couldn't remember the numbers anyway, and from the look of Michael's smile, it wasn't as big of a secret as she thought.

He left the elevator, and as soon as the doors closed, they were falling. Her feet never left the ground, but her stomach rose into her chest.

She was glad when it was over. Her feet felt oddly light, and her organs tumbled when it got the memo that she was planted on the ground again. The elevator door opened, and they were in a quiet lobby. It was a decent looking hotel with a large seating area and bar. A man behind the bar eyed them until he saw their shirts. He nodded.

Allison dragged Katie to a couch. "Don't tell me you aren't. It's written all over your face.

"Aren't what?" Katie said as a woman walked through the lobby doors. Katie stole a look out a window. The outside was lit up like downtown at night. Katie *pretended* not to know what Allison was talking about, but pretending wasn't hard when she was genuinely interested in what lay beyond that front door.

The elevator chimed. Four more people got out and moved towards them.

"Kay, Tristan isn't the only one who can read you like a book. You're always staring at him like—like that. That goofy look you get when you hear his name." Allison smiled. "You two are pathetic. It's so cute it makes me gag."

"What do you mean, *you two?*" Katie waited. Butterflies took off with her innards—stomach, guts, and all. Did Allison think he liked her too? Not, *too.* She didn't like him. Not Tristan. Not like that. He was—the person who was making her smile right now.

Fiddlesticks.

The elevator chimed again. "You both get that same look when you see each other. I'm totally jealous. Someone needs to look at me like that," Allison sighed.

Did he?

The elevator chimed again and again, and Allison went on talking about someone's ugly shoes, but Katie didn't hear a word. Not until Mr. Carver was herding them out into the city.

It was the moment Katie had been waiting for.

She took her first step out into Gray City and stopped. It was—normal.

A city.

People walked up and down the illuminated streets. Cars drove by and stopped at red lights. Chatter and city noise filled the air. The only strange thing was it was dark.

Everyone drifted off into their groups, and even Allison

lagged behind with Adam, who'd beaten Katie in the preliminaries. It turned out he *was* nice, but she still never talked to him much.

Katie tried to stay close to Mr. Carver. He didn't seem to notice that everyone else was ignoring him as he played their tour guide. He pointed out the hospital and historical homes belonging to well-known vampire families. The city, he explained, had been around for over a hundred years now, one of the newest underground cities to be built.

To the left, down 8th Street, was the werewolf district. Many werewolves owned restaurants, and a few were notable among the underground cities of America. "I sometimes find the meat a little too raw though." Mr. Carver chuckled.

Katie shrugged. Maybe it was supposed to be a joke? As they crossed the street, she caught a glimpse of a sign: *The Pub*. It was a bar. Apparently werewolves were *a little too* unoriginal too.

"Here," Mr. Carver said directly to her, now that he realized she was the only one next to him. "Down 12th Street is called Shadow District. This street, specifically, is the fashion district. A little Soho, if you will."

Despite its name, it was not any darker or ominous-looking than Main Street on a Saturday afternoon. How—odd.

"Mr. Carver?" Allison said behind them. "Have you ever been to SoHo?"

Mr. Carver shook his head, and Allison gave him a five-minute speech on why 12th Street was not a little SoHo.

Katie still couldn't believe it. It was all so grossly *normal*.

People passed by her. Vampire? Werewolf? She couldn't tell. For all she knew, she wasn't even underground.

Mr. Carver stopped the group as a man walked up to him. The man pointed up and down the streets as they talked. Katie looked around. They were across the street from a club that pumped indie music.

"Oh! Remember that night Brian got plastered?" Michael said to Ethan and Christi. They were staring at the same bar. Katie had gotten used to ignoring their existence, even more so now that Brian wasn't with them, but now she leaned in as they spoke.

"I wonder if his puke is still on that mailbox," Ethan laughed, pointing across the street. Three cars sped by.

Maybe they don't have speed limits in Gray City.

Katie leaned closer but they eyed her and dropped their voices.

Whatever.

"They're just allowed to go out like that? Into clubs and drink?" Katie asked Allison.

"No, but they don't really card down here," Adam said. He looked bashful that he'd said anything. Maybe he thought Katie still held a grudge from the preliminaries—or her horrible attitude early this year. She smiled.

"How many times have you been down here?" she asked him.

"Unsupervised? Ten? Fifteen?"

Katie nodded. This entire time she'd been thinking Gray City was some uber shady place with dark alleys and rampant gun men.

Adam said something, and Allison laughed.

Katie wished Tristan was standing next to her. Of course he saw this place differently. *He'd* been here more than ten or fifteen times. He knew the nooks and crannies.

Then again, he promised her he wouldn't come down here anymore. Maybe that's why he skipped out on the field trip. He was keeping a promise. Katie smiled again. She felt so stupid and happy and in…

No. Definitely not that.

∗ ∗ ∗

Mr. Carver finished the tour up with showing them more popular destinations and guardian hubs. There was a guardian hub on every major street. Hotels, bars, restaurants, trinket shops. People owned actual stores down here, and even a blood shop, where Lucinda must have bought blood for Tristan. And, to everyone's disappointment, they spent half an hour in a "Getting To Know The New You!" community center—where Mr. Carver mentioned extra credits for weekend volunteer work.

On the way back to the "topside" as Mr. Craver called it, Katie tried to stay engaged with Adam and Allison as they talked about studying for midterms, restaurants they'd been to with their mentors, and people they'd met down here. She couldn't. She looked up and down the streets for Tristan.

Katie knew he wasn't there, and yet, he was on the face of everyone she walked by. He was in the windows of the shops they passed, maybe that guy looking for hats, or that guy boarding a bus. He was everywhere.

"Kay. Kay? She's gone again," Allison said.

"What?" Katie turned around. She'd walked past the hotel everyone was walking into. "Oh."

The ride up the elevator wasn't as bad as the ride down, but the drive back to the school was long. Love songs were on the radio, and she hid her face in the window every time Allison looked at her. Was it that obvious? Why was she thinking about him like this? Katie knew from experience that friendships are better left at just that. What if she kissed Tristan, and it turned out to be like kissing a fish? No. Not with lips like his—full, never dry, probably soft.

No.

No.

No.

The bus pulled into the school. The thoughts had to stop. She was only thinking them because—it didn't matter *why,* they just needed to stop. Her life was complicated and awkward enough without him hearing *those* thoughts.

"What thoughts?"

Katie jumped and smacked against her open locker door. What was he doing there? *When* had he got there?!

Her heart seized. *Good grief.*

"What are you hiding?" His voice drifted from behind her locker door. She couldn't look at him. Not now. God. Not right now. "Katalina," he sang, holding out the 'ahhhh.' Why did that make her smile?

Her locker began to swing closed, and there he was. Smiling

from ear to ear. "How was the field trip?"

"It was fun." She fidgeted with her mouth, trying to suppress a smile.

"What am I not supposed to hear?" he said, moving closer to her. She caught a whiff of his hair. Bar Soap. Clean. He bent down to her eye level. Blue. They were so blue today. Blue and unblinking. His nose was very close to hers.

It was coming back.

No.

Tristan smiled bigger. "What did you do? You are acting *very* suspicious." His eyebrows were bouncing. What an idiot. A cute—

His eyes got bigger.

"NO!"

"You think my eyebrows are cute? I get them from my mom you know," he winked.

Katie laughed and pushed him. To her surprise, he lost balance and fell backwards.

She laughed again.

Tristan squinted his eyes and smiled. "I'm giving you a five-second head start."

She took off running with him hot on her trail.

13

HALFBREEDS & EGGNOG

SNOW BLANKETED THE ground around them as Tristan went over Lucinda's mini boot camp for the Christmas holiday. They had to get more serious about their training ever since Lucinda caught them throwing mud at each other and called them clowns, but they still used any opportunity when she was distracted to goof around.

Katie didn't mind boot camp though. She loved training and the dull burn she felt every morning when she stretched her muscles, and running with Tristan shouting out, "Detour!" every time they got close to Lucinda's house.

She didn't have so many bruises now, and she was getting faster and faster every day. She *felt* stronger and lighter. Even now, after a long morning practice, she felt fresh—except for the hole in her stomach that wanted to consume all of the cookies Lucinda was making. She could smell the sugar cookies now, mixing with the thick cold wet outside. They were probably right out of the oven.

"Boot camp, Katalina. No Christmas cookies for you," he said, poking at her stomach.

She jumped at the touch and laughed, slapping his hand out of the way. They sat down on the porch and stretched.

"Grinch. I'm eating at least six. Even if I have to fight you for it."

"Is that a challenge?" he said, throwing a light punch. She dodged it and punched him in the arm, harder than she meant to. He grabbed his arm. "You're getting good. Really good."

"Got that right." She flexed her arm. Her muscles were defined. She *was* good. "You really think I've gotten good?"

"Doesn't matter what I think. You've got less bruises to prove it," he said.

Yeah, but what do you think of me?

He studied her. She blushed under his gaze. It was like the one from a few days ago, long and contemplative. She'd caught him looking at her legs. What she would give to know what he was thinking.

He smiled. "That I have to start pumping more iron to keep up with you."

◈

It snowed every day leading to Christmas Eve. Lucinda went crazy, putting up decorations in any space she could find. Will hid from Lucinda after she made him rehang the stockings over the living room fireplace. Brian was making more of an appearance, but he left early and stayed out late. Every day before practice, she'd hear Will yelling at him.

Katie made Tristan help put up—even more—Christmas lights in the front yard. His face was dark against the mounds of snow on the ground, and his pink lips and blue eyes popped more than usual.

She couldn't help but laugh as he attempted to make the lights look nice. They'd always droop where they were supposed to hang and hang, where they were supposed to be in a line. "Have you *ever* put up Christmas lights before?" She pointed at a sad little cluster of red.

"No," he said stiffly.

She brushed hair out of her face. "Seriously?"

"Never." He wore his crooked smile, but it didn't fool her.

"Didn't you celebrate Christmas?"

"I don't like to remember." His face hardened and he looked at her. She felt The Black Void brooding under the surface, and she was glad he let her feel it—glad he didn't mind being exposed in front of her.

She focused on fixing her sections in silence. As they worked, The Void eased away, but there was still a stark loneliness around him. It was in the blanket of untouched snow and in his footprints when he'd disappear around a corner.

⋅⊛⋅

The Andersons had their Christmas Eve party that evening. Every year, people came dressed in their best. They'd always gape at the majestic winter wonderland that was once yard; they'd admire Lucinda's modern, yet traditional color scheme—red and green with gold metal works—and gasp at the transformation of the house into a ballroom fit for a gala; and Lucinda would modestly deflect admiration for her custom-made gown onto the catering company or hired entertainment.

This year was no exception. Katie looked forward to it every year. Even more now that her dad was not only invited, but had also agreed to go. It would be awkward, but she knew she'd at least enjoy the pumpkin bars and Tristan's disapproval as she stuffed as many down as she could.

This year, she wanted to dress up and be pretty. She didn't dare let herself say why because she knew it was stupid. Tristan never treated her like more than just a friend—except yesterday, when he snuck up behind her and tousled her hair. His fingers had moved through her hair slowly, but quick enough to not be considered anything more than just that—a friendly hair tousle.

Katie got dressed with Allison at Lucinda's house after helping with the last of the preparations. Allison loaned her a pretty dress. None of Katie's old dresses fit properly anymore. They were loose and baggy. This dress was a red a-line with a cut-out back. She loved everything about it except that the top of the dress fit tightly around her breast. It was too much.

"I'm falling out everywhere," Katie said, looking at herself in the mirror. Allison fixed Katie's hair in a decorative bun and finished by placing a jade-green butterfly comb on the side of it. Her breasts were not only visible but accentuated by the dress. So was her necklace, the green-and-gold turtle matching perfectly with the comb. Maybe she should take it off? It looked kiddish next to the dress.

In the room, she felt pretty—maybe sexy—but if she left the room, it was too much.

"You aren't eight anymore. You're seventeen. It's okay to be semi-sexy. Besides, you think anything short of a turtleneck shows off your tiny boobs. You're so paranoid." Allison wore a dark green curvy dress, her hair pulled up with spiral curls, and a smile that could stop traffic. A chic red-headed elf. Katie wished she could be as confident as her. Allison could wear a paper bag and be bold and beautiful.

Katie was torn between practicing an over-the-shoulder glance she could use on Tristan and finding a nice sweatshirt to throw over her body, but Allison pushed her out of the room. She focused, instead, on making it down the hall and to the stairs without somehow messing up her makeup or hair.

Everyone must have been at the party already because the house was full of moving bodies laughing and hugging. Katie prayed she wouldn't trip going down the stairs and have a wardrobe malfunction. The last thing she wanted was a room full of people staring at her boobs. *Even if they are small—thanks Allison.* The thought of that alone made her sway a little before she got to the bottom step. She sighed, relieved when Will walked up with a drink.

"Merry Christmas. Take a sip. Just don't tell Lucy." Will passed them his glass of eggnog. She tasted it and wrinkled her nose, passing it to Allison. The smell of alcohol always made her dizzy. They gave him back his glass, and he winked, leaving them to enjoy the party.

Katie and Allison moved through the room, saying hello to old, familiar faces and new ones. Mr. Reynolds and Mr. Carver laughed loudly with a group of men by the fireplace. Mr. Reynolds, searching around the room, locked eyes with her. She blushed. The last time she saw him, he was cursing about his hand. He probably thought she was crazy. He raised his glass to her before directing his attention back to the group.

Mrs. Barnes was there, but Katie hardly recognized her. It must have been the dress, bright green and squeezing and pulling. It made her normal Frankenstein-body, frogish.

Many faces smiled at Katie. She felt pretty.

"Allison."

"Hi, Mr. Heckler. How are you?" Allison said, shaking hands with the tall, thin-lipped man Katie had met the day she met Tristan. The man who'd brought Glock.

"I'm doing well," he said, smiling. He extended his hand out to Katie.

"Katie Watts. It's a pleasure to meet you again. Mr. Carver won't stop talking about his three favorite students. I expect nothing but the best from the daughter of Katalina Rockwell and Drew Watts. That is fine lineage. The Rockwells date back to the fifteenth century. Fine lineage. This Tristan, I thought he was a little strange, but he turned out to be a star. Where is he?"

"Nice to meet you again, Mr. Heckler. I'm not sure where Tristan is," she said, shaking his hand.

"No matter. Mr. Carver is saying you've broken records. A bright young lady, like our rising star, Allison." He flashed a smile at Allison. "I look forward to writing you both recommendations for Elite Force entry positions. I always say, '*it's the amazing young women who pave our future.*' Do you know my son, Michael?"

Katie and Allison shared a look. "He's in a few of my classes." Katie held back a laugh. *He's also the most annoying kid in those classes.*

"Michael is around here somewhere, I'll make sure he says hello to you girls."

Katie and Allison nodded, smiling graciously until they got far enough to make faces.

"I swear, every time I see that man he's trying to set some poor girl up with his son. I bet he'd like you dating Michael with your *fine Rockwell lineage,*" Allison said, impersonating Mr. Heckler.

Between *Silent Night* playing softly above them and the normal-ness of it all, Katie felt amazing. She even caught her dad talking to a few people she didn't know. He looked happy enough.

Katie danced with Allison, who got an unexpected peck under mistletoe by Adam. Katie made a face at Allison, but she pretended not to notice. Even Brian seemed to be in high spirits. He laughed loudly and gave Katie a hug when she bumped into him, almost as if he'd forgotten he was supposed to avoid her.

Even Christi was at the party—Brian must have invited

her. She smiled at Katie, wearing a sleek black dress Katie would have thought was cute if anyone but her was wearing it. She remembered what Christi had said a few months ago, about them seeing a lot of each other now that she was a guardian. It must have been Lucinda chastising Will, as he sang a loud rendition of *"Grandma Got Run Over By A Reindeer"* over the string quartet, that put Katie in an over-the-top Christmas spirit, because she smiled back at Christi and sort of meant it.

Katie had been around the room two or three times with Allison, small talking to people she didn't recognize. All the while, she looked for Tristan, the one person she really wanted to see. The *only* person she wanted to see. She left the party and checked his room and the rest of the house, but he wasn't anywhere. The last place was the backyard.

He was standing by one of the large pine trees, they'd decorated, that lit up the snow covered yard.

"Tristan," she said, wishing they were in his warm room and not out in the cold.

He turned around and stopped short, giving her a long look. Katie wished she'd grabbed that sweater. What had she been thinking wearing something like this? She obviously looked like she was trying way too hard to get attention, and he was probably laughing at her—and hearing everything right now.

She stared at the blinking lights and decided she didn't care.

He smiled.

"I just wanted to see where you were. You should come inside." She heard the start of *Jingle Bells.*

"I don't know anyone in there." He was handsome in his black suit. He looked like he belonged in there more than anyone else.

"You know me." She rubbed her arms. He knew her better than anyone else at the party. She watched him watch her. The fresh smell of pine coming off the tree filled her nose in the thin, cold air.

"Go inside before you get cold."

"It's no fun without you," she said, chattering her teeth for extra effect. He was alienating himself because inside were a bunch of people who had Christmas' and families and stories to tell. He wanted his own family and his own stories. The ones he had were too much to talk about. She understood that. Every time she glanced around the party, she'd wonder what it was like to see her own mom laughing and singing Christmas songs. If her mom would have bought her a dress and taught her how to be pretty. She almost had that.

"That's a bit grim, Katalina."

"Then help me clear my mind. Come in with me. Have fun with me."

"On one condition," he said, walking over to her. His usual smirk appeared on his face. It made her smile. Not the closed mouth kind, but the kind where it seemed like a no matter how big or long she smiled, it wasn't enough.

"Sure."

"I get to tell the pervert story."

"Tristan!" she hissed. "Jesus, can you forget that already?" She couldn't stop her cheeks from burning.

"I'll never forget anything as vivid as that—just like when you tried to honeypot me."

"I was not. You seriously have a dirty mind."

"*You* were holding *me* down and biting me. I don't even have to mention your shocking Russian accent. I don't even think it *was* Russian." He laughed his contagious, easy laugh.

"You know what? I give you permission to fantasize about it however you want. I know what really happened."

"So I have permission to fantasize about you now?"

She burned so much the snow around her melted. Her stomach dropped into a free fall. She swallowed, trying to slow the banging in her chest.

"I didn't mean it like that. You don't have to go all stiff on me. It was a joke, Katalina. Stop staring at me like I'm a perv."

"I wasn't." She half-laughed, cursing herself.

There it was, that weirdness that sometimes happened to them. Like a train that just jumped tracks.

"We should probably go inside."

She nodded and took the biggest breath of her life. Why was she such an idiot? Tristan nudged her with his elbow. "You look really nice. No pervertedness intended."

She blushed, the words '*thank you*' caught in her throat because she was scared of what saying it would give away. "Tristan, I don't think you're a pervert."

"Oh, I know. You're projecting *your* true feelings on me," he said, opening the back door.

"Really?" she laughed, stepping inside. "That's your theory?" He closed the door behind her.

"Who honeypotted who?"

"Stop saying that," she said, moving toward the growing voices. She stopped in the hallway before turning the corner, and peeked at the party. She didn't want to be a part of everyone else yet.

"Why?" he said right behind her. His breath brushed the back of her neck. His chest pressed against her back as he peered over her shoulder. The pressure was warm. Her stomach jumped up, down, sideways, and around in circles. It took a world of strength to turn her body into him casually.

"Why what?" she said, stretching her neck to look at him. He didn't move back or give her space. He didn't smile or blink.

"Why don't you want to go in there?"

She swallowed. She couldn't say it. *It* was a lump in her throat burning to be out. She forced herself not to think it, even though it was obvious.

"It's really not. You—should say it."

Her chest thumped so loud she was sure it could be heard over the music. Her throat burned as she opened her mouth to say what she'd been feeling—what she *was* feeling. That she… but she couldn't. She stood so still, she shook.

He leaned closer, just as still as she was, his heart pounding hard against her back. She felt every beat, just as fast as hers.

They were too close to pretend it wasn't what it was. Did this mean he was meeting her halfway?

Katie leaned in closer…

"There—you are," Allison said, making them both jump apart. Her eyes grew wide as she realized what she had walked in on. "Uh—a few of us from school got together in the dining room. We're gonna playing cards. Just thought I'd find you before we start."

Katie lost her voice. It was still stuck in between her and Tristan. His lips were so close to hers. His eyes were on *her* lips.

Katie nodded, taking deep breaths, and followed Allison to the dining room, aware of Tristan's arm brushing against her as they went. He let his fingers brush against hers, and if they happened to connect for a second, he made no effort to pull them away, and neither did she.

Her insides were smiling again. She walked with a little bounce, scared, and yet hoping he felt it.

When they got to the dining room there were only two seats left—next to each other—and she smiled again. "Do you want anything to drink?" Tristan asked. His voice was a little raspy. He cleared it. For the first time ever, she saw his cheeks turn pink.

"Soda. Thanks," she said, finding it hard to look at him. Not without her heart jumping around like a caged maniac. He left, and she sat down.

She was surrounded by Brian's new friends: Ethan, who was staring at Allison in a creepy kind of way; Christi, who was talking Michael's ear off; Adam, who was smiling at Allison; the girl Jenn Black who beat the crap out of her in preliminaries; and, of course, Brian, who was getting up from his seat across from her. Probably to run and hide.

To her surprise, it was exactly the opposite. He sat in the seat next to her. "Hey." He smiled and his eyes formed little rainbows. There was a hint of alcohol and eggnog on his breath, and his face was tinged with pink.

"Hi." They sat quiet for a second, listening to everyone else's conversation.

"I'm sorry. For everything. I really am. I miss you. A lot." He looked at her, probably waiting for her to say something back. But she didn't have anything to say. She had been waiting so long for this apology that she'd forgotten all the lines she had prepared. "I'm not just saying this because you look really pretty, which you do. I'm sorry. This is coming out all messed up." He took a deep breath. "I've wanted to say something for a while now, but you're always with Tristan. I don't know how many times I've stood by the back door waiting for you to take a water break." He stopped and closed his eyes. "That sounded even worse didn't it? I'm sorry."

"No, it's okay," she said, wanting to stop him. She had imagined him groveling for her forgiveness a thousand times, but seeing him do it, listening to him try, hurt something in her—like watching him fall in training. "I get it. Water under the bridge."

"Friends again then?" he said, grabbing his cup from on the other side of the table. He took a drink and smiled at her.

"Sure," she said, smiling back. He grinned and hugged her. A laugh escaped her as he gave her a squeeze. They let each other go and laughed again.

"Okay, enough girl stuff," he said with a wink.

She sank when Tristan walked in the room carrying a single glass of fizzing soda. As soon as he saw Brian, his blue eyes hardened.

He handed Katie her drink. "You're in my seat," he said.

"There's a chair open right there," he said, pointing to the one across from them.

"Then go sit in it."

Katie cringed. They were like bulls kicking up dirt, ready to charge.

"What's your problem?" Brian said a little loudly. Everyone looked up. Tristan narrowed his eyes and opened his mouth.

"Okay, let's start the card game. Poker? Go Fish?" Allison said loud and overly cheerful. Katie offered Tristan a smile, but he frowned, moving to the empty seat across from her.

"I like Poker. Go Fish sucks," Jenn said. She had pretty green eyes that matched her strapless dress.

"I second that," Adam and Allison said, almost at the same time. They looked at each other then laughed. No one else said anything.

Allison dealt the cards, and Katie looked at her hand, completely confused. She didn't know how to play. Allison disappeared and brought back a bag of candy canes, Starbursts, M&M's, Skittles, and little Reese's cups. She gave everyone candy and explained the rules, but Katie didn't hear. She stared at Tristan.

He was watching her.

She pretended to play, but got lost in which candy was worth how much. It didn't help that Tristan threw random candies at her from across the table. Every time she looked up, he'd smile that crooked smile and his eyes would shine.

"Tristan, stop throwing money," Allison scolded.

Katie threw a candy cane back at him, aware of everyone's eyes on them. It made her feel superior in a way. No one else was in on their joke. They were the only two people in the room, and they belonged to each other. And everyone knew it.

"I don't know if that's more or less than what I've thrown at you," he said.

"This is why you don't throw money. Do I need to explain the currency again?"

Tristan threw two candy canes at Allison. "Is that enough to shut you up?"

Katie laughed so loud everyone stared at her, hiding their own laughs as Allison rolled her eyes.

"Michael! Would you eat a hundred dollar bill, Michael? Because that's what you're doing right now. That candy cane was a hundred dollar bill," Allison said.

Michael turned red and put his half-eaten candy cane back on the table. "Is it still worth fifty?"

Katie found Tristan's eyes, and they laughed. Laughing with him made her feel invincible. If she were wearing a garbage bag it wouldn't matter. He made her feel pretty. Katie grabbed a few of Allison's Skittles, sending Allison into a fit. "Stop eating my Skittles, Kay," she yelled, throwing her cards onto the table. Katie laughed so hard, she choked on Skittle juice.

She caught her breath and looked around the table. Everyone was laughing. They were all as red-faced as she felt, even Allison, who graced them all with her cancer curing smile. Faces she had grown to dislike and was envious of were smiling back at her. She'd always spent her time with Tristan and never considered the others as potential friends.

"How about we stop playing cards and just eat candy?" Jenn said. She had a nice smile too. Katie would have liked her if she hadn't slapped her in the head three times.

They all threw their cards into the middle of the table and unwrapped candy. Everyone except Tristan. He looked uncomfortable, stuck between pretending to eat, like he did at school, or sticking out. Katie stood up and grabbed his candy.

"You just got jacked by the candy ninja," she said before she realized how stupid it was.

"What?" Adam said, starting to laugh again.

"I don't think it's ninja if I saw you," Tristan said, stealing back a skittle. He popped it in his mouth and scrunched up his face. He squinted his eyes and swallowed hard.

"What's wrong? Don't like food?" Brian said, draining the rest of his eggnog.

"I almost forgot you were here," Tristan sighed.

"I live here."

"So do I."

"I did too once," Katie said. "You live down the hall, right?" She looked at Brian. "I *knew* you looked familiar."

"You *all* live together?" Christi asked. Her voice startled Katie. She had been so quiet—*how unlike her.*

"I don't anymore..." Katie trailed off. Talking about it felt like an invasion of privacy. She never should have mentioned it.

"Oh. How about you Tristan, you're Brian's cousin, right?" Christi wasn't taking the hint.

"Something like that," Brian said, raising his eyebrows.

"Sorry, it's just this is as much as I've heard you talk. You only hang out with Katie and Allison. Not that there's anything wrong with that." Christi gave Katie a look. The look bothered Katie. There was something behind it, like she was saying, *"it's true,"* or *"that's a good thing."*

Tristan raised his eyebrows and shrugged. Everyone in the room averted their eyes, pretending not to see his indifference.

"We might have all hung out last semester, but Brian kind of ditched us," Katie said. "I didn't mean ditch—" she turned to Brian and offered an apology.

"Well he did," Allison said under her breath.

"Don't be a bitch, Allison." Brian twirled his glass.

"Piss off." Allison smiled back at him.

If looks could kill...

Brian flicked Allison the middle finger—he always had to have the last word.

"Why *did* you guys stop being friends?" Michael said, sucking on the rest of his candy cane. "I thought you were like one step away from getting together."

"Seriously, Michael? Because that's not the most awkward question to ask right now," Jenn said.

Me and this girl could be friends.

Christi sat up straight. "Well that doesn't matter anymore. You and Tristan are like inseparable now, right?" she said, nodding her head. Katie wanted to hit her. Why was everyone talking about her love life? No. She didn't *have* a love life, they were making it into that.

"She can have more than one *friend*, Christi." Brian frowned.

"That's right, only you dump off one set of friends for the other, right?" Tristan said.

Katie cleared her throat. "How about we *all* be friends? Kumbaya? Anyone bring a guitar?" Katie forced a smile, but no one smiled back. She was no longer in control of the situation. It was turning into something—something dangerous.

"I only stopped because she started hanging around you," Brian spat back at Tristan.

"Okay, that's a lie," Katie said.

"No, it's not. You two were inseparable the day he got here," Brian said with astonishment scribbled on his face.

"You've *got* to be kidding me. You started avoiding me the day after preliminaries, and you know why. Don't give me that bullshit you're spewing. I'm not stupid."

"Bullshit? You've been 'buddy buddy' with him, rubbing it in my face. Like *you've* found a new best friend."

"You're delusional, Brian." She flung M&M's across the table by accident, but she was too mad to apologize.

"And you're spiteful, Katie," he sang back.

"Spiteful about what? You ditching me when I needed you?"

"You're so full of yourself."

"*Me? I'm* the one with a ego problem?"

"Yes. I made new friends and you can't stand that. Ever since then you've been a spiteful little shit."

"I am not some clingy little girl," Katie yelled.

"*Ha!*" Brian twisted his lips into a cruel smile.

"If anything, I think she'd be spiteful about you using her as target practice," Tristan said.

Michael grabbed a few stray M&M's "Wait, *you* shot *her?* I thought Katie shot *Jenn* in the head during preliminaries. I did hear that right, right?" Michael said, stuffing M&M's into his mouth.

"It was an accident," Brian mumbled.

Tristan smirked. "Like you being a guardian?" An eruption of laughter from the adjacent party filled the room. It was obnoxious. Unwelcomed.

"Ouch," Ethan chimed. Katie wanted to get up and rip his throat out. Where had he come from? He was like a fly on the wall, big and irritating. A disgusting fly. She wanted to set fire to his wings and watch him fall off.

"Hey, guys," Lucinda said, poking her head in the room. "Everyone come out I have an announcement to make." She winked at Katie before she saw the frowns on all their faces. "Everything all right?"

"Yeah, just ate too much candy," Katie said, trying to paste a smile on her face. She left the dining room feeling like the music was too loud, there was too much laughter, and too many smiles.

Lucinda waved Tristan up to the fireplace. Tristan tucked his hands into his pockets—a sign that he was annoyed.

"This year's party is more than just another Christmas party." All the talking dwindled. "We are also celebrating the fact that we have a new addition to our home. He's just as stubborn as me, but a wonderful boy all the same." There were kind laughs and light cheers as Lucinda raised her glass of wine in the air and everyone toasted to them.

Katie was taken aback. She smiled, but couldn't help feeling uneasy as she watched Brian in the corner, his head tossed back, draining another glass of eggnog.

"This is from Lucy and me," Will said, smiling bright. He handed Tristan a small box. "Don't worry, just a Christmas Eve present."

Inside was a homemade stocking for him, no doubt handmade by Lucinda. Tristan's face was unreadable. To everyone, he looked happy and thankful, but to Katie… She knew him too well to know that it wasn't a smile. It was a mask. He searched the crowd for her, and when their eyes met, she knew he hated the stocking. It meant that he had a home and was wanted. It meant he had to let go of all the anger and resentment that swarmed around his thoughts.

"That's just what this family needs. A halfbreed," Brian slurred. The chatter died as he made his way towards the fireplace, another glass in hand, this time full of a dark liquor. He wasn't even hiding it now.

"Where did you get that?" Lucinda said between gritted teeth.

Katie quickly moved to him, grabbing his arm. "Let's go, Brian." She needed to get him out of the living room before everyone noticed he was drunk out of his mind, and before Lucinda unhinged. But no one was looking at him. They were looking at Tristan.

"Get off me," Brian yelled, shoving Katie. His fingers caught in her necklace and it pulled, snapping off her neck. She crashed into a woman and hit the ground covered in eggnog and Brian's alcohol. Rum. She could smell it, and her mind started to spin.

"Tristan, don't!" Lucinda yelled. In an instant, Tristan moved toward Brian, and Katie was filled with his hatred.

I should have killed him, she heard him think.

Will stepped in front of him, and they stared each other down. Tristan's jaw was stiff. He breathed in and out rapidly, his nostrils flaring. "Does he have to *shoot* her again before you believe me?" Tristan said, only loud enough for her and Will to hear. He offered Katie a hand. Her hand touched his, and she felt it. All the eyes on *them*, shocked as if she were touching a rabid animal.

"You think you're better than me? You'll never be anything but halfbreed scum. You'll never be a part of this family," Brian yelled, red in the face. Spit flew from his mouth. "You think you can replace me?" Will back-handed him across the face. Brian fell back a few feet, and the room was filled with gasps. Eyes flickered between Brian holding his face, Will daring his son to say one more thing, and Tristan.

But the eyes of disgust lingered on Tristan. Somehow, he was worse than the toxic waste that oozed from Brian. Murmurs erupted throughout the room. What if they realized she was like him? People she had known for years. What would they call her…Katie or halfbreed?

Her dad was making his way towards them.

"Come on, Kay," Allison said, picking up the necklace from of the floor. It was lying in a puddle of eggnog. Tristan pulled his hand away and ignored her as she reached out to him.

She stared into his stormy blue eyes. The Black Void sent chaotic waves of rage and misery between them both—but he turned from her, pulling it all away. She felt nothing. Nothing but her own fear and fury.

Allison pulled her out of the living room, and Tristan disappeared from her sight.

14

WEREWOLVES & LIES

THE PARTY WAS dying. Katie could hear it die from upstairs. Allison was trying to get the eggnog out of the dress and cursing Brian to hell. There was a knock on the door. Katie opened it. Her dad. His eyebrows rested above his eyes as if to say, *"What did I tell you?"*

"Can you excuse us, Allison?" When the door closed he sighed. "Now do you see why I didn't want you to know? You saw the way they turned on him, and with just one word."

Katie said she didn't care, but it did unnerve her. Her dad looked out the window as people spilled out of the house like it was the site of an outbreak and they were all in danger of contagion.

"Will and Lucinda are going to lose face with all these hypocrites," he said, shaking his head. "They'll be lucky to keep their jobs. No one will want to work with them knowing they've been lying about Tristan."

When he finished his rant, she said goodbye to him, and he went home. She had packed a bag to stay the night. She had expected the party to last a lot longer than it did.

Will screamed at Brian nonstop. Though his voice was muffled, isolated words like, *"This is it,"* or *"Boarding school,"* floated through the wall. *Boarding school* bothered her more than anything else he said. Allison said that was code for where kids who got their memories erased. Will would never do anything like that. He was a calm man. But she never thought he'd hit Brian the way he did either. Always a light slap on the back of the head when he wanted to get his point across. Tonight he hit Brian like a man.

Lucinda kept creeping into her room and asking if she was all right, apologizing for Brian as if Katie were a stranger and she, completely embarrassed, was unaware of where the rage had come from, or that it was even there.

When all the noise settled down and Katie washed the eggnog out of her hair, it was a little past midnight. It was Christmas. She looked out the window, wrapped in her towel. Snow blew everywhere, big white puffs covering everything in sight. At least one thing had gone right amongst all the drama. She felt guilty. Tristan. What was he thinking right now?

She sat down at her desk and picked up the book she'd gotten him. She had gone back to the bookstore and bought that old copy of Othello. Touching it now made her sure he'd like it—leather-bound, soft, and a little droopy, the way an old worn book is. She could give him his present now—it *was* officially Christmas.

She put it back in the gift bag on her desk and brushed her hair. She put it in a braid, then decided it looked better loose. She put on her best tanktop that showed off her arms. She wished she'd actually packed the matching pajama bottoms. Instead, she'd packed the sweats that hung low. At least they'd show off her toned stomach.

She picked up the jade turtle Brian had given her. It was still sticky with eggnog, and it smelled sour. She put it back on the dresser.

What about her face? Lip gloss. She needed lip gloss.

She rummaged through the bottom desk drawer, shifting through candy wrappers, old essay papers, pencil shavings, and loose index cards she'd left here from a few months ago. Finally, there it was, a perfect stick of pink. Sweet cherry rolled across her lips. She used her towel to wipe most of it off, so they didn't look too shiny.

She grabbed the gift bag and eased down the hallway. She went down the stairs two at a time, skipping the last one that creaked. She started to knock, but held back a smile as she turned the knob instead. He'd know she was there.

It was locked.

"Tristan?" she whispered, feeling embarrassed. The door clicked and opened.

"Katalina?" he looked her over and half-smiled. She looked away, trying not to blush.

"I got you something," she held out the gift bag.

"Let me guess, Othello?" he said, taking it from her. "I heard you thinking about it a few minutes ago."

She felt deflated, silly, and stupid all at once.

"Sorry."

"It's okay. Just killed the surprise."

"The surprise isn't what makes it the best gift I've ever gotten."

She couldn't look at him, not with the stupid huge grin on her face. "So you like it?"

"Of course. It's from my best friend."

Best friend.

He walked to his desk and pulled out a package from the top drawer.

"You got me something?" The butterflies made it hard for her to breathe. She hadn't expected a gift.

"Yeah, a while ago." His thumb rubbed across the package as he studied it. Did he think she wouldn't like it? His eyes met hers.

"It's not the gift that makes it the best gift I've ever gotten." Her stomach leaped at the small smile he gave her. She took it. It was heavy. She opened it carefully to preserve the thoughtfully wrapped paper. She took the lid off a thin brown box and opened and closed her mouth until she said, "Wow."

In the box was a twin set of knives with ivory grips and printed pink roses climbing the grips in spiraling vines. Next to the knives was a silver-plated pistol with a grip that matched the knives. They shined with expensive beauty. "How much did these cost you?" She was afraid to touch them.

"Doesn't matter. That pistol will never misfire on you, and those knives are handmade to perfection."

She picked them up, one by one feeling the grace they exuded. They were light to the touch, an extension of her arm. Perfection. "Tristan, this *really* is the best gift I've ever gotten."

"I'm glad you like them."

"I love them." She looked up, ready to throw her arms around him, but he looked away.

"I've been thinking we should really push harder in training. Your hand-to-hand is pretty good, but you've got to work on being completely comfortable with a knife." He sat down on the other side of the bed. Pluto was closer to her than him. He wasn't looking at her, or being relaxed. He was calculating. "We have a good week before school starts back up. I bet we could get a lot done if we ask Lucinda to train three times a day."

Why was he acting like he couldn't hear her? If he knew she got him Othello, if he had been listening to her thoughts, he would have known she was coming down to give it to him. Why did he lock the door? If he had been listening, he would have known why she put on the cherry lip gloss and the stupid too-tight tank top.

"Is there something you're trying to tell me?" she said, feeling dumb and disgusted.

He stared at the floor. "What do you mean?"

"You're being—weird."

"Since when is me talking about training weird?"

"You know what I mean."

He raised his eyebrows and shrugged. That display of indifference and mock confusion. Pluto was also much warmer. But it was something more than that, something she hadn't felt for a while, until now. His wall.

"If you have something to say to me, just say it." She pushed back the hole she felt growing from the pit of her stomach out. It was eating everything in its path, leaving behind panic.

"Don't be a girl, Katalina. You're making this more than what it is."

"If I'm being a girl now, what was I before?"

"I don't know, normal."

"So I'm only any good if we're wrestling out in the backyard and making jokes?"

"We don't wrestle."

"Because *that's* the point I'm making."

"Well, yes—I mean no."

"Did you honestly just say yes?"

"I didn't mean that. I meant when we're training and joking around, that's normal. This, I don't know—you're being weird."

You might as well have called me ugly.

"That's not what I said. You don't look ugly. You're not ugly"

"So now you can hear me? If me being a girl weirds you out so much, why'd you open the door?" She balled up her fist, torn in between punching him in the face and crying.

"You don't see how I might think what you're feeling now is weird?"

She stood up and grabbed her box. "Thanks for the present, asshole."

"Katalina," he called as she swung his door open. She didn't care about being quiet as she ran up the stairs and to her room. She put the box on her desk and sat on the bed. She was shaking, she was so mad. She hated, absolutely hated him. How much of a jerk did someone have to be to go from nearly kissing her to complete indifference? She felt like a complete idiot. She opened up to him, treasured the fact that he let her in. Now she was paying for it, but she had learned her lesson.

⁕

Christmas was as pathetic as her relationship with Tristan. Will packed up Brian and flew him out to Seattle to live with his uncle. Lucinda cried in her room. Tristan didn't come out of his room, and at home Katie just sat in front of the TV with her dad watching *The Christmas Story*. It was a pathetic day. She couldn't think about anything except how she now hated Tristan with her every fiber. But she didn't, did she? Not really. If she did, she wouldn't have gone to bed early and cried.

Every day for the rest of break all she did was train, from sun up until she passed out. Lucinda worked them harder each day. And they accomplished a lot, now that they didn't talk. Katie almost skipped every lesson, but Lucinda was not in the mood to be crossed and Katie couldn't stay away anyway. She hated herself for it. It was always better to hate Tristan while he was standing in front of her, than if she didn't see him at all. Though, when she did see him, she let him hear just how much she hated every little thing he did.

She ignored everything he had to say if it wasn't how to punch straight or get more range when throwing a knife. When they were in the same room, he treated her the same way he used to—like she was going to laugh at one of his jokes at any moment. But he was finally starting to get the hint.

"He's a jerk," Allison said, sitting across from her at Jimmy Bean's Coffee shop. They were sipping on hot chocolate with marshmallows at a table next to a window. "But that's expected of him."

"Why?" Katie said. She had been patiently waiting to see if Allison was bigoted like Brian and everyone else at the party. She wanted to know if her best friend would look at her the way all those eyes had looked at Tristan.

"Because that's just how Tristan is. Mean and jerky." She took a sip of her hot chocolate. "Too bad you didn't get to make out first. I'm really sorry I interrupted."

"Allison, are you serious?" This was her chance. "He's a halfbreed."

Allison cut Katie a look that could have drawn blood. "Shut up, Kay. You don't even know what that word means. And if you do, you're not the person I thought you were." Allison's face was just as red as her hair.

"Allison…"

"No. No one should ever be called that. Like they're some

sort of animal. How would you feel? I'll never forgive Brian for what he said," she spat. "Just because his parents are elite, it doesn't make him royalty. Him and his stupid friends strut around like they're better than everyone—and *you*. Using that word."

"I didn't mean to…I didn't know it would bother you that much. That was stupid."

"Yeah, it was."

"I'm sorry." Katie couldn't help but smile to herself. She should have known better than to doubt Allison. Then again, she thought she knew Brian, and she thought she understood Tristan. They had fooled her. She didn't know who they were at all.

She finished her hot chocolate and pushed the cup to the middle of the table.

"I love her boots." Allison stared at the feet of someone behind Katie. She turned and saw a girl wearing a thick, but form-fitting, black sweater and pretty black boots over dark denim skinny jeans that she knew Allison would have killed for because they looked designer. She had tiny braids that went down to her butt and—was staring directly at Katie. The girl looked familiar. Did she go to their school? Whether she knew her or not, she was about to, because the girl walked straight to their table. Allison's eyes were still glued to her shoes.

"You don't remember me, do you?" the girl said. Her skin was smooth like slowly melting dark chocolate. She had a heart-shaped face with full lips and perfect eyebrows. "It's okay, I hardly recognized you. You look much better now than you did before." She pulled up a chair and sat down.

"Where did you get those boots? Those are the hottest things I've ever seen in my life." Allison said, looking at the girl for the first time.

"I don't remember. I think a small boutique in Manhattan," she said, looking Allison up and down. "You have good taste. In everything."

Allison blushed.

The girl looked back at Katie and a jolt shot through her. It was the eyes. They were beautiful. Hazel, with long lashes, just like the werewolf from the alley. The girl laughed, and it sounded like music. She pulled her shirt and sweater to the side to show a tiny scar on her shoulder.

"It's almost all gone now. I'm going to be really pissed if there is so much as a speck of scar left."

"You're the *werewolf?* The one from the alley?"

The girl nodded and glanced at Allison. Allison scrunched her brows.

"She's a guardian," Katie said, thinking the girl might have thought talking in front of Allison wasn't safe.

"I know she is," she said. "And it was me. Tristan and I weren't too far from here when he flipped out."

"Mercedes," one of the guys behind the counter said. The girl stood up and excused herself. The barista handed her a cup with a hand warmer, and she came back to the table.

She knew Tristan. She was *with* Tristan. Katie felt a rush of jealousy. This girl was beautiful. She was graceful *and* she was beautiful.

"What exactly are you guys talking about?" Allison knew Katie was keeping something else from her. Allison was told that Brian had an accident during a training exercise with Will that put him in the hospital. She didn't know anything of the alley.

Katie shrugged it off. "I was meeting Lucy and Tristan here the other day to—uh—see a werewolf. She was the werewolf."

Allison didn't believe one word. It was all over her face.

Mercedes sat down and looked between them. "Anyway, I've been looking for Tristan for the last few weeks. He stopped dropping by the pub," Mercedes said, crossing her legs.

Tristan went to pubs? And met up with girls like this? Her heart sank. She knew nothing about him.

"How do you know I'm a guardian?" Allison said abruptly.

"Because you smell like one. Pleasure with a hint of caution." Did Katie imagine the way she looked at Allison's shirt like a piece of rich chocolate? "That perfume is to die for, and that shirt—it's a ZaneFlo fall collection isn't it?" Allison's eyes lit up like stars.

"You're good," Allison said, jaw dropped. They raved about designers Katie never heard of and fabrics she didn't know existed.

"Why have you been looking for Tristan?" Katie said.

Mercedes paused and looked at her. "To be honest, in that shirt you're an eyesore. How could you let her out in public like that?"

Katie frowned and wrapped her arms over her baggy, faded, blue and green striped sweater.

"You should have seen the yellow one she had on before I made her change," Allison sighed.

"Yellow? With that complexion?"

"That's what I said!"

"Guys!" Katie nearly yelled. The last thing she needed was two Allisons picking on her. Mercedes' face shifted from confusion to contemplation. She was considering her words carefully.

"Just wanted to catch up with him."

Katie was as still as stone. She tried not to give away her desperation.

"Anyway, if you see him, can you let him know Mercedes has an answer for him?" Katie stared at her, blinking. An answer to what? What had they been talking about that required an answer? Katie didn't need to ask. She knew. You don't go to bars to talk about the weather.

Mercedes winked at her before getting up to leave.

"Wait," Katie said. Mercedes saved her life that night. Even if she was some secret Tristan was hiding from her, Katie owed her.

"Yeah?" she said, arching one of her perfect eyebrows. Why didn't Katie have eyebrows like that?

"Thanks. For that night—uh, for showing me what a werewolf looked like." Katie shifted her eyes towards Allison.

Mercedes took another sip of her coffee and left. Both Katie and Allison watched her walk across the street and disappear out of view.

Katie got up to get another hot chocolate. A tall man bumped into her nearly spilling coffee on her sweater.

"My apologies," he said, staring at her and raising an eyebrow. What? Could he see the look of utter defeat on her face? He was handsome for an old guy. Katie nodded and moved past him, back to her table.

Allison looked at Katie with a little pity. "I'm pretty sure they're just friends."

Katie hated that Allison knew what she was thinking. "She said he stopped seeing her. It was around the time you guys got pretty chummy right?" Allison said.

Katie glanced around the coffee shop, trying to hide from Allison's gaze. The man who'd nearly seared her with coffee was looking at her again. Even from here, she could see how his leering eyes were watching her. *Do I look that pathetic?*

"You'll never guess who just walked in," Allison said.

Katie turned but snapped right back around when she saw Tristan. "He can sit here if he wants. I'm not talking to him."

"Even if he apologizes ten more times?"

"Whose side are you on?"

"What? I said he was a jerk, but you can't say you didn't know that from the beginning."

She heard a chair scoot against the floor behind her. Allison shrugged, and Katie took a peek. He was sitting behind her, as if he hadn't noticed she was there, and reading the book she got him for Christmas. He'd have to do better than that.

She rolled her eyes at Allison and sipped more of her cocoa. Something soft hit the back of her head. She ignored it. Again, she felt a soft projectile smack against her hair. A tiny sugar packet hit the ground. Gripping the cup, she thought of all the ways she could beat him up without causing a scene.

Another packet hit her head, but this time it snagged onto her hair. That was it. She'd give him what he wanted. She'd say something to him. Something witty that would make him feel stupid. Another packet smacked the top of her head.

She turned around and faced him. "You know what? You're gonna have to pay for those packets you wasted. This is a coffee shop. People use those."

He threw a packet at her forehead. "That wasn't witty."

She stared him down, mad that she'd said something so stupid.

He smiled that crooked smile she hated. He smiled bigger.

"I hate you," she mumbled.

"Don't say that."

"I hate you."

"Think of what the divorce will do to the kids. Think of the kids, Katalina," he said, scrunching up his eyebrows.

Allison stood up. "I'd love to stay and watch this, but it's kind of uncomfortable."

Katie eyed her as she walked off toward the counter. So much for being on her side.

"Katalina."

She turned back to him. Trying to keep a straight face, trying to keep her mind quiet. But his eyes kept probing her, and she missed that stupid smile that was easing onto his face right now.

"I knew you missed me."

"Almost as much as I miss school."

"Don't be cruel." He pulled the sugar packet from one of the curls in her hair. She'd forgotten it was there. "Do you really hate me?" He fiddled with it in his hands, turning it over and over. When she didn't say anything, he looked up at her, eyes wide, like the world wouldn't continue to spin without her answer.

"No."

"Then you forgive me?"

"Do I have a choice?"

"Nope," he said, staring at his sugar packet.

"Then I guess we're friends again," she slapped his arm, because that's what friends do, not girls who are still a little angry at a giant idiot of a guy.

"You guys kiss and make up?" Allison said, walking up to the table. Katie shot Allison an evil eye.

"I'll make it up to you. How about we ditch practice?" He smiled. "Let's all go to a movie instead."

"Oh, I want to see the one about the zombies," Allison said, way too excited. Whose side *was* she on?

"Come on, Katalina. I'll meet you there at six." He stood up, not even waiting for her answer. "Six!" He smiled again and left.

She couldn't help but watch him until he disappeared from view. She would have preferred he'd stayed than go wherever he was going.

"You've got it bad," Allison said, digging through her purse. It could have easily housed two families and a dog.

"I do not."

"Kay." She stopped and looked at her. "You've had that same dopey look on your face for almost a month now."

"And look where that got me."

Allison delved deeper into the purse, half her arm consumed by it. "No one ever said you had good sense," she said, pulling out a stick of gum.

◦◦◦

They walked around downtown to kill time before the movie. It was getting late, and Katie hated being out past dark. She was always more deliberate with where she walked, more aware of her surroundings. She took note of who was on the street and where, like the couple arguing across the street. The odd man sitting in his parked car looking down at—maybe a cellphone? A weird—looking boy slouched over a bike rack down the alley they'd just passed. She saw them all.

Allison sighed. "My dad was supposed to call, like ten minutes ago. I swear, it's like he doesn't even have a daughter."

"He's not that bad. At least he didn't erase your memory."

Allison laughed, a short *humph*. "He tried once."

"What?" Katie looked at her profile, half her face covered by her sunglasses. An easy smile appeared, and it made her stomach knot. It was the smile Katie never liked. The one Allison used to mask the part of her she never let anyone see. Not even

Katie. Katie's eyes stayed forward on the road, and she waited for Allison to go on.

"It was last year. Right before the school year started, he asked me over and over if I was sure about the decision I'd made a year before. Half way through the school year, I was already the top in all my classes. Mr. Carver even asked me if I wanted to start preparing for my entrance exams for the Elite Force." She glanced at Katie. "That's a big freaking deal. I told my dad as soon as I got home, and all he said was, *'Carver's always been a teacher, never a doer. I'm surprised they let him pick the students for the exams.'* That night, after dinner, he said if I wanted, he'd take me to an omitter. That I still had a chance to be, *'just a girl,'* that the Elite Force wasn't for everyone."

"Seriously?"

"No, I made it all up." Allison frowned.

"That's not what I meant. I just can't believe it.

"I can't believe your dad erased six years of your life."

"I know," Katie breathed.

Allison moved her sunglasses to the top of her hair as they passed by the entrance of a spaghetti restaurant. "We should eat there after the movie," Allison said, sniffing the air.

Katie agreed, not really listening. She wondered where Tristan went. Had he seen Mercedes before he came in? Was he with her now? She hated herself for caring. For being excited that he invited her to a movie. It wasn't really a date because he'd invited Allison too, but still it was the first time they'd really do something outside of practice.

Tristan was waiting for them when they showed up at the theatre. He smiled when he saw Katie, and she pretended she didn't see him. They stood in line for tickets, and Tristan announced that he'd pay for them all. Katie wondered where he got the money, but realized it would always be a mystery, like his trips to the *pub*.

Tristan shot her a look, and the smile dropped off his face.

"That's thirty-dollars, please—Excuse me—"

Tristan tore his eyes away from her and paid.

As they walked toward the concession stands, a girl older than Katie approached them. "Hey, you. How've you been?" she said to Tristan. She was tall, she had sweet brown eyes, and more breast than Katie could ever hope for.

Tristan looked behind him as if she could have been talking to someone else.

"Tristan?" she said, smiling. She turned to Katie and Allison. "Oh hi, I'm Nicole."

Katie tried to hide how much she wanted to die. She had no choice but to smile and introduce herself. No wonder it creeped him out when she tried to be pretty. He was hanging out with girls like this.

"I'm sorry, I really don't know you." Tristan looked between them.

Don't lie for my sake. Katie excused herself and walked off to theatre number five. She seethed and even wanted to cry. He should have run after her. He didn't. Of course he didn't. She was the idiot, still wishing for him to make some romantic gesture.

The movie was crap. That was what Allison said. Katie didn't watch it. She sat there ignoring how Tristan looked at her every five minutes. Allison tried to talk through the tension, but it didn't work. Katie just wanted to go home.

They walked Allison home first because her house was the closest to the theatre. She looked relieved to leave them.

"Katalina—" Tristan said after ten minutes of silence.

"Don't talk to me."

"What have I done?" Tristan spat.

Are you kidding me?

"I didn't *do* anything. I—uuughhhh. You drive me crazy."

Katie got pleasure out of that.

"I didn't even know that girl. Even if I did, why is it a big deal? *We're* friends."

Katie walked faster.

He grabbed her hand, but she yanked it away. She hated it when he touched her. It made it worse. He knew that. He had to know that.

"Katalina—"

They were at the corner of her house. "Just go home. Leave me alone, Tristan." His name came out weak. She couldn't start crying now. Not in front of him.

"Katalina—"

"Go."

He stopped following her. "Fine." He sounded defeated. He was walking away, she could tell. She could always feel when he wasn't close anymore.

A boy who was in love with the girl who'd just told him to leave her alone would have followed her—*begged* her to hug him. He wouldn't have walked away.

She sat on her porch. Tristan didn't have the right to be upset. This was all his fault.

It was cold outside, but she took off her sweater anyway. She wanted to feel the cold on her skin. She wanted most of all to stop loving him. Because she did. That was what made her hurt the most. The fact that she loved him, he knew it, and he didn't care.

She welcomed the numbness climbing up her body, as new snowflakes danced from the purple sky and into the white dense fog surrounding her.

She closed her eyes and breathed. The night was quiet and lonely…

Crunch.

A footstep? She opened her eyes, and a bearded man stared back at her from across the yard. He smiled. The numbness turned into sparks of fear. She didn't move, and neither did he. Just the fog between them.

She stood up and stepped back towards the door. She could make it inside before he came closer. This was what she'd been waiting for. The paranoia she'd had. It was for him.

He shook his head, still smiling.

She took another step and everything went black. A bag was thrown over her head and tied around her neck.

She clawed at the fabric, but pulling at it was useless.

"Help!" The word was muffled, and a fist smashed into her ear. Her head blossomed into pressure-filled pain. She was clutched against a large body. They were running with her, and fast.

Her legs buckled under her, and they burned against snow and asphalt. She was being kidnapped.

"Help!" she screamed. She heard the sound of a car door opening. She wasn't going to let someone take her. She kicked her legs out, but it didn't stop her attackers. She called on her power, but nothing came. She couldn't concentrate. She was tossed in the air, a free fall, until her body crashed against metal.

Doors slammed, and she heard the roar of an engine.

"Go. Go!"

"Help!" she screamed, tasting blood.

A hand collided with her throat. Still, she kicked and punched into the darkness. They weren't going to take her without a fight. If she was going to die, she was going to take a piece of them with her.

The van skidded forward at a high speed.

This was it. She was going to die.

"Hold on to something. I'm going to crash the van," Tristan's voice said in her mind. A spark of hope. She felt for something in the darkness, anything to hold onto, but it was too late. She flew, suspended in the air, and slammed against a body.

The screeching of metal filled her ears as she was propelled again, like a rag doll, backward into another body.

She reached for the back of her neck and pulled the bag loose, ripping it off her head. She was in the back of van that was on its side. She scrambled for the doors, but was yanked back. The bearded man squeezed her leg, but she kicked him in the face, freeing her leg.

The door wrenched open before she touched it.

Tristan. He grabbed her arm and pulled her out of the van.

"Behind you," she shouted. A man the size of a house was behind Tristan and throwing a punch. Tristan ducked it and punched him in the bottom of his stomach. A liver shot, he had taught Katie. The man spasmed as if having a seizure and fell to the ground, face first.

She turned around, hearing a muffled scream. A man slid out from the passenger side door and threw himself on the ground. He twitched as his muscles rippled. Before her eyes, he transformed.

It was the most horrifyingly majestic thing she had ever seen. He morphed as if his body was originally created to *be* a dog. Before she knew it, a beast growled at her, hunched on all fours and salivating. Murder in its eyes. He was nothing like Mercedes. He was twice the size, and his slick silver pelt blended in with the night fog.

"Get away from him," Tristan yelled as he ran full speed at the beast. She caught a glimpse of his eyes as he passed her. His were the same as the animal before her. Murderous.

They collided like thunder. The werewolf snarled as it snapped at Tristan, but Tristan was fast and just barely avoided the dagger-like canine teeth.

She heard shuffling behind her and turned. She threw a

punch straight into the stomach of the man who had abducted her. He was strong, but she had learned to hit the major arteries.

However, she didn't expect him to take the hit. Not directly. He back-handed her and knocked her off balance. She tried to regain her footing, but wasn't prepared to take a hit in the stomach.

He threw her to the ground and pinned his knee into her back, pressing her rib cage down. She could barely breathe. Her face stung, scraping against hard ice and road.

Another muffled scream sounded by the van. Katie guessed it was the bearded man morphing. He growled as she saw a blur of fur stalk towards Tristan and the gray wolf.

She watched, tears burning her eyes, as Tristan yelled out in pain. He grabbed onto his limp arm.

Tristan pulled out a knife as he dodged a set of teeth that would have torn him apart. He found an opening.

He ducked under its mouth as it snapped forward a second time and jammed his foot into its front leg, snapping it backward. The wolf howled as Tristan moved to its back leg and broke the bone.

The second wolf ran towards him.

Tristan ran dead at it. What was he doing? She expected them to collide, but instead Tristan held out his knife and threw himself on his back. The wolf, unable to stop, ran over Tristan and the knife. It slammed on its side, spewing blood as it collapsed.

Tristan stood up, drenched in blood. His blue eyes settled on the man on top of her.

The pressure on her back lifted, but she was pulled against the man and felt cold metal against her head. Why was this happening to her again? She tried harder to fight against him.

"Make one move and—"

A gunshot cracked through the air, and she was released. Warm blood coated the top of her head. Tristan pulled her toward him, and she spun around to see her captor fall to his knees and her dad just behind him.

"What happened?" a man said, jogging up to them. She gulped, trying to fill her lungs with air. The street was filling up with men and women with guns and curious faces. Questions and gasp filled the air as people looked between the dead wolf, the incapacitated wolf, and the dead man. Their eyes traveled to her, barely able to hold herself in the upright position, and Tristan dripping with the wolf's blood.

"What happened?" the man said again.

"Back up, Peter," her dad said to the man while staring between her and Tristan.

"They kidnapped me. I was on the porch and they threw a bag over my head and put me in that van." Katie pointed to the van. She hadn't noticed before, but there were shards of glass all over the icy road and a large concave dent in the middle of the van. The fence across the street was busted through. "Tristan saved me."

Mr. Heckler pointed at Tristan. "So this was your doing," he said, stepping out from the crowd. Jim Heckler, from the Christmas party and the board.

Tristan didn't answer. He ignored Mr. Heckler and completely turned to her. His arm was still limp, and he held it close to him.

"You okay?" he asked.

"I'm alive. How's your arm?"

"I'll live."

Mr. Heckler shouted orders for groups to detain the unconscious man, sedate the snarling but immobile werewolf, and clean up the blood-covered street and the eviscerated wolf that lay in the middle of it.

Lucinda's truck sped up the road toward them. She flew out of the car like a hurricane.

"Don't wait until it turns back. Just get rid of it now before someone sees it," Heckler said.

"Turns back?" Katie said.

"Yes," her dad said, while checking her for injury. "While dying, a wolf transforms back into a man again. It usually takes a little bit of time. But if it hasn't changed back yet, I don't think it will," her dad said, staring at the mass of slick brown fur. Her dad and Mr. Heckler had said "*it*," not him. As if the body was just the carcass of a dead animal. As if there was no man inside of it.

Katie used her sleeve to wipe the blood off Tristan's face. He looked like a horror movie. Lucinda was stopped by a few people before she got to them. She checked Katie, even though her dad had just finished looking her over. Katie's dad grunted, annoyed, as Lucinda questioned him. "Did you check her pupils? There's blood on her head."

"She's okay, Lucy."

"We better get you checked out just in case. You too, Tristan. That arm—all of you looks bad."

"Hold it," Mr. Heckler said. There were still a few spectators left not cleaning or off patrolling the street, but no one looked surprised at the existence of werewolves, just the appearance of them so close to home.

"Jim," Lucinda warned.

"Look, Lucy. I'm not judging you for your choice of house guests, but this?" He gestured to the wolves. "This is inexcusable."

"You say that as if it's their fault," Katie's dad said. "She was nearly taken. They did what they had to do."

Mr. Heckler turned his attention to Tristan. "Why didn't you call security? We have procedures for situations like this."

"Do your procedures include letting three werewolves snatch a girl off her porch?"

Mr. Heckler's face turned purple. Spit flew out of his mouth as he spoke. "Innocent people could have been on these streets."

"Well you should have been protecting them. *You have procedures for situations like this.*"

Mr. Heckler moved toward Tristan, but thought better of it. "Watch it boy. As far as I'm concerned, you're the reason they were on this street!"

"He saved my life," Katie said, feeling her own rage. Her ears still pounded from hearing a gun go off so close to her head.

"We wouldn't have let anything happen to you. We would have—"

"Done nothing. I was in the back of that van. I was as good as dead without him. You didn't even have the decency to show up until it was all over. Those wolves could have killed us." She didn't know if the fire she felt was from her pain or anger. How dare they blame him for what happened? How dare they look at him like he was a monster. Like he was a *halfbreed*?

"Enough. Let's go, Katalina," Tristan said, holding out his bloody hand to her.

She grabbed it. The look of pure disdain on Mr. Heckler's face did not go unnoticed. "The school does not look kindly upon discrepancies like this. We have procedures."

"Bigot," she shouted at him. Mr. Heckler stiffened, and the street fell silent. All eyes were on her. The same expressions from the Christmas party. Shock, horror, and disgust.

"Excuse me?"

She couldn't stop herself. Tears fell freely and she was engulfed in such a rage it shook her aching, cold body. Tristan had *saved* her. And yet they all looked at him like *he* was the threat. What if they knew she was a *halfbreed*? Would they have even cared to save her?

Mr. Heckler stepped closer to her, sensing her disgust for him. He dared her to say it again.

She wanted to shout it to all of them. She dared them to look at her the way they looked at Tristan. She would tear their eyes out.

"Katalina." Tristan stepped in front of her. "Let's go." He caressed her hand with his thumb, smearing blood all over its bruised surface.

"He saved me. You would have let me die. Who's the monster?" she said, before letting Tristan pull her away.

Even Lucinda stayed frozen in her spot. Possibly, because she knew what Katie really meant…or maybe because she knew Katie was right.

~ 15 ~

Revelations & Isolations

THEY WENT TO her upstairs bathroom. Her dad was right behind them but disappeared into his room before returning with an old shirt and a pair of shorts. He offered to pop Tristan's shoulder back into place. Katie had to look away.

"Go shower up, you're scaring everyone." Her dad said in his usual gruff voice. He was so calm. How was he so calm? "Katie, why don't you use my bathroom?"

She started the shower. This was the second time. The second time she'd been attacked by people. This time they were werewolves. How had this happened? Why was someone targeting her?

When she got out the shower, she changed and went back into her room to get rid of her dirty clothes. Tristan was sitting on her bed. Staring at her mirror. He looked a little small in her dad's big t-shirt. His hair was still wet from the shower and stuck to his face. She sat next to him. She couldn't pretend to hate him or be angry, not after what just happened.

"I don't know why," Tristan whispered. "I didn't know them. I swear, I didn't know them. I don't know why they tried to take you. I swear—" Tristan's voice was desperate.

"I'm fine. That's all that matters." She said it, but she knew he knew the truth. She was terrified. If it weren't for him...

"I'd die for you."

Katie sucked in a breath. Hearing him say that changed something in her. She lay back on her bed and he followed her. He grabbed her hand and held it. He squeezed it, and she could feel how close he wanted to be. He didn't have to let his wall down for her to understand that.

She wanted it. To be in his arms, feeling his warm skin against hers.

He rolled on top of her, and her stomach hurt with anticipation. Her breaths couldn't keep up with the beating of her heart.

He kissed her. His soft lips pressed lightly against hers. He pressed his body harder against her.

Their soft kisses became harder and faster. She couldn't get enough, and the way he ran his hand up her shirt told her he couldn't either. The higher his hand went, the more her breath caught in her throat. It didn't help that his lips had moved from hers to her neck.

The tips of his fingers set fire to every inch of skin they touched. She let out a gasp as he squeezed her. He hovered above her, breathing just as hard. He looked crazy, his hair standing up from her hands moving through it, his beautiful blue eyes looking right back at her.

He kissed her lips and ran his hand down her side. When had his body moved in between hers? They were moving in sync. Her shirt lifting higher with his hands.

Someone knocked on the door.

"Whatever you're doing behind this closed door, it's inappropriate," her dad said. They sat up and moved to the opposite sides of bed. She tried to straighten out the sheets. The door opened, and her dad looked at them. "At least have the decency to get *off* her bed."

Tristan shot up and moved to the other side of the room, looking like a five-year-old caught stealing cookies. Katie was mortified. They were supposed to pretend like they weren't doing anything. Why did he look so guilty?

She couldn't keep her hands still. She straightened her shirt out, which looked even worse. She could still feel his hands under her shirt and all over her skin. She'd meant to put on a bra when she got out of the shower…she hadn't expected him to be in her room.

Her dad watched them for a moment. Did he know?

He left, but made it a point leave the door wide open.

Tristan kept a three-foot gap between them after that. They sat, and Katie pulled out a board game. It was silly. Playing monopoly when she was almost kidnapped, when, just moments ago, she was spread out on her bed with him in between her legs. Playing the game kept her hands from shaking, but from fear or pure joy she didn't know. The feelings were almost the same. The way Tristan looked at her, even now as she rolled the dice, staring back at him—it set her ablaze.

Lucinda called him downstairs, but he hesitated before he stood up. Katie stood up to walk downstairs with him.

He grabbed her and held her so tight she felt like she'd melt into him. The back of her shirt was gripped between his fingers. He kissed her again, hard, before pulling away, but they held hands for a second before they went downstairs.

"I'm going to go home and get a few things. We've decided it's best to stay here for the night. It's not a coincidence that Katie's been attacked twice in the last two months," Lucinda said, grabbing her car keys.

Katie almost thought someone should go with her, but when Lucinda stood up, Katie saw the gun strapped to her waist. She still wished her dad would go with her. It would give them at least twenty minutes to see just how far they were willing to go.

Tristan coughed. Loud.

"Was there something you wanted me to grab?"

Tristan shook his head still coughing.

"You'll be sleeping down here, on that couch," her dad said, pointing out the couch to Tristan.

Tristan had guilt written all over his face. It made Katie feel like her dad and Lucinda knew what they'd just done. Katie was too embarrassed to even deny it. She couldn't even open her mouth to deflect the way her dad was looking between them.

⋅⋅⋅

It didn't matter where her dad wanted him to sleep. They didn't close their eyes once that night. Katie didn't know if it was because she was afraid to close her eyes, or if she just wanted the moment between her and Tristan to last. They sat at the kitchen table putting together a puzzle. At first it was all four of them silently working. Katie never thought she'd see her dad and Lucinda sitting so close without screaming. When they retired, Katie and Tristan stayed working, pretending they actually cared about the puzzle.

When her fingers ached to be interlaced with his, he'd brush his fingers against hers to pick up a puzzle piece. Grab her hand and take the piece she had. Any excuse to touch her. How long would it last? He still kept his wall up. They were frozen in this time and space. At any moment it was going to crack and they'd have to decide which direction they were going to go in.

⋅⋅⋅

She was right. All she had was that night. Nothing was the same after that. Tristan was on thin ice with the school, and she was on lockdown. One-hundred percent lockdown. She wasn't even allowed to go to school. Her dad put her on leave, and only Traci, Lucinda, and Allison were allowed to come over. All at her father's request. Traci volunteered to grab her books and notebooks out of her locker, brought at least two tons of classwork, and didn't read the mood when Katie was too busy wondering why her dad was being such a jerk and banning Tristan from the house.

Her dad went so far as to try and train her. He was miserable, he took breaks every ten minutes, and she felt like she was working *him* out. Lucinda nagged him until he finally came to his senses and added Tristan to the list of people allowed to enter the house.

She thought he'd be as excited to see her as she was him, but she was wrong. He was back to treating her like a friend. He wasted no time getting back to their old routine.

Every other day he had something insulting to say: "*Reflexes like that are why you got kidnapped.*" Or, "*Yeah, eat more pie. Maybe next time they won't be able to pick you up.*" And her personal favorite, "*Stop sucking.*"

"I don't *suck*," she said for the third time. They had been practicing all night in the backyard. She still ached from the car crash, and Tristan constantly added pains on top of her existing ones.

"You wouldn't hurt if you drank," he spat. Whenever Lucinda was out of earshot, he'd say that to her. She wouldn't do it. She'd never touch blood again. "Fine. Quit letting me beat the crap out of you. Stop taking hits and fight back."

"What if I can't fight back? That guy took my hit like it was nothing. Everyone who's attacked me has been stronger than me. I won't win."

"If they're stronger, you just have to be faster."

"How?"

He threw a punch straight for her face. She threw her hands up and braced herself. Instead, he pushed her hard on the ground. "One, stop being afraid. You're being pathetic. You were better than this two weeks ago. Two. Drink."

"That's unrealistic." She stood up and felt another bruise forming on her hip.

"What are you afraid of? Pain? I've landed so many punches tonight I'm surprised you're still standing."

"No, I don't care about the pain."

"Is it dying? Because it's not *if* you die, it's *when*. Everyone dies. That phenomenon is called life."

"No—I don't know!" Katie looked for Lucinda and lowered her voice. "Why are people targeting me anyway? I can't sleep at night." How could she live life when people were always out to get her?

"You're in control of whether you let someone kill you or not. If I let my opponents scare me we'd both be dead right now."

"I'm not like you!"

"Not like me how? I fight to survive."

"I'm not strong. I can't kill someone like it doesn't matter. I'm not a—" She didn't have to say it. The word was already in her mind. Monster.

"*Surviving* isn't what made me a monster."

"What's that supposed to mean?"

Tristan stared at her.

She changed the subject to something he'd really been avoiding. "Where have you been going? You don't even come every day."

He turned his back on her.

She knew. He'd been going back to Gray City. He was being shady again. He'd made a promise and he broke that. For how long? Did it have something to do with why she was nearly kidnapped? "At the pub, hanging out with your friends then?" Mercedes was a werewolf, what a coincidence. She'd been saving it for the right moment.

He turned on her.

"Yeah, I know about your werewolf friend. She stopped by the coffee shop that day. Apparently she didn't know you've been playing us both." Katie's voice shook a little.

Tristan's face turned from annoyance to confusion. "Mercedes talked to you the day you got kidnapped?" It came out like a whisper.

"Yeah, I can see why you were hiding her," Katie said, getting her confidence back. He was caught. The ever elusive Tristan was caught.

Katie scowled, remembering exactly what Mercedes had said. *Tell him I have an answer for him.*

"Katalina." He stared at her. "Why didn't you tell me?"

It was her turn to be silent and walk away.

"Katalina!" His voice sliced through her.

She spun back around. "Don't shout at me. I don't care if you missed your chance to—"

"You're so goddamn annoying! There is nothing going on between me and her. She's a friend."

"Like I'm your friend. Yeah, I get that."

He shook his fist and yelled. The way he jerked his body put her on edge. He was pissed. "She's been helping me find out about the man who killed my parents—you idiot. There is *nothing* going on between me and her." He was red in the face and pulling on his hair.

She felt stupid, but she didn't want to lose, no matter how wrong she was. She wanted to be angry because he kept yanking her around like a ragdoll. Tossing her here and there like what she felt didn't matter. "How was I supposed to know? You don't tell me anything."

"Just shut up."

"What about the other girl then? At the movies?"

He stared her down. "It wouldn't matter if I told you I've never seen that girl in my life or if I told you I sleep with her every Tuesday night. So I'll let you guess that one."

She reached to slap him but he grabbed her hand before she touched him.

"Hey? What's all this yelling about? I swear, I turn my back for three breaths and you two are either goofing around or gearing up for a fight," Lucinda said, appearing from the back door with bottles of water and a few sandwiches.

Katie pulled her hand away and went inside.

⁘

He never came back.

At first she thought he was going to ignore her for the week, but one week turned into a week and a half—then two. She threw herself into the homework Traci had given her. It was the only way to distract herself. If she let herself think too hard about him, she could easily imagine him with that girl, kissing that tall, pretty girl the way he'd kissed her. Rubbing on *her* body the way he'd rubbed on hers. In between *her* legs—but with no clothes separating them.

"Katie?" Traci said when Katie broke her pencil. She'd been thinking about it again.

"Sorry,"

"Katie, this is important. This will definitely be on the final exam next month," Traci said.

What did it matter? She hadn't been to school in three weeks, and it was starting to feel like she would never go back.

Traci sighed and flipped the page in her book. "You're not even on the right page." Traci had been less cooperative with her lately. Always sighing, always taking deep breaths. "Read from pages three-hundred-forty-seven to three-hundred-fifty-eight. Then we'll talk about it. I'll grade—this." She said, looking disappointed at Katie's math work.

Katie looked down at the book. It was about *Royal Vampire Families.* How exciting. Katie flipped through the pages but stopped when something caught her eye. A short passage entitled: *"The Keeper's Vow."* Her heart sped up as she read it.

"The royal families were divided into two groups, the ruling family and the sister family. In order to protect the status of the current ruling

family from siblings and cousins in the sister family, a blood oath was used that could only be done between those with vampire blood in their veins. The sister family was forced to protect the ruling family with their lives. In the event of the death of the ruling family, the sister family would be eliminated. Some documents speculate the bond created a close kinship between siblings at a young age. They were bound telepathically and all inner family assassinations ceased. This vow was often used to tie servants to noble families and even slaves to their buyers. Later known as the Keeper's Vow, was abandoned with the loss of vampire fertility and the royal kings during the Dark Ages."

Katie flipped the pages looking for more. Nothing. That was what Tristan had kept from her that night she'd asked him. He was tied to her. His *life* was tied to her. He hadn't just been protecting her. He'd been protecting both of their lives. Katie didn't bother pretending she was reading the rest of the book.

He'd been protecting himself.

She wished he'd come back to her house so she could confront him. This was why he'd protect her with his life. She fought back every ugly tear that welled up inside of her.

⁘

Later that night, Lucinda and Allison came to her house. It was Friday, so she wasn't expecting them, and she really didn't want to talk to anyone. It aggravated her even more when she found out they hadn't come to talk.

"I don't know what has happened between you and Tristan, but I'm fed up. He hasn't showed up for a practice in two weeks. Two weeks, Katie," Lucinda said in her stiff, *'you've done it now'* voice. "Did you two forget that I'm your mentor and that I expect you to continue doing what you're supposed to be doing?"

"It's not my fault he stopped coming," Katie said. Why was she being attacked? She was here—against her will, but still here—and Lucinda wasn't exactly all present either. Ever since Will and Brian left, she'd barely even put together their training schedules.

"No, it's both your faults. You do not solve problems by avoiding—I see I'm going in one ear and out the other." Lucinda rolled her eyes. "Anyway, that's not the point. Go change into something and meet me in the backyard."

Katie sucked in air between her teeth.

Allison followed her up the stairs. "The drama around here is unrelenting."

"Don't want to talk about it," Katie said before she realized how harsh it came out.

"Okay, then." Allison stopped following her. "I'll just meet you outside."

When she went out to the backyard, the first thing she did was apologize to Allison. Allison shrugged it off, but Katie knew she wasn't really over it. Everything in her life was turning into one big ball of fiery anger, and she didn't know how to control it.

Lucinda laid an airsoft gun on the table and loaded the clip with little white pellets.

"What exactly is that for?" Katie asked, not looking forward to the answer.

"I can't push you physically like Tristan can. No one can, honestly, so we're going to be a little creative today. You're going to fight me and Allison. I have a gun and she doesn't. Between the two of us, we will make up for Tristan's speed and then some."

"You're going to shoot me with that—OUCH!"

Lucinda answered her with a pellet in the arm. She could feel the welt rising. Lucinda was sicker than Tristan. What was wrong with these people?

.◦◦◦.

It wasn't fair, the entire hour that they trained, it wasn't fair. Allison was taking her revenge for Katie's aloofness, and Lucinda was being sadistic. By the end, Katie was covered in dirt and welts.

Katie could see her dad watching from the window. He was no help. When ever she looked at him, he shrugged as if saying, *"You asked for it."* Maybe they were all taking out their frustrations on her.

"Stop. I'm done." Katie said, getting up after Allison dropped her to the ground.

"No, you're not," Lucinda said sternly.

"Yes. I am." Katie didn't have to take any of this anymore.

"Allison. Go inside. Get some water." Lucinda's eyes never left Katie.

"I'm done, Lucy," Katie said. She stood her ground. She was sick of people bullying her.

As soon as Allison closed the door, Lucinda moved in close. Katie silently dared her to say something. She couldn't wait to take her anger out on someone. Especially since that someone just spent an hour lighting her up with plastic BB's.

"What are you going to do?" Lucinda said. "Go cry in your room? So I'm hard on you. Tough shit, Katie."

Katie seethed. Words were piling up in her throat.

"Allison is running circles around you. I watched you and Tristan every day, and you've gotten better than her. You're faster than this crap you're doing today. You've been slacking off."

Katie grit her teeth. Lucinda didn't know the half of what she'd been through. When was the last time she'd gotten thrown into the back of a van? "I'm done," she said for the final time.

"Then let's call an omitter because *that's* what happens when you want to be done. That's what happens when you slack off."

Katie laughed in her face, but it was full of angry jitters. Lucinda was a hypocrite. Katie had heard her Christmas Eve begging Will not to send Brian away, to give him another chance. She'd heard Will tell her she was going to get her own son killed. "Is that what you said to Brian? Wait no. You begged—"

Lucinda slapped her. Pain cracked across her face, but Katie was used to pain. "You're not *my* mother. You don't get to—"

Lucinda slapped her again and left Katie standing in the backyard holding her face.

Lucinda came back the next day, and every day for a week after that. They never talked about what happened. They pretended it never happened. Her dad, who she knew saw it, didn't say anything, and she suspected Allison had seen it because she ignored the tension that surrounded Katie and Lucinda too well.

There was space between her and Lucinda now. Katie shouldn't have said what she said. Katie couldn't look Lucinda in the eyes.

"Katie," Lucinda called one day after practice. Allison wasn't there. Lucinda had Katie do target practice with the airsoft gun and targets set up around the yard.

They didn't talk during practice anymore, so when Katie said, "*Yes?*" it barely came out.

"You're doing better," she said, taking down the targets one at a time. Katie nodded, even though Lucinda's back was to her.

Katie noticed it too. She was getting back to her normal self. She was a match for Allison now.

To think, over six months ago, she couldn't even get an honest score in the Preliminaries. She could probably make it to the top now. It felt like a long time ago, the Preliminaries. She was so different now. Everything was different.

"You still aren't where you should be. You should start drinking," Lucinda said. She was staring directly at her now.

"No." Katie had made up her mind a long time ago after Tristan force-fed her. The thought still made her want to vomit. Plus, she wasn't a vampire, or a half-vampire, or whatever. She was Katie Watts. A girl. A human girl.

"I don't think you have much of a choice. You're getting better, but you're still too slow."

What was Lucinda saying? Wasn't she the one fighting for Tristan to get away from her when he was pouring it down her throat? "You know what the difference is between you and

Allison? She pushes herself every day and makes strides to reach her maximum potential. She knows her limits and she works through them. You don't. You can't. You don't even know your full potential. You're hitting a ceiling that isn't supposed to be there." Lucinda waved her into the house.

They walked into the kitchen. Her dad was sat at the table, reading the newspaper through his glasses. Lucinda pulled out a lunch box from the refrigerator. She sat it on the table and opened it. Three packets of blood were stacked in a row.

Her dad looked over his newspaper and went red in the face. "Get that crap out of my house. You're going too far, Lucy."

"Drew, you admitted it yourself. She's hitting a wall."

When had they talked about her? Hadn't they barely become friends again?

Her dad gripped the paper and looked at her. Katie pleaded for him to talk sense into Lucinda, but the more she talked, the more she saw his face change from rightful anger to sympathy.

"Dad?—Dad?" she said.

"You know it's inevitable, Drew. Tristan said she moves her body like she's drunk and he's right. She's off. Even at her fastest, there's a sluggishness about her."

When had Tristan talked about her with Lucinda? She felt betrayed. Why had he been *allowed* to talk about her?

"No," Katie said, trying to put her foot down. As soon as she saw her dad's face, she knew it was pointless. They were going to make her do it.

"Katie, it will make you better. You're not meant to be like you are. Your body isn't meant to survive on food. You're starving it every day," Lucinda said.

Katie didn't care. She was scared. The last time—

The last time she drank, it burned her throat. Last time felt like someone holding her face first in it.

"Come on, Katie Bug." Her dad stood up and wiped away her tear. He walked her over to the sink and pulled down a glass. She wanted to sob like a baby and throw a tantrum. Maybe he wouldn't make her do it. He didn't know what it was like.

He poured a packet into a glass. It filled the tall glass with a little left over.

"She only has to drink one pack every two weeks," Lucinda said, holding her own arms like she was the one who might fall apart.

Her dad picked up the blood and sniffed it. "It's not so bad. It's probably better than my cooking," he laughed, but that didn't comfort her. She took the glass when he handed it to her.

She held her nose.

"Don't sip it, Katie Bug. Just try to gulp it down. That works best," her dad said, rubbing her back.

She didn't even get so much of a mouthful down before she was throwing it up in the sink. Her dad held her hair, and Lucinda took the glass. Her stomach spasmed until she was throwing up nothing.

The sink looked like a murder scene. Her dad rinsed out the sink and gave her a glass of water. She washed out her mouth.

Nothing could rinse out the taste of blood. It didn't taste like it smelled. It was thick, pungent rot.

Lucinda gave her the glass again.

Katie steadied herself and swallowed down her urge to gag. After a moment, she tried again. She drank and swallowed. Drank and swallowed. Drank and swallowed. Her body shook as she concentrated. She hated throwing up. She could never breathe and it made her panic. She cried, drank, and swallowed until it was gone.

It never got easier. She set the glass down in the sink, and the sound echoed in her head. She turned around, too fast, and nearly fell. The lights were getting brighter and she was taking in too much air.

"How do you feel? Do you need to lie down?" Lucinda asked.

It was the exact opposite. Every second that passed, she felt more and more like she needed to run. So much energy, so much—

Silence. This house is just like the other. Silent…

Katie stopped. That wasn't her thought.

I hate this…

It was Tristan. She just knew it. Who else could it be in her mind? And he didn't know she was there…

"Katie?" her dad said. He and Lucinda were watching her like she might sprout wings and fly out the window.

"I'm fine," she said too loud. Everything was too loud. And bright. "I just need to go, sit or something," she said. The world was coming at her on full blast. But it felt good. Her body felt so good. Was this what it was like for Tristan?

I hate this…

There it was again. He came in and out like static on a radio.

"Why don't you go lie down?" Lucinda said. They were moving toward her like she might collapse at any second.

"Yeah, I'll do that." She backed away from them. She could feel the space around her. They were too close.

She went up to her room and took off her shoes and socks. As soon as her feet touched her furry rug she flipped out. It was too much fur at one time. She jumped on the bed, but that was almost no better.

She breathed. This must have been what snorting cocaine felt like. She could hear Lucinda and her dad even though they were downstairs, still in the kitchen. She could see the dust floating around in her room. She blinked. It was really a feather that must have escaped her pillow when she jumped on it.

She was tripping out. She spent hours in her closet feeling her clothes, running from one side of the room to the other. She'd jump over her bed effortlessly and landed as quiet as the feather that drifted to the floor.

She stopped when she felt him getting angry. It was like a slap in the face. She could see Lucinda as clear as day, sitting at the dinner table. It was just the two of them. He was so angry.

"Are you trying to say you want me to drop out?" he said.

"I don't know what they'll do. No one is answering my calls."

"Then stop calling."

"And do what? Sit around and wait? I won't let them think they're better than me."

"You can't control what people think about you," he said.

"No, Tristan. I've spent my entire life building up my reputation. I can't just let them discredit me because I'm—"

"Related to a halfbreed? Just admit it. You hate it."

"You know that isn't what I mean."

"Do I?"

"I would never say that!" Lucinda slapped her hand against the table.

"I don't care what you think. Don't you get it? You asked me to stay here. You want me here because you want to prove to yourself that you're not a terrible person. You wanted to prove you're not someone who would throw a kid out on the streets."

"Tristan!"

"If you weren't so busy trying to prove yourself a saint, you would have seen how pathetic your son is."

Tears streamed down Lucinda's red face. *"You don't think I know that?"* she screamed. *"You don't think I'm in my own personal hell because of all this?"*

Lucinda used her napkin to wipe the tears off her face. Her tears were coming from somewhere deep. It made him angrier.

He was leaving, but Katie couldn't see where. He was moving too far maybe, or she wasn't good enough at listening. It faded into a small whisper.

An idea struck her. She was going to follow him. She'd have to sneak out. Her dad would never know she was gone if she waited until *Law and Order* started. He was always out like a light before the middle of the show.

She took a shower and yelled that she was going to bed. He never checked in on her. She'd be able to leave and come back before he'd notice. She put on a dark pair of skinny jeans and a tight black shirt. She was going to have to do some climbing if she was going to get in and out. There were light sensors on the ground, so she couldn't go through the door, but she could use the tree next to her window. If she took the longest branch and swung a little, she could land in the neighbor's backyard.

She grabbed her cell phone, turned out her lights, and opened her window. Wind blew through her hair. She should have been cold. Nights in March were always cold, but she wasn't.

Climbing and swinging from trees was much easier than it should have been. Her body was strong, and she held onto the branches like she'd been doing it her whole life. Climbing over the neighbors fence was an easy hop too.

She was free. She hadn't realized what being trapped in the house day in and out was doing to her. She was a bird spreading its wings after being clipped and caged.

She took off running through the wind. It was exhilarating. Her lungs were full and light. Her legs took her faster and faster. She was laughing before she realized she was out of her neighborhood and spinning in circles.

As she breathed in the night air, she felt him. He was close. Her body turned like a compass and he was the magnetic pulse. He was going toward Gray City. Katie stopped. What was she doing? What would she do when she found him? They still weren't talking and she still hated him.

She called Allison.

"Kay? What do you mean you're going to Gray City? It's a school night and you're supposed to be in your house. This is screaming bad idea."

"Allison, it's either yes or no. Are you going to come with me?"

It took Allison thirty minutes to meet her downtown. It was a normal Thursday night in Boise. The college students were all out getting ready to drink their weekend away. A few guys stopped to shout cat calls at Katie. It made her uncomfortable at first, but she liked the attention. She wished she were wearing something more sexy. She hadn't bothered to do her hair or put on makeup. She pulled it out of her high-pony just as Allison appeared around the corner.

"What exactly are we doing?" Allison said. She'd bothered with the makeup.

"Do you have your makeup bag?" Katie pointed to Allison's purse. It was smaller than her usual pick and strapped around her body.

"Of course. Kay, would you like to explain why I just snuck out of my house at eleven at night?"

"Let's go to a club, where they don't card us," Katie said, feeling dangerous. She wanted to dance. She wanted to feel sexy and she wanted boys to stare at her and shout things as they passed.

Allison looked skeptical, but the sly smile didn't go unnoticed. Katie started to walk toward the bistro, but Allison stopped her. "Kay, we can't go in there. They'll call the school if we take the elevator alone. That's a guardian entrance. We have to use another one." Allison took her to the a large warehouse that acted as a concert hall for bands. There was a concert going on and a line of people showing their IDs to get in.

"Well there goes that plan," Allison said, sighing.

"Where is the elevator?" Katie asked, thinking of something she never would have before her body felt like it could fly.

"It's behind the stage, why?"

Katie grabbed Allison and took off to the door. Allison protested behind her but once Katie pushed through the girl looking at IDs she picked up speed. There were footsteps behind them, but as soon as they started moving through the crowd inside, the music and jumping bodies blocked them out.

Allison pulled on Katie's arm. "Are you flipping crazy?" Allison looked wide-eyed, but she was smiling just as hard as Katie. They started giggling. "Come on," she screamed through the music. Allison led her backstage. No one was guarding it—it must have been a local band on stage. The room Allison led her to was locked. Allison knocked three times and kicked it.

A guy opened it and looked them over. "Bathrooms are on the other side."

"Two tickets to Gray City, please," Allison said, trying to push her way through the door.

"Oh," the man said. "It's *you*. Aren't you supposed to be supervised or something?" The guy had a long, thick beard, two gauges, and a nose ring with spikes.

"You gonna rat us out?" Allison said, holding her ground.

The guy finally let them through, closed the door, and locked it. "Whatever, my shift is almost over anyway." He led them down a hallway to a small room. Katie could have burst into giggles. They were doing *it*. Whatever *it* was, and it felt good. The guy pushed a few buttons and told them to hold on. Katie remembered the last ride and held on tight.

This elevator was much faster than the last one, but she was balanced and centered. This was what it felt like when she drank blood. Was it worth the rancid taste?

She smiled.

The elevator opened, and they were free in Gray City.

16

Gray City

THEY STEPPED OUT onto the street, and Katie knew exactly where to go. It was like a pull. He was definitely here and close. The vibe was different down here at night—not as docile as it was during the field trip. It was alive. More lights, more people, more cars, and more noise.

If she didn't know any better, she'd think she'd just stepped out onto the streets of New York City.

She watched as a man pushed a woman against a wall of a short, yellow brick building. They were in the shadow, but she could see them clear as day, making out. The guy even had his hand up the girl's skirt.

Allison squinted into the shadows. "Apparently things don't change no matter where you are," she said, catching onto what

Katie was looking at. "Some people just don't have the decency to get a room."

Katie blushed. That night in her bed—how far would she and Tristan have gone if no one had knocked on the door?

As they walked through the streets, Allison pointed out a pet store where vampires frequented for discreet meetings (she learned from listening in on one of Will's conversations), restaurants to find werewolves, and where *not* to go because fates were notorious for spiking drinks. It was a better tour than the one Mr. Carver gave. This time she wasn't wearing a dorky shirt that everyone glanced at. This time, as she walked down the streets, she saw things. Things even Allison hadn't seen. The people with Silver eyes. They were most definitely vampires. They all smelled the same, (not that she'd gotten up close and personal, but it was hard to miss). Like stale blood.

As they walked past a short, green, sunken-in building, she saw a shadow curl into itself—watching her. She blinked—it was impossible, but silver eyes blinked back.

"That place gets busted every other month. Fates lure drunk humans by the masses down there and *do* things to them." Allison pointed at the green building. The sign on it read *"The Pony Express."*

By the look on Allison's face, Katie knew that whatever they did, it was something wrong.

"Once I waited outside when Will went in, and a guy asked me if the fur matched the drapes." Allison shook her head.

As they continued into the heart of the city, she didn't see any more living shadows, but there was a new living buzz in the air. They stopped outside of a club blaring electronic music. Flashing blue and red lights lit up the sidewalk. It was called "*Hot Flash.*"

He was there.

"You want to go in there? Looks good to me," Allison said, swinging her hips.

Katie stopped her. "Put makeup on me." Katie started to get nervous. What would she do when she saw him? She'd made it this far. She couldn't go back yet. But what would she say? What would *he* say?

When Allison was done applying her makeup, Katie tried to make her shirt look less—shirty. It wasn't working. She tried to stretch the neck a little. It ripped.

"Crap, Kay. Who are you? The Hulk?"

Katie started to panic. Allison grabbed her shirt and tore it more. Katie almost yelled until she realized what she was doing. It was genius.

When Allison was done, her shirt looked like it was supposed to be torn, and showing a good deal of cleavage. Allison the savior. Katie was ready. She didn't know what she was going to find in there, but she was ready to do it.

Getting in was just as easy as everyone had made it out to be. They walked up to the door, the guy at the door opened it, and they walked in. I might have helped that the guy at the door was checking out her chest. As soon as she stepped into the club, she felt Tristan's eyes on her. She couldn't see him, but he was there and watching her. She felt his confusion.

Allison pulled her onto the dance floor and Katie let her. They danced to the beat as she felt him closing in. She focused on the music. It bounced off the walls and radiated from the bodies that surrounded her. People swayed around her, and shouted lyrics to songs she'd never heard. She moved her hips and found she was more bendy than before. What she wanted her body to do, it did.

She wasn't the only one to notice.

"You're a good dancer," a voice said behind her. It wasn't Tristan. She turned her head around to a brown-haired guy with deep brown eyes. He swayed behind her and smiled.

She smiled. When did *this* ever happen to her? At school dances, she always found herself dancing awkwardly with Brian or as a group. Now, electricity flowed through her veins and with each breath she floated above shyness.

He moved closer behind her until his body was against hers. She put her arms in the air and he wrapped them around his neck. She tingled—and liked it. Someone paying this close attention to her body. She knew he was staring down her chest. His hands gripped her waist, pulling her closer. She was mixed with embarrassment and pleasure when she felt his nether regions pushing up against her.

It never escaped her that Tristan was there lurking. She still hadn't seen him. She didn't have to.

"What's your name?" she yelled behind her. The song had changed and they moved faster.

"Sean," he said in her ear.

"I'm Katie," she said back, in her throatiest voice. She felt stupid, but he seemed to like it.

Allison raised her eyebrows at Katie, then at Sean.

Sean moved his hands from her hips to her stomach, and she felt dirty. Like she was cheating. How stupid. She had no one to cheat on.

He moved his hands higher and higher. She stopped him, and he took it as an opportunity to move them lower. Just as she was about to add a little space between them, she saw him. Tristan. A wave of heat and anger permeated around her as he stared at them. To be honest, she couldn't decide whose heat or anger it was. His or hers? Why were they always like this?

His face was unreadable, but she heard every curse he was spewing in his mind. She wasn't the only one trying to look her best, he was wearing a black blazer over a white, expensive-looking v-neck. She didn't even know he owned a blazer aside from his uniform.

He marched toward her, pushing people out of the way.

He grabbed her arm, but she pulled it away. He squinted his eyes and looked her over.

"Hey, man," Sean said, stepping between them. "Back off."

"Katalina. What the *hell* are you doing here?"

"I said back off, man," Sean said, looking back at Katie.

"Say one more word and I'll break your face," Tristan said, moving closer to Sean.

"Since when do you care what I do?" Katie said. The electronic melody filled her ears, making her charged and ready for battle. She grabbed Sean's hand and it felt so wrong, but she wanted to make a point. She moved him deeper onto the dance floor.

"Katalina!" Tristan's voice cut through the music. The world, the music, and time stopped. Her heart ripped, as torn as her mind.

"You know what," Sean said, walking back towards Tristan. "Nobody likes a sore loser—"

Tristan punched him in the face.

Katie and group of girls shrieked as Sean backed into them. "TRISTAN!" Katie screamed, but even she started to drown in the wave of violence he was swimming in.

Sean swung back, in Tristan's stomach. Tristan took the hit and grabbed his face. Sean screamed as Tristan forced him back and into the bar. People parted. Sean slammed his fist into Tristan's side, panicking.

Tristan's grip tightened, and Sean began to spasm. Tristan let him go and kicked him into the bar. Sean's face had red burns scratched across them.

"Fucking untouchable?" Sean gasped, holding his face.

Three guys pushed past Katie and grabbed onto Tristan.

He fought back, kicking one into a concrete pillar.

Allison grabbed Katie and pulled her back and away from the other two guys trying to hold Tristan down. They couldn't hold him.

One guy yelled in pain. "Get back, he's an untouchable."

Another guy with yellow teeth and yellow hair pulled out a gun. "Look, kid. Calm down or we'll have to put you down."

Tristan snarled.

Katie pulled away from Allison and tackled Tristan. They fell into the bar and Tristan's head smacked against the ground. He grabbed her, and she thought he'd throw her off for sure. He squeezed her and yelled, "Get off me, Katalina, or I swear—"

"Then stop," she yelled back. "Just stop." She wouldn't move until his breathing steadied.

A different guy walked up to them wearing the same black polo as the other three guys. "Boss wants you to bring up those three." He was pointing at Katie, Tristan, and Allison.

Katie contemplated running.

"Get off me, Katalina," Tristan growled.

As soon as she got up, one of the guys grabbed her. It was the door guy.

Tristan charged him.

"Stop!" She pulled her arm away, but it was too late. The guy with yellow hair shot him. Tristan's body shook, and he dropped to the ground. They'd tasered him.

"This kid is a beast," said one guy as Yellow-hair helped pick up Tristan's body. Tristan was still fighting, but they were able to hold his arms back.

The three of them were herded down a hallway and into an elevator.

"I hope this is what you had planned when you came here," Tristan said, slurring his words. "I hope this is *exactly* how you planned it."

"All right, kid. Calm down," Yellow-hair said. They marched them down another well-lit hallway covered in marble tile. They stopped at the door on the far end, and the guy holding Katie knocked. He'd relaxed his grip on her.

What had she gotten them into? Katie looked at Allison. She was just as terrified as Katie. The door opened, and Katie's jaw dropped when she saw the man staring back at her.

It was Larry. Larry from the ice cream parlor. Except he wasn't wearing a blue polo with a fat cat licking ice cream. He was wearing a tailored black suit and looking at Katie's outfit, thoroughly disappointed. She blushed, wishing she had something to cover up her chest.

"La—Larry?" Allison stuttered.

"I told you to get a new boyfriend, Katie." He waved them in.

"Thanks gentlemen, I've got it from here—oh I know he's got a temper. I think we'll be fine from here." Larry closed the door and offered them a seat on the cream-colored couch next to a large window that overlooked the city. "Please, do sit. From what I understand, you're probably exhausted after wrecking my club."

"S—sorry," was all Katie could say. She still couldn't wrap her mind around the fact that Larry was walking over to a mini bar and grabbing two cokes. Allison's purse fell and everything splattered across the floor. The noise was louder than anyone had expected.

"Excuse me," Allison said, picking everything up quickly.

Silence.

"I'm guessing you don't want one," he said to Tristan. "You usually like your drinks stronger, right?"

Tristan's eyes were burning holes through Larry's head. "What's your game?" he said, flexing his fist.

"Well, I was sitting at my desk doing paperwork when I got the message that *you* started throwing one of *my* customers around *my* club." Larry handed Allison and Katie each a can of coke. He started to sit down, but took off his jacket first. "Please, Katie, put this on."

Katie was mortified. She looked like a hooker. She'd known Larry long enough that it was like being caught by an uncle. An uncle that did not just own an ice cream shop with delicious ice cream, but also a club. In Gray City.

Tristan stood up and took off his own jacket, holding it out, roughly, to Katie. He was staring Larry down.

"Just take it," Tristan said between his teeth. Why was he making this already awkward situation worse?

He looked at her. *"Goddamn it, can't she just trust me for once?"*

Katie squinted, *"I did that and got burned,"* she thought back.

"Dammit, Katalina." Tristan held his head. His hand still twitched a little from the taser.

Larry looked between, them and a dark look crossed over his face. He folded his jacket in his hands and nodded for her to take Tristan's. She put it on. His smell covered her, and she almost suffocated. Her heart pulled and twisted as if encased by barbed wire.

"I guess it has become obvious to you that I am not just an ice cream shop owner," Larry said, smiling at Katie and Allison.

Tristan shifted in his seat. He wanted to leave. He wanted to grab her and leave. He was contemplating it and thinking hard on it. Katie wished he'd shut up. His thoughts were beating at her, making it hard for her to think.

Larry looked between them again. "In fact, I didn't buy that shop until I moved here."

"Let's go." Tristan grabbed her hand.

Katie didn't move. Fear was sinking into her like maybe she should run, but she couldn't just stand up and walk out the door. She knew Larry.

"It's not your choice, Tristan." Larry looked tired.

"She doesn't care about what you have to say," Tristan spat. "Now, Katalina."

Katie looked to Allison, but Allison shrugged.

She pulled her hand back. What was wrong with him? He'd spent two months ignoring her, and now he was acting like a raging lunatic on steroids, beating people up and deciding what she did and did not want to hear.

"For once, will you stop thinking about yourself and just trust me?"

"When did you take the vow?" Larry said abruptly.

All three of them turned to him. How did he know? How could he possibly know?

"I can see it in the way you two look at each other. Not many can recognize the signs, but I was one of the last few to ever take the vow. I thought it was no longer in practice, but now I see—I was wrong." He cut a dark look at Tristan. As if maybe it were Tristan's fault that he was wrong.

Katie shuddered. Who was this man? This man that smelled so powerful? Katie blinked at the thought. How could she smell power?

"It doesn't matter who he is. Let's go now," Tristan said, but she wasn't looking at him. She was staring at Larry. His accent—the reason she couldn't place it. The textbook said the vow hadn't been used since the dark ages. He was a vampire—that she had figured out the moment she stepped into his office. But vampires couldn't walk out in the day time. Not unless they were half. Or pure.

Tristan pulled her out of the chair, and she decided maybe he was right. Maybe they should leave. Something about Larry didn't sit right. A pureblood vampire running an ice cream shop. Giving her free ice cream every Friday…it was beyond creepy.

"Your friend is worried that I'll say something he'd rather keep quiet. But I only want to ask when Ivan did it. When did he bond you both?"

This time it was Tristan who stopped. "Don't talk about my dad. Don't ever say his name."

"He was my friend before he was your father," Larry said. "I thought we'd already reached that understanding. You're too old to play that game, Tristan. Let me—"

"I still don't want or need your help. Katalina is no different." Tristan said.

"You've—you knew him? Before you met him at the ice cream shop? That's why—who are you, Larry?" Katie said.

Larry and Tristan watched each other for a while before Larry said, "A friend. I knew his father. When I found out what happened—I decided I'd best keep an eye on you two."

Tristan's grip on her hand eased a little. Was this the man Tristan stayed with? Larry? Why didn't he ever say anything?

"Please sit back down. I only want to talk," Larry said.

Katie moved her hand from Tristan's and sat back down. Whether he wanted to or not was his own prerogative. She'd known Larry for years. If he'd wanted to kill her or do any number of demented things, he would have done it a long time ago.

Tristan hovered by the couch, but didn't sit.

"Why did he do it?" Larry said, almost to himself. "Do you know why we ended the Keeper's Vow? Why we made sure our fathers were the last to ever utter the words?" He was looking at Tristan, but his eyes ended on Katie.

The words *keeper* and *vow* rolled out of Allison's mouth. They all listened to her as she tried to remember something they all knew.

Tristan was rigid again. He was about to open his mouth to redirect the conversation. He still didn't want her to know, but his eyes widened as he listened to the answer rise in her mind.

Yes, she knew why they'd stopped doing it, how barbaric it was, and how it forced one person to protect the life of the other.

"Because. If I die, he dies," Katie said.

"So you know?" Larry said, raising an eyebrow.

"Only because I read books." It was a gibe aimed at Tristan, but Larry looked apologetic. "I mean, I had to find out from a book. No one bothered to tell me."

Now it was Allison who looked offended. Katie tried hard to pretend she didn't see the stern look on her face. Katie forgot she'd never told Allison. No—not forget—she never wanted to. It felt like a dirty secret—a secret she never wanted to be true.

"I can't imagine why he'd speak the words that tore so many families apart." Larry was talking to himself.

"He felt obligated," Tristan said, burning holes through Larry again.

Larry's face went apologetic again. "You've had to endure a lot, no doubt. It's not an easy burden to bear."

"I'm not listening to this crap," Tristan laughed cruelly and left.

Katie was caught in between running after him and sitting awkwardly with Larry the ice cream man turned vampire. It was odd, but after the initial shock, it really didn't bother her. Her shock levels were recalibrating again.

Katie stood up. No, her body did. She meant to stay sitting because it was the polite thing to do. "Sorry—uh—he's—not easy to get along with," Katie said, feeling him move further and further away. He wasn't moving fast though. He wanted her to catch up.

Larry released a deep breath. "You used to be a caterpillar. Now I can see you've turned into a butterfly. Strange, I thought when it happened I'd be delighted, but it saddens me in a way."

Creepy.

Super creepy.

What was she supposed to say to that? Could he tell she'd drank blood only hours ago?

"I suppose you'd like to go check on him?" he said.

"Uh—yeah, sorry," Katie said, a bit out of sorts. Could she ever go back to that ice cream shop now?

Katie turned to leave, but not before waving at him awkwardly.

Allison stood up. "I'd like to apologize for the damage we caused, and say thank you for all the discounted ice cream. I hope what we've done hasn't changed your opinion of us."

"Just children being children. The next scoop is on me, alright?" Larry said, crossing the room to open the door for them.

Why hadn't Katie thought to apologize? Why hadn't she thought to say thank you for not busting them? She was almost angry at Allison for being so damn good in situations like this. Why did Allison always know what to say and do?

Katie said goodbye again and walked in silence to the elevator, through the club—avoiding eye contact with Yellow-hair, who was staring at her for way too long—and out onto the street where she followed her Tristan-compass.

Allison didn't say anything, and Katie didn't want to touch

whatever she was fuming about with a ten-foot pole. Not when Allison probably had a knife in her pocket and knew how to use it.

It wasn't long before they caught up with Tristan. He wasn't exactly making it hard to follow him, but as soon as they were close enough he picked up his pace and led them out of Gray City.

It was strange to Katie how completely different she'd felt when she'd taken the elevator into Gray City. She'd been overflowing in excitement and adventure. Now she was quietly cooking. Even though she was standing in a small elevator, moving towards the above world, she couldn't hear Tristan's thoughts. Maybe he'd caught on that she could hear them easily. Maybe, like Larry, he could tell she'd drank blood. Maybe she looked different—or smelled different.

Anyway, his silence was undeserved. If anything, he had gotten them into this mess. So she showed up at the same club as him. He didn't own the place, and she had the right to dance with whoever she wanted—

Tristan banged his fist against the elevator wall and Katie and Allison jumped. The doors opened, and a morning haze drifted in. They had to squint and adjust their eyes.

"Anyone have the time?" Allison said, opening her purse. She searched through it faster and faster. "I don't have my phone. I lost my phone. Katie, call it."

Katie? Allison *was* pissed. Katie looked at her own phone. It was dead.

Tristan was off walking again. He always had a watch on. He could have told them the time, but as Katie looked closer, it wasn't there. Maybe he'd given it to one of his girlfriends. Or maybe the girl he slept with every Tuesday—

Tristan spun on her like a cornered cat. "SHUT UP!" His voice traveled down the empty street.

"Don't tell me what to do. It's not my fault you can hear me and I don't give a damn. Hear it all, asshole." Katie's voice grew louder and louder with every word.

"Why did you follow me here tonight? To prove a point? Well you did, and you looked like a slut while you did it."

He slung the word at her like mud and she was ashamed at how dirty she felt because of it. "Why are you here? WHY TRISTAN? Why did you ever come back? You should have just stayed where ever the hell you were and left me alone. No one wants you around! My dad hates you. You only piss off Lucy and you've ruined her life, Will's life, Brian's life, and the numbers keep growing because you've *completely* destroyed mine."

As Tristan stared at her his, eyes went dead. He walked toward her, past her, and back into the elevator. He pushed a button and the door shut, severing everything that held them together. The magnetic pulse she felt, his thoughts, the sense of him. It was all gone.

She'd gone too far. What the hell had she done? She'd gone too far.

She pushed the elevator button, but it wasn't working. "Allison, how do I get back into the el—" Allison was walking away. "Allison!" Katie shouted. She needed to get back down there and find him. She'd gone too far.

Allison kept walking.

"Allison!" Katie reached out and touched her arm.

Allison grabbed Katie's arm and flung it off her.

"Alli—"

"When were you going to tell me?" Allison ground her teeth. What was she talking about? This wasn't the time to get upset because she didn't tell her *everything*. Allison wasn't her personal diary. Katie could keep whatever she wanted from her.

"Tell you what?" Katie was out of breath. It was her heart. It had been pounding ever since she'd gotten out of that elevator.

"The *Keeper's Vow*, Katie." Allison said her name like it was a joke. "I read books too."

"Allison, get off it. So I didn't tell you. It's not something to tell."

"Not the *vow*, you idiot. The fact that only vampires can take it. The fact that you have to at least be half-vampire to be bonded that way." Allison flexed her hands in and out of fists. "You're half-vampire and you didn't tell me. You dragged me out tonight not because you wanted to hang out with me after being a complete and utter bitch for the last two months, but so you could follow *him* down there and make him jealous. It's *always* about Tristan. I am so sick and tired of taking a back seat to whatever boy is in your life. We were never friends. I was just someone you bitched and complained to when Brian made you angry, and when Tristan showed up—don't even get me started. Do you even *know* what's going on in my life? Do you even know that my parents are filing for divorce because my dad has been cheating on my mom for a year? That he missed my preliminaries because he was picking up that woman's son from a baseball game? Or that I broke up with my boyfriend two days ago?"

Katie took a step back. She stuttered, but nothing came out. Her dad had been cheating? A divorce? When had Allison *gotten* a boyfriend? Who? Why didn't she tell her? "I—I didn't know—"

"Of course you didn't *fucking* know! YOU DON'T CARE ABOUT ANYONE BUT YOURSELF." Allison was done. She didn't wait for Katie to respond, or for Katie to say she was sorry, or say that Allison was being a little unfair.

Katie followed behind Allison until Allison made the left turn to take her home. She never once turned back to see if Katie was behind her or not. Katie wanted to scream. She wanted to slump down onto the sidewalk and scream. Of course she didn't. She'd have to wait until she was in her bedroom face-first into a pillow.

She tried to focus on how she'd sneak back in. It was better than seeing the dead look in Tristan's eyes and the way Allison's red hair swung after she'd turned her back on Katie. She decided to go up the same way she'd left. It wasn't so hard, not with her new body.

As soon as she put her head into the window, it was over.

"YOU SNUCK OUT?! AFTER YOU WERE ATTACKED BY A WEREWOLF AND SHOT BY A VAMPIRE, YOU SNUCK OUT TO GOD KNOWS WHERE? DO YOU KNOW HOW MANY PEOPLE ARE LOOKING FOR YOU?" Her dad was pacing. He'd flung over her bookcase in a rage. Why was everyone in her life so violent? He went on for at least twenty minutes telling her that she'd never leave the house again, that he was going to take her to an omitter because she wasn't responsible, that she'd wasted people's time and energy, and again and again, how stupid she was.

When he was done, he called Lucinda to tell her that Katie had been found, and Lucinda spent thirty minutes screeching through the phone, repeating everything her father had already covered. One word hovering—*selfish*.

Katie didn't cry. She was numb.

Everyone hated her.

She took a shower and fixed her bookcase. Her favorite Peter Pan book was pinned under the case. The cover was bent, and the spine tore when she pulled it from under the bookcase. She tried to fix it. Stupid book. She never liked the story. Never even read it. Why was she trying to fix something that was never going to be whole again?

She charged her cellphone, and it blew up with missed calls and text messages. She didn't dare listen to any of the voicemails. She started to delete them all until she came across a strange number. She listened to it.

"Hello, Katie? It's Larry. I think your friend left her phone in my office. I'll bring it by the ice cream shop. Don't let me forget next time you stop by. See you soon. Oh—I've been thinking about adding frozen yogurt to the selection. I've ordered a few different ones. Free "fro-yo" if you girls can tell me which ones are best. See you soon."

Katie breathed deeply and fell back onto her bed. She didn't feel every fiber like before, not unless she paid attention. It was almost eight o'clock, and she hadn't slept at all. She wasn't tired either. Must have been a side effect from the blood, like her ability to see, smell, and hear, and piss people off to exaggerated extremes.

She rolled over on her side. Traci would be here any moment, and the last thing she wanted was to explain why she hadn't touched any of the work she assigned her. She wasn't in the mood for it.

⁘

"Katie did you do *any* of it?" Traci said in her squeaky voice. The squeaks used to be endearing but that was when she saw Traci once a day for an hour.

"I got busy, I—"

"Busy doing what? You just don't care. I can't help you if you won't help yourself."

"I'm not allowed to slack off for *one* day?!" Katie ran her hands through her hair. Her fingers got caught in a tangle.

"One day off? Katie, I'd be glad if you only took *one* day off. When's the last time you did all the work I asked you to? When was the last time you did an entire assignment? You're full of excuses."

"I'M TRYING!" Katie screamed. They were all attacking her today. It wasn't fair.

"Do you even use the planner I got you?" Traci waited for an answer, but Katie wasn't going to give it. It was still in the back of her locker where she put it after Traci gave it to her. Traci shook her head and grabbed her purse. She rummaged for a second and pulled out the planner that was supposed to be in Katie's locker—the locker Traci had to go through to get her books. "You never even opened it." Traci flopped it on the table, packed her things, and left.

She was the third person that day to walk out on her. She could handle Tristan, because maybe, maybe she could fix it. She could handle Allison, because Allison always forgives her. Her dad and Lucinda, they were just angry parents. But Traci was never disappointed in her. Traci always gave her those lame motivational speeches and worked with her.

Katie laid her head on the table and cried. They were all right. They were right about everything.

17

Broken Pieces

No one talked to her for a week. It wouldn't have been so bad if she could sleep, or leave the house. She was surprised that her dad never put bars on the windows. She tried to make it up to him by cooking every day and cleaning the house, but it didn't work. The only way they communicated was via grocery list and short commands. An actual conversation about anything other than what she should, or could do was nonexistent.

She never ate what she cooked. It was like stuffing food down an already stuffed body, but as the week went on, she could feel her body growing more tired.

Lucinda still trained her, but she never saw Allison. Lucinda made gestures and gave lectures when she wanted Katie to do something, which was only shoot, because that was all they did for a week straight. After training, she'd discuss what Katie did well, what she needed to do better, and what they were going to do next. That was it. No friendly chats, none of the small talk Lucinda was known for. Only lectures, instructions, and feedback. Traci mumbled a word here or there, but Katie never knew if she was talking to herself or not.

Since Katie didn't need her nights to sleep, she did her homework and tried to catch up on the things she'd never bothered to do. Traci sometimes seemed impressed, but she never really said anything.

⁕

She was allowed to go to school starting tomorrow. It was a good thing. She could hear other voices besides the ones on the television. Her teachers would probably talk directly to her, and she wouldn't feel like she'd break out into tears every time Lucinda looked at her with disappointed eyes.

Katie stayed up that night working on math. She was getting better at it. So many patterns. She laughed at herself when she started looking forward to doing the next problem.

She lay back on her bed, taking a break. She couldn't wait for school tomorrow. It would be nice to spend time seeing something other than her four walls.

"TELL ME!"

Katie shot up. It was Tristan. Her body filled with dizziness and rage. She even tasted alcohol.

"I told you, I don't know." In her mind, she saw a small guy with red hair and bright blue eyes. He was shaking. *"Look man, you've had a few drinks, maybe you're confusing me with someone else."*

Tristan was laughing maniacally. She could feel his rage boiling over. *"You're making this harder"*—Tristan grabbed the guy's face and slammed it into a brick wall—*"Than it has to be."* The guy scratched at Tristan's hand, but the pain felt good. Tristan let go, and the man's head flung backwards. Blood stained the wall. *"Tell me."* Tristan was breathing harder.

The redhead cried and held his head. *"Don't kill me. Please. I don't know."*

Tristan walked away. He flexed his fist and laughed.

Everything went blank. But Katie could still taste the alcohol and the echo of his manic laugh. Her heart pounded, threatening to break her chest. What was he doing?

She tried to focus her dizzy mind on math. But she was kidding herself. Her hands shook—they ached. It was him. She was feeling too much of him. She tried to slow her breathing. She didn't want to see something like that again. But it was too late, she was sucked in again.

He was pounding back drinks. So many he started to throw up. Katie ran to the bathroom quick enough to make it into the toilet.

Tristan?

If he heard her, he was ignoring her.

And still drinking.

It went on for hours. Until six in the morning. She'd see flashes of him beating people, getting drunker and, right before he passed out, fighting three people at once. They'd knocked him out. But she knew he was alive. She'd caught a glimpse of Mercedes throwing water on his face.

It was almost time to go to school, and Katie lay curled up on her bed. She didn't want to go. Her stomach pinched, and she couldn't get her body to stop shaking. She'd felt one of those punches. She even checked a few times to make sure her hands weren't bleeding. The Black Void. It was back, but she was no longer floating above its surface. She was in the deep end.

⟨◦◦⟩

She went to school, but spent half of it in the nurse's office when he started having nightmares—she hoped they were just nightmares and not memories. One of a D-range vampire breaking through his front door. He was a little boy, maybe eight. It was the first time he'd ever killed someone. The sound of a neck cracking, as if there were a thousand tiny bones popping at once. That night. It changed something in him. She could tell by the way he'd wake up filling her mind with his scream every time he stabbed the D-range in the head. He'd wake up, take a drink, and go back to sleep. Those dreams were real…but the others, she hoped *so bad* they weren't.

A Death Dealer. He lied. They weren't a police force. They were executioners.

⟨◦◦⟩

During the week, she tried to pay attention in class, but she was merely walking in the dark. Flashes here and there. And screaming, always screaming. She had been right to call it the Black Void because it never ended. Perpetual darkness. She waited for a twilight, a glimmer of hope, but whenever silence settled, something else crawled out. Once it was a little girl. A D-range. The others wanted him to kill her, but he couldn't— she was just a little girl.

They did it and made him watch her head snap back as the bullet went through. It didn't kill her though, it only stopped her long enough for them to throw her out into the rising sun. He ran after her, but by the time he'd reached her body, it had shattered into crystals—she felt like fine sand.

Katie woke up crying in her math class. She couldn't stop. She didn't know when she'd fallen asleep, or when she'd been led to the office, or when they called her dad. She kept seeing that little girl's face and the bullet going through her head. They never closed her eyes. They just tossed her. And he wasn't fast enough.

Katie screamed.

"Katie? Katie Bug, talk to me." It was her dad. He was shaking her.

"I'm sorry," she said. She was talking to Tristan, but only her dad heard her. Her dad took her home, and when Lucinda came to train her, she didn't look surprised to find Katie curled up in her room.

"Katie? When was the last time you drank? You have to every two weeks or you'll start having withdrawals. Do you feel dizzy? Murky? Lethargic?"

No. She couldn't drink anymore. The visions were less detailed as the week went on. If she drank again, she'd feel him more. She'd feel it all. She couldn't. When he was drunk, there was no wall. Katie stayed curled up on her bed and gripped her pillow.

"How does this work, Lucinda?" her dad said.

"I don't know."

"Ask the boy."

"He's been missing. Actually, I wanted to take Katie to Gray City to help me find him. I know they can sense each other,"

Katie looked at Lucinda. How did she know?

"I've watched you both train. You lived at my house. These things don't escape me. Tristan always saw you before you walked into a room. He spent most of your practices answering questions you never said out loud. And you just confirmed it."

Katie shook her head. She didn't want to go to Gray City. She didn't want to see him. It could get worse the closer she'd get to him. For the first time, she was truly afraid of Tristan. Not because he was half-vampire, but because of what he kept locked up inside. The real reason he'd always kept her out.

And like that, Katie caught a glimpse of a woman flying into light. Katie—no Tristan—had scratches and bites on his arms from where she'd tried to hold on.

Katie shook her head.

It took an hour for Lucinda to convince her to go. Lucinda told her he'd been creating noise amongst some of the guardians establishments in Gray City, but Katie knew that. It was the fact that Lucinda was worried that changed her mind. Tristan hadn't returned home since the day he shut the elevator doors in Katie's face. It was her fault.

Lucinda kept looking back at Katie while they drove into downtown. Tristan hadn't started drinking yet, but the nightmares, or memories, were starting up.

"What's going on, Katie?" Lucinda said.

Katie shook her head. Katie didn't want to tell her just how deeply she could sense Tristan. It would be a violation if she did.

They took the bistro down into Gray City, and Katie felt him like a magnet. This time, going to Gray City was very different from the last. She was afraid of what they'd find. He wasn't far. He was in a small bar that Lucinda said was owned by an ex-guardian turned werewolf.

When they walked in, Katie saw him right away, sitting at the bar, staring down at his drink. He didn't notice them though. Not until Lucinda was two feet from him.

"Tristan? Why haven't you come home? What are you doing in a bar? You're not old enough to—"

"Leave me the hell alone." He turned back to the drink in front of him. It would be the first one since he woke up.

"Tristan—"

"I said back the fuck off."

Lucinda stood still and steadied her breathing. Katie wanted to warn her. Tristan was a rumbling volcano, but only Katie could feel the earthquake beneath her feet. He sat still as stone, looking at his drink.

Lucinda tried to grab his drink, but he smacked it onto the ground right before she touched it.

"HEY!" the bartender yelled. He was a burly man with thick sideburns. He reached for something under the bar.

"It's alright, Birmingham. He's my nephew."

Tristan stood up. "I'm nothing to you. No, I take that back. I'm a blood-whore's baby. You remember that letter? I bet you do. It made my mother cry for months."

"Hey, get out kid," Birmingham said, wiping the spilled liquor off the table. He didn't take his eyes off Tristan.

Tristan moved past Lucinda and towards Katie. He didn't look at her. He was walking past her as if she didn't exist.

"Tristan." It came out a whisper. But she couldn't let him walk out the door. "Tristan."

He stopped.

"Please, stop. Just—"

When his eyes met hers, a shudder ran down her entire body. She felt everything. His anger. His sadness. His regret. Everything. And it was all meant for her. He hated her to his core.

"*You* are the worst. While you grew up with two families and a clean conscience, I lived in solitude like a prisoner. No one wanted me. Because I'm the real version of what you are. Even the man who locked me away spent all this time waiting to give you free ice cream. While you *have* a life, I have to live mine tied to yours because your whore-mother took that away from me. From the day you were born and until the day I die, it will *always* be about you."

His nostrils flared, and he dug his nails into his hands. She could feel the pain on her own hands. "I fucking *hate* you."

Hot tears ran down her face. She wished…she wished that he was lying. Saying it to hurt her. But all she felt was his hate mixed in with loss, loneliness, fear, and regret. All of it thundered in her until she couldn't breathe.

Tristan walked out the door. Inside, her heart burst, and she dropped to her knees. She could even feel his heart turning to stone and crumbling into tiny pieces. The shards stabbed at her insides. This is what they had done to him. The way she couldn't breathe, the way she couldn't stand, or feel Lucinda pulling her up. This is what *she* had done to him.

18

Purebloods & Ice cream

How DO YOU fix something so broken you can't even recognize the pieces? Katie could see now that his entire life he'd been trying to glue the pieces of himself together. One by one, he tried to make himself whole, but glue never holds up. He had come back into her life because he couldn't do it by himself. He'd needed them. He'd needed her.

After seeing him in the bar, the visions got no better or worse, they just changed. She was his nightmare. All those times she'd thought of him as a monster, gotten angry with him for being reclusive, the way she'd said he ruined her life. It was all there, laid out for her to see while he pounded back more drinks. He was always drinking.

Katie was on her way to school, alone, because Allison never walked with her anymore. Or talked with her. Or looked at her.

Katie got as far as the school steps before she turned around. She hadn't drank blood and she was almost a week overdue. Her vision was fuzzy at times, it was hard to hear, and she'd tripped over her own feet twice already in the last five minutes. She needed to drink, but more blood meant more Tristan. She didn't want the distinctive burn and taste of vodka right before he threw it up.

She wandered around downtown in a daze. The first time she was downtown with Tristan, he'd followed her around from shop to shop until she confronted him. He couldn't just tell her that he could hear her thoughts. No, he always had to be indirect.

For him, being indirect was making an effort. He always wanted her to meet him halfway. She'd spent their entire relationship expecting him to do all of the work.

Katie stopped in front of Larry's ice cream shop. He was in there scooping out ice cream for an older woman. She went to open the door. It would be her first time seeing him since that night. What would she say?

He was waving her in.

She opened the door and sat at one of the tables. She didn't want ice cream. Why was she here?

He waved to the woman as she left the store, and took a long look at Katie. He walked over to the door and locked it, flipped the open sign over to closed, and sat down across from her.

"You don't look well." He didn't sound like Larry, the friendly ice cream man. He was Larry, the nightclub owner. Things had changed.

Katie smiled. It was weak. She felt like she was going to cry. And then she was. Why *was* she crying in front of Larry in his ice cream shop? Her head was down on the table, and he patted her back until she stopped. He didn't ask her what was wrong, or tell her everything was going to be okay. He just let her cry.

"I'll tell you a story." She heard him shift in his chair. "My father used to hate me because I didn't need blood *and* food from the earth like him. Everyone but him saw me as a blessing from God."

Katie looked up.

"He tried to kill me when I was ten. That was when I found out I had the ability to heal myself."

Katie raised her eyebrows in question.

"He and a few others saw our births—me and the other royal children—as a curse. The women stopped being fertile, and we were the only ones ever with gifts that were supposedly from the God that had originally damned us. It was a very complicated time.

"Ivan was really the one who saved me. We were best friends growing up. Inseparable—until he moved to the New World." Larry eyes drifted and stared out past her. "I had been screaming because my father was pushing iron nails into my hands and feet. He was going to crucify me, and told me if I was really from God that I should be glad to die. He told me neither God, nor God's blessings had a place in his house. Not when the rest of them were cursed to live in the shadows.

Ivan was smaller than me then, but he had the strength of a thousand men. My father was about to put the final nail through my skull when Ivan hurled him across the room and said he'd kill him if he ever touched me again. Ivan had thick black hair like Tristan, but it was at his shoulders then. And that night he looked like a demon with it slick and pulled back from his bony face.

No one knew what his gift was. I was the only one to ever see him use it. I kept his secret, and he kept my father away from me until the day came when we had to kill our fathers."

Katie swallowed.

"Tristan reminds me of Ivan. He hardly ever smiled, and when he did it was always a mocking smirk that, most times, I wanted to slap off his face. And he was always…cryptic. It was easier to make a cat walk on water than it was to get him to speak openly."

Katie sat up in her chair. "Tristan stayed with you after, didn't he?"

Larry nodded. "I kept him in my house in New York." Larry was quiet for a while.

Katie tried to make sense of it. There had to be a reason.

"Tristan is a—troubled boy. I can't say I approve of you having a relationship with him. Let alone being bonded."

Katie looked away. First, they *didn't* have a relationship. Second, Larry wasn't exactly someone who could approve or disapprove. Third, Tristan wouldn't be so troubled if he'd raised him instead of leaving him in a house to raise himself like a potted plant.

"I can tell by the look on your face—you didn't like what I just said," Larry chuckled. "You're like your mother."

"How'd you know my mother?" Katie said, feeling intruded on.

Larry stood up and walked over to the counter. He grabbed something and came back. He handed her Allison's cellphone. "Maybe we'll talk about that next time? I can't make any money if I'm closed, and you never pay." He smiled at her teasingly, but there it was. Evasion. How had he known her mother? Why did he own an ice cream shop near her neighborhood called 'Kat's' ice cream?

She left. She didn't want to open that can of worms. Not now. Not tomorrow. Not ever. Nope.

～○○○～

She waited outside the school until the last bell rang. She went in and waited by Allison's locker. They still weren't talking to each other, but she needed to give her her cellphone back.

As soon as Allison saw Katie, she scowled. She opened her locker and put her books away, all the while acting as if Katie wasn't there.

"I have your cellphone," Katie said.

The locker door slammed. "You had my phone this whole time?"

"No, I—"

"*Unfreakingbelievable.*" Allison grabbed it from her.

"I didn't have it. You left it—forget it." Katie turned to walk away.

Allison stopped her. "What's been up with you?" Allison looked a little sheepish, like maybe she was talking about the weather and not worried.

Katie almost lied. But when she opened her mouth, the truth poured out instead. "My best friend hates me. Tristan told me that he hates me. My dad and Lucinda won't talk to me. Traci thinks I'm a failure, I can't see most of the time, I'm tired. I think I might puke again—for the third time today. I have day-mares and nightmares without even closing my eyes. And I think the ice cream man is my father."

Allison stared at her. "Wait. Have you gone to the hospital—Larry? You think Larry is your dad?"

"No hospital. Lucinda says it's withdrawals. And yeah, Larry. He all but told me just now. My father is the ice cream man. I think I might puke again."

She did. Allison waited outside the bathroom stall.

"So before we attack that beast of a reveal, tell me what you're withdrawing from?"

Allison's voice was dangerous.

"I'm not on drugs. Is there anyone else in here?"

Allison's footsteps clicked up and down the bathroom. "No."

Katie opened the stall and splashed her face with water. "Blood."

Allison's mouth dropped. "You've—how long? What's it like?"

"First time was the last time, as far as I'm concerned. It tastes like rot and—" Katie couldn't continue. She couldn't tell her about Tristan. She could never tell anyone. "It's been a rough few weeks." Katie looked at Allison through the mirror, avoiding her own face, which had adopted a grayish look. She tried her best to pretend she was still okay. Still herself. "How about you?"

"Me what?" Allison cocked her head to the side. Was Katie that bad of a friend that Allison didn't know she was asking, *'how are you?'* Was that such a foreign concept to Allison?

Katie's stomach tightened.

"How are you handling the—breakup and stuff?" Katie wanted to ask about the divorce, but maybe she wasn't considered privileged enough to bring it up. Allison was keeping her distance and looking a bit nonchalant.

"Oh. Adam and I are talking again. Turns out he thought I stopped liking him because I was snapping at him all the time. I was just mad about my parents' divorce. If I'd had just told him we could have avoided it all. I probably could have talked to him about it. His parents are divorced too. It's really not that big of a deal. I mean it's not like they were the perfect couple or anything. To be honest, I'm kind of glad my dad is moving out. Anyway—"

Katie nodded.

Allison nodded.

"Sorry," both said at the same time.

They were never good at making up from fights. They would usually pretend like the fight never happened and move on.

Allison took a deep breath. "So Larry. How—creepy."

"Tell me about it."

They were out of the bathroom and walking downtown, making sure to avoid the ice cream shop. Allison brought up good points: it made the free ice cream less creepy, it was cool to have a vampire dad, at least he was *in* the picture, and he never specifically said it, so she could be jumping to conclusions, though it was highly unlikely.

They also agreed on the faults: it was still one-hundred percent creepy that he owned an ice cream shop, her mother left him for a reason, and worst of all, what he did to Tristan. How could he neglect his best friend's kid, or any kid for that matter?

Their conversation shifted to Tristan, and Katie told Allison about the last time she saw him.

"Wow," was all Allison muttered. Katie had hoped Allison would tell her something uplifting and reassuring. All she did was confirm Katie's worries.

"He'll never forgive me. I know he won't. I told him everything I said because I knew it would hurt him. Instead, I think I broke him." Katie sniffed back a few tears.

Allison rubbed her back as they sat down on a park bench in Findley Park. The park where Tristan and Katie spent the night. Now that she thought about it, he probably did put his shirt over her. It was something he'd do, but never take credit for.

"He doesn't hate you. He's Tristan. He's in love with you. I've never seen him light up for anyone else like he does for you.

You're the only person who ever got him to try food. Every day, during lunch, he'd taste something because *you* asked him to. He's always reminding Lucinda you don't like tomatoes on your sandwiches. If he's not sitting next to you, then he's looking for you, because he acts like he needs you to breathe."

Allison sighed. "To be honest, I hated him for a long time. He stole you from me. We used to be that close. About everything. But he didn't steal you, he needed you. He still does. If you're his friend—if you love him—you'll be there for him."

Deep down, Katie knew it was true. She should be there for him, no matter what. But How could she when his hate ran so deep? "You weren't there, Allison. He hates me. To his core."

"He hates that you're a selfish ass. That you don't see how much you mean to him. Anybody would hate that. You hated it when he was indifferent toward you, didn't you? When he started treating you like you guys were just friends."

"But—"

"It's the same thing, Kay."

Allison was right. Katie always wanted him to chase her and deliver grand romantic gestures. He'd been chasing her all along. Chasing her, and saving her, and loving her.

She was a monster.

⚬◈⚬

When Katie got home, she dropped her bags in the kitchen and went straight to the refrigerator. Her dad wasn't home to hold her hair back and talk her through it. It was her decision, and so she had to do it alone.

She pulled down a glass and filled it to the brim with blood. The smell alone almost sent her overboard. There was no going back. If his life was tied to hers, she could at least endure his nightmares with him.

Tristan told her once that drinking never gets better. He failed to mention that each time feels violent and worse than the last. She did it though, and just as she suspected, she was back in the darkness. The darkness where he'd lost his heart.

⁂

She spent a week avoiding Larry, but she couldn't run away from that too. She sucked it up Saturday morning and went to his shop. When she saw the sign—*Kat's ice cream*—she wanted to gag. The whole time. It had been there the whole time.

Larry looked relieved when she walked in. Katie had rehearsed what she'd say. She'd try to make it as nonchalant and matter-of-fact as possible, but Larry never gave her the chance.

He locked the door, switched the sign, and started off into another story. This time about his travels around the world, and what it was like to see a Shakespeare play on stage for the first time. He told her what it was like coming to America and how it was a different kind of wild than he had ever seen before in his life. And how he had started to question his purpose in life when he was in Germany.

Katie asked him if he had ever tried to use his gift of healing to help people, and he laughed, saying she was exactly like her mother. They sat in silence after that, and he pretended he didn't see her incredibly embarrassing '*I'm about to freak-out*' face.

After a while, he told her that his *gift* was just as much of a curse.

"I call it healing, but it is really a gift of life and death. I tried when I was young, but quickly realized that I didn't know whether the person I put my hands on would heal or die. I started only using it when I knew that the person would die whether I intervened or not."

"Well, that's a little better," Katie said, thinking of the lives he could save.

"There is a catch, my dear Katalina."

Katie cringed. He'd never called her Katalina before. Yet, it sounded so natural. She hoped that wasn't what he called her mother, but there was no use lying to herself. "The more I heal, the more I die."

Katie looked away from the window and at him. "What?"

"I didn't know it until the time I healed your mother. I started coughing up blood, and my heart slowed down."

He shifted in his chair when he realized she was intentionally looking away. Why couldn't he just say, *I'm your father'* and be done with it? On the other hand, she could say something too, but—

"You know, your mother and—I…"

Pandora's box needed a padlock. "So what happened to her?" Katie said. She was just as much a coward as he was. Maybe that's where she got it from? *Ugh.*

"We were in New York. It was a cold winter that year. She was attacked by werewolves. Ten of them. I did everything to save her. She wasn't completely happy with the results, but I saved her life. It left me weak and near dead, but your mother was on death's doorstep. Energy is neither created nor destroyed. Do you know what that is?"

"Energy conservation." *And one point goes to Traci.*

"When I use my gift, it has to come from somewhere. And it took me a long time to realize that it comes from myself. I give a piece of my life to heal another. And other times, whether I want to or not, I take life from another. That is why mine is a curse."

"Tristan said his dad felt the same way about his strength. Tristan doesn't though." Katie said it, but Larry raised his eyebrow to confirm it. Maybe his gift had passed down to her? If she *was* his daughter…

Neither of them touched that.

"How is Tristan?" Larry asked.

Katie hesitated. "I don't know. He's stopped talking to me.

"I see."

"I can't make him hear me either." She'd tried that. Maybe he was too drunk to hear her.

"If Tristan doesn't want to hear you, there is nothing you can do. Except apologize for whatever it is he's sore about."

Katie sighed. What if she wasn't brave enough to apologize? What if she never saw him again? "What if one of us died? The other would feel it, right? I mean—is it true?"

Larry frowned and nodded. His eyes drifted out the window. "You would feel it if he dies. But if you die he will die soon after."

"What if we never talk or see each other again? Does the bond go away?"

"No." After a moment Larry added, "You are a good person. Good people are always forgiven."

"Some things are unforgivable," she said, looking down at the table.

"Would you like to hear another story?"

Katie smiled. Larry was weird.

"I used to be the leader of a pureblood brotherhood in Europe. I was charismatic, I had common sense, and when it counted, I was kind. I was all those things to everyone except my real brother."

Katie never picked Larry for someone with siblings.

"My brother was born ten years after me. He didn't have an easy life. My father refused him because he was halfborn, a product of his kitchen whore. He threw Eshmael out to die. I took him to his mother, our Turkish kitchen slave, and she named him and raised him. My father was furious. He made us take the Keeper's Vow as a punishment."

"Why?" Why was his father crazy?

"Because my father was a demon in a man's body. I'm no better. When I think about my brother, Eshmael, now I wonder if I should have left him to die—don't look at me that way. In a way, Eshmael and I are the same. We both hated our father, and we both don't want to be anything like him. The problem is, you can't escape the demons your parents pass on to you."

"You *can* help who you are," Katie said, not believing Larry. She was trying to change herself now. She wanted to be a better person. Not someone who was too selfish to see when her friends needed her. "Anyone can change."

"Perhaps, but you can't help what you believe to be right and wrong. When we were still boys, I used to be ashamed of Eshmael. He called that slave woman his mother, he was a brat, and he even had a slave name. He used to follow me and Ivan around playing tricks and making my life hell."

"Isn't that what all younger siblings do?" she said.

"Eshmael spent his life trying to kill me. We were hardly siblings. He always failed because I was smarter and stronger than him, and because I could heal myself. I'd always rub it in his face that he was nothing and I knew I was wrong for it. —I take that back, Ivan always told me I was wrong for it. Sometimes, Eshmael would hurt himself in one of his own traps and I'd heal him—not because I loved him, but because I wanted him to see how much more powerful I was compared to him. I was as bad as our father was to him. The only good thing I did for him was kill our father." Larry sounded regretful, but of what, Katie wasn't sure. Every time he said his brother's name disdain followed.

He continued. "When Eshmael was still fifteen, he saw our father rape and kill his mother. She was the only person he ever loved. I heard her screaming and when I went, Eshmael was unconscious on the floor and my father had just killed her."

"Why? Why would he do that?"

Larry looked deep in her eyes. "Because he could. Maybe he saw Eshmael laughing with her, maybe he saw how she loved him. It didn't take much for him to end a life, he spent most of his life in shadow form.

I killed him then, with my bare hands. I didn't understand why he had to pick her. The only thing Eshmael had in the world. There were plenty of women throwing themselves at him every day, yet he had to take the one who didn't belong to him. When he was dead, I told myself I did it because of a prophecy, but I really killed him because I thought it would rid us of his evil," he said more to himself than to her.

"I was wrong. Eshmael became more of a devil, and I, who should have shown him the right path, let him make his own of death and destruction. I never reached out to him like a brother should have. Though we came from the same father, I had a friend to keep me from a life of abhorrence. Ivan forced me to live an honest life. I should have done the same for Eshmael. We were flesh and blood brothers, yet I cast him aside like he was a peasant. I was a fool. I was envious."

Larry didn't look at Katie, and she felt his shame. "Envious of what?" It seemed to her that there was nothing to envy Eshmael for.

"Because a brother always wants what the other has. I had power and I never wanted him to be able to take that from me. He had a mother who loved him…"

"What happened to him?"

"He lives to destroy me."

"He's trying to kill you? That's a bit…much."

"No. He doesn't want to kill me. Just everything I love. Everything that brings me happiness. It's my job to forgive him and show him that it's possible. That even now he can also forgive me."

"If he keeps trying to kill everything you love, I think you guys are past forgiveness." Eshmael was dangerous. People like that were labeled as sociopaths today. Didn't Larry know that?

"That is my retribution, Katalina. At least my father cast him out to die. I saved him and showed him a life full of hate and inhospitality. In a way, that makes me more of a demon than my father. If I can hope for forgiveness from my brother, you can hope for forgiveness from Tristan."

The sun blinded Katie as it settled just above the window. A few rays slipped directly into the shop. "Do you like to paint?" he asked suddenly.

Caught off guard, Katie shrugged her shoulders. "I've never really tried."

"How about tomorrow we go to a studio? It's next door."

Katie agreed, but she felt a little guilty. Like she was cheating on her dad with her maybe real dad. Who wasn't exactly her dad, but someone who knocked up her mom. Maybe.

⚬⚭⚬

Painting was fun. They did it often. It helped to talk to Larry. Slowly, she started to tell him about how hard it was sometimes to see things Tristan saw, but she never went into detail, and he never asked her to. He'd tell her to try painting the good things she saw. And sometimes she did. She had never realized it before, but sometimes Tristan did flood her with good memories. They just seemed like nightmares because they'd always sent him drinking. Especially the ones of her.

"What is that?" Larry asked once.

Pointing at a yellow-gold blob, Katie had replied, "a honeypot."

She was becoming numb though. As numb as he was.

The only thing that brought a little ease to her numbness was painting with Larry. She let out all her anxieties into bad sunsets and lopsided oceans. She wasn't good at it, but there was something about blending colors that made her less numb on the inside.

"You've forgotten to drink, haven't you?" Larry asked, signing the bottom of his painting of a landscape with a castle.

"Are you painting that from memory too?" Katie answered. Before, he had painted a picture of a boy that looked just like him, with gray eyes, mud-colored hair, a look of contempt sitting on his face. He told her it was Eshmael when he was fifteen.

"Yes. It was where I stayed in Germany. Where I met your mother. Why aren't you drinking?"

"You always drop 'mom bombs' and never stay for the fallout," she half-chuckled.

"What are *mom bombs*?" he asked, watching her. He told her to add shadow to a tree that was really an accidental blotch. He was using his father tone again, he did that without knowing it, but she had grown used to it.

"You just mention my mom but you never talk about her. Like how you knew her."

"You know, you're really not so good at painting," he said, shaking his head.

A laugh caught in her throat.

"I met her in Germany."

Katie put another black glob on the canvas, careful to pretend she wasn't paying attention so he'd talk freely.

"I think she was twenty at the time. She had a big reputation in the underground city there. I never imagined she'd stroll right through the door of my house and chastise me for not punishing the members of my brotherhood that sometimes went—astray," Lawrence laughed. "I can still hear some of them screaming out "injustice" in their thick Dutch. I fell in love with her that day. Love at first sight sounds silly, like something from Shakespeare's plays, but it happened to me.

"She didn't make dating easy. I followed her to New York, where she lived, and she avoided me at all costs. I spent countless hours thinking of ways to win her over. She came from a pure untouchable family, and she was the only child to be a guardian. She had a twin sister who chose to have her memory erased, and I think she felt she had to make up for it. Her father was a purist, and he was ashamed by her lame sister. When I found out, I tried to stop seeing her. I was on my way back to Europe when she showed up at my front door.

"During the time your mother and I had our affair, I was the happiest I'd ever been in my life. We met together for ten years or so and no one ever knew. Eshmael—he found out about us. It all changed when she got attacked by a pack of werewolves."

Larry stopped. He started a new canvas. There was a lot of red.

"I was on my way to see her—I killed them all before they took her." More red. "But—I had to change her. She'd lost too much blood. If I knew she was pregnant—anyway, she cursed me when she awoke as a vampire. She'd lost everything that made her who she was. *'You killed me Lawrence. You killed me.'*" Larry picked up another brush and spread black across the canvas. "That was the last thing she ever said to me. But when you think about it, if I hadn't changed her, you would have died. One life for another."

Katie stared at her canvas. She couldn't bring herself to look anywhere else.

"I'm sorry, Katie. I'm all out of stories for today." They didn't talk after that. Just painted as the light outside grew dimmer.

It was official now. He was her biological father. A man who loved her mother.

19

SPITFIRE

KATIE PACKED HER things to leave. "I'm going to head home now, Larry," Katie said, still not really comfortable making eye contact.

"You can call me Lawrence. I never liked the name Larry much, but it seemed to fit with the ice cream shop."

Katie nodded.

"Do you mind coming with me to the shop first? I have something else to tell you."

Larry—or Lawrence—led her into his shop and unlocked the door. He left the lights off and disappeared to the back room. He came back with a glass in hand and a packet of blood.

Katie swallowed hard.

"You need to be regular with drinking. I've seen you go into withdrawals, and that's dangerous. It can mess with your mind. You can go mad and become a fallen." He opened the packet and poured it into the glass.

"A fallen?"

"Your people call them D-ranges. The fallen get trapped in their shadow form and search to fill their bloodlust. You've seen them in the shadows of Gray City. They can never change back, and the only way to free them is to kill them by exposing them to sunlight."

"That's cruel." Katie said, shivering from the visions she'd had of Tristan doing just that.

"It's crueler to let the shadow consume their souls. Some of them don't have a chance. They are created recklessly and are left to starve when they are reborn. But you, you have a chance. Now that you've started drinking, you can't go back."

Katie remembered the silver glinting eyes from the night she'd been with Allison in Gray City.

"Drink."

Katie's stomach turned. She started to make an excuse, but Larry wouldn't hear any of it. She drank it. It was just as horrid as the last time.

"It's strange. To you, my brother, and all other halfborns, it's unpleasant. To me, it's like eating rainbow sherbet ice cream every Friday." He smiled, but Katie didn't return it. Not while her stomach was still threatening to bring it back up. As always, it was only a matter of seconds before she started to feel better.

She left Larry at the ice cream shop, and her feet took her to Lucinda's house. She'd been avoiding this place. She told herself it was because Tristan was gone, but the truth, she knew, was because she was avoiding Lucinda. Allison had told Katie that Will had left her. He never came back from Seattle with Brian, and it didn't look like he was going to come back.

Katie didn't believe it. She couldn't. Allison was all about divorce now that her parents' were getting one. She saw it everywhere. It was all she talked about. She had to be wrong.

Katie rang the bell, and Lucinda answered. "Why do you always ring the bell, Katie? You know where the key is."

Katie shrugged.

"Want a sandwich? I was going to make myself one."

Katie shook her head. The thought of food made her feel overstuffed.

"Ah, that's right. Well, come in. I'm working on some paperwork in the living room. Why don't you pop a movie in?"

They watched the movie and talked. And talked. And talked. When was the last time Lucinda had someone to talk to? She was alone in this big house now.

Lucinda got a phone call, and Katie went to Tristan's room. It was a pull. She'd been itching to go in there since she'd stepped into the house, as if maybe she'd open the door and he'd be in there smiling at her like usual. It never failed. He always knew she was coming, and she always looked for that smile.

It wasn't there this time. Her heart still sank, even though she knew it wouldn't be.

The room was the way it was before, as if Tristan had never come to this house. No. There was one thing different. A book sitting on the desk. It was never there before. After all, she'd bought it for him for Christmas. Katie touched the leather binding remembering the night she gave it to him. It all seemed so petty now.

It hurt that he left it.

She picked the book up and fanned through the pages. The pages suddenly stopped, and Katie pulled out the paper that had stopped it. A picture. Wrinkled and worn over the years. It was a picture of him and his family. Tristan wasn't looking at the camera though, he was looking at his dad.

"Katie?"

Katie put the picture back in the book and closed it.

"I wondered when you'd come in here." Lucinda stood in the door frame. "I haven't been in here since he left."

Katie sat on his bed. It was cold.

This was her fault. This empty room.

"Don't cry, Katie." Lucinda sat next to her. "I know he'll come back."

Katie shook her head. Lucinda didn't know the things he thought. If she did, she'd know he'd never come back.

"He doesn't really hate you, you know. He was just angry. I can't blame him. I failed him. I'd be angry too." Lucinda sighed. "Those knives you use in practice—he gave them to you, didn't he?"

Katie felt her waist and nodded. She always carried them now. She was still too anxious to walk around with a loaded gun.

"I've seen them before. A long time ago." Lucinda stood up and walked over to the window. She ran her fingers down the curtains softly. "My sister came home with them one day. We always told each other everything, but she wouldn't tell me where she got them." Lucinda cleared her throat. "We stopped being friends that day. And by the time I'd found out she was dating Tristan's father, I was too mad to see how ridiculous I was being. All I did was spout propaganda at her like she needed saving."

Katie watched Lucinda pick at lint on the curtains.

"We wrote each other letters for a little while, after she left. I thought if I could get her to leave him and come home, everything would be better again." She rubbed the fabric. "I found out she was pregnant and—and she had become like him. I called my own sister a blood-whore." Lucinda cleared her throat and opened the window to the room. "I was a terrible sister, but I can be here for her son."

⁂

It had been a long day, and yet, Katie didn't go home. She'd made up her mind. Either she was going to be there for Tristan and share the burden he'd been carrying, or run away forever. Being tormented by his memories wasn't enough. It was time for her to be the person she was born to be, to grow up and be brave. She wasn't going to abandon him. That wasn't who she wanted to be.

She walked by Larry's shop, expecting him to nod as she passed by, but the shop was closed.

Odd. But she couldn't say she was sad he wasn't there. She didn't want anything to distract her from her purpose. She passed by the movie theater, Joe's Coffee, a few thrift shops, but her feet kept moving, taking her deeper and deeper into downtown. Tristan must have been close by. Underneath her somewhere. Sometimes, she would skip school and let her feet take her around downtown. She moved until her feet told her to stop. Start again when they felt like moving. It was him. However, she never mustered up the courage to go down into Gray City. After going through the trouble of pulling out the elevator passcode from Michael, she'd find herself, countless times, in front of the bistro or the Knitting Factory. She wanted to take the elevator down and follow her feet until she found him—no doubt sitting at a bar stool. However, each time was a fail.

Maybe today she could do it.

The bistro was crowded. A perfect time to slip into the back room. She did what she had done three times already. It wasn't hard. She walked between the tables and towards the bathrooms. When no one was looking, she eased into the large room and pushed the button for the elevator.

She had done this already. Even sat inside it for fifteen minutes once.

Katie pushed in the numbers: 6743256.

Her finger rubbed over the enter button. She couldn't stop it from shaking. What was she afraid of? He already said he hated her. What more could he say that would hurt as bad as that?

The elevator doors opened and Katie jumped.

"Er, hello. K—Ka—I'm sorry, I'm not good with names. But you're the girl that almost took off my hand."

It was the werewolf from her evaluation. Mr. Reynolds. British accent and all. He had a peppered five-o'clock shadow that made him look younger than he was.

"You're not supposed to be here, are you?"

Katie moved towards the elevator doors. He blocked her way and pushed the green enter button. They started to move.

He smiled. "I'm not going to tell anyone."

Katie gripped the metal bar behind her. They were moving down into Gray City.

"What brings you to Gray City?" he said, tilting his head towards her.

"A friend."

"Your halfborn friend?" He looked at her. "I take it they haven't found out about you yet."

Katie froze.

"I'm not going to tell anyone about that either." He turned to her. "Guardians like to pretend people like you and your friend don't exist."

"H—How did you know?"

"Any good wolf can smell a shadow. Even the ones who haven't drank. But I see that's changed about you too. You should be careful. You're lucky Carver is too dense to realize why you were able to use your power so quickly. He doesn't know the other part of you helps you control it." He paused. "You live in a lions den. What you are is like a disease to them. They don't like that you're more powerful than them."

Katie stared into his dark eyes. They were warning her. "How do you know so much about how my power works?"

"My brother was halfborn." The doors opened, and Mr. Reynolds stepped out and into the hotel. "When you find your friend. Keep him close. He's the only one who will ever understand what it means to be what you are." Mr. Reynolds winked.

"Yeah," Katie said. She stood in the elevator and watched him leave.

He knew. Ever since that day.

What did he mean his brother *was* half? Half what? Vampire? Wolf?

She ran out of the hotel and onto the street, but he was gone. Cars blurred past her, and the sounds of Gray City filled her ears.

.৩৫৩৯৯.

It didn't take long for Katie's feet to find the right direction. Her heart pounded with every footstep.

8th street. The werewolf district. Maybe he would be with Mercedes. Maybe she was the one who stood by his side now. Katie shook the thought from her mind. Her feet stopped on the corner, unsure where to go. She looked up and down the street, moving out of the way of a small boy who sneered at her. His mother was close behind and smiled apologetically. The crosswalk blinked green and she almost crossed the street when a sign caught her eye.

The Pub.

She stared at the little white sign. It was *The* Pub. She'd seen it before, maybe, but that wasn't what bothered her.

The Pub.

Mercedes had said Tristan had stopped coming to *the pub.* Maybe she meant *The Pub.* An actual place, not a nondescript bar.

Katie jogged down the street and ran across the road. She couldn't see in the window—it was blacked out. The actual building itself was next to a dark alley where she heard quick and fast grunts.

She blushed as a sharp gasp escaped from someone.

What happened if she was wrong. What happened if the place she was walking into was a whorehouse? Or worse, what if the people here took her for someone who would walk down a dark alley and do something similar?

She had come this far. What did she expect? She'd spent weeks seeing what he saw, trying to block out his violence. Just because he was quiet now didn't mean he was sitting in a park somewhere staring up at the stars. She'd made up her mind when she'd gotten out of the elevator. She was going to find him no matter what. She was going to help him put the pieces of his life back together. Even if he hated her.

Katie opened the door. Laughter erupted from inside. A few heads turned to look at her but turned back to the bar after sizing her up. It was dim. Music played in the background, but nothing loud. Conversations bounced back and forth, and more laughter ensued.

"See, Mer. This is what happens when you let one blood-licker in. The others start thinking it's okay."

Katie swallowed and stood her ground. Tristan had been here before. The funny-looking guy with the handlebar mustache must have been talking about Tristan.

"Get off it, Clyde." Mercedes arose from behind the bar and set a crate of beers down. Her long braids swayed. She locked eyes with Katie. Katie's chest eased a little. She was in the right place. "Come sit. Have a drink."

"Mer!" Clyde the Handlebar gasped.

"I said get off it. My bar, my rules. She doesn't bite."

"Not if I bite her first."

Katie tried to act nonchalant, but her hands shook as she sat on the only open bar stool—next to Clyde.

"What's your name?" Clyde asked as if he hadn't just threatened her. Katie took in a deep breath. Time to grow up. Be hard. Act like Tristan.

"I'll put it on your tombstone," she said holding eye contact with Clyde. If he stood up, she'd lose it and pee on herself. She was stupid. Tristan wouldn't have said that. No one would have said anything to Tristan to begin with.

Silence.

Clyde laughed. "Why would you put *your* name on *my* tombstone? You can stay, Spitfire. You're much cuter than the other one anyway." He took a swig of his beer.

Mercedes smiled. "Don't pay attention to Clyde. What's the saying? 'He's all bark.'" She pulled down a glass and then stopped. "What's your poison?"Mercedes bounced her perfect eyebrows up and down. What was this, a saloon in the seventeen-hundreds?

Katie shook her head. "Thanks, but I'm fine."

"Nobody's ever fine." Mercedes put the glass back and leaned over the bar. "You're here for him aren't you?"

Katie didn't need to say anything. There was no other reason she'd show up at this place. Her stomach turned over and over. She was so close.

"I haven't seen him since the day before yesterday." Mercedes arched one of her perfect eyebrows. "He does that sometimes though. He comes and then disappears."

"And he tears the place up."

"Clyde," Mercedes said, in warning.

"It's bad for business, Mer."

"Me putting my fist through your face is bad for your health. Don't think I won't do it. *Again*."

Clyde grumbled and picked up his beer.

"Clyde's not a fan of our friend."

Clyde opened his mouth, but closed it when Mercedes cut him a look.

Katie looked down at the bar. He wasn't here. But she was led here. Maybe he was close. Maybe he was coming. Her heart sped up a little. "What time does he usually come?" she said.

"Around this time. To be honest, I thought you were him. I smelled you out there. Actually everyone did, and they were placing bets on how many drinks it would take before he went off." Mercedes said.

Katie looked at the door instinctively. The door didn't budge.

"Your face is priceless. You look more scared than Clyde did when you opened the door."

Katie stuttered. She was afraid. What would she say to him? What would he say to her? This was what kept her from pressing the button in the elevator.

"He talks about you a lot." Mercedes watched the door with her. "It's not always pleasant, but nonetheless, he's usually going off about you."

Katie wanted to know more. What did he say when he was sober and closing his mind to her?

"He rants and raves, but when he passes out and wakes up screaming, talking about you is the only thing that calms him down."

Katie shook her head. Half the things he woke up screaming about had to do with her. She couldn't believe that. Mercedes must have seen the disbelief on her face.

"Then tell me why I know you hate tomatoes, or that you used to have a gerbil, but you dad ran it over? Or that you could eat your weight in rainbow sherbet ice cream, your left hook is killer, you still watch Saturday morning cartoons, and you collect ratty old books? Not to mention your room looks something like a botched crayon abortion—his words, not mine."

Katie held back the smile.

"Also, you have a bit of a jealous streak?" Mercedes smiled wide. "You know, I don't date shadows. I like my men hairy."

Katie blushed. He *told* her about that? "Tristan said you were helping him," Katie said, hoping Mercedes would stop grinning.

"I was."

"Did he find what he was looking for?" Katie couldn't say it. The man who murdered his family and her mother. It was unreal to her, like a movie. She'd caught glimpses of the story Tristan told her, but he never told her how he saw the bodies of his parents—that his father was missing his head, and that the last memory of his mother was her covered in blood.

"He did." Mercedes wiped down the bar.

Another laugh rumbled from the corner as a man fell off his seat.

"How far are you willing to go for Tristan? What are your limits?" Mercedes said. How was Katie supposed to answer a question like that? "When he walks through that door, he might not be the same Tristan you last saw. He's turning into someone who likes the sight of blood. I've seen guys go off the deep like that. Bringing them back isn't easy. And if I'm right, when shadows get bloodlust, they don't come back. Ever."

Katie nodded. She knew what Mercedes meant, but that didn't stop her from flinching as the door opened.

It wasn't him.

"I—I'd—" The rest of her words caught in her throat. She was falling. She hit the floor and screamed. Pain erupted in her body, and she shook from head to toe.

"Katie?" Mercedes jumped over the bar and knelt next to her. She touched her, but snatched her hand back. Everything went black for a moment. The pain still throbbed, but the bar came back into view.

"Katie?" Mercedes was touching her again. "What the hell just happened? Are you epileptic? Should we take you somewhere? Don't just stare at me—talk to me. You're freaking everyone out."

Katie looked around, panting as beads of sweat formed on her brow. The bar was in complete silence. Someone had even cut the music. Katie stared them all in the faces as if they were the ones who'd done it. They were the ones who'd caused the pain.

"Tristan. Something's wrong."

Mercedes nodded for Clyde to come over. He offered to help Katie up, but she waved him off. She needed to get out. The feeling of him was moving away from her. This wasn't like anything she'd felt before. Katie's own body felt wrong. Breathing was painful, like something was squeezing her ribcage.

A hand planted firmly on her shoulder. "You want to tell me what's going on?" Mercedes said. Katie turned and looked around the bar again. They were all watching her. "Mind your own business," Mercedes snapped. The music started and conversations picked up again, but Katie knew they were all still watching.

"I don't know. I just know something's wrong." Katie sucked in her breath and held on to the bar.

"Quit fighting. He wants you alive. Don't act like you haven't been following us around for the last week. This is what you want, isn't it."

Another surge of pain shot up through her bones. She gripped the bar harder and steadied her breathing. He'd been taken by someone. "Who's he been following?"

Mercedes looked alarmed. "How'd you know?"

"Just tell me. He's been taken by someone. They knew he was following them." Katie gripped her side.

Mercedes cursed. "Eshmael. I knew it was too easy. I told him it was too easy."

Eshmael.

The name echoed through her mind and grabbed her insides. Larry's brother.

Katie ripped into her pockets for her cell phone. "Lucy? Lucy, listen. Tristan's in trouble. I can find him, but you have to come quick. I don't know how long we have."

"Katie, slow down. Where are you?"

"Gray City."

"Katie, you know you aren't supposed to be there—"

"He's in trouble! You just have to trust me."

"Tristan can handle himself. You stay put."

She didn't understand. This wasn't a stupid bar fight. "Lucy, he's in serious trouble. He's hurt. I don't—"

"Don't move, Katie. I'm going to make a few phone calls and get some people together and then I'll find him, okay? If the situation is as bad as you say, you need to go home right now."

Katie hung up the phone. Lucinda didn't get it. Katie's blood was on fire. They'd done something to him. He didn't have time for her to make phone calls. She needed to talk to someone who understood how urgent this was.

She searched through her phone for Larry's number. It was still the only number without a name in her call history list. She never deleted it or saved it. Mercedes was shouting orders around the bar as the phone rang. Katie didn't even know if this was a number to the ice cream shop, his cell, or his club.

He answered.

"Larry, Eshmael has Tristan, and he going to do something to him. They've already done something to him. I can find him. I can feel where they're taking him."

"Katie, I know. Where are you?"

"I'm in Gray City at a bar. He's still close by. Maybe ten minutes away from me. I don't know but I *can* find him."

"I know Eshmael has him. I have informants that work for him. I'm on my way to the place their taking him. Everything will be fine. I'll get him back. What bar are you at?"

"It's on 8th street. Why?"

Larry cursed. "Stay where you are."

Everyone wanted her to stay. They didn't feel the blood he was losing. Her phone beeped. It was her dad. Lucinda must have called him.

"Katie?" Larry's voice called. "Don't go anywhere. Eshmael is dangerous. He won't hesitate to kill you. Or anyone else who was in his way."

Katie pulled the phone away from her ear. In Eshmael's way

of doing *what?*

Her mother, Tristan's father they were both people Larry cared about.

He hadn't save them.

She ended the call.

Mercedes grabbed a set of keys and tossed them to Clyde. "Clyde. Watch the bar. You six are on standby. Follow behind us, but not too close. We don't want anyone knowing the pack is moving. We need to attack in small numbers. They won't be expecting us, so let's keep it quiet." Mercedes pointed at two guys already waiting for orders. "You're not going to like where we're going."

A tall guy smiled at Mercedes. "Never do, but I like watching your ass as we go there."

Mercedes didn't react to the comment. She stared at Katie. "Looks like you didn't have any luck," she said, pointing at Katie's phone. "If it's Eshmael who's got him, we're going to have a hell of a time getting him back, but I need someone to lead me there. How far are you willing to go?"

Katie's heart pounded. She was scared out of her mind. "As far as it takes."

"That's the right answer. Let's go."

20

INTO THE LIONS DEN

KATIE'S ADRENALINE PUMPED as she gave Mercedes directions.

Mercedes never let up off the gas pedal. It was just the two of them in the car, but the two guys behind them were right on their tail.

"You're taking us to Eshmael's house. I know where it is. Might take us about twenty minutes to get there."

Katie sat back gripping the door handle. He was losing blood. Slowly. Since she left the bar, they'd done something to his wrist. Hers burned.

"I'm not going to pretend that this isn't weird," Mercedes said. "You're like psychic or something." Mercedes took a hard left. Cars swerved to miss them.

She might die before Tristan.

"It's not like that. It's hard to explain." Katie braced herself as Mercedes hit the brakes. They'd almost hit a woman. Mercedes cursed and sped off. Somehow, the other guys were still right behind them. They never missed a beat.

Katie held onto the door.

"I know how to drive," Mercedes said, maneuvering through cars.

"Just not used to driving like this." Sharp Right. "How do you know Tristan?"

"He saved my life once. Back when he was a Death Dealer. Our old pack leader hated the threat of another Alpha in the group, even if it was his own daughter. He hired Tristan's lead commander to kill me, you know, under the table. Tristan made sure I stayed alive long enough to take my father's seat at the top."

Why did everyone have terrible parents or people out to destroy them? Katie counted herself lucky—her dad just drank too much and forgot to come home at night. Then again, her other father neglected the only child in his care and had a psycho brother.

"We are almost at Eshmael's."

Katie didn't need her to say it. She felt it. Her skin burned with every turn that brought them closer.

"My guys, Franco and Johnny, will do whatever I say. They'd die for me. But I don't want them to. I don't want them dying for you either."

Katie cringed. "I'd never want them to."

"You led us here. It can end there. You can wait in the car, or I can let you out a few blocks away, call your people and have them pick you up. We aren't walking into a tea party. Shadows will be shooting at us with the intention to kill."

Katie swallowed.

"If this is as far as you can go, I'd understand. Tristan would understand."

The car stopped. Did Mercedes mean for her to get out now? Katie couldn't move. He was so close. Her body hurt, not just from him, but from being this close. The closest they'd been in weeks.

"If you're going to get in the way, you'll get us killed. We can handle ourselves and the shadows. But if we have to protect you too, one of us will end up dead. I can't lead my guys in there to get killed like that."

Katie fidgeted in her seat. The words weren't coming out, but she couldn't get out now. Mercedes leaned over her and opened the door. "Get out."

"No," Katie said. "I'm going. I won't get in the way. I can't abandon him because it's dangerous. He'd save me."

He'd always saved her. Every time. No matter what. Maybe because he was bound by the bond, or because he cared. It didn't matter. He put his life on the line. She couldn't walk away. Not now.

Katie closed the door. "Do you have an extra gun? I have knives and I'm good with them. I'm good with a gun—"

"It's not just about if you're good. You'll have to kill someone. Tristan understands that. He's killed before. I know you haven't.

A girl who's killed before doesn't walk into a bar scared of a few drunk men. We're going in to kill. Not take prisoners or make friends." Mercedes opened the glove compartment and put a forty-five pistol, two clips, and a holster on Katie's lap.

Katie picked it up. It was heavier than she remembered it should be. She wasn't a little girl anymore. She was a guardian—no, she was half-vampire. Lucinda didn't teach her how to shoot for fun. Always before every lesson Lucinda would say: *"Don't aim unless you're willing to pull the trigger."* Lucinda was preparing her for the day she'd have to point a gun at a living person.

"I'm going to do whatever it takes to get him back. Drive."

Mercedes nodded and drove down a few blocks before stopping the car again. They were surrounded by classic Victorian-style city houses. Wrought iron fences around each home and old-style lamp posts lighting up the street. "We have to walk the rest of the way."

Mercedes signaled for Franco and Johnny to split up, and they slipped into the darkness. Mercedes led Katie silently in the shadows. They crept over garbage bags and scaled iron gates that irritated her hands.

Katie surprised herself and Mercedes with her stealth. She was in the zone. Her objective was to get Tristan back. No matter what it took. She told herself that over and over, as she gripped one of her sheathed knives.

"You better use that power you have. We're here." Mercedes pointed across the street. A single man stood on the steps of the biggest house on the street—nearly half the city block. He sucked on a cigarette and looked up and down the street. "It's a shadow nest. Maybe ten or fifteen will be in there. I have no idea which room Tristan will be in. You have to lead me there."

"How are we going to get past that guy?" Katie watched him throw his cigarette. Her question was answered before the cigarette hit the ground. Franco emerged out of the darkness, and a knife flew into the back of the vampire's head.

"Shadows shouldn't smoke. It makes it hard to smell when a dog is creeping up from behind." Mercedes smiled as Franco dragged the body into the darkness.

Johnny signaled for them to cross the street. Katie took in a deep breath as she leaned against the brick. She was closer. Tristan was very close.

They scaled the fence around the house. It wasn't real iron.

"Everyone ready?" Mercedes said. She touched Katie's hand. "I told you. Use that power you have."

Katie panicked. She didn't know how. She'd only been able to do it for a few seconds before it flew out of control. Now, she would never be able to concentrate long enough.

Mercedes cursed. "I should have left you in the car."

Johnny waved at them as he peeked around the corner. They ducked.

"Where's Randall?" a voice said from around the corner. A door open. "Damn idiot and his smoke breaks. This place reeks." The door closed again. What was the plan? Walk through the front door and go all action movie on them? Would they jump behind couches and shoot up walls? Katie heard a noise. She looked behind them.

Nothing. Then a screech like metal scrapped across cement. The others heard it too. They crept farther down the side of the house until they found the origin. A small window at the bottom of the wall. Katie peered through. Down below, a man dragged a filing cabinet across the floor. Katie felt the pull. Tristan was down there somewhere. He wasn't up top in the house.

She pointed at the window, and Mercedes nodded. Katie could hardly make out the muffled voices.

"It's not down here—you look then—when's the last time he's even seen his golf clubs?"

Golf clubs? Tristan was somewhere being tortured, and they were looking for golf clubs. Another sick thought filled her. What did they want the golf clubs for? The man left the room. The window was small, but Katie could fit through it if she tried. The drop to the ground would be far. She pulled at it. It didn't budge.

Mercedes pushed her aside and started working on the lock.

Franco appeared from the darkness. "The body's gone, but there's no way in except the front door, and we're too big to fit through that window," he whispered.

The lock clicked. "You and Johnny stay out here and keep an eye out. If it gets noisy, call in for back up. If it looks like we're dead, don't stick around. Go back, and you better avenge me or I'll haunt you until you die." Mercedes smiled, but Franco didn't return it.

"You aren't going to go in there by yourself. I don't care how good you think you are."

"I'm not going alone." Mercedes winked at Katie.

Franco frowned. "I'll find an opening in the front. Johnny and I will be enough of a distraction for you to slip in, find the blood-licker, and get out."

Mercedes and Franco watched each other for a moment. "Don't die. You're second in charge."

"You don't have to do this, Mer. You don't owe him anything."

"I owe him my life."

Franco pulled her up and to him. "What about the pack? What about me?"

Katie blushed.

Mercedes pulled away. "If you wanna keep watching my ass, you better go and make a good diversion." Mercedes turned away from him, opened the window, and shimmied through.

Katie looked back, but Franco was gone.

This was it.

She put her knife away. Working her legs through, she dropped through the window. She landed on her feet, but didn't lost balance. She tripped, but Mercedes caught her.

"Sorry," Katie whispered. She looked around the room. It was a storage room. Piles of boxes and furniture lay scattered throughout.

"Be more careful."

"I mean about Franco. I didn't know you guys were—you know."

Mercedes' hazel eyes flickered. "Don't get me killed, and there won't be anything to feel sorry about."

Katie nodded and followed Mercedes to the door. Mercedes motioned for her to wait on the other side.

"He's on the other side of the house." Katie's wrist burned, and she felt Tristan jerk in his chains. He knew she was there. Hysteria filled him, and Katie lost her balance.

"What's the matter?" A voice said to him. She couldn't see, but the voice was clear. *"She's coming isn't she?—Oh. You didn't know that I knew, did you? How about we give her a reason to hurry?"*

Katie fell to the ground and Mercedes jumped on top of her and covered her mouth. Katie screamed, but it didn't matter if anyone heard her. Tristan's scream was much louder. Katie curled onto her side. He'd cut him with more flames. Iron.

It was iron, slicing down his chest.

Mercedes' eyes widened and she looked to the door. They waited. Had anyone heard her? Seconds passed, and the door stayed closed. "Did he kill him?" Mercedes whispered.

Katie shook her head and Mercedes uncovered her mouth.

"We better hurry up then." Mercedes got up and began to open the door.

Katie stopped her. "Eshmael knows I'm coming. He—he knows."

Mercedes searched the room with her eyes. "Then he's going to have the front door guarded." She opened the door slowly and sniffed. "There are only four bodies down here—and a lot of blood." She closed the door again and looked towards the window.

"What about Franco and Johnny?" Katie said.

"I don't know. There are a lot of bodies in this house, but I don't know exactly where. Franco and Johnny will be fine. They're night hunters." Thunder struck the house, and Katie pressed her hands over her ears. Brick and cement rumbled as the building shook. Mercedes smiled. "And they've just started." Mercedes grabbed the door once more. "Are you ready?"

Katie pulled the gun out of her holster. She cocked it. The metal screeched and echoed. Chills slid down her back. It was like the very first time she'd shot a gun. Tristan had told her then that there was no going back.

"Ready."

Mercedes nodded and opened the door slowly. A rush of footsteps thudded above them. People screamed and single shots fired off from different parts of the house. Voices shouted commands to go left then right. It was chaotic. Mercedes signaled to her. "Watch my back." They left the room, and Mercedes held out her gun ready to shoot anyone in her path. They walked down the long hallway, but it was a dead end. They circled back and found a staircase.

Katie steadied her hands.

Wood creaked, and cement and brick crumbled as it fell from the wall. Every noise made Katie grip her gun. She tried to steady her breathing. Dust from the debris started to fill the hallway. It thickened as they climbed a staircase.

Mercedes fired off two shots, and two bodies dropped. She saw the tops of their heads snap back. Or maybe not. Maybe she'd imagined that. Clouds of dust and smoke filled the light in the darkness. Katie did all but scream as Mercedes pulled her into a room.

"Did you see it?"

Katie didn't see anything. It was hazy, and she was too busy watching that last body jerk back as it fell. Katie swallowed.

More shots fired off and more footsteps changed directions. What had Franco and Johnny done? Set off a bomb?

"Down the next hallway, it looks like there is a staircase. There are still some bodies up here. Maybe two, I can't tell exactly from all the smoke."

Mercedes led her out of the room and they made their way down a clouded hallway. With every step Katie checked their back. When they passed a room, Katie double checked for any sign of life. Mercedes stopped at the end of the hall. There was a big gap from where they were to the next hallway. Furniture pieces and wood littered the floor. This must have been where Franco and Johnny set off the explosion. Light from the outside filtered in. They were near the foyer.

In front, Mercedes cleared it and they started to cross. Katie saw a man out of the corner of her eye. He was in the doorway and lifting his gun right at Mercedes back.

Katie put three bullets in his chest. One right after another. The fourth shot came from Mercedes, and it flew right through his head. His blonde hair swayed back with his head as he hit the ground.

He didn't move. Of course he didn't move. He was dead.

Mercedes grabbed her hand and pulled her down the hallway. Katie gripped the gun. She was supposed to feel like a murderer, to feel like she'd stolen something that belonged to someone else. She didn't feel anything. Only the ache in her side as she got closer and closer to Tristan.

Mercedes stopped quick and pointed her gun into a room with an open door. She lowered her gun and sighed. "You've caused quite the mess." Mercedes waved Katie into the room.

Franco was in there checking one of the windows. "We got most of them. Johnny set up a few traps outside and lured them out. I smell a lot of blood down that staircase, Mer."

"We're almost done. Just one big man left," Mercedes said, checking the hallway.

"He's one of the old ones. He'll pick us off before we get through the door—that's not even the worst of our problems. The second floor might cave in at any moment. The explosion hit two beams."

On cue, the house groaned. They all looked up. Franco picked up a chair and smashed it through the window. "We need to get out. Now."

Mercedes looked from the window to Katie. Katie shook her head. She wasn't going to leave without Tristan. She wasn't going to leave him trapped under a house with a crazy man. The house creaked as wood began to snap. Mercedes moved to grab her hands, but Katie ran out of the room as the hallway started to collapse. Mercedes screamed her name, but Katie didn't stop until she was at the bottom of the staircase. She pulled at the door at the bottom. The house cracked more. The second floor was threatening to fall right on her head. She pulled at the door, but the frame that held it together was crushing it closed.

Katie flung herself at it, but it didn't move. The walls started to crack and snap. She pulled out her gun and shot the rest of her rounds into the middle of the door. She flung her body against the hole-ridden door and flew through just as a bathtub crashed down where she was standing. Katie backed up as the house collapsed into the hallway. Dust pushed past her as the last of the doorway crumbled.

She was trapped. There was no way out. The only way left was where Tristan and Eshmael waited.

21

ESHMAEL

A LAUGH DRIFTED DOWN the dark hallway. "Are you going to keep us waiting?" It was the same voice. It was Eshmael. He faintly sounded like Larry.

Katie unsheathed one of her knives. Tristan always taught her to keep one hidden.

Run.

Katie gripped her knife. No. She wasn't going to run. Not this time. She stopped at the end of the hallway. He was behind this door. What if she opened it and Eshmael just shot her dead?

What did it matter now? She couldn't turn back even if she wanted to.

She opened the door. She had to adjust her eyes to the light. Her knees buckled when she saw Tristan. His shirt was torn to pieces, his face and chest was bruised and bloody, and his wrists were held up with chains. They were raw.

He wouldn't look at her.

"Hello," the voice said.

Katie flicked her eyes across the room. He was sitting in a chair on the far side smiling at her. He looked so much like Larry, except he was more handsome. His gray eyes studied her.

"I knew you'd come," he laughed. "This is so perfect. Much better than my original plan." Eshmael's face was more angular, and his eyelashes made his eyes dark. She'd seen *this* face before. Somewhere. "Why don't you take a seat. I was just going to tell Tristan about my plan for tonight."

Katie didn't move. She gripped her knife.

"Put that down." It was a command.

Katie didn't move. Tristan always told her never to make the first move. In a fight where you're outmatched, look for weaknesses, don't rush.

The back of Katie's head split open with pain and she fell to her knees. Someone stepped on the hand that held her knife, forcing her to let it go. She was being pulled up by her hair. She grabbed the other knife hidden around her ankle, stabbed her attacker in the stomach, and pulled up. She felt the wet of his blood spilling on to her.

She was let go immediately and faced her attacker. She knew him. His eyes widened as he fell to the ground. Blood poured from his stomach. Katie couldn't catch her breath. This time she felt something. He was dying. Right before her. He was fighting for life. His body jerked and his breath quickened in sharp intakes. He was one of the bodyguards at Larry's club. He was the guy that had carried her to Larry's office. He was Yellow-hair.

He reached for her. Katie moved back. What—what did he want?

His breaths stopped, but he never stopped looking at her. She'd killed him. His blood was still warm on her hands. She wiped her hands on her jeans.

"Idiot. No one told him I needed his help. Now he's useless to me." Eshmael rolled his eyes. A man bled out on his floor and he just rolled his eyes. "It was hard enough finding him. Lawrence, surprisingly, has a loyal following."

"He was a spy," Katie said, staring at his open eyes.

"Lawrence thought so." Eshmael waved at her again. "Please, sit. Have something to drink. You must be tired."

Katie turned to Tristan, but he still wouldn't look at her.

"Fine. Stand. Die of thirst. Just don't ever say I'm inhospitable."

Katie's head throbbed.

"You know, I never wanted you. I never knew you existed." He watched Katie. "I hired Daren, Tristan's old lead commander, to lure Tristan back into the city so I could get closer to him. I really do have Daren to thank for this—turn of events.

"He noticed you. Thought if he took you, Tristan would follow. He was right, but the invalid never realized that Tristan was stronger than him." Eshmael stood up from his chair. "Are you sure you don't want a drink? I've got this really nice bottle of Scotch. My brother's favorite."

Katie looked back at Yellow-hair. She couldn't stop staring. *She* did that to him. It was too easy. The knife slid in with no resistance.

She choked back vomit.

"—I thought it was peculiar that Tristan had saved you. Maybe it was a coincidence that he was nearby? I don't believe in coincidences, Katie." Ice clinked and clanked against a small glass.

"I sent my good girl Nicole out to test the waters. See exactly what your relationship was. I hear you're very dramatic." Eshmael smiled. "Yes, I know all about that. You see, I had fates follow you and Tristan. Everyone thinks they're killers, but really, they prefer to watch—for whatever reason. I don't claim to understand the minds of the sick and twisted. Anyway, I thought, what if they've taken the vow? That would be an interesting thought. Why, that would mean she's not a human girl. Walking around in the daylight? No, she's not a shadow born either. She's half. How did our sweet boy Tristan find himself a halfborn girl to fall in love with? How would they ever know the words to the Keeper's Vow? Now, I had a crazy idea. Wild really. But I needed to test my new theory."

Eshmael sat back in his chair and drank a little scotch.

"You talk too much," Katie said. A numbness fell over her. "Your brother is on his way. Most likely right above us."

Eshmael stopped. "Then I guess I should just kill you both now and go along my merry way." Eshmael frowned. "Don't threaten me girl. My brother's on the wrong side of town. He has a habit of showing up when it's too late. I like to make sure of it."

Katie gritted her teeth. He'd been watching them? If he had been ahead of them this entire time, how was she supposed to make it out of this room alive, let alone with Tristan? They were both going to die in this room.

Eshmael cleared his throat. "Are you listening? Today's youth—a bunch of selfish prats if you ask me." He sat his scotch down on the table next to him and pulled a gun out of his jacket. "Listen, or I'll shoot your friend."

Katie held up her hands. "Okay, Okay, you wanted to test your theory."

"Ah—yes," Eshmael smiled, "The kidnapping. I wanted to see if Tristan would *know* you were in danger. And of course— he's very predictable—he came running back. So now, I thought to myself, *why this girl?* Who *is* this girl? I had a hunch. A few years ago I killed his father, and coincidentally my brother's lover was there. But I told you, *Katie*. I don't believe in coincidences.

"Do you know why I want Tristan? Because he's Ivan's son. He has a power that I want. I didn't get to take it from Ivan that night. His wife made sure of that by cutting off his head after I'd shot him—but he had a son. Now, don't get me wrong, I was delighted that I got the chance to kill your mother too, but what was she doing there? So far away from home. With Ivan? The only thing they have in common is Lawrence. I had to see you for myself. You were sitting in a little coffee shop. After I saw you, little girl, with your gray eyes and—your name—how do you say it, Tristan—*Katalina*. I knew. I knew you were his daughter."

Eshmael grinned again. "So this time. I decided I wanted both of you. Tristan made it easy. Whatever happened between you two, he came running down here with his tail between his legs following me around like I'm too daft to notice. I could have killed him days ago. But I didn't. I took him because I knew you'd come running."

Eshmael stood up. "But you're right, I talk too much. My brother should be on his way back after finding out I fed him a false lead. We have maybe an hour or so. Let's give him something to find, yes?"

Eshmael moved towards her. The hair on her neck stood up. He was powerful. She didn't have to fight him to feel that. It seeped from him. She grabbed her knife and gripped it. She'd fight him. No matter what.

Tristan spoke for the first time, "You're wasting your time on her. Lawrence doesn't care about her. If he did, he would have kept her the night he found us."

Eshmael frowned. "Maybe you're right. He's still in love with her mother. Holding on to the memory of her. This little girl is nothing but a piece of that memory. Like you are nothing but the memory of his beloved friend. Or maybe. Just maybe, like with you, he kept his distance so I'd never go after either of you. Alas, what I'm about to do to her *now* has little to do with him."

Katie backed up. The smile and pleasure that eased out of his voice gave her enough reason to be afraid. She thought once that he was a sociopath. Maybe she was right.

"You see, Tristan. I asked you earlier. What did she mean to you? You told me nothing. You lied to me. You're like your father. He used to lie and tell my brother that he wasn't evil spawn. That he wasn't the demon he is. Your father was wrong. You said earlier that I took everything away from you. I want to show you that you're wrong."

Tristan yanked against his chains. Katie gripped the knife. She wasn't going to let this maniac touch her.

He was quick.

She sliced the air between them and kept him at bay.

Eshmael laughed and backed up. It wasn't over, but all she had to do was fight long enough for Larry to get here. She could do it.

Eshmael locked eyes with her. "You're a fighter, I can tell. Your eyes tell me that you are ready to die right here. But you've got one weakness." In one fluid movement he moved toward her and pulled out his gun. It was pointed at Tristan's head. "Drop your weapon."

"Don't," Tristan said.

Eshmael pulled the trigger.

Katie screamed and lunged at him. He grabbed her arm and spun her around.

Tristan wasn't dead. A bullet hole rested right above his head.

"Drop your weapon or the next one goes between his eyes." Eshmael's breath was on her neck.

Tristan's eyes were on her. He shook his head. "Don't, Katalina."

Katie dropped the knife.

"Good girl—now turn around and look at me." His hand still squeezed her arm. "You're very beautiful."

Katie's insides squeezed and dropped. It was in his eyes. He was going to touch her.

"Get away from her." Tristan's voice was hoarse, but she heard him fighting against his chains. "Just kill me. Leave her alone. Just kill me. You were right. I lied. Please." He sobbed.

"If you move, I will put a bullet through his skull." Eshmael whispered in her ear. Katie choked back tears. She didn't want Tristan to hear her cry. She tried to blank out her mind while Eshmael let go of her arm and ran his free hand up her back. "I won't make it hurt. You'll enjoy it. Women say they enjoy me. But I do have to warn you"—his hand wrapped around her neck lightly—"what I do really is an acquired taste." He started to squeeze.

Katie swallowed and his palm pressed against her throat. She grabbed his hand and pulled at it.

"Remember what I told you. If you move I will put a bullet through his skull."

Katie's hands shook. He added slightly more pressure and her body told her to pull at his hand. She fought herself.

"Fight, Katalina. Dammit. Fight." Tristan thrashed against the wall.

Eshmael kissed her cheek, then her forehead. Tears clouded her vision. A blackness seeped up in her mind as she fought for every ounce of air.

"You know, I'm not going to kill her. Just suffocate her, fuck her, and leave her brain dead." Eshmael tightened the grip around her neck, cutting off all her air supply.

Katie twisted. Her body forced her to fight. She reached up and scratched at his face, trying to reach his eyes.

He screamed and let go.

She bit down on his arm. She would be damned if this psycho thought he was going to rape her.

Her head exploded into pain, and she realized he hit her with his gun. She couldn't breathe. The hysteria made her push through the pain to fight. She slammed her heel into his knee.

He hit her again, and she stumbled away from him, dizzy and confused. She looked up and met his glare as he grabbed at her. A frenzy filled Eshmael's eyes and he swung to hit her but missed as she dodged. His eyes flicked like flames—burning everything. Destroying everything.

"KATALINA."

She tasted blood. Eshmael flexed, readying himself for another hit. Had he made up his mind? Was he going to try and beat her to death?

She blinked as her eye began to swell. She didn't see him grab at her throat. She reached out and pulled whatever flesh she could—his ear until he let go and Katie dropped to the ground coughing and choking on air.

She braced herself ready to tear him apart with every bit in her, but he stopped.

"You're right on time, brother. That's a first." Eshmael began to straighten out his jacket. He sniffed and wiped his red face.

Katie turned her throbbing head and saw Larry. He faltered at her face. Did she look as bad as she felt? She could hardly blink without pain rushing through her entire head.

"Let me explain, brother. You see, I was going to do to her what you let our father do to my mother. Do you remember that day? How you only killed him *after* he'd taken her from me?"

Larry was behind Katie. When had he moved there? "Are you all right?"

Was he really asking her that?

"Kill him, Lawrence. Kill him." Tristan's face was red, and his voice lethal. He pulled at the chains. The wall began to crack, as his wrists bled.

"The boy's right. If you don't have plans to kill me, you should just let me finish what I started."

Larry pounced on his brother and squeezed his hands around his neck.

"Just—like—you—used—to." Eshmael choked out. Katie dragged herself over to Tristan. She touched the chains, and they burned her hands. Iron.

That was how they kept him here. It was slowly draining him.

"Katalina, don't. Don't. I can do it—your hands. Please, stop." Tristan begged her, but she couldn't leave him here chained up. She needed a key. She rummaged around the room as Larry started punching Eshmael. Katie searched the drawers of Eshmael's desk and found it.

The iron burned her skin as she moved the chains to get to the lock. They started to fall off, and Tristan dropped to the ground. He grabbed her.

"Your face. Katalina, I'm sorry. I'm so sorry." He squeezed her in his arms. It hurt, and she winced at the pain. He let her go. "I'm sorry he—" Tristan moved towards Eshmael and Larry. He picked up one of Katie's fallen knives and shoved Larry to get to Eshmael.

Tristan brought the blade down.

Katie will never remember how exactly it happened. She'd been right behind Tristan. To do what? She didn't know. But when the blade came down, it was Larry who was underneath it. Tristan twisted the blade and ripped it out before he could stop himself.

"Why?" Tristan dropped the knife and backed away from Larry.

Larry coughed up blood.

Eshmael crawled from underneath him. He grabbed his throat, coughing.

"You can heal yourself," Katie said, kneeling down over Larry. It was amazing how fast her hands pressed down over his bleeding chest.

He shook his head.

"I could do it." She said it and she meant it. She was his daughter. She could fix it. All she had to do was try. Tears clouded her vision and burned as the salt touched her face.

He pushed her hands away and stared at his brother. He shook his head.

Eshmael grabbed his own chest and gasped. He tried to stand up, but fell back down. The bond. It was breaking. One brother was dying, and so was the other.

"Brother." It came out a whisper. "Don't let us die." Eshmael shook in spasms. His eyes turned silver, and his body began to fade into darkness. "You made—me—who I am."

Tristan knelt next to Larry. "You were there that night. You let him live after he killed my father. *You let him live.* He killed the woman you loved and you let him live—you're a coward."

Larry blinked back tears, and Katie held his hand. Tristan was right. He let the guilt of what he'd done to his brother hurt the people he loved. Larry squeezed her hand. He tried to talk but only blood came out.

Katie shuddered. "Shhh."

A tear escaped his eyes as they turned bright silver. He was gone.

There was a final scream as Eshmael clutched his chest. Both their silver eyes watching her.

Dead.

Tristan turned her away from them as she cried.

It was over.

22

PROMISES

KATIE AND TRISTAN climbed out of the room using the path Larry had created. When they emerged out of the final hole, they must have looked like death itself. Mercedes, Johnny, and Franco watched them like they were wild animals. They asked what happened, but neither Tristan nor Katie told them.

It was a silent ride back to The Pub. Mercedes offered them one of the rooms above her bar.

They sat on the bed, unmoving and quiet.

"I hate him." Tristan's voice broke. "He left me in that house for eight years. It was a prison cell. I wanted to know. What had I done to deserve that? And so far away from you."

Katie rubbed Tristan's back with her bruised hand. The one Larry's bouncer stepped on. She was sure one of her fingers was broken, but she was slowly starting to heal on her own.

"He was hiding me. That stupid, coward was hiding me from his brother." Tristan turned away from her so she wouldn't see his tears.

Mercedes came in a little later with packets of blood. Tristan chugged two packets before Katie finished one. Mercedes made faces as they drank and offered a few jokes. When that didn't work, she told Tristan how Katie shot the guy who would have killed Mercedes. Katie frowned, but Mercedes smiled and told her she hated owing people.

Katie washed up in Mercedes' bathroom while Tristan used the one in the room. Her face horrified her. The swelling was going down, but the bruises were what made her jump at her own reflection. She washed the dirt and blood off and borrowed a tanktop and pair of shorts from Mercedes.

"You should probably call your parents," Mercedes said, holding out a bag for Katie's soiled clothes. She was right. Katie called her dad, then Lucinda. They each screamed and demanded to know where she was, but she only told them that she was safe and would be home soon, with Tristan. She didn't want to deal with the drama. Not after watching Larry choke on his own blood. He wanted to tell her something. She'd never know.

Tristan was out of the shower when she walked back into the room. He watched her with red eyes. He looked better after his shower. He was still bruised and cut, but he looked better. At least he was looking at her now. But she couldn't read his expression or his thoughts. He was blank. Maybe he still hated her.

"I can go," Katie said. He was safe. That was all that mattered.

"I came looking for you because I wanted to say sorry. I was selfish. You were right, everything you said about me was right."

"You had no right coming down here," Tristan said, not looking at her.

"I'm—I'm sorry—but I'm glad I did."

Tristan sat in silence. He opened up and let her feel his thoughts, but it was just confusion. His and hers.

Was this it? Were they going to say goodbye forever? What were they supposed to do when the future felt no farther than the seconds they spent in this silence?

The thought gripped her heart, and she wanted to fall. Katie grabbed onto the doorknob. If this was it, she wanted to leave with everything right between them. She promised herself to wait until she was far away before she'd let herself feel anything.

She breathed in deep and turned the knob. *Goodbye.* She couldn't say it out loud. Not if she wanted to keep her other promise.

She felt the panic rising up both their throats before she felt his arms around her.

"—I love you," he said, squeezing the breath out of her.

She hugged him back. "I love you too."

"I'm sorry, Katalina. I'll never lie about it again. Not to myself or you. I love you."

A Vow of Their Own

KATIE WENT BACK home. She walked into her room with her dad threatening to ground her and closed the door in his face. She wasn't a kid anymore. She'd killed two men and held the hand of a dying one. Life wasn't about cutting corners in school so she could sleep in. She wasn't a girl anymore—and she wasn't half-vampire.

She was a new Katie Watts. Someone who realized how important it was to protect the people she loved and not be afraid. There were scarier things than death. Watching Eshmael point a gun at the boy she loved showed her that.

Katie looked around her room. It wasn't hers anymore. The empty gerbil cage, the clay pots she'd never painted, the books on cinema that she never read, the basket of yarn left over after she'd only knitted one ratty hat. Her infamous hobbies. All along she'd been trying to find herself and she never bothered to look in the mirror.

Katie waited for her dad to go to sleep before going to the garage and collecting a few boxes. She spent hours going through her room and filling them.

Last was her torn Peter Pan book. She could never read it. Katie tried to see if she could fix it, but the spine of the book was broken. She wrapped it in paper, put it in her last box, and started taping it up to go away with the rest of her incomplete things.

"What are you doing, Katie?" her dad said, walking in her room in the early hours of the morning. She finished taping the box.

"I'm putting some stuff away. Not everything, just a few things that I don't need anymore."

"Look. I don't know what happened to you, but you just can't come home after being missing for a day then throw away all your stuff." He was starting to stumble over his words. He was afraid. He was afraid he was losing her.

Katie put the tape down and hugged her dad. This was going to be her job now, to help the people around her stop running. "I'm here, Dad. I can't be the old Katie anymore. I have to be who I'm meant to be. I have to be me."

"What the hell happened? It's him, every time he comes into our lives, you suffer. No more." He was shaking his head.

"Dad. For once, stop blaming him for the things he's suffered from. He was a boy. We were the same age. If you can't accept what he is, then you can't accept me."

"Katie, there are people out there who will damn you for what you are. You don't understand the world we live in."

"Let them. It's not going to stop me from being who I am. I am not a coward. I'm not going to hide anymore."

⁕

They both stopped hiding, Katie and Tristan. Katie made it a point that she supported Tristan, and if anyone asked she was just like him. They finished out the last month of school being ostracized by everyone except Allison and those too ignorant to care what they were. None of the teachers treated them differently to their faces, but Traci argued that she had her suspicions. *I may be bad with a gun, but I'm not stupid. Not as stupid as everyone else at least.*

Traci helped her and Tristan study for their exams. During the final exams, they even got a meeting with the members of The Board in the guidance counselor's office. Jim Heckler and Henrietta Sterling—it seemed Will's position had not been filled yet.

"You know, it is going to be very difficult for you to continue your schooling here at Hamilton," Henrietta said. She looked the same as when Katie first met her, almost a year ago. When Katie's life had changed. Here she was again at the other end of the pendulum swing.

"Life is hard outside these walls too. I can't run from that," Katie said, looking into her stark blue, unblinking eyes.

"We will not look kindly on ill behavior," Jim said. He looked appalled when Katie confirmed the "rumors" of her being half-vampire. There was no need for a meeting. It was a show. It was a warning to them. Tristan had still yet to say anything.

"And I do not look kindly on your bigotry," Katie said, staring Jim down. He had not expected that.

"Do not wrap yourself so tightly in your woven web of victimization. You will end up suffocating only yourself," Henrietta said. "What Mr. Heckler means to say is, you will still be expected to follow all school rules, which may or may not come into conflict with your new self-discoveries. Going to Gray City unattended is still forbidden."

"Even if all of the students do it?" Katie argued. Tristan put a hand on her shoulder.

"The rules are for everyone, regardless of those who break them. Though, I would like to thank you for bringing that to my attention." Henrietta said. She dismissed Katie and Tristan to go back to their class.

"She's right," Tristan said as they walked down the hallway. "You can't let people like Heckler turn you into a victim."

"I only spoke the truth," she argued.

"Yeah, you did. But it's only been a few weeks since we've been back, and you already have a chip on your shoulder. You attack anyone who looks at you, and you wear *what* you are on your chest like it's *who* you are." Tristan held her hand. "I never wanted this for you."

He was right. But she was just trying hard to be herself. Whoever that was. When she was with Allison and Tristan, she never thought about *what* she was. Only here at school with everyone reminding her. Asking her questions, not looking at her, whispering when she wasn't looking.

It was harder than she thought.

"You're strong," he said, pulling her closer. "Even stronger than me."

*

It was a normal day. As normal as it could be. It was the first week of summer vacation, and Lucinda watched them practice in the backyard. She was still tip-toeing around Tristan, not sure how to apologize, if she should, or what needed an apology. Tristan made it awkward because that was always his way of doing things, but none of them expected Brian to walk out of the door and into the backyard. Even Tristan, who was great at pretending Brian was nonexistent, stopped what he was doing and looked.

Will was right behind Brian, and from the look on Lucinda's face, she had no idea they were coming. She moved to hug Brian, but stopped as if somewhere along the road she'd stopped being his mother, and maybe he had found a new one. Brian filled the gap between them and hugged her first. Will put his hand on Lucinda's back, and she started to cry.

Katie wiped her eyes and let Tristan take her from the backyard. Practice was over. A family was reshaping itself, and hopefully for the better.

They went to Tristan's room. Tristan took a deep breath and sat on his bed. Katie moved to sit next to him, but he pulled her on his lap.

Katie blushed. They had never talked about that night at the hotel, and nothing had happened ever since. They'd been better about keeping their thoughts to themselves, but more often than not they were lazy and shared most things. *He,* the mysterious Tristan, shared things with her freely. That was as close to the night he said, *"I love you"* as they got.

"What are you thinking?" he said, placing his head on her back.

She burned. There was no way he couldn't feel how hot her skin felt now. Why did she feel so shy? As much as they'd been through, as many times as they'd seen each others raw, naked thoughts, she should feel…open.

It was because up until now, they had been busy. Always battling one thing after another—tests, the school, the past, themselves. Now—now everything was quiet, except for his hands starting to travel up her back.

"Is this how you've always felt? Going crazy with wonder? Hating silent answers?" he said.

She laughed and leaned into him. It was Tristan. Why be guarded now? *Because he's a boy and you're not good at this. Last time he touched you, he left and pretended his hands had never touched your body the way they did.*

Katie sighed and started to stand up. They needed to talk this stuff out. Figure out what they were doing and what his intentions were.

He pulled her back to him and kissed her. The more they kissed, the more his hands touched her like they might never get to again. He pulled her onto him and touched more. His hands rolled down her back and back up with her shirt.

What were they going to do? She looked into his eyes. Lust stared back. He kissed her, and she melted into him. He kissed her neck and—stopped. He started to move her off him.

This! This is why she was guarded, because he was always doing *this*.

"Tristan, I swear—" she started.

"Katalina. Turn around," he said, not looking at her, but over her shoulder.

"Why?" Did he want to bite her? Like in those romance novels—

"Don't be a pervert," he said, turning her around and looking at her back. His fingers were soft on her skin. She felt naked.

"Did you know you have the tattoo?"

"What tattoo—*the* tattoo. Like yours?" Katie craned her neck but couldn't see it. Tristan traced it with his finger. Under her shoulder blade. It was small, he said. He kissed it as the door opened.

"Tristan—Oh my god. No. Not in this house. There are *rules*. Katie put your shirt on—*What is that on your back?*" Lucinda's face turned red. Katie slammed her shirt over her head, but as soon as Lucinda was done lecturing them and shaming her out of considering sex for at least another ten years, she went to the bathroom with a second mirror and looked at her back. There it was. Faintly glowing a little silver. Just like Tristan's.

The Mark.

⊗

Katie was relieved to find out Lucinda hadn't called her dad and told him about her and Tristan. They tried to tell Lucinda that he was just looking at her back, but she wasn't buying it and was a little insulted. She did threaten to call her dad about the tattoo until Tristan showed her his. It must have been the blood. It was the only explanation that any of them could think of. Now that she was drinking blood, it started to show up.

Their theory proved right. After a few days it came in better and better. Katie always made it a point to ask Tristan to look at it when no one was around. He'd always start gingerly lifting her shirt, and it always ended with them making out on a couch. He was an addiction. But, in the back of her mind, something stirred.

⊗

Katie fumbled a set of keys in her hand. She finally knew what had been bothering her for weeks. She slid the key into its lock and opened Larry's ice cream shop for the first time in months. Tristan put his hand on her back as they walked into the dark, cool shop.

Katie wandered through the shop silently. Larry left it to her, along with a gross amount of money she'd never be able to explain to her dad. What was she going to do with an ice cream shop? She opened one of the freezers. They were on a timer and the ice cream was still cool and edible. The smell of chocolate, cookie dough, mint, and vanilla swirled in her nose and she closed it.

"What are all these?" Tristan said from the back room. He was unfazed by all of this. He had rolled his eyes when he found out Larry had left him the house in New York. *As if I want to go back to that prison cell.*

Katie took a deep breath and found Tristan thumbing through a few dozen receipts. No, they weren't receipts—they were stubs for paintings. She had one in her wallet now for a painting she had to finish and pick up next door. The shop stored paintings there until they were either finished or taken home. It cost a lot to do that, but then again, Larry was loaded. Now she was loaded.

Katie grabbed some of the stubs and exhaled. *Keep it together.* "They're stubs for next door. Let's go," she said.

Katie held her breath with anticipation. She needed to get out of the ice cream shop. She wanted to see some of his work again anyway. A pang squeezed her chest as she remembered the way he'd instruct her on blending. The way his accent rolled thickly off his tongue when he corrected the way she moved her brush.

She handed the front desk clerk a few stubs and was led to a room. "Actually," the woman had been talking, but Katie only heard her just now, "all of his paintings are in here. He had so many we just stored them all in the same place. Is he all right?"

Katie ignored the last part and stepped into one of the many tiny storage rooms. There were dozens. All here sitting, waiting. They were all organized by date starting from a few years ago. Katie shifted through them, looking for something but never finding it. He'd painted pictures of castles, symbols, his brother, her mother, but nothing of her. She didn't know why she wanted to see one of her—or why she wanted to prove that he actually cared about her. Her real father. The one who never even really said it.

"He locked me in a house for eight years without uttering so much as a word. He's not the sentimental type of guy," Tristan said, holding her.

She'd gotten her tears and snot all over his shirt. Of all times for him to read her mind, this was the first time she really didn't want him hearing her ugly thoughts. The ones that meant she actually really cared.

"If it means anything," Tristan started, "he moved here and watched you grow up. He cared. He was just a coward and couldn't say it the way you wanted him to."

Tristan pulled away from her, and pulled out painting after painting. More than half were of Eshmael. They went from his adolescence to a face speckled with blood. In all of them, the overlapping letters *KV* were tattooed somewhere on his body. Keeper's Vow.

As they studied each painting, Tristan said aloud what Katie thought. "He painted what haunted him. This is borderline obsession."

"We would be normal if they hadn't ruined our lives," Katie said, looking at an unfinished version. What she thought were symbols were just the letter K and V overlapping in different angles.

"The vow ruled their lives. It drove them crazy," Tristan mumbled. Katie felt a wave of his fear and uncertainty.

"No. It wasn't the vow. They were selfish. They never looked past themselves to truly see the other person for who they were. They couldn't do what we did. What we've done," she said.

Tristan's blue eyes linked with hers. He understood without her uttering the words.

They loved each other.

Even if they were no longer together—even if they'd settled on just being friends—they would always love and understand each other. They had seen too much of each other's souls to let pride or irrational anger get in the way.

Tristan took her hand in his, and they left the shop. The paintings could stay there until the shop got rid of them. She didn't want them. She didn't need them.

They had each other and nothing could tear them apart. Not even the Keeper's Vow.

✎ACKNOWLEDGEMENTS✎

There is nothing as relieving and slightly emptying as reaching the end of a book. I am relieved because I actually did it—I'm empty becuase I'm not sure how to feel after having my emotions tossed about like ice in a blender. There are many people who helped me get here—who helped me deliever this to you—and I really want to throw out 'thank yous' from my mouth like confetti. (Forgive the comparison my son is running around my desk shooting off confetti poppers.)

A special thanks to Juan my husband for believing in me and being my bruttally honest developmental editor.

A big hug and thank you to Kim my cover degisner. I never, in a million years, thought scomeone could capture everything I wanted with such beauty and precision. Thank you also, to Leah for believing in Katie and Tristan enough to convince me that they do deserve their full story told; to Alan Heathcock for being a true mentor and enstiling the Truth of story in me; to Chamong and Mindy for being my beta readers; to every reader who has sent me an email telling me about their experience with the story; and to you for making it to the end with us.

Guardians: Book Two

Darkness Comes At Dawn

Christmas 2016

www.ingramcontent.com/pod-product-compliance
Lightning Source LLC
Chambersburg PA
CBHW051206120726
47905CB00004B/1002